Prince of Secrets and Shadows

Cursed Fae Courts

Book Two

Heather Hildenbrand

Prince of Secrets & Shadows

Cursed Fae Courts #2

Cover Design by Fay Lane

Edited by Dawn Y.

www.heatherhildenbrand.com

Moriori Isles

Rada People

Concordia
The Winter Court

Concordian Mountains

Ravenna
The Midnight Court

Lightshore
The Spring Court

Grey Oak
The Autumn Court

The Broadlands

Osphiris River

Troloch Forest

Emerald Forest

Rosewood

Sevanwinds
The Summer Court

Vorinthia
The Calidium
Empire

rica

Pronunciation Guide

Characters

Aurelia Valeen – Aur-el-ee-ya Vuh-leen (Princess of Summer)
Sonoma Eko – Suh-no-muh Ek-oh (Aine warrior)
Tyrion Valeen – Teer-ee-on Vuh-leen (King of Summer)
Celeste Valeen – Suh-lest Vuh-leen (Queen of Summer)
Heliconia Kucera – Hel-ihh-cone-ya Cue-seer-uh (Conqueror of the north, self-declared Queen of Winter
Rydian Nytherra – Rid-ee-in Nigh-terra (Second son of Duron)
Callan Ashfall – Call-en Ash-fall (Autumn prince)
Duron Ashfall – Der-on Ash-fall (Autumn King)
Lesha – Lee-sha (Aine warrior)
Amanti – Uh-man-tee (Aine warrior)
Daegel – Day-gull (Rydian's friend & confidante)
Meerdra – Meer-druh (Oracle in Grey Oak)
Koraz – Core-azz (Duron's top advisor)
Lemuel – Lem-yule (Duron's advisor)
Vanya – Vah-n-yuh (Aurelia's first maid at Grey Oak)
Beryl – Bear-uhl (Aurelia's second maid at Grey Oak)
Talthis – Tal-thiss (Lightshore emissary)

Naliadne/Nali – Nal-ee-ad-nee (Princess of the Osphanis/River People)
Patamoi – Pa-tuh-moy (King of the Osphanis/River People)
Winyra – Win – eye-ruh (Former Queen of the Midnight Court)
Cadira – Kuh-deer-uh (Queen of the Midnight Court)

People Groups

Verdant – Verd-ant (Healer tribe with powerful magic that lived a thousand years ago
Moriori – Mor-ee-or-ee (Pacifist people from an island in the northwest sea)
Rada – Rah-duh (Sea fae)
Naiad – Nigh-add (Mermaid fae)

Places

Menryth – Men-rith (Name of the realm)
Concordia – Con-cor-dee-uh (Winter court kingdom)
Ravenna – Ruh-ven-nuh (capital city of the Midnight Court)
Calidium Empire – Cuh-lid-ee-um (Once a great southern empire before it fell during the Great War)
Alorica – Al-or-ee-kuh (Western continent across the sea)
Vorinthia – Vor-in-thee-uh (The last kingdom to wield strong magic before it fell in the Great War)

A Quick Recap

In Kingdom of Briars & Roses...

Princess Aurelia Valeen of the Summer Court has spent seven years trapped behind enchanted walls, her kingdom cursed into an endless sleep. The curse—set in motion by the dark conqueror Heliconia, self-proclaimed Queen of Winter—has stripped Summer of its magic and left Aurelia with only one option: Fulfill a long-standing political alliance with the Autumn Court in hopes of saving her people.

She promises herself to Prince Callan Ashfall, her charming ex-fiancé and the heir of the Autumn Court. On the journey to Autumn, Aurelia survives attacks by enhanced Obsidians (Heliconia's soldiers) and begins to realize that her own magic isn't as dormant as she's been led to believe—especially when she kills one of the creatures and absorbs its life force.

Enter Rydian Nytherra, Callan's illegitimate half-brother and a stranger from her past. Cold, lethal, and openly hostile toward Aurelia, Rydian clearly knows more about her magic—and about Autumn's secrets—than he lets on. Despite his warnings that Callan and King Duron Ashfall will try to use her, Aurelia is forced into Grey Oak as a political prisoner disguised as a fiancée.

In Callan's court, Aurelia uncovers unrest among Autumn's people, fueled by Duron's brutal taxation and exploitation. Rebels attempt to assassinate her, believing she is complicit in Autumn's oppression. Meanwhile, Duron pressures Aurelia to hand over her magic as the "offering" required to finalize the alliance—confirming Rydian's fears.

As Aurelia searches for answers about her true power, she learns a devastating truth: her magic isn't merely fae. She is the daughter of Ire, a god they call a Furiosity and ruler of Hel. Not only that, her death-fueled power is tied to an ancient bargain involving the Fates (female gods of the light), Furiosities (the gods of Hel), and Heliconia herself. Aurelia is the Chosen One, destined to one day confront Heliconia and save the realm.

Caught between political manipulation, rebellion, and forbidden desire, Aurelia shares a single night with Rydian—knowing it can never last. But when it comes time to wed Callan, she chooses independence over submission, attempting to flee Grey Oak and fight Heliconia on her own terms.

As Autumn collapses into chaos, Rydian makes a devastating choice: To "save" Aurelia, he forcibly delivers her into the hands of the infamous Midnight Court, a kingdom full of deadly monsters that will likely torture and kill her before saving her from anything.

Book one ends with Aurelia vowing vengeance—not just against Heliconia but against Rydian for his betrayal—as she embraces her heritage, her fury, and the fire of Hel burning in her veins.

THE
LOVERS

Chapter One
Callan

The Autumn Court burned beautifully around me. Ashen leaves fell from the sky like embers, then curled at my feet, leaving a cloud of smoke thick enough to make my eyes water. I hadn't witnessed who'd started the fire, but somewhere amid the chaos of clashing swords and fleeing guests, a spark had caught.

The trees beyond the gardens glowed against the night sky—gold and rust and scarlet. More smoke curled above the keep's towers, carrying the scent of oak and ash. The blackened vines along the outer walls dripped with water, thanks to some guard's quick thinking and the buckets they'd hauled from the stables. But damage had been done in more ways than one tonight. My father's kingdom—bleeding from every edge.

And somewhere beyond the gates, a black carriage rolled into the dark, carrying precious cargo.

The Summer princess who should've been my queen.

The woman who'd refused me before the entire realm earlier tonight.

I cut down another Withered rebel before thought could root too deeply about what I'd done. The creature I'd slain—once fae, once loyal

—collapsed in a hiss of blackened breath, his veins hollow from where my father had drained him dry at one of the magic donation centers.

The rebels had chosen tonight to strike. Of course they had. It was all a distraction, a perfectly timed assault to give Aurelia room to run.

Her rebellion had begun with a single word at the altar aimed at me: *no.*

And now, here I was, fighting the ghosts of my father's cruelty while the only person who ever saw the boy beneath my crown disappeared into the night.

"Your Highness!" Holt's voice cracked across the courtyard. "We've secured the gate and the section of wall they breached for entry."

"Take any prisoners you can. Kill the ones who fight back," I snapped, turning away from the drained fae I'd killed. The Autumn fae. Withered or not, they were my people. Bile rose in my throat, but I shoved it down and looked to my brother.

Half-brother by blood, we shared a father. And a common experience of that man's abuse in both of our childhoods. Though, I was the one my father was cruelest with. Maybe because I was his heir. Either way, Rydian and I had never been best friends, but we'd been united against a common enemy long enough to forge a tenuous bond.

Tonight, that bond had broken forever.

I glared as he stepped from the smoke, blades drawn, eyes bright with cold fury.

"Still alive?" he asked.

"Disappointed?" I parried a strike from another Withered, the clash of metal ringing between us before I flung the gaunt fae to the ground where the guards set upon him. "You could have warned me half our people were turning on us tonight."

"I thought you'd notice when they started trying to kill you," he said evenly.

Bastard.

"You knew about this."

"I knew Aurelia wouldn't stay."

I froze, my skin as cold as if winter had come to the court. "You helped her."

He didn't answer. Didn't have to. His eyes flicked toward the gate—

the one just now beginning to swing shut, the road beyond it swallowed in fog and darkness.

"You were supposed to keep her safe," I roared.

"I did," he said simply. "She wanted to be free."

"She humiliated me tonight." I stalked toward him, my blade still slick with blood. "She could've left quietly. But no—she had to turn it into a show. In front of every noble, every emissary—"

"Maybe she wanted them to see she wasn't afraid of you despite your attempts to control her."

I laughed—harsh, broken. "Afraid of *me*? I would've given her everything."

He tilted his head. "Except a choice."

Rage burst through me, and I lifted my bloodied sword, unthinking about what I'd do next—and what the consequences might be.

Fletcher came running, breathless, armor stained with ash and gore.

"Your Highness!" he panted. "The king— He's dead!"

The world tilted. My sword hand fell limp.

"What?" I uttered.

"Your father," Fletcher said between breaths. "Burned to ash. They say it was... furyfire."

He glanced between us uncertainly. But I barely noticed. The word itself froze me. *Furyfire*. Aurelia's magic.

"She wouldn't—" I started, but the truth turned the words bitter in my mouth.

She would.

She'd already burned me. The other night in the library. Her control had slipped past her temper.

"She killed him," I whispered in disbelief.

Rydian's voice came low. "You don't know that."

My gaze snapped to his as my blood began to heat. "I know she had motive. And I know you didn't stop her."

"She wanted to survive," he said quietly. "Duron made that impossible."

"Your Highness," Fletcher said again.

"What is it?" I snapped.

"Advisor Koraz was also found dead. Run through the heart with a blade."

Again, a darting glance toward Rydian.

My half-brother's expression never flickered away from the calm stoicism of relief. And I knew then he'd been the one to do it. Not just because they'd hated one another but because it was Rydian's kill to make.

Still, after everything else he'd done tonight, I couldn't allow it.

"You don't deny it," I said.

"I don't."

Something inside me snapped. "Guards," I said, my voice gone sharp and cold. "Take him away."

Rydian didn't even flinch as they circled him. "You'll regret this, Callan."

"There are many things I may live to regret. Locking you up is not one of them."

"Your guards and chains won't hold me if I decide to go."

"You're right. Although, I could persuade you to stay without any of this."

His gaze flicked to my hand. He knew what I meant even if the rest of the court didn't. His frown told me he would keep my secret a little longer, though I dared him to try to use it against me now. His crimes were far worse than my own.

"Take him to the dungeon. I have a crown to claim and dead to bury."

When they were gone, I walked to the garden where my father's remains lay strewn about from the breeze. Ashes and bone, that was all that remained of the former Autumn king.

Above, the moon hung low, pale as bone, watching me struggle not to fall apart. I sheathed my sword, hands shaking. The blood on my knuckles gleamed in the moonlight.

The monster I'd feared all my life was gone. And still, I felt like nothing more than an echo of what he wanted from me—small, angry, hollow.

"Majesty?" Holt asked softly. "What are your orders?"

Orders. Because that's what kings gave.

"Find her," I said. "Bring her back to me."

He hesitated. "Alive?"

I didn't answer.

He bowed low and disappeared into the smoke.

The night wind swept through the courtyard, scattering burnt leaves and ash. Scattering him. Underneath the scent of it, I caught the faintest trace of blue vervain smoke from the herb I burned to silence my power.

I breathed it in for the last time and whispered to the dark, "Long live the king."

THE
LOVERS

Chapter Two
Aurelia

Every flutter of my eyelids dragged like cotton soaked in water. I stopped trying to pry them open and inhaled slowly, taking stock. The first thing I noticed was the smell—woodsmoke and damp stone, threaded with something sharp and herbal that clung to the back of my throat.

The second thing was sound. A hush, broken only by the faint crackle of a fire somewhere nearby. No voices. No footsteps. Just silence, the kind that reminded me of all those years spent among my sleeping kingdom. The kind of silence that pressed like a weight on my ribs and brought a twinge of panic that I'd been transported right back to the nightmare of the past seven years spent inside my sleeping kingdom.

Maybe the last few weeks were nothing more than a strange dream. Sonoma's death, the secret she'd kept from me until the end—that she was my mother and a god of Hel was my father, Callan's marriage proposal. His father's plan to drain my magic for the sake of a pretty lawn. Rydian. Thinking of all that had happened, I wasn't sure whether I wanted it to be real or not.

Either way, I was awake now. And reality could not be ignored much longer, especially not my bladder.

My limbs were heavy, sluggish, every movement tinged with the wrongness of muscles that shouldn't ache this badly, considering the softness of the mattress I found myself on. My mouth was dry, and when I swallowed, nausea climbed my throat.

Drugged.

The realization crawled over my skin like cold sweat. Followed quickly by the memory of how it had happened in the first place.

My furyfire burning King Duron to ash. His advisor, Koraz, with a blade through his chest. Rydian pushing me into a black carriage. The driver's armor emblazoned with the silver sigil of the Midnight Court.

My eyes flew open, my heart racing as I tried to breathe through the panic. I blinked at the sight of the smooth ceiling, slanted and high, exposed rafters gleaming in the soft, orange light. Beneath that, the walls were stone, uneven and old, and a faint draft whispered through cracks.

I was lying on a large bed layered in thick blankets. A single window was shuttered tight. Two doors stood across from me. One hung open, revealing a glimpse of a massive bathing chamber. The other was closed, the faint glint of iron along its latched edge telling me what I didn't want to know.

Locked.

I hadn't dreamt it after all; I was a prisoner.

Another quick glance around the space revealed no sign of my personal belongings, including my beloved swords: Dorcha and Latha.

Panic flared in my chest, sharp enough to shove me upright. My pulse hammered in my temples. But the ache in my head was nothing compared to the fresh pain splitting through my chest. My heart broke all over again as the truth settled like stone in my lungs.

Rydian had betrayed me.

He had used my feelings for him as a lure, dangling his own affections like a bait and switch. By the time I'd decided to flee Grey Oak, I'd given up the idea that my alliance with Callan would have worked, but there were plenty of other courts I could have run to. The only one I never planned to cross paths with was the Midnight Court. Cowards and monsters—the lot of them.

And now, I was here—wherever *here* was—locked away, drugged into compliance.

An heir without a throne.

A warrior without a sword.

A woman who had trusted the wrong prince—only to be ruined by him in the end.

My fingers curled into the blankets until my nails bit through the soft material. I had to get out. Now. Before my new captors realized I was awake and came to torture me for whatever information Rydian told them I had. Or worse, maybe they wanted what Duron had coveted: my magic.

I slid from the bed, my legs unsteady, the floor tilting beneath me as if the whole world had been knocked askew. I faltered at the sight of the simple nightgown clinging to my frame. Not the wedding gown I'd been wearing when I fled. Which meant someone had dressed me. And undressed me. Bile rose in the back of my throat, but I shoved it down.

My palms found the smooth, exposed log wall, steadying myself as I shuffled to the bathing chamber. When I was finished, I splashed water on my face and drank deeply from the faucet of cold water being piped in. The attention to detail in this place was on par with royal houses. It reeked of luxury rather than the filth I'd expected.

On my way back through the bedroom, my gaze caught on a large pack sitting against the wall. I went to it and peeled it open, surprised to find all my belongings I thought I'd left in Grey Oak, including the jewels and Aine armor I'd brought from Sunspire. Dorcha and Latha, my swords, were still missing, which only reminded me of the fact that I was, in fact, a prisoner despite the accommodations.

I straightened again and went to the bedroom door. The heavy iron latch gleamed faintly in the torchlight.

I pressed against it anyway.

Locked. A clear message. But I was no good at obeying.

I opened my hand, willing furyfire to spark to life in my palm. A single, sad ember sizzled then winked out. I tried again. And again. Nothing.

My stores of magic were still depleted, thanks to whatever they'd drugged me with, but I rummaged through my bag again and managed to come away with a hairpin. Picking the lock took far more time than I wanted, but eventually the lock sprang free, and the door opened.

Stumbling out of the bedroom, I tried to breathe through the pounding in my head. Gripping the wall, I hurried forward, bare feet brushing over worn rugs, my pulse thudding loud in my sensitive fae ears.

The hallway opened into a larger space that was clearly the living area of a massive log cabin-style residence, and I was so surprised by the fact that it wasn't a dungeon, I halted and stared.

The space was high-ceilinged yet warm, with the glow of firelight spilling from a hearth built with gray stones the size of my head. Before it, a comfy sitting area beckoned, complete with fluffy pillows and a throw blanket tossed over the back of the deep-cushioned sofa. A pair of reading glasses was perched on the coffee table as if someone had only just set them down before getting up and wandering off.

Along the far wall, built-in bookshelves were stuffed and brimming with books. In the corner, beneath a window, a large desk stood with papers stacked in haphazard piles.

It felt almost... cozy.

Other than the fact that the walls bore blades of various shapes and sizes, lined up in neat, lethal order with tiny placards beside them, likely listing the number of enemies their wielder had slain.

Still... this place was lived-in. Comfortable. Something about it reminded me of Rydian's townhouse in Grey Oak. Which, now that I thought about it, made it all so much worse than a dank prison cell in the bowels of a drafty castle.

A male stepped from the shadows near the door. I didn't recognize him. Midnight fae, I assumed. He was tall and broad, his cloak failing to hide the sword pommel protruding from his hip. He wore all black except for the small silver sigil of the midnight court emblazoned on his lapel.

"You shouldn't be out of your room," he said, voice low.

I dropped into a fighting stance, fists raised, my body already moving on instinct. My magic sparked, embers of furyfire flickering at my fingertips. Hopefully, the male wouldn't know embers was the extent of my stores just now.

"Try to stop me," I hissed.

The fae lunged.

I braced, ready to fight until the walls ran red—

"Enough."

The voice cut clean through the haze, sharp as a blade but achingly familiar.

The male stopped.

I whipped around, heart slamming into my ribs.

A female stepped into the firelight. Her dark hair was cropped short and almost jagged on one side, her arm bound in a sling, wings scarred and torn but unmistakable.

Her eyes were steady, bright, unyielding as ever as she took me in.

My breath left me in a rush. For a moment, I could only stare, too stunned to move. "Amanti."

THE
LOVERS

Chapter Three

Aurelia

The Aine warrior smiled, eyes crinkling at the corners. "Hello, Aurelia."

My bare feet slapped against the rug, my pulse louder than the fire crackling, and then I was in her arms. My cheek pressed to her shoulder, my fingers digging into the coarse weave of her tunic. Gods, she was so much thinner than I remembered. For a terrifying heartbeat, I thought she might vanish. That she was some phantom conjured by the drugs still crawling through my veins. But she was solid. Warm. Alive.

And then her arm came up—the one that wasn't bound in a sling—and wrapped around me. Hesitant at first, then steadier. The scent of her as she hugged me—earth and sky and something faintly sweet, like resin, or the sap of trees—was familiar in a way that cracked something raw and aching inside me.

"Amanti," I whispered into the fabric at her neck. Grief poured through me like water. She smelled like home. Like Sonoma. My mother—

No, I couldn't think about her now.

"You're alive," I said, joy brimming just as full as my grief.

"Barely," she said dryly.

I pulled back just enough to look at her, but my hands stayed braced on her arms, unwilling to let go completely. Her face was sharper than before, cheekbones cut like blades, skin stretched taut. Her hair—once a long, shiny black curtain—had been hacked short on one side. The longer side was braided and tucked over her shoulder.

But the worst was her wings... My throat closed at the sight.

Torn. One hanging off-kilter, the other stiffly tucked at her back, scarred and broken.

I swallowed hard. "I thought you were—"

"Dead?" She gave the faintest tilt of her mouth, not a smile but the shadow of one. "Close enough."

Her eyes flicked past me to the fae warrior still lingering near the door, hand resting on his blade. Was Amanti their prisoner too? Is this where she'd been all this time?

"What happened?" I asked.

"I went south like we discussed. For weeks, I searched for any sign of the Verdant healers, but there was nothing left of their old tribe." She frowned and added, "There was nothing left of any tribe, in fact."

"What do you mean?"

"The southern outposts were emptied. The nomadic tribes who still make their home in Vorinthia's rainforests were nowhere to be found."

"What happened to them all?"

"I don't know. There was no evidence of a battle, but... if they're still alive, they clearly don't want to be found." Her voice dipped lower, roughened by something deeper than injury. "Despite that, it turns out I wasn't the only creature roaming the southern forests. A Brindalorn attacked me—"

"A Brindalorn?" I echoed in disbelief. "Impossible. They've been extinct for centuries."

"Apparently not," she said. "The blasted thing nearly made me extinct, though."

"And Lesha? Did she find you?"

"Lesha?" She frowned. "No, I thought—" Confusion flickered, turning to concern. "Is she not at Sunspire, holding the wards with Sonoma?"

My shoulders fell. I shook my head. "She went to look for you. We hadn't heard any news from her before..." I couldn't bring myself to tell her what had happened to Sonoma. What she'd given up to protect Sevanwinds for me.

"We'll find her," Amanti said, voice firm.

I nodded, borrowing her confidence. "I'm just glad you're all right."

A shadow passed over her features, highlighting the dark circles beneath her eyes. The paleness in her complexion. "The healing process has been slow. My wounds were ... substantial."

No wonder. Brindalorns were vicious by all historical accounts—striped hide sharpened to points along its back, patches of its body armored in stone-like plates. Its eyes were pits of pale fire, its jaws wide enough to snap its prey in half. Nearly unkillable, born of cursed magic and a corrupted line of glimfangs, it hunted anything warm-blooded, and it never stopped once it picked up a scent.

"How did you defeat it?" I asked.

"It took every last drop of my Aine magic," she said quietly, and I could feel her sadness at the loss. "Draining myself that way nearly killed me. I was almost gone when Rydian found me."

"Wait. Did you say Rydian?" My hands tightened on her arms. "Rydian Nytherra saved you?"

She nodded. "He brought me here a few months ago."

Her words stunned me. The idea that she'd been a prisoner here while Rydian pretended to care about me was a rage heating my blood, but I couldn't let myself think about Rydian right now. Not when we needed to find a way out of here.

"I'm so glad we found one another," I told her. "So much has happened that I have to tell you. And I want to hear more about your time in the south." I dropped my voice low, leaning in so our captor couldn't hear. "But first, we need to find a way out of here."

"Out?" Amanti's brows knitted. "Why would we do that?"

"You can fly us out and then we can—"

Her expression fell so far that I stopped, bracing for what she was going to say. "My wings... They don't carry me anymore," she said quietly. "They might again, with time. But not yet."

My chest caved. My mouth filled with bitter ash. Amanti—*my*

Amanti, warrior of the Aine, chosen by the Fates, fierce, indomitable, untouchable—was earthbound.

"It's okay." I swallowed back my own panic at the idea of how helpless she was, how trapped we both were. I kept my voice low, hoping like Hel the midnight fae in the corner couldn't hear me. "We'll run. South, east—wherever it takes to get out of this gods-forsaken court. They've taken my swords, but I'll find another weapon. I won't leave you here."

Her voice cut through my rush of words. "Aurelia."

Something about the way she said my name made me stop.

Her hand, warm and soft, closed over mine. Her gaze didn't waver as she said, "I'm here willingly."

The floor seemed to tilt beneath me. My mouth opened, but no words came out. For a long, stuttering moment, I thought I'd misheard.

"What?"

Her tone was patient, calm, infuriatingly level. "I'm not a prisoner here. The Midnight Court is our friend."

"No." I shook my head so hard that strands of hair fell into my face. "You can't mean that. Amanti, they drugged me. Locked me in. I—Why?" The word tore out of me, thin and broken. "Why would you want to stay here with these monsters?"

Her expression softened, and that terrified me most of all. She had never looked at me with pity. And now, she'd done it twice in the last two minutes. "Because Rydian Nytherra is my nephew."

I blinked at her, stunned into silence. "Your...what?"

"My sister's son," she said evenly.

"That's insane." My laugh was brittle, too sharp. "That's not—you never said—you never told me you had family—"

"There are things," Amanti said carefully, "that could not be spoken of until the time was right."

The words transported me back to another confession. In another castle. Another time. I'd survived Heliconia's curse on my people—leaving them all perpetually slumbering while I carried on with only the Aine to keep me company.

Seven years later, as she was dying, Sonoma had admitted the truth: that I was not the Summer fae daughter I'd been raised to believe.

I was the product of a forbidden romance between an Aine warrior and a Furiosity. With the blood of a Fairy and a demon god running in my veins. But more than that, I was the answer to an ancient prophecy, one which promised a darkness that would blot out the light. Heliconia.

Her obsession with power had been foretold Ages ago. And when she'd come—and so had I—the Fates saw their chance to balance the scales. And I became their Chosen One. Fates-blessed and deemed their own personal savior. Destined to destroy the Dark Queen. If and when I ever got around to figuring out how that was supposed to work.

I'd spent the first seven years of the curse protecting my sleeping kingdom from within Sunspire's walls. Sonoma and the other Aine had provided a ward of protection, using their Fated-gifted magic, and for a time, it had been enough to keep us safe. But then that magic had begun to fail. The Fates had vanished from Menryth altogether, and their power waned in their chosen warriors.

I'd spent the last several weeks banished outside my home after Sonoma's death, and her bargain with my uncles, the gods of Hel, had sealed the wards around the place. This time, more powerful and unbreakable than before. Until I found a way to break the curse, there would be nothing and no one in or out.

I'd been so foolishly convinced I could find a way to break the curse and wake them all through an alliance of marriage to Callan Ashfall, Autumn Prince. Now, Autumn's king.

But my pitiful effort had been doomed from the start.

Not only that, but I was the last to know it.

The last to know who my parents were. The last to know what kind of male Callan really was, which didn't even begin to cover the fact that he possessed compulsion—a magic long gone from bloodlines in this realm. And the last to know Amanti was still alive—thanks to her secret family. A blood relation to the male who betrayed me most.

"Was it all a lie then?" I asked, nearly choking on the words as I looked at her now. "Some ruse to spy for the Midnight Court. To learn our weaknesses. To bring us down."

"Of course not," Amanti insisted, eyes flashing. "I am an Aine, by vow and by choice." Her indignation softened to affection. "And I love you, Aurelia. As I always have. I would never do anything to hurt you."

Her words were genuine, but I couldn't find an answer inside me. Not after so much failure and loss. So many secrets hidden away.

"Rydian and Slade found me when I was injured and near dying. They brought me back here. Keres has been healing me."

Rydian had found her? Saved her? When? Certainly before he'd come to Grey Oak with me, where, all along, he'd known she was alive and hadn't bothered to mention it. The truth of it choked me.

I wanted to scream. I wanted to hug her until her bones protested and make the world small enough to fit my hands. I did neither.

"Why didn't you send word?" I asked.

"Communication was too dangerous. Heliconia's spies are everywhere. Aurelia, my loyalty and love for you are true."

The silence stretched between us, taut as a bowstring.

And rather than break it with anything so futile as words, I turned and walked away. Back to my room where I shut the door with a firm click.

A prison cell after all.

THE
LOVERS

Chapter Four
Aurelia

Someone knocked. I didn't answer, though my body tensed, waiting to see if they'd let themselves in. A moment later, I listened to a few muted clinks, and then it went quiet again. Even then, I stayed where I was, curled on the soft bed with the blanket twisted in my fists, counting breaths and the beats of my anger until both blurred into one.

Hours drifted like a lazy current. Some part of me felt the urgency of figuring out my next move, of pushing past my hurt and shock that Amanti was alive—and had kept secrets yet again. But it wasn't just Amanti's presence or lies I struggled to process.

It was all of it.

Callan's betrayal. The way he'd used his compulsion on me all this time. Duron's attempt to trap me so he could drain my magic. Just like he'd been doing to his own people all this time. Sonoma's death. The fact that my father was a king of Hel.

Rydian.

Somehow, his betrayal made everything worse. And now, lying in this bed alone only made me think of another bed. One we'd shared. A single, reckless night where I'd forgotten how many secrets were between us. How many reasons I had not to trust the male, who, in the end, I bared myself to anyway.

I couldn't stay in this room forever. But in order to keep moving, I needed a plan. And settling on one that wouldn't get me killed was proving difficult. Instead, I nursed my hurt and my outrage for as long as this room's amenities would allow. Eventually, my stomach betrayed me with a low, traitorous growl.

Hauling myself out of bed, I rifled through the pack of clothes someone had left and found a pair of pants and a loose-fitting tunic to wear before stuffing my feet into my boots. By the time I was dressed, I was light-headed, and my stomach was knotting from hunger.

When I cracked the door at last, the corridor was empty.

A tray of food waited on the floor: a heel of bread, a wedge of hard cheese, thin-sliced salted meat, a little dish of something pickled and bright. The tea in the lidded mug was lukewarm and mint-bitter. I sat down right in the center of the open doorway and pulled the whole tray into my lap.

The food steadied the worst of my trembling hands. The fog at the edges of my sight thinned. But the quietness of the house offered no clues about my captors. Or, as Amanti put it, her *friends*.

When I finished, I wiped my fingers on my pants, gathered what remained of my pride, and stepped out to face whatever waited.

The main room was empty. Not even the guard was around. I briefly considered making a run for the front door. But in the hearth, a fire crackled with enough fresh logs that I knew I wasn't truly alone.

Instead, I decided to study the space until I had my bearings. I wandered slowly, taking in the trinkets that sat on shelves. The weaponry on the walls, some of which I recognized from history lessons about the Great War, some of which were completely foreign to me. The placards mounted beside them offered information in a language I couldn't decipher.

The bookshelves were the same way. Leather-bound texts in languages I'd never learned. The common tongue was shared by every kingdom in Menryth, so I'd never needed anything else. Whoever this collection belonged to had a different opinion. Or an obscure hobby.

Some small noise made me look up.

I found Amanti watching me from the other side of the space. Her expression was wary but patient.

She was giving me time, I realized. Ironically, it was the one thing I knew we didn't have much of. Not after what I'd done to Duron. Or whatever the Midnight Court had planned for me. I still wasn't willing to take Amanti's word for it that this court wasn't a threat. I'd done that with Callan, and look where it'd gotten me.

"We should talk," I said at last.

"All right."

Her arm was still in a sling, her ruined wings tucked at her back. Every time the mantle of her dark hair shifted, I saw the ragged edges again, and worry scraped my ribs raw.

I paced in front of the fire, thoughts racing through all the things that needed to be said between us.

"You're going to wear a trench in this floor," she said at last.

"Good." I kept pacing. "Maybe that damned guard will break his ankle in it, and I can see myself out."

"It'll take a lot more than a rut in the floor to stop Thorne," she said mildly.

"Exactly what will it take?" I tossed out, only half-joking.

"That's a good question," she mused. "For starters, you'd have to get past three Midnight fae, all elite warriors with gifts from the gods."

"Wonderful," I muttered. "So, it was a communal kidnapping."

A low voice drifted from the doorway. "We prefer rescue."

I whirled. The guard from earlier leaned a shoulder against the frame, a hulking silhouette with a neatly kept beard and eyes the color of slate before rain. A section of hair had grown longer than the rest and hung in three small braids at his shoulder. He'd swapped the cloak for a dark wool shirt, sleeves rolled to forearms corded with quiet strength. I had the distinct impression that the sword at his hip wasn't a threat so much as an extension of his body.

"One of my *rescuers*, I presume," I said, the word laced with sarcasm.

He offered a mock-bow. "Thorne Varros, at your service, Your Highness."

"Where are my swords?" I demanded.

"They were removed for your safety. And ours. Though apparently the blades weren't the primary threat." His gaze flicked to my hands as if he'd seen the embers spark from my skin earlier. "At any rate, you'll get them back when you're recovered."

"Recovered?"

"The drugs we gave you," he said and had the decency to look slightly embarrassed by it, "are pretty strong. They'll take another day or so to fully leave your system. Until then, you'll be a bit off balance."

I crossed my arms. "I'm not off balance."

"Of course not," he said gravely.

I frowned, remembering how the food had helped steady me, how it took the edge off my shakiness and blurred vision. Maybe it had been more than just hunger.

Before I could ask what, exactly, they'd given me, another figure appeared behind Thorne. Another male, older, broader in the shoulders, quieter in presence, though no less imposing. And familiar. Recognition hit me like a punch in the gut.

"Daegel," he said as if to remind me.

As if I'd forgotten.

"I know who you are." The words came out thin as a blade. "Rydian's third."

Something like warmth moved through his eyes—friendliness, unguarded and infuriating, considering he was one of my captors.

"You remember."

The way he said it, like it was a compliment I'd given him, only sent irritation rushing through me. "I don't think I'll forget you. Not since you helped kidnap me."

"Rescue," he corrected.

Thorne gave me a look as if to say, "See?"

A third figure pushed past them both—female fae, brown skin, dark braids coiled at the nape of her neck. A scar nicked one eyebrow; another bisected her lower lip and tugged one corner downward in a perpetual frown.

"This is her?" she asked the others.

Her gaze landed on Amanti behind me, who must have offered silent confirmation. The female fae frowned at me.

"I'm Keres," she said, breezing past without waiting for my response.

She carried a wooden tray with a steaming bowl and a mug that smelled like crushed mint and bitters. She set them on the low table near the sofa and glanced at Amanti in a way that was not deference so much as fondness curbed by discipline.

"Eat. You'll stop shaking."

"I'm not—" I began.

Keres cocked her head. "I wasn't talking to you."

I watched in mild shock as the Aine warrior lowered herself to the chair and took the mug Keres handed her.

"Thank you," she told Keres.

Keres nodded once and moved to the hearth, where she checked the clean bandages drying on a rack set near the heat of the flames. Her back was turned to me, which made her either formidable or naïve.

Weighing my chances for escape, I stole glances at the others. Thorne remained in the doorway, watchful. Daegel took three steps into the room and stood with the patience of an old tree, not to mention the solidarity of one. Whatever this was—rescue, kidnapping—they weren't letting their guard down.

"How long have I been here?" I asked no one in particular.

"Two days," Amanti said. "Nearly three."

"Two days?" I blinked. "And the journey here took…"

"Another three days before it," Daegel said.

Keres hissed at him for it.

"I've been drugged for five days," I said, wondering what I'd missed. What state the realm was in now. With Duron gone, with Callan likely now king… and with so many witnesses to my furyfire that night. A power imbued by Hel itself.

Would the realm have guessed me a demon's daughter by now? Would they turn on me for it?

"They had no choice." Amanti's eyes softened with that damnable patience. "Heliconia's scouts have doubled. We couldn't risk you slowing them down in any way."

"Ah. Well, I wouldn't want to burden you with my slowness while you were busy kidnapping me to another kingdom." I glared at each of them one by one. Daegel and Thorne looked slightly sorry, but Keres didn't even blink.

"Where are we?" I asked into the tense silence.

Keres said nothing. At least she didn't hiss. Apparently, that was all the permission Daegel needed.

"At the edge of the Trolech Forest," he said. "Just south of the city."

The city. Did he mean Ravenna? The capital city of the Midnight Court?

"And this is your house?" I asked him.

He looked to Keres, who answered for him.

"This is Frithhold, an outpost dedicated to the court's protection. Thorne and I live here now, but it belongs to us all," she said.

All? As in, the three of them? Or were there more?

I looked at Daegel. "You're midnight fae."

He nodded slowly. "I am."

Did Rydian know that? He must since he's the one who put me in their carriage.

I looked from him to the others. "You all serve the Midnight Court then?"

Keres's gaze narrowed a fraction. "We serve our queen and her appointed general."

"And will I be meeting her?" I asked. "Your queen?"

No one had ever seen the Midnight queen in person. Not anyone I'd ever met, anyway. Not even Tyrion, the male who had raised me and King of the Summer Court, had ever taken a meeting with her directly. Her name was Cadira. She'd inherited the throne several years before Heliconia had cursed the Summer Court. The former queen, Winyra, had been reclusive before she'd been killed, but Cadira was worse. They said she was nothing more than a shadow when she wanted to be; that was all I knew of her. All I'd ever cared to know, considering she'd left the rest of the realm to Heliconia's destruction.

"She knows you're here," Keres said evenly. "If she wants to meet you, she'll send for you."

"And if I want to meet her?" I challenged.

The three of them exchanged a look, but no one offered an answer.

Amanti reached out and set her fingers lightly on my wrist. "Tell me what happened after I left."

I tensed, thinking of all that had happened in her absence. And the listening ears here to witness me utter it now. At my pointed look toward Thorne and Daegel, Keres merely said, "You can say it while we're standing here, or we can pretend to leave and listen from the other room. Your choice."

I sighed, knowing there was nothing I could do to stop them from listening. I could refuse to talk, but if I was right, and this was a kidnapping, they might attempt to torture it out of me. Then again, Daegel, at least, likely knew all this already, thanks to Rydian. Either way, Amanti deserved to know about her Aine sisters.

I spoke slowly, the words scraping on the way out. I kept my attention on Amanti, doing my best to shut out the others as I told her almost all of it. The fraying wards, Lesha's departure, Sonoma's decline, her death. And then Callan's arrival. My decision to marry him in exchange for his help breaking the curse.

"That brat has never cared about anyone else in his privileged life," Keres muttered, earning a warning look from Amanti for her interruption.

"Go on," the Aine said to me, patting my hand.

So, I told her the truth about Duron—how he was draining his own people to feed his land. And his ego. So no one would know that Autumn was weakening. Judging from their lack of surprise, they already knew that part too.

Finally, I told her about the party in Grey Oak that was supposed to be my wedding. The Withered agreeing to attack as a distraction for my escape. Koraz. Duron.

When I reached the part about my furyfire, the air in the room thinned to a thread. Keres didn't stop her work, folding and stacking the clean bandages, but her movements slowed. Even Thorne seemed to lean in.

There was no point in lying about it, though. Rydian knew it all—everything I was capable of—and he'd already sold me out. Besides, the realm would know it too now that I'd used it to murder a king. Telling them this part would hopefully save me from their attempts to torture it out of me later. There were plenty of other secrets worth dying over; this wasn't one of them.

"I didn't mean to kill him," I said. "He would have chained me up and drained me dry. He would have—"

"You were cornered," Amanti said. "You chose the only path out that didn't end in your death."

"Or worse," Keres murmured. "There's always a worse."

I swallowed past the ash in my throat, refusing to put my emotions on display for these people. "And that brings us to my kidnapping," I said pointedly.

"Rescue," Thorne and Daegel said in unison.

I said nothing, glaring pointedly.

Keres set the folded bandages aside. "If we'd meant you harm, Princess, I wouldn't have bothered with the tea, which contained a healing tonic to help speed up your recovery, nor the food, which means less resources for us, by the way."

"Or blankets," Thorne added. "Or letting you attempt to set fire to our house."

How did he know I'd tried it?

"Or giving you the nicest guest room with the bathing chamber attached," Daegel said with what I could have sworn was a pout.

Okay, these were fair points. This entire scenario was so far from what I'd imagined waiting for me on the other side of that carriage. But I couldn't let my guard down—not yet.

"Why bring me here then? Why not let me take my chances escaping Autumn on my own? Did Rydian pay you? Did you pay him? What kind of secrets do you think I possess?"

"You think Rydian paid us?" Thorne asked, and I could have sworn he looked amused by the idea.

"Unbelievable," Keres muttered.

Amanti glanced toward the female fae, the firelight catching in the dark sweep of her lashes. "Rydian sent a request to extricate you somewhere Autumn couldn't reach you," she said at last. "He was worried what would happen after your wedding to Callan."

I wasn't sure what to say to that. Rydian had come to me. That final night...everything between us had felt like a goodbye. I'd assumed he was giving up on his feelings because I would soon be wed. But now I wondered… had he been saying farewell before sending me away?

What would happen to him now as a servant of his new king? His brother? Would he continue following orders, fighting to protect Autumn from Heliconia's attacks?

Would I ever see him again?

I shook off the last thought, reminding myself I shouldn't want to.

Amanti squeezed my hand. "You weren't taken for punishment or torture, Aurelia. You were taken because Heliconia's scouts were already hunting you. This was the only way to keep them from finding you."

"How do you know that?" I asked.

"Our spies in Grey Oak found a trail not long after you arrived at Grey Oak," Daegel said grimly. "Obsidians entered Sunspire when the ward lines fell—"

"You found their trail back in Sunspire?" I cut him off sharply.

"They followed us back to Grey Oak," he went on, eyes glittering with a regret that made me wonder if he felt responsible somehow.

"The attack in the Emerald Forest," I murmured.

He nodded. "A few got away. They likely reported back to her. And then a couple of weeks after you arrived in Grey Oak, they infiltrated the city. Got inside the castle walls, in fact."

"Duron blamed Callan for it," I remembered. The black eye he'd brandished when he'd come to my room that night. Drunk, no less. And wanting me to comfort him. To forgive him everything that had happened between us like it was nothing at all.

"How do you know they were looking for me?" I asked. "Maybe they were trying to get to the king."

"You mean besides the fact that they kept hissing your name?" Thorne asked pointedly.

Daegel slid a small oilskin packet from his vest and set it on the table. "Because we took this off one of them."

I flipped the flap with two fingers and eased out a square of vellum, edges singed. A charcoal likeness stared up at me—my face, hastily but unmistakably sketched. A braid over one shoulder. The small moon-and-stars tattoo inked on my neck.

Beneath the sketch, symbols had been etched with dark ink.

"What does this say?" I asked, frowning. That made twice I'd seen a language in the old tongue in the past hour.

Thorne translated. "Alive if possible. If not, return the heart."

The room went silent.

Keres took the vellum and slid it back into its case. "You should know that we intercepted a royal emissary from Grey Oak headed for the Spring Court on our way here. He carried news of Autumn's recent coronation," she added, mouth flattening, "and a bounty."

Thorne's gaze flicked to me, steady. "It names you the late king's assassin and a traitor to the Autumn crown. The bounty is impressively high. Dead or alive."

Amanti swore softly.

My pulse thudded in my throat, too fast, too loud. "So, I have the Autumn Court on one side," I said, voice strangely unruffled, "and Heliconia on the other."

"And us in the middle," Thorne said.

"Lucky us," Keres said.

"Does that mean..." I swallowed the emotion that wanted to rise. "Will Rydian be ordered to look for me? As the king's soldier, won't he be tasked with retrieving the bounty—"

"Rydian will not return to this place," Thorne said, and the finality in his words suggested something more than just an assurance I wouldn't be hunted down for my crime.

Daegel's tone gentled. "There's more." He tipped his chin toward my hands. "Autumn's proclamation named the weapon that killed Duron as your furyfire. The realm knows what you are now. And where your gifts come from."

A laugh scraped out of me, ugly and small. "Great. I'm sure I'll be welcomed anywhere I go now that all of Menryth knows I'm Hel's Chosen One."

So much for torturing me for secrets. It seemed they were all out in the open now, thanks to my recklessness.

Keres stepped closer. Not coddling. Braced. "So, embrace it. Become what they fear."

"Easy for you to say," I said in a hard voice. This female, whom Amanti seemed so fond of, had been less than welcoming since the moment she'd walked in. I wasn't in the mood for any more of her snarky comments. "You don't have the weight of the realm on your shoulders. Nor are you being hunted by an entire army made from the dark queen's stolen power."

"No, instead, we're risking our own necks by offering you refuge. If you're caught, we'll be targeted now too."

I scowled. "No one asked you to do that."

"Rydian asked," she snapped. The way she'd said his name—like she knew him well, maybe even intimately—grated on parts of me I didn't want to admit. "Apparently, he cares about you. Maybe more than you care about yourself. Or the realm you were chosen to protect."

"How dare you?" I said. "You don't know anything about me or what I care about. And despite what Rydian says, I can take care of myself."

"Prove it," she said, smirking in a way that had me wanting to rip the expression off her pretty, scarred face.

"Don't tempt me," I snarled.

"Keres," Thorne said with a sigh. "This isn't the time."

"I'm serious," Keres said. She nodded toward the front door. "You want to be free of us? This is how. Train. Learn to wield your magic. Control it. When you don't need our protection anymore, we'll go our separate ways."

"Keres," Daegel warned, but a look from her cut him off.

"She has to stand on her own," Keres said, pinning me with a measuring look.

Daegel hesitated but then nodded.

"What do you say?" Amanti asked quietly. "Will you stay and train with us?"

No one said anything, all of them waiting for my response. Part of me wanted to refuse. They'd taken me against my will—kidnapped, not rescued, I didn't care what they tried to call it—and drugged me for days. Keres obviously hated me and, in this moment, the feeling was mutual. But I couldn't walk away from Amanti. Not after losing Lesha and Sonoma. For better or worse, she was the only family I had left.

Besides, the entire realm knew I wielded the power of the Furiosities. Where could I go that was safe now?

"I'll stay," I said at last, the words rough as gravel. "For you, Amanti. Not for your queen." I didn't even let myself look at Keres as I added, "Not for any of them. For you, I'll stay. For now."

Daegel breathed an audible sigh.

Thorne slapped Daegel's shoulder and said, "See, Keres? And you thought we'd have to tie her up."

THE
LOVERS

Chapter Five
Rydian

Three days stretched into what felt like three hundred as I sat in the bone-chilled dungeons of Grey Oak Keep. Water trickled somewhere nearby, though I didn't bother to look for it. Not when it would likely be moldy or worse. The air smelled of unwashed bodies and rat dung. Every so often, chains clinked; the only sign I wasn't down here alone. No one spoke to me except a guard on day two, who told me, "The king will see you when he's ready, and not before," which was not a response so much as a door closing on what power I once might have wielded in this court.

Power that had been relinquished when I'd run Koraz through with my own sword. When I'd stood by as Aurelia unleashed furyfire on the Autumn king—my father.

I hoped the bastard rotted in Hel. Koraz with him. Thanks to the magic-infested wound Koraz left at my hip, I wasn't convinced I wouldn't be joining them.

At least, Aurelia was safe.

I could only hope the others would remain at her side, showing her the way the gods had laid out for us all.

On the morning of the third day, boots stopped outside my cell.

Keys scraped. Light cleaved the dark as the door swung inward, and a captain I half-remembered said, without looking at my face, "Up."

They took me not to the gallows but to a guest wing where a bathing chamber containing a basin full of steaming water greeted me. A servant kept his eyes on the tiles and handed me a razor. I washed three days of grime from my skin and let the heat loosen the ache from my shoulders.

When I emerged, clothes waited: a clean tunic, trousers that still smelled of lye, boots that fit.

"Why the charity?" I asked the captain when he returned.

The captain looked at me then, and I saw the regret flash. "You deserved better than a cell for all you've done for the Autumn people."

"Thank you," I told him.

He cleared his throat, blinked—and the kindness was gone. "The king has summoned you," he said gruffly. "Don't keep him waiting."

"Wouldn't dream of it."

The corridors of Grey Oak were too quiet for a palace that had just crowned a new king. Torchlight skimmed the stone like oil. Servants moved in hushes, their eyes averted, as if sound alone might crack the veneer holding the halls together. The scent of damp earth threaded with smoke drifted in from the courtyard beyond—rain had come and gone, carrying away the ash from where Duron's body had been burned to dust on that fateful night.

I didn't slow. My steps found the old paths without thought—past the east gallery where Duron's hunting trophies leered from their mounts; through the colonnade the sunlight never fully reached; down the wide hall that had been so intimidating when I was a boy walking these halls.

A guard outside the royal antechamber shifted his spear to bar my way. Fletcher, of course. He'd always been one of Callan's favorites. "The king is—"

"Waiting," I said, and pushed the haft aside with two fingers.

The door clicked shut behind me.

The hush inside the chamber was different—thicker, clotted with something that didn't break apart when I crossed the threshold. Something that nearly pulled me forward, whether I willed it or not.

Callan stood at the table beneath the south window, crown set beside a spread of maps. Rain left pearls on the panes; the storm had left the glass streaked, and the light came through in broken bands that cut his face into pieces—light, shadow, light.

On the table between us, placed carefully over the maps he studied, lay a jeweled crown. I recognized it vaguely from Duron's collection, but even he rarely wore such an ostentatious piece. It was far more ornate than necessary, especially in private company, which meant it was a message. To remind me of who each of us had become in this kingdom. To remind me of who held power—and who didn't.

"You won't be charged with treason," he said, voice scraped flat.

A dozen answers rose and fell in me. I chose none of them. "No?"

"Several members of the court," he went on, "have given statements that you were... attempting to apprehend Aurelia at the scene." A muscle ticked along his jaw. "They claim she assassinated my father with her demon-gifted magic, then escaped with aid from the Withered—and the Midnight Court fae she is clearly working with."

The words landed carefully between us.

I let a beat pass. "You and I both know that's a ludicrous claim."

His chin came up, his jaw hardening. "It's the truth, and the people have a right to know it."

"Do they have a right to know *I'm* half-midnight?"

"Of course not." He didn't flinch. "How would that look," he asked softly, "if my midnight-fae brother helped my fiancée kill my father?" He breathed out, and a crack showed beneath the new edges. "They would wonder what was between them to cause the bastard prince to do such a thing." Rage flashed, sinking beneath the surface of his calm façade. "That is a story I prefer not to tell—especially as I begin my rule as king."

I watched as he inhaled shakily, collecting himself again.

"What do you want from me, Callan?" I asked.

"Gone," he said bitterly. "I want you gone. This is no longer your home."

"It never was my home," I said.

Something flickered in his eyes—hurt or history, I couldn't tell. "If that is how you want it, then we'll do it your way. If you are found inside Grey Oak's borders again, I will treat you as the law would treat any foreign spy and have you executed."

He moved then, not away from me, but toward, closing the space with that controlled grace he liked to pretend was gentleness. I suddenly realized why the room had felt so thick when I'd arrived. Callan was no longer dulling his power. The scent of vervain, his little trick for suppressing it, was long gone from where it had once clung to his skin.

His mouth twisted as he crowded me. "Where is she?"

"Alive."

"Where," he said again.

Over his shoulder, the rain scratched at the glass like a thing trying to get in.

I didn't answer, wondering how long before he touched me. Before he compelled the truth from my tongue.

He took the last step. His fist came with it.

The first punch exploded brightly behind my eyes. The second forced me back a step. Pain rang clean and absolute, shuddering all the way to my still-tender hip. I did not give him a third.

His fist landed in my palm. For a moment, I did not yield it to him, and his eyes blazed with fury that I knew would never truly extinguish between us as long as we both lived.

He stepped back, yanking his hand with him, and I let him have it. Gingerly, I touched the new bruise blossoming on my cheekbone. The bastard had a stronger left hook than I imagined. Good for him.

"Are you finished?" I asked.

He turned away and braced both hands on the table. His right knuckles bloomed purple already.

"You had no right to take her from me," he said.

"You were going to put her in chains."

"I was going to keep her safe." He lifted his head, anger scalding his grief clean. He pushed off the table's edge, straightening. "The court is already saying she bewitched me. That she murdered him to make room for herself. That I—" He bit the word in half, and the room swallowed it.

"So tell them the truth."

"Which truth is that, brother? Your betrayal? Hers?"

"About Duron. What he intended to do to her. What he should never have done to his own people."

His gaze met mine—king and boy at once.

"Where is she?" he said, softer. Not a demand. A plea.

"Somewhere you will not follow."

"You think there's anywhere in this realm I won't find her?"

"There are places even you can't go," I said. "Doors that will not open for even an Autumn king."

He held my stare.

"You always told me she was wrong for me," he said. "All this time—it was you who was wrong for her."

I pretended he hadn't hit a mark.

He cocked his head. "Oh, you thought I didn't know? That I was too stupid to realize you touched what was supposed to be mine?"

"We never meant to hurt you, brother."

His expression twisted, and I realized, too late, it was the wrong thing to say. "I don't have a brother anymore."

I didn't bother to argue for myself. There was too much history between us. And too much of our father in the male who stood before me now.

"Her role is far more important than whatever you think you feel for her," I told him.

His eyes closed a fraction, and for a second, I wondered if I'd finally talked reason into him. When he opened them, the king had returned.

"You're banished," he said—each syllable deceptively soft. "From Grey Oak. From Autumn's borders. If you're seen inside them again, I'll make good on every threat I've just spared you. Same goes for her. If she's caught, she'll be charged with murder and treason and dealt with accordingly."

"Will you turn your back on an alliance with the Chosen One then? Risk your kingdom's destruction over your own broken ego?"

The muscle along his jaw worked, then eased. A dozen answers moved behind his eyes. "You always hated me," he said finally, but there was no bite left in it. "From the first day you arrived in this hall, dripping with your stupid shadows."

"I never hated you," I said. "I hated him for what he did to you. And who you became."

His breath shuddered out. It almost sounded like a laugh. Almost. "I should have killed you in the yard when we were twelve," he said, voice hoarse.

"You couldn't then," I said sadly. "You can't now."

"Get out," he spat with enough force that I turned to go.

The guards closed around me like a tide, releasing me only once I'd exited the castle and reached the outer gate.

Outside, the rain had eased to a mist that made the lamps gutter. The courtyard smelled of wet stone, wet iron, wet leaves—everything washed, but nothing clean.

My eye and hip both throbbed in time with my steps. I couldn't bring myself to feel relieved that he'd let me go. That I'd see her again after all. To be banished from Grey Oak, to be at odds with its king, only meant this would be harder in the end.

Outside the gates, I did not turn toward the road that led to my townhouse in the city. Instead, I turned my feet toward the only place in this realm that didn't require a blood oath from me for entry. Frithhold was a hidden hinge in the crook of a mountain made from ancient midnight magic. In a place where time stood still. Where Fate waited for a choice from us all.

THE
LOVERS

Chapter Six
Callan

The bruise on my knuckles bloomed before the one on his face would. Still, I consoled myself with the fact that I'd left him damaged. And laced with a little magic, it would last long enough for *her* to see it. To be forced to think of me when she looked at him.

It was a small comfort.

The great hall was empty, though I felt anything but alone among the ghosts that clung to this place. The echo of the door closing behind my half-brother still vibrated through the stone. It sounded like laughter. His, probably. He'd looked almost satisfied when I struck him—like he'd been waiting years for proof that I was exactly the vile creature he thought I was.

Or maybe my father's spirit taunted me from the Afterlife.

I flexed my hand. The pain was small, sharp, mercifully quick to heal. It wouldn't do for a king to be wounded that easily.

Outside, Grey Oak groaned under another cold wind. The vines on the outer walls were dying, leaves crisping to ash instead of amber. A sign of the Winter queen's reach, the advisors said. Another reminder that everything my father built was rotting faster than I could pretend to save it. Even with the donation centers operating at full volume, it would not be enough. My father must have known it and had done nothing about it except try to trap a Summer heir to drain instead.

Now, for better or worse, I had no plan at all.

"Majesty."

Lemuel's voice could sour wine. My father's advisor appeared in the doorway, already mid-bow, already displeased. Thin, gray, smelling faintly of mildew and superiority, he looked at me like I was the runner-up.

"What?" I demanded flatly.

"You dismissed the prince rather abruptly," he said.

"I struck him and tossed him out," I said. "Let's call things what they are."

Lemuel's mouth flattened. "The court will expect an explanation about your brother's expulsion and his role in what happened here."

"The court can expect silence. They thrive on it."

He drifted closer, hands tucked into his sleeves. "Your father would never have tolerated—"

"My father is dead." I hadn't meant for it to sound like that—relief disguised as a statement—but it did.

Lemuel's eyes narrowed. "May his spirit judge us all," he murmured, the ritual phrase sharp as a knife. "And may you prove a stronger king than he believed you could be."

I turned away, retracing my steps back to the table where I stared down at the maps of the villages Heliconia's soldiers had burned. According to our scouts, she'd entered our borders three days ago, attacking every village along the way, taking no prisoners. It was concerning, the Winter queen's sudden act of war, and required a king's response. But mostly, I stared at the maps, unseeing, because I refused to let Lemuel's words find a mark.

"He left you a kingdom bleeding from the roots," Lemuel went on. "If we do not enrich our borders before the Winter queen finishes sucking the life from the land, Autumn will rot."

"And what would you have me do? Drain our people? Empty their life force so thoroughly that I no longer have subjects to rule?"

He didn't answer. He didn't need to. The suggestion hung between us like a specter. *Increase the donations. Imbue yourself with power. At any cost.*

"Close the donation centers," I said.

"Your Majesty?" Lemuel blinked. "What will we do—"

"We will allow our people to retain their magic so that they may fight and defend their kingdom," I snapped.

The advisor hesitated.

"Do you defy your king's commands?" I asked, debating the merits of simply putting my hand on his arm to make it so.

But the elder sorcerer shook his head. "No, Your Highness."

"Then do as I say."

Lemuel swallowed but said nothing. When he finally bowed out, the silence he left behind felt heavier than his oppressive presence ever had.

THE
LOVERS

Chapter Seven
Aurelia

Agreeing to stay hadn't magically made Frithhold feel less like a cage. It just meant I'd picked my prison. Night came anyway, sliding down the mountain in slow, gray sheets. Lamps were lit one by one, a warm glow in the great room that made it look almost inviting from the shadowed corridor outside my bedroom.

Almost.

I tried—and failed—to sleep. Restlessness drove me out again. I wrapped my arms around myself as I stepped into the main space, half expecting to find Keres waiting with a smirk and a new way to insult me. But the room was empty.

The fire banked low in the hearth, all coals and soft orange light. Shadows climbed the log walls, licking across stone and leather and wood.

Weapons lined every surface that wasn't already taken up by shelves. Blades older than anything I'd seen in my lifetime. Axes with double heads and inlaid handles made of gemstones. A spear whose tip shimmered faintly with its own internal light. Each one mounted on a plaque etched with curling script I couldn't decipher.

I drifted closer in spite of myself.

The nearest sword had a bronze hilt, the metal worn smooth where countless hands had gripped it. A dragon's head curved along the pommel, jaws open in a silent snarl. The plaque beneath it was a small strip of metal bolted to the stone, the words engraved in the old tongue, the letters sharp and elegant.

My fingers itched to trace them.

Eventually, my gaze drifted back to the shelves.

If I was going to be stuck here for the foreseeable future, I might as well learn something. The thought surprised me. A few hours ago, I'd been plotting escape routes. Now I was thinking about settling in. The thought of sitting by the fire with a good book left an ache in my chest.

I thought of all the endless nights I'd spent in the library at Sunspire, scouring every book in Tyrion's royal collection for some clue about how to break the curse on my kingdom.

I'd drunk a lot of whiskey those nights. Amanti had too. Some nights, we'd laughed more than we read. Other nights, I scoured page after page, tome after tome. And come away without a single answer in the end.

I wasn't sure if trying it again in this library made me a fool or utterly determined.

Sonoma would've teased me as the former. Then she would've picked the heaviest, driest tome on the shelf and made me read it out loud until we were both cross-eyed.

The ache that thought left in my chest nearly sent me back to bed. Instead, I crossed the room.

Up close, the collection was even more intimidating. The nearest shelf held thick volumes bound in dark leather, their spines tooled with unfamiliar characters. Some looked like claw marks. Others like vines. A few were stamped only with a single symbol in the center.

The Old Language, I assumed.

I reached out, then hesitated as something tugged at the skin of my wrist.

My sleeve had ridden up. The mark there caught the firelight—a small, inked curve of lines and arcs, the Verdant rune the oracle had etched into my flesh back in Grey Oak.

A favor owed.

I rubbed my thumb over it. The skin warmed, the magic stirring faintly like a sleeping animal shifting in its nest. Someday, she'd come to collect that favor. I could only hope it would be one I was capable of giving.

"What do you want from me?" I whispered to the mark.

It didn't answer.

When I lowered my hand, my gaze snagged on a spine directly in front of me.

A symbol had been stamped there in faded gold. Not identical to the one on my wrist, but close—same shape, same curve, the lines intersecting in a way that made my skin prickle.

My heart thudded once, too hard.

Slowly, I slid the book free.

It was heavier than it looked. The leather creaked. Dust motes spiraled in the firelight as I carried it to the table near the hearth and set it down.

Up close, the rune on the cover was even clearer. The same shape as the one on the spine, with additional flourishes at the edges. A more elaborate version of the Verdant mark on my skin, but undeniably related.

"All right," I murmured. "You have my attention."

I reached for the cover.

"That's an ambitious choice," a dry voice said.

Every muscle in my body tensed.

I turned.

Thorne Varros lounged in the archway, one shoulder propped against the stone, arms crossed loosely over his chest. The lamplight traced the edges of him—broad shoulders, hair pulled back and braided at his nape, eyes sharp enough to slice.

He'd traded his cloak for a simple black shirt and worn leather trousers, but nothing about him looked relaxed. Even leaning, he was all potential energy, like one wrong move would snap him into motion.

As a child, I'd heard horror stories of midnight fae—blood-suckers and teeth-gnashers. Creatures of nightmare. These fae were much more civilized than the legends claimed, at least as far as I'd seen, but I hadn't seen a whisper of magic from a single one of them yet. That didn't mean they weren't a threat.

"Do you make a habit of sneaking up on people?" I asked.

"Do you make a habit of talking to books?" he countered.

He pushed away from the wall and walked toward me, steps soundless on the stone. When he drew close enough, the air shifted. A faint hum threaded through it, just below hearing. It might've been my imagination. Or it might've been a warning that Thorne was a threat.

"I couldn't sleep. I thought I'd see what sort of contraband my captors keep around."

"Rescuers," he corrected automatically, then sighed. "That one isn't exactly light reading."

"You say that like you know what it says."

"I should hope so, considering it's part of my collection."

"All of these are yours?" I slanted him a look. "Trying to impress your dates?" I asked. "Or are you just compensating for something?"

His mouth curved, almost but not quite a smile. "I'm not the one who can't read what's in those pages."

It dragged an unwilling huff of amusement out of me. I hated that. I turned it into a scowl.

"What does this mean?" I nodded to the rune on the cover while making sure to keep my own tattoo covered. "I've seen something like it before."

His gaze dropped to the symbol.

"The old tongue has many layers," he said. "But if you want the simplest translation?" His fingers brushed the edge of the cover, not quite touching the rune itself. "Life."

Life.

The word settled in my gut like a stone dropped into deep water.

On my wrist, the Verdant tattoo warmed again, responding to the echo of his word. Life. Favor. Promise. Debt. All knotted together.

"Of course it does," I muttered.

His gaze flicked up at that, from the book to my face and then lower. To my throat.

I realized too late that my hair had shifted, exposing the small crescent of ink just below my ear. The moon-and-stars mark I'd woken with after Heliconia's curse had failed to hurt me seven years ago. The one the bounty sketch artist had apparently gotten a good look at.

Heat climbed up my neck. I resisted the urge to cover it.

"There's magic in that," Thorne said quietly.

"In what?" I asked, feigning ignorance.

He didn't bother to hide his look. "It's humming like a nest of hornets."

I swallowed. The tattoo tingled, a slow, spreading warmth under the skin. It had always felt like a part of me, but lately, the magic inside it had grown more insistent. Like it knew something I didn't.

"It's just ink," I said.

"Nothing in this realm is 'just' anything," he replied. "Not if the gods had a hand in it."

"And you would know?" I asked, arching a brow.

He tipped his head as if considering how much he wanted to say. Then, with visible reluctance, he sat on the edge of the low table opposite me, the book between us.

He drew his hand up, and slowly, dark lines appeared from his fingertips. They seemed to draw upward from the floor rather than shooting out from his hands. Like he was drawing power inward rather than pushing it out.

"What is it?" I asked.

"Ley lines."

Ley lines were a reference to the very magic that gave Menryth life. The courts whose season sustained itself year-round—that was all thanks to ley lines. The magic fae fed on and in turn dispersed back to the land as a renewable source—also, ley lines.

I'd never known anyone to wield them.

"What can you do with them?" I asked.

He closed his fist, and the dark webbing vanished. "If a ley line flows near me, I can draw from it. Borrow strength. Lend stability. But it's not free. It takes something back."

"What?" I asked.

He met my gaze. "Whatever it can get."

That sent a chill skating down my spine that had nothing to do with the mountain air.

"Sounds miserable," I said.

He shrugged one shoulder. "We don't get to choose our gods-gifts. Any more than you chose yours."

I bristled. "Mine's not a gift."

"No," he agreed softly. "It's a weapon. And a warning. Most gods-gifts are both."

We sat there for a moment in the thick quiet, the fire throwing slow shadows around us.

My fingers drifted toward the book again. "And this?" I asked. "More stories about fae gifts?"

"It's a compendium," he said. "Old accounts of the creation of Menryth. The way the ley lines were mapped and anchored." His mouth twisted. "The sort of thing that's useful if the realm becomes imbalanced."

"Is it imbalanced now?" I asked before I could stop myself.

He didn't answer right away. His gaze slid past me, toward the far wall, as if he could see straight through to the world beyond. For a heart-beat, the air hummed again, that faint vibration in my bones.

"It's... shifting," he said at last. "That's why I brought the books here. Closer to where the lines converge."

"Here." I glanced around the cabin. "Frithhold."

"Frithhold sits on a knot in the network," he said. "If something goes wrong, I'll feel it from here sooner than I would anywhere else."

"And the books—you want to protect them?" I asked.

"I want to preserve our history. So that we don't repeat it."

"Are there any books here about the Verdant?"

"Why do you ask?"

"Before I left Sunspire, we had reason to believe the Verdant healers might know of magic strong enough to break Heliconia's curse on my kingdom."

His expression softened to one that looked infuriatingly like pity. "The Verdant don't break curses."

"How do you know?" I asked, my voice rougher than I'd intended.

"Because my mate was one."

"Well, can I talk to her—"

"She died eight years ago."

Guilt and grief panged in my chest. True mates were rare these days in Menryth. Celeste and Tyrion had loved each other more deeply than anyone I'd ever known, and even they hadn't been true mates. The fae believed it was likely from fae magic waning to nothing more than a weak trickle of what it had once been. But there was nothing weak about Thorne. His iron-clad stoicism as he said the words was proof enough.

"I'm sorry."

His silence made it clear the subject was closed for questions.

"You said earlier," I began, then stopped, choosing my words carefully. "You said Rydian will not return to this place."

"Did I?" His voice was mild, but his jaw tightened.

"You said it like you knew something." My fingers curled around the edge of the table. "Is he never coming back to Frithhold then?"

The question felt like yanking a splinter out of my own chest. I hated that he heard the thread of rawness in it.

Thorne studied me for a long moment. In that look, I caught something I hadn't expected—understanding. Maybe even a flicker of sympathy. It made me want to lash out.

Instead, he glanced down at the book again.

"Rydian has his own path to walk," he said finally. "Destiny tugs at him, same as it does the rest of us, even if his power runs darker than most. I can't tell you where he is right now."

"Can't?" I pressed. "Or won't?"

"Both," he said simply.

I scowled.

The fire cracked, a coal collapsing in on itself.

I stared at the rune on the book, at the mark on my wrist, at the faint outline of my neck tattoo reflected in the polished metal of a nearby sword.

Life. Favor. Debt. Gods-touched power that felt more like a curse.

"You're reassuring, you know that?" I said.

He huffed out a quiet laugh. "It's a gift."

"Another one you didn't ask for?" I asked.

"That one I might have," he said, and there it was again—that almost-smile, gone as quickly as it came.

He rose. The faint hum in the air diminished as he straightened, as if he were taking it with him. Maybe he was. If the ley lines were something he took into himself, maybe that was why it felt like he always sucked the air from the room.

"You should sleep," he said. "Training starts early."

"You're very confident I agreed to that," I muttered.

"You said you'd stay," he reminded me. "And you don't strike me as someone who likes wasting time. Or potential."

He had me there, damn him.

He took a few steps toward the archway, then paused. "If you're set on that book," he said without looking back, "start with the illustrations. The text will give you a headache."

"And if the book bites?" I asked.

"Then you'll have learned something from it," he said. "Which is more than most can say."

He left me with that and the lingering hum of his power, the room feeling both emptier and more crowded in his absence.

I looked down at the book, at the rune for life glinting faintly in the firelight. At the mark on my wrist, warm and waiting.

Slowly, I opened the cover.

The first page was an illustration, inked in elegant detail. Seven thrones, each carved from different elements—stone, ice, oak, ivy, and something that looked like solid flame—spread out in a circular design. Lines threaded between them, a web of power, the same inky threads I'd seen under Thorne's skin when he'd drawn power from the ley lines.

At the center of the circle, another shape waited. Not quite a throne. Not quite a void. The ink there seemed thinner somehow, as if the artist hadn't been sure of the shape.

Unease prickled along my spine.

Life, the rune whispered. Favor. Promise.

Debt.

I traced the circle with one finger, feeling the faint thrum of magic in the page, and wondered which one of those I was meant to pay.

THE
LOVERS

Chapter Eight
Aurelia

The day after Keres baited me into training with them, I stood in the grass behind Frithhold and breathed in the sharp, cold air, the clearing before me soft with fog and edged with frost-bitten pine. At the far edge of the yard, the ground dropped away into a sheer overlook, and through the mist that clung stubbornly to the mountainside, a city lay faint and ghostlike below—its towers blurred to smudges of silver and shadow. Close enough to see. Far enough to never touch.

"What city is that?" I asked as Thorne walked by.

"Ravenna," he said.

I looked at him sharply. "That's the Midnight Court down there."

"Yes."

So, we weren't inside the city after all.

"Will we visit it?" I asked.

"That's not up to me," he said and walked off.

After another glance at Ravenna, I turned back to the yard. A circle of stones marked the training area, the dirt tamped flat by years of boots and blades.

By now, the sun had risen to directly overhead, but the wind remained brutal and unrelenting. The cold climbed through my feet, up my spine, rattling my insides. The fog that had rolled in before dawn never lifted—only softened until the trees looked like they'd been painted with a wet brush.

Even out here, the cabin's kitchen exuded the scent of warm bread and simmering roots, soothing in a way that made me angrier than if it had been all chains and iron. Captivity wasn't supposed to be cozy. But outside made up for it. The wind was a scraping blade that cut to the bone if you stood still long enough to let it.

So, I didn't.

"Again," Daegel said before I'd come to a complete stop.

He stood at the edge of the circle with his arms folded, patient and immovable, beard catching the fog's fine droplets.

I tightened my grip on the sword in my right hand. Latha, Sonoma's last gift to me, hummed low against my right palm. Dorcha rode my left; lighter, eager—the blade of my childhood.

From inside my palms, my furyfire burned as it licked from around the edges where I gripped my swords. All day, Daegel had been pushing me to wield both at once. So far, doing so had proven harder than it sounded.

I barely conjured a spark before I was done with the next sequence.

"You lift your left shoulder when you're angry," Amanti called from where she sat along the stone circle. "Keep it down."

"I'm always angry," I muttered.

"Then learn to be angry and precise," she said without missing a beat.

She still wore the sling, and after her own one-handed hour of sparring with Thorne, sweat clung to her tunic and matted her hair. One wing lay too still across her back, dark scars weaving through it like stitches of the dead. The other wing remained tucked tight, stubborn. Every time she'd shifted her stance or parried Thorne's blade, I saw the torn edges, and something inside me caught. But the dark circles no longer carved hollows under her eyes. She was healing. Slowly. Far more slowly than she would have as an Aine. But I'd take it.

Keres sat to her left, braids coiled, sleeves rolled. She held a blade and a whetstone, the steady scrape of steel on stone filling the silence. She hadn't said much today, which was fine by me. I'd heard plenty yesterday and had no desire to hear more of her self-righteous opinions of me.

Thorne leaned against the far post, eyes on the tree line, attention flicking between me and the horizon. Earlier, when he sparred with Amanti, I'd watched the way he moved—fast, clean, not just his blade work but the grace with which he spun and leaped. Only the Aine moved like that. Now, his stillness was another gift. Maybe the ley lines had something to do with it.

Daegel's throat-clearing called me back. I blinked then fell into my stance and began working through the steps. When I'd finished, my breaths were labored, and sweat dotted my brow despite the wind chill. It had been long weeks since I'd trained properly, and it showed.

Then again, I'd never attempted both furyfire and swords at the same time.

"Again," Daegel said when I stopped.

"After a break," I panted. "And some water."

"Do as he says," Keres snapped. "Water breaks are for soldiers who follow directions."

Scowling, I began again, concentrating on the form Sonoma had drilled into me until my muscles knew it better than my mind—cut, turn, shoulder-check with the heel pivot, guard up, slide, feint. Latha sang through the air, Dorcha following, while blackened flames licked at the edges of my grip on them both.

Twice more, I ran through the sequence. My flames grew each time but barely. My frustration grew along with it. On the third sequence, as I spun and sliced, a dark shield sprang up before me. It swayed and swirled like I'd seen from Rydian's shadows, but when my blade struck it, the clash rattled my teeth. Furyfire shot from my hands, their flames eating through the shadow-shield until it winked out again.

I stumbled back, breathing heavy, as I steadied myself enough to glare at Daegel. "What the Hel was that?" I demanded.

"Motivation," he said.

I stared at him, debating whether to attack with my sword or toss a ball of furyfire at his head. "You could have warned me."

"That would have defeated the purpose," Keres said dryly.

I didn't bother glancing at her.

Daegel held my gaze then finally shrugged. "I'm a ward."

"What the hell is that?"

"How it sounds. I can create wards—shields of protection."

Wards. Shields of protection. It was kind of impressive. If he hadn't been using it to knock me off my feet.

"When were you planning to tell me?"

He shrugged. "Now seemed like as good a time as any."

I glared at him.

"Oh. And don't overextend on the strike," he said mildly. "If your opponent is worth the iron in his blade, he'll take your wrist and your pride with it."

"Got it," I said through my teeth.

"Again," he said, the word somewhere between suggestion and request.

I complied, mostly because I wanted to see that stupid shield again. To learn what it was made of or how to pierce it. I never figured out either one, but we went again and again and again. Until my knees buckled, my arms screamed at the idea of holding my swords high, and my furyfire was nothing but a plume of gray smoke.

Daegel didn't look bothered. "You did well."

Despite the exhaustion of my muscles, I hadn't felt more like myself in ages.

"I'll take the blades," Daegel added before I could exit the stone circle, still gripping them.

I handed both blades over before my mouth could protest. Agreeing had less to do with trusting these fae and more to do with the way Amanti's expression eased when I did.

Daegel wrapped the swords in oiled leather, careful as if he understood they were more than metal. "Thank you," he said quietly.

"You're welcome for the privilege of disarming me."

"I'd hardly call you defenseless," Thorne said.

"Don't worry, I'm not going to roast you in your sleep," I told him.

Keres snorted. She looped a fresh sling over Amanti's shoulder with competent gentleness and tightened the knot. Thorne stepped in to lift

Amanti's hair from the strap, fingers careful not to graze the torn edge of her wing.

"Hovering again, Varros?" Amanti asked.

"Supervising," he said, solemn.

Amanti patted his cheek. For a heartbeat, he looked younger, and she looked ancient.

Keres pressed a tin into Amanti's good hand. "Salve. You're not a blacksmith's anvil. Stop treating yourself like one."

Amanti shot me a look that said she wanted to argue but wouldn't.

We filed inside and ate warm bread with dried meat and soft cheese. Thorne leaned in the doorway, watching clouds slide past like a hunter waiting for a sign of its prey. Daegel finished first and stood, muttering something to Thorne that I couldn't hear. Then the two of them left together.

A few minutes later, Amanti excused herself to take a nap, leaving me with Keres.

Great.

We finished eating in silence, and I prepared to return to my room. Or maybe wander the shelves to see if I'd missed a book or two printed in the common language. Anything to pass the time so I wouldn't have to think about what waited for me out there. And not just the threats either. Rydian was in my thoughts far more often than I liked.

I was determined to chase him out again.

"We can go again this afternoon if you want," Keres said, and I looked up in surprise at the offer.

"Daegel already put my swords away," I told her.

"No blades. We'll work on controlling your magic."

"You say that like it's easy," I muttered, tearing off another hunk of bread that practically melted in my mouth. Whoever baked it had a gift.

"It could be," she said simply. "If you stopped fighting everything and everyone."

For once, I had no good retort.

~

Twenty minutes later, in the shade where the Trolech loomed and fog laced low through the branches, Keres lifted her palm to face me. A thin filament of darkness rose from her middle finger. It arced like spider-cast silk and hung between us, impossibly fine.

"What is it?" I asked, noting how similar it looked to the threads woven into Amanti's broken wings.

"Shadow-thread," she said. "I can stitch flesh and armor with it. Or I can use it to cut your throat in less than the time it would take for you to reach for your sword."

"Delightful," I murmured.

"Meet my magic with yours," she said.

"No way. Mine would burn you alive."

"Not with your whole furyfire. With a thread. Like mine."

Tentatively, I held out my hand. Heat gathered—eager, curious, deadly. I curled a fist, took a breath, then forced it open again. A thin line of black flames licked at the thread. The webbed stitching held for a heartbeat, two—then sizzled out with a sound like butter in a hot pan.

I tensed, wondering if I'd hurt her, but Keres didn't flinch.

"Again," she said, already spinning more threads from her hands.

My jaw ached from clenching. I tried again. The thread took more fire before failing.

"Better," Keres said. "Again."

We did it until my hands shook and the air tasted like burnt leaves.

"It's not working," I said. "What I have... it's too big."

"You're not opening to it."

"If I open to it any more, it'll kill you."

She smirked. "I doubt it."

I thought of the moment I'd lost control with Rydian and unleashed my furyfire on him. It hadn't even singed his clothing. Was Keres also immune to its destruction?

My furyfire jumped, zapping Keres with a hot ember. She yanked her hands back and glared at me. I had my answer.

"How do I keep it small enough without snuffing it out?" I asked.

"Don't think of it as small or big," Keres said. "Think of it like threads inside you. Find the one that leads to the source of your power. Separate the signal from the noise."

"I don't have a signal," I said. "I have a pack of glimfangs fighting over a single piece of meat."

"Glimfangs can be taught," she said.

I snorted. "You ever met one?"

"As a matter of fact, I was raised by them."

I blinked.

She merely smiled with eyes colder than the whipping wind and walked toward the house. "We'll try again tomorrow."

I turned to find Amanti sitting alone at the edge of the stone circle. When I moved to join her, she waved for me to remain standing.

"Walk with me. I need to stretch," she said, grunting as she pushed to her feet. I didn't offer to help her. I knew better.

We took a narrow path skirting the house that led through a copse of trees before spilling into a small meadow. Waist-high grass rippled like someone ran fingers through it, bending low against the brittle gusts. A ledge dropped off sharply, offering a view of mountain ridges stacked in the distance like sleeping beasts. A hawk made a slow circle overhead.

If not for Heliconia hunting me and the bounty on my head, it might have felt almost peaceful. My thoughts drifted again to Rydian. I snarled at myself and shoved them back.

Amanti kept close to the woods, one hand trailing leaves like she needed the touch to remind her body that the ground was real. She didn't look winded. She didn't look well, either.

"I need to tell you something."

Her words, the seriousness held in them, stopped me. "What is it?"

She looked away. "The Brindalorn's attack injured me gravely, but that's not the reason I haven't healed." She turned back to me as if forcing herself to meet my eyes. "Not long after my attack, I felt something shift within the magic I'd been gifted by the Fates. Our Aine magic has been fading for years, but this... This was different. And it is not something I can come back from."

"You're no longer Aine."

"I'm no longer Aine."

I searched her gaze, trying to decipher why she seemed so braced. "Do you worry I'll think less of you for it?"

"I worry I won't be enough to help stop her," she admitted quietly.

"Everything I was gifted, everything they imbued in us—it should have been the realm's to use. To stop Heliconia. And instead... it's gone. All of it. And I'm sorry for it, Aurelia. I know what it's like to feel the realm's hope rests solely on your shoulders."

"Amanti, to me, you have never been just one of the Aine. You are the one who taught me how to shoot with a bow. How to hunt. How to drink." We both grinned at that one, undoubtedly thinking of our late nights spent in Sunspire's library with a bottle of whiskey between us, but my humor faded quickly to longing. "You are my family just as Sonoma and Lesha are. I don't need you to be Aine. I only need you to be here with me. To love and support me."

She grabbed my hand in hers, her brown eyes welling with tears in an expression I'd only ever seen once or twice in my life. "I will do so always."

"That is all I need," I whispered.

She squeezed my hand. And for a fleeting moment, I was transported back to those years in Sunspire—my days spent with Lesha, Sonoma, and Amanti. A family of protectors. Of warriors. Sisters and friends. No matter what. Grief stole my joy as those memories washed over me.

"What is this?" I looked down, noting the mark the oracle had given me.

Amanti's hand closed over my wrist and pulled my sleeve back to reveal it fully.

"I made a bargain with the oracle in Grey Oak," I told her.

"Meerdra." She dropped my arm, not nearly as upset as Rydian had been about it.

"She said you told her I would come."

"Sonoma said she'd had a vision," Amanti told me quietly. "I delivered the message about eight months ago. Before I went south."

"Sonoma never mentioned visions to me before," I said, trying not to hate how many secrets my mother still carried even from the Afterlife.

"I suspect it was more of a message," Amanti said. "From your father."

Of course.

We walked on in silence, my memories drifting back to the past. To the three Aine who had raised me. Become my family. Two of them lost now.

"You are troubled," Amanti said, noting my expression.

"I keep thinking about her," I admitted. "Lesha."

Amanti's expression pinched. "Me too."

"I should've gone with her," I said, the truth cutting its usual path straight to guilt. "If I had—"

"If you had, you'd both be lost," she said. "She made a choice to protect you. That doesn't become your failure just because you survived."

Her words cut at wounds inside me that had been there so long I'd forgotten to tend them.

"She might still be out there," I said.

"If she is, we will find her. Together."

I swallowed hard, tears burning. "Promise me."

She didn't hesitate. "On my blade and what's left of my wings."

Her mouth quirked at that.

I shook my head. But the knot in my chest loosened just enough to let air in.

"Okay?" she asked.

I nodded, not trusting my voice.

We started walking again.

By the time we'd rounded the meadow and returned to the cabin, a draft had slid over the yard, colder than before. The sun had dipped behind the horizon, casting long shadows across the stones, but it was more than just sunset heralding in the twilight.

Beyond the cliff's edge, something approached.

Amanti didn't comment, but I felt her tense, bracing for something. Or someone. Thorne and Daegel were suddenly there. At the edge of the clearing. They didn't draw their weapons, though. They only waited; their gazes trained on a narrow dirt path that wound away over my shoulder into the trees before descending sharply.

I felt him before I saw him—like a storm rolling in. The hair on my arms lifted.

Bootsteps found the edge of the yard and stopped.

I turned.

Rydian stood in the fading light, half his face cast in shadow. Across the space, his gaze found mine. His mouth tipped, not kind—never that—but edged with something I wished didn't make my pulse climb.

"Hello, Furious," he said, voice low enough to scrape across my skin. "I've missed you."

THE
LOVERS

Chapter Nine
Rydian

The sight of her nearly knocked the breath out of me.

I'd spent the entire journey telling myself I wouldn't feel a damn thing when I saw her again. That the secrets, the way she'd planned to run from Autumn without me, the betrayal she undoubtedly thought I'd dealt her would be enough to harden me. My role in her life was too important to let my feelings get in the way. So, I resolved to keep my distance. But the second her eyes met mine, all of it burned away like fog in sunlight.

Aurelia Valeen.

Furyfire in a mortal frame.

My heart taken a female form.

On the surface, she looked the same. Her blonde hair was braided, but strands had come loose, tangling around her face in the whipping wind. The expensive gowns she'd worn at the Autumn Court had been replaced with fighting leathers and her Aine armor. Her boots were caked in dirt, her shoulders squared like she'd been waiting for a fight since the moment she woke. Or maybe she'd just finished one. I couldn't tell if I wanted to drag her into my arms or let her throw that fire of hers at me just to feel something from her again.

Instead, I said the wrong thing.

"Hello, Furious. I've missed you."

Her expression flashed as something dangerous tightened around her mouth. The others felt it too. Thorne shifted his weight, Daegel took a quiet step back, and Amanti didn't move at all. She just watched me like she'd already figured out everything between me and the Summer heir.

Aurelia turned and walked straight into the cabin.

No words. No rage. Just dismissal.

The others followed her, as if they all knew it was best to get this over with, but I stood there for a few breaths longer, letting the cold scrape through me before I went in after them.

The house smelled of freshly baked bread, Thorne's specialty. Aurelia stood near the hearth, arms folded, chin high. A tangle of hair had slipped free from behind her ear. Her pale blue eyes were cold enough to make me forget how to breathe.

"Why are you here?" she asked.

I didn't answer right away, choosing carefully the reason I wanted to offer up. "Because I needed to see for myself that you were alive."

Her laugh was humorless. "Alive? That's rich. You drugged me, hauled me across the continent, locked me in a room, and call it rescue."

"I didn't like doing it," I said evenly. "But it kept you breathing."

"I didn't ask for your help."

The firelight caught her face, throwing her in gold and shadow—half fury, half heartbreak. I wanted to reach for her, but that would've been suicide.

"If you'd stayed in Autumn, you'd be dead. Or worse."

"Don't you dare pretend you care what happens to me."

"I'm not pretending."

The silence that followed had an edge to it. Keres was the one who broke it, dragging a chair to the table and sitting with deliberate noise. "If you two are going to kill each other, do it outside. I just cleaned up in here."

That drew a strangled laugh out of Thorne, though he quickly smothered it when Aurelia shot him a look that could peel paint.

Amanti stepped between us, voice calm but firm. "We're fighting on enough fronts; let's not do it with each other. Now that you're home, we need to talk about what comes next," Amanti added.

"What comes next," Aurelia told her with a pointed look at me, "is me leaving."

"We've been over this," Thorne said before Amanti could answer. "The Obsidians are all over the mountains."

"I can't stay here," she said viciously. "Not with him."

Her eyes met mine on that last word, and whatever air was left in the room vanished. Every line of her body said she was ready to bolt if someone so much as blinked.

Daegel shifted, uneasy. "No one's keeping you prisoner, Aurelia. But Thorne's right. You wouldn't make it half a day's walk."

"I've made it farther on worse odds."

Her voice was flat, and it wasn't bravado. It was truth. That scared me more than her anger.

Before I could respond, hoofbeats thundered outside—fast, urgent. Everyone froze. Keres was already moving toward the door, hand on the dagger at her belt, when the bird call sounded.

Keres halted, releasing her grip on her blade.

The rest of us exhaled.

Thorne crossed the room in three strides, yanked the latch, and the door swung open to reveal a rider dismounting in a spray of mud.

Slade.

He'd stayed behind to tie up loose ends. I hadn't expected him for another two days. He looked like he'd ridden through Hel to get here—cloak soaked, blood streaked down one arm, eyes wild with exhaustion.

"You're supposed to be in Grey Oak," I said.

"Plans changed." His mouth was a grim, flat line.

"What happened?" I asked.

"A message from Heliconia was sent to Autumn. Meant for Duron."

"What message?" I asked.

He glanced past me to Aurelia before handing over a folded piece of parchment. "Read for yourself."

I scanned the words quickly, my gut tightening at the words meant for a dead king.

"What is it?" Keres asked impatiently.

I cleared my throat and read it aloud: "I have the last living Aine in my possession. If the Summer heir is not surrendered, she dies, and any hope of aid from the Fates dies with her."

"Lesha," Aurelia breathed.

She and Amanti shared a look before the princess whipped her gaze back to Slade's.

"Where?" Aurelia asked sharply.

"A war camp. Somewhere along the northern border."

"That still leaves miles of ground to cover," I said.

"Our scouts are working on pinning down the location," Slade said. "We'll know more soon."

Aurelia's eyes brimmed with moisture that she blinked back. "Alive," she whispered, and then louder, steadier, glancing to Amanti again, "We have to go get her."

Slade shook his head. "The message is meant to draw you out."

"But soon, she'll know I'm not in Autumn," Aurelia argued. "She'll think I never got the message. We have an advantage right now."

Slade's expression only tightened. "When Heliconia finds out you're no longer in Autumn, she'll be even more on guard. Even if we find your friend, she'll be heavily guarded. You wouldn't make it in, much less out again."

"Then we go together." She looked around the room, wild determination sharpening her edges.

Thorne shook his head. "You're talking about seven of us against hundreds. Maybe thousands."

Aurelia's hands curled into fists. "I'll figure it out. Find allies. If we can rally a force—" She stopped abruptly and turned toward the others. Daegel. Keres. Amanti. "What about the Midnight Court? Will they fight?"

The air in the room changed. Thorne's expression shuttered. Daegel's gaze flicked to Keres, then to me. Even Amanti looked uneasy. No, *guilty*. We all looked guilty.

Aurelia caught it instantly. "What is it?" she asked, voice low. "What are you keeping from me?"

Keres stood slowly. "Now isn't the time."

"I think it's exactly the time." Aurelia took a step closer, furyfire sparking faintly at her fingertips. "For days, you've had me in this cabin on a mountain high above your precious court. Acting like I'm here for my safety when we all know it's more than that."

"I told you, you're not a prisoner," Keres said tightly.

"Prove it. Take me into the city. Let me meet with your queen and let her decide if her court will stand with me."

I looked at Keres then, the truth twisting in my chest. She shook her head as if to say, "Not now."

"Whatever secret you're sitting on," Aurelia continued, "Whatever reason you've stashed me in this cabin instead of taking me to the city, tell me now. Or I leave. Alone."

Her voice didn't waver. The heat from her magic rolled through the room in waves.

Amanti's eyes met mine. "She deserves the truth, Rydian."

My throat felt dry as dust. "Now's not the time. The queen will explain—"

Keres's jaw tightened. "The queen isn't coming."

Aurelia's gaze snapped to the female warrior.

Keres ignored her, eyes fixed on me. "She said it would be safer this way. To keep her away from the city. Away from the court. Until it's time."

The words hit like a blow. The queen had refused to meet Aurelia, all over her own fear and resentment. I should've expected it, but the confirmation still cut deep.

"She knows what this will look like to our people," I said, anger building. "The message it sends."

Keres's expression didn't change. "I'm sure she did what she thought was necessary."

Aurelia's voice was ice. "You mean she abandoned us. Just like the Midnight Court abandoned Concordia when Heliconia invaded. Just like they abandoned my kingdom when we needed them most."

"No," I said, meeting her glare. "She's protecting you. But she should've explained."

The fury in her eyes was sharp enough to wound. "You did this," she said. "You sent me here, and for what? To keep me from fighting for my kingdom? To make sure you remain in control of all the moves?"

"That's not what this is."

"Then what is it?" she demanded. "Because from where I'm standing, it looks a lot like another male deciding what's best for me without giving me a choice."

I didn't look away. "Was I supposed to just leave you there with Callan—alone, hunted down for a king's death?"

She stepped closer, so close the air between us hummed. "You did leave me."

I felt the heat of her breath, saw the crack in her armor where grief and fury met. Gods, she was beautiful like this—angry, alive, unstoppable. And I was an idiot for noticing when I'd already lost the right to ever touch her again.

"I made a choice to keep you safe," I said. "If that makes me the villain, fine. But you're still standing."

"I would rather have taken my chances with the Obsidians if it meant never seeing you again."

Her voice shook. Just once. It was enough to remind me that, under all that steel, she had once looked at me like I was worth saving. And I'd broken that trust.

Slade cleared his throat, breaking the moment. "I'm going to ride out and wait for word from our scouts. See if we can get a location on the Aine."

"Thank you, Slade," Amanti told him. "It's good to see you again."

"Good to see you back on your feet, Aunt." He hugged her, exchanged a few words with the others, and left.

"Rydian," Amanti said into the tense silence. "She can't do what's needed if she doesn't understand. Tell her."

I closed my eyes for half a second. When I opened them, Aurelia was still watching me, jaw set, firelight tracing the planes of her face.

Waiting.

Gods, I had wanted to do a better job of this part. Instead, I'd made it all worse.

"The Midnight Court isn't what you think," I said quietly. "The reason no one came to aid Concordia or Sevanwinds is because they can't."

"What do you mean they can't? Are their hands tied behind their backs? Are they cursed to perpetual slumber like my people?"

"Not quite like Summer, but in a manner of speaking, yes, they are trapped."

The fight in her eyes turned to wariness. "By whom?"

I sighed, knowing that once I put the truth between us, there'd be no taking it back. It would be a barrier, unbreakable, that would only create more distance. But she needed to know.

"Long before the Great War, the gods favored the Midnight fae, gifted them, and imbued them with dark magic that rivaled any other kingdom in Menryth. We respected that power and were careful about how it was wielded. We kept to ourselves. Nurtured our own people. Allowed the rest of the realm to rule their own lands how they saw fit. Ten years ago, those same gods who'd preserved our power threatened to take it away again."

"Why?"

"In the aftermath of the Great War, the gods struck a precarious truce that lasted centuries. Three decades ago, another power rose. A new one that violated that truce, threatening to plunge the realm into pure darkness as a result."

"Heliconia," Aurelia said, anguish brimming in her gaze now.

"So, the gods came to us and made a new deal," I continued. "One that ensured the survival of the realm—and our kingdom with it."

"What kind of deal?" Aurelia asked warily.

"The Midnight heir swore an oath to the gods." Keres scowled, as she always did about this part of the story. But I ignored her. What was done was done. We could only go forward now.

"What oath?" Aurelia demanded.

"A blood vow to protect and fight for the one fae who would prove powerful enough to stop the rise of evil and destruction. Someone chosen by the gods themselves. But until such time, in order to preserve our power and our people for the moment they were needed most, the gates to our kingdom were sealed shut. And they remain so until the Chosen One we've been waiting for unlocks them and calls us to war."

Aurelia paled.

"And so, we wait, our people locked inside their kingdom until it's time," I told her quietly, watching as she processed it all.

Her part in it.

What it all meant.

What she was expected to do.

"Are they awake?" Aurelia's question broke the silence—and my heart.

I nodded, knowing she was thinking of her own family. "Yes. They are awake and alive and well inside the walls."

Keres and the others didn't say a word, but I knew they were all biting back the rest of that truth: Our families were inside the walls, but we remained out here.

"That's good." Aurelia's eyes searched mine for a long moment, as if she could find another meaning there, some softer truth. But there wasn't one.

"Which gods sealed the gate?"

I felt the others' eyes on me, but I ignored them, not letting my gaze waver in this moment. It was one of the questions I knew would ruin things between us. Even so, I found myself relieved this was the one she'd chosen to ask.

"Was it the Fates?" she pressed. "Because this tattoo they gave me—"

"It wasn't the Fates," I told her. "And they're not who gave you that tattoo either."

"What are you talking about?" She shook her head. "The morning after the curse, I woke up with this. It's a symbol of the gifts they bestowed—"

"The Fates don't possess the gift of furyfire," Keres said.

Aurelia frowned, reaching up to touch the inked mark on her neck. Her gaze cut to Amanti. "You told me—"

"You assumed," Amanti cut in gently.

Aurelia's hands fisted. Black smoke escaped.

"Princess," Keres warned.

"I know," Aurelia snapped. She forced her fists open, and the magic winked out. A moment later, her breathing calmed.

I shot a look at Keres, impressed.

The fae warrior simply crossed her arms.

"The tattoo is the gods' mark for their Chosen One," Keres said into the silence. "It's imbued with their power. Part of their whole mission to right the balance or whatever."

Daegel muttered something at her, but she threw up her hands, saying, "If everyone else is going to tiptoe around it, what do you expect me to do? She deserves to know. She's not made of glass."

Aurelia shot me a pointed look. "Glad someone thinks so."

"Aurelia," I began.

"Which gods," she said again.

Out of the corner of my eye, I saw Keres open her mouth. But I beat her to it, taking the fallout onto my own shoulders as I said, "The Furiosities."

Aurelia swallowed hard. Then nodded slowly. I braced myself for furyfire or some weapon aimed at my head. But she didn't even move.

The silence stretched.

The others just waited, but I remained tense, prepared for a fight. An interrogation. An inferno.

Finally, she looked at me and said, "What happened to your face?"

Thorne snorted loud enough for it to echo off the walls.

THE
LOVERS

Chapter Ten
Aurelia

Rydian glanced at his aunt and, almost as if he'd spoken aloud, Amanti rose. Her hand brushed my arm. "We'll give you space." She tipped her chin, and Keres fell into step with her. Thorne was already out the door. Daegel followed. In their wake, the latch clicked, the house settled, and then it was just the two of us.

Rydian stayed on the far side of the sofa as if distance might keep this from getting worse. He looked steady, but the bruise along his cheekbone had darkened to plum. I hated that I noticed. Hated that I cared enough to ask. But I needed a distraction from the things he'd told me. About the gods. The gates. Me.

Eventually, the silence stretched too long. "It's none of my business—"

"Callan hit me."

I blinked. "Did you deserve it?"

"He thought so," he said dryly.

"Did you... hit him back?" I asked tentatively.

His humor vanished. "No."

"Why not?"

"We'd both lost enough." His eyes flicked to the hearth. "And he's your past. Punching him back wouldn't change that."

"And your hip?" I asked.

He frowned.

"You're limping," I added. "Did Callan injure it?"

"Koraz's last gift," he said quietly. I opened my mouth to ask more, but he waved me off. "It's healing. Slow enough, but it'll be fine."

We stood in silence for a beat.

"He hit you because of me."

"He hit me because of himself. His insecurity, his own pain. But yes, he was upset about losing you." His voice gentled as he added, "And losing our father."

I flinched at the reminder of Duron. "There's a bounty on my head."

"Yes."

"He wants me dead."

"He'll cool off."

I shook my head. "How can you say that? I killed his father."

"The man was a bastard." His voice twisted until it was nothing but sharp edges. "He deserved so much worse than that. Callan knows it. He'll come around."

"He gave Callan a black eye," I said. "The night those Obsidians broke into the castle. As punishment."

Rydian nodded. "Did worse than that, but the healers managed to put him back together again."

I blinked, startled to know it had been worse.

"Why did he leave the bruise on his eye?" I asked and then knew the answer immediately. "He wanted me to see it."

Rydian remained silent, but I watched the muscle in his jaw tense.

I looked down, thumbs worrying the frayed edge of my tunic. A dozen things crowded my throat. None of them were safe to say.

"I grew up believing the Midnight Court was full of monsters and nightmares," I said.

"Those stories have truth in them."

"And cowards," I added.

He scowled, and I could see the argument brewing in him. The insult that grated every time I uttered it. The way he took it personally.

"Those stories weren't all true. You may be a monster, but you're no coward."

I expected defense. Or temper. Instead, I saw weary acceptance that made my stomach twist. He didn't deny it.

Rydian was Midnight fae.

"How?" I asked. "Duron—"

"Was my father," he said quietly. "My mother is Midnight fae."

"You could have just told me the truth."

"Maybe I should have."

"Why didn't you?"

Rydian's gaze slid past me to the shimmering lights. No answer came, and I knew none would.

"If I open the gates?" I asked. "What happens?"

"Two things," he said. "One: The city will answer. You'll have an army at your back with more magic than any other kingdom combined. Two: The power that's currently being used to keep the gates sealed will flow into you."

"And that's a bad thing?" I asked, noting the wariness in his eyes.

"Depends on whether it works. We're not talking about a little bit of power. This would be a torrent. The power of the gods imbued into a living mortal fae."

My chest swelled with something dizzying—hope, perhaps, for the briefest impossible moment. An army. Enough magic to destroy Heliconia. To rescue Lesha. To break the curse. Visions I'd held as scattered promises snapped into the shape of a real plan. I tasted victory.

Then his next words cut me sharply. "But it is not a gift without a cost."

"What cost?"

"If you are not prepared to take on that kind of power," Rydian said quietly, "it will not bend to you, nor will it join you. It will destroy you."

There it was. The reason for his wariness. He wasn't sure I could survive it. And if I failed... this realm would fall to Heliconia. And the Midnight Court would remain trapped inside its own walls forever—right along with my own kingdom trapped in their immortal slumber.

"Is this what you meant about choosing a side?" I asked. "You needed to make sure I wasn't going to take that power and run as Heliconia had? Or worse, fail and keep your people trapped forever?"

Rydian's jaw flexed, but he didn't look away. "I had to see that you were willing to fight. To sacrifice for the fate of this realm."

The furyfire pulsed beneath my skin, hot and restless, begging for somewhere to go. Had I not already sacrificed everything?

"Show me how to open the gates," I said. "We can use the army to free Lesha. To defeat Helconia. To—"

Something like regret flickered in his dark gaze. "No."

Fury coursed through me at that. My hands fisted at my sides.

"I know what you're thinking, but the power inside those gates is far greater than anything you can imagine," he warned. "The strength it will take to harness it, the control—it would destroy you from the inside out."

"You think I'm too weak," I said.

His jaw tightened. Shadows lifted at his heels like a tide restrained by sheer will. "I think it would kill you," he said. "And I've buried enough warriors to know the difference between sacrifice and slaughter."

Beneath the anger, something inside me splintered.

"I'm going to bed," I announced.

Rydian didn't try to stop me.

THE
LOVERS

Chapter Eleven
Rydian

A biting wind whipped across the ridgeline where I stood, stirring the frost and bringing the scent of pine resin and woodsmoke. Beneath it, I could still scent her—embers and sunlight and fury barely contained.

She had asked me to let her open the gates.

And I had told her no.

Not because I thought her weak. She'd proven the power she possessed the night she'd rendered Duron to dust. I told her no because I knew the ancient, otherworldly magic that slept inside those gates would devour her whole. And because some part of me—coward or lover, I couldn't tell which—would rather damn the realm than risk anything hurting that woman.

The bruise beneath my eye pulsed in rhythm with my thoughts, a dull reminder of the king who'd given it to me and the woman we'd both lost in the same night. It should have healed by now, which meant Callan had used magic to make sure it lingered. As punishment. For me or for Aurelia, I wasn't sure. Or maybe just for sport.

Below the ledge where I stood, the Trolech Forest spread like an ocean of wet ink. Down in the valley, the wall that encircled my kingdom gleamed faintly—dark stone and silver wards that caught the moonlight and reflected like scales. The Midnight Court slumbered beneath that shimmer; my mother locked inside its powerful ring of protection.

A protection that hadn't always been there for her. Back when I'd taken the blood oath to Duron, the gates had been wide open. And she'd been exposed. Vulnerable. With only me standing between them.

Now, at least, she was safe, even if she was being stubborn about using her gifts to visit this side of the wall. To meet Aurelia.

When I finally went back inside, the air shifted—from knife-edge cold to the heavy warmth of fire and pine smoke. The hearth burned low, its light catching on the walls and weapons, the steel edges gleaming like teeth.

Amanti sat near the flames, her injured arm tucked into a sling, her right wing spread wide to catch the heat. The left one trembled faintly where it lay tucked against her back, the torn membranes glinting with scar tissue that crisscrossed Keres dark sutures. The others were nowhere to be seen, but that didn't mean they weren't listening.

Busybodies, the lot of them.

Daegel especially, though surprisingly, it had been Thorne who seemed most amused by Aurelia's ire aimed at me.

Amanti didn't look at me when she spoke. "You told her."

I leaned against the doorframe, dragging a hand through my hair. "She deserved the truth."

"She deserved it long before tonight." Her tone wasn't cruel, just tired. "But I suppose late is better than never."

"She wants to open the gates." I crossed the room, the floorboards creaking under my boots. "She thinks it's the only way to reach Lesha."

"And you told her no."

I sank into the chair opposite hers. "I told her what would happen if she tried."

Amanti shifted, and the firelight revealed the hollow beneath her cheekbones. "You're afraid."

"Yes," I said. "But not for me.

If my aunt was surprised by the admission, she didn't show it. But I knew she missed nothing, which meant she'd already likely guessed there was more between Aurelia and me than there should be.

She adjusted the sling, her gaze never leaving the fire. "Your mother is afraid too."

"Don't," I said, shaking my head at what already felt like a fight.

"Cadira doesn't want to lose you to this, Rydian. She believes you can find another way."

I exhaled hard through my nose. "That doesn't make me forgive her for snubbing Aurelia."

Amanti turned her head then, meeting my eyes. Her gaze was sharp enough to cut. "No. It makes you her *heir.*"

"What if I don't want to be the heir?" I asked, exhaustion lining every word. "You're her sister. You have just as much a claim as I do."

"You know I gave up all claim when I became one of the Aine," she said.

"The Fates are gone, and so is your magic. You're not Aine anymore," I said and then immediately regretted it.

Amanti flinched. Her mouth flattened. "The Midnight crown is yours, Rydian. Whether you wear it or not. That's how it's always been meant."

"I'm sorry," I said, guilt pressing my shoulders down. "I didn't mean it."

"I am Aine," she said quietly. "Until the Fates take my breath from my body."

"You are. And I am the heir," I said, shoving the words out.

"As much as it pains you," she added quietly.

My fingers tightened against the armrest. I stared into the flames until they blurred, taking on the shape of the former Midnight queen. My aunt Winyra, third sister to Amanti and my mother. She had been a formidable and wise ruler who cared deeply about all fae. Until she was killed nine years ago and the weight of the crown had fallen to my mother. For now.

"And when Aurelia finds out what I am?" I asked.

"That depends," she said, "on whether you tell her, or she learns it when her army of Midnight fae answers not just to her, their Chosen, but also to you, their future king."

The hearth crackled, resin burning sweet and sharp. Somewhere outside, a nightbird cried once and fell silent.

The door opened, and cold rushed in, curling through the room like smoke. Slade stepped over the threshold, his cloak heavy with frost. His gloves were still damp from snow; his dark hair stuck to his brow.

"Any news?" I asked.

He shook his head. "Likely be a day or two before they make contact."

"Where's Daegel?" I asked, "And the others?"

It was too damn quiet in here, considering Amanti's words. Usually, the others would have popped up by now to stick their noses in my business. Especially when it came to my crown.

"They went to do a perimeter check." He removed his cloak and slung it over his arm. Snow fell, dotting the floor in wet drops.

"You mean they're waiting until the worst has passed," I said. "In case Aurelia and I killed each other or burnt the house down trying."

"We didn't think you'd kill her," he said mildly.

I huffed a laugh at that.

But his humor faded quickly. "Are we going then?"

"Where?"

He shrugged. "Wherever she's decided."

"We're not going anywhere, and neither is she. Not until we come up with a plan."

He shook his head and turned for the hall where he kept a bedroom here.

"What?" I demanded. "You have something to say; spit it out."

"She'll go," Slade said. "You know she will. You can't keep her from it."

"I can delay her," I said. "Long enough to come up with a plan to keep her from doing something stupid."

Slade gave a short, humorless laugh. "You? Delay *Aurelia of Sunspire*? I'll fetch a shovel now for when she buries you in the yard on her way down the mountain."

"She's the Chosen One," I said with a scowl. "If she falls into Heliconia's grasp..."

Amanti finished for me. "Then the gates will open at Heliconia's command."

The fire popped, sending sparks skittering across the hearth. For a moment, none of us spoke.

Amanti rose slowly from her chair. Her wings dragged faintly across the stone, the sound like paper tearing. "She'll ask again," she said. "To show her how to open them. And if you refuse, even if it kills her, she'll try on her own. For Lesha."

"I know," I said.

Slade's gaze lingered on me. "You'll have to tell her soon," he said. "About what you are."

I didn't look at him. "I know."

He studied me for a beat longer, then turned and left, the door closing on another gust of cold.

Amanti remained by the fire. "She'll hate you if you keep this from her."

"She already does."

Amanti's gaze softened, her voice a whisper against the crackling wood. "And still, you'd die for her."

"Not for her," I lied. "For what she'll become."

Amanti stared silently into the fire.

Finally, she turned away, headed for her room.

The fire hissed as sap burst in the logs. Shadows climbed the walls like a tide rising. I stared into them and saw the shape of the city below—the dark towers, the silver gates, the pulse of the vow that would one day wake them all.

THE
LOVERS

Chapter Twelve

Aurelia

The following afternoon, the cabin's walls felt like they were closing in on me. I'd been pacing for the better part of an hour, wearing a groove into the ancient floor while Rydian pored over maps and correspondence at the massive oak table. The scent of ink and aged parchment mingled with the ever-present chill that slid in through the cracks and crevices.

Flames crackled in the hearth, the pop of the embers reminding me of another fire. A flame that had been more lethal than cozy. I remembered the look on Duron's face as my furyfire consumed him, reducing him to nothing but ash and memory. It had been necessary, killing Duron, and would be again before this was all finished. But the burden it left was heavier than I'd expected.

For Lesha, though, I'd kill again.

Rydian insisted we needed a plan before rushing into action. I wanted to argue that unlocking the Midnight army was the best plan—the only plan. But I bit my tongue.

The truth was, I was short on allies. On friends. And we still had no idea where Lesha was even being held. Until word came about her location, there was no point in leaving anyway. Still, now that I knew she was alive and in danger, I couldn't sit and do nothing.

"You're going to burn a hole through the floor," Rydian said without looking up from his maps.

I stopped, turning to face him. Shadows pooled in the hollows of his face, cast by the flickering torches mounted on the walls. Even exhausted, even bent over battle plans with tension carved into every line of his body, he was devastatingly beautiful. I hated that I noticed.

"We need to talk about opening the gates," I said.

His quill stilled. "No."

"You didn't even let me finish."

"I don't need to." He looked up, those storm-grey eyes meeting mine with an intensity that made my breath catch. "The answer is no, Aurelia. It's too dangerous."

"The realm is a dangerous place," I retorted.

His brow arched, and he nodded toward the window. "You should join Amanti in her workout. Daegel would be happy to spar with you."

I planted my palms on the table, leaning forward. "Lesha helped *raise* me, Rydian. She's family. I can't just sit here and do nothing. I have to open the gates—"

"You're not ready." He stood abruptly, the chair scraping against stone. "Do you have any idea what kind of magic lies inside those gates? What Heliconia has been building in the north? The magic inside the Midnight Court is enough to stop her and every Obsidian she's ever created. Whoever opens those gates must be strong enough to receive that magic. To control it. You can't even control what you already have."

I held up my hands, and for a moment, I could have sworn I saw embers dancing beneath my skin. I closed my fists, forcing the sensation away. "I killed Duron. I know what I'm capable of now."

"And do you embrace it? Or do you continue to fight it?" His voice softened, just slightly. "To push it away out of fear of what it will mean if you're marked by the Furiosities? If the realm finds out your magic is gifted from the darkness rather than the light?"

I snorted. "The realm already knows."

He rounded the table, stopping a careful distance away—close enough that I could feel the warmth radiating from him, far enough that we weren't touching. "You're afraid of your power. I can see it in the way you hold yourself, the way you flinch every time your magic rises to the surface. Even with Duron, you held back. And that scares you."

I wanted to deny it. The words formed on my tongue, sharp and defensive. But they would have been lies, and we'd had enough of those between us, thanks to him. I refused to add to the pile.

"So, what am I supposed to do?" The question came out smaller than I'd intended. "Let Lesha die? Let my people sleep forever while Heliconia conquers the entire realm? Let the Midnight Court remain trapped inside those walls forever?"

Rydian's jaw worked, a muscle ticking beneath the sharp line of his cheekbone. "We'll find another way to get her back."

"There is no other way."

"There's *always* another way." He moved closer now, close enough that I had to tilt my head back to maintain eye contact. "You think I don't want to save your friend? You think I don't wake up every morning, thinking about your people, about mine? About what they've lost? I won't watch you burn yourself out or let Heliconia tear you apart because you rushed in before you were ready."

The protectiveness in his voice made my chest ache. This was the Rydian I'd fallen for at Grey Oak—the one who'd shown me tenderness in a world of thorns. But it was also the same protective instinct that had led him to send me away, to make decisions about my life without consulting me.

"You don't get to decide what I'm ready for," I said quietly. "Not anymore."

Something flickered across his face—pain, maybe, or regret. "Aurelia—"

"No." I stepped back, needing distance, needing air that didn't smell like him. "I'm not asking for your permission. I'm going to get Lesha. And if you won't help me, then I'll find allies who will."

His expression turned wary. "What allies? The Withered? There's still a bounty on your head."

He was right, and we both knew it. The Withered, Autumn fae whose magic and life force had been drained away by Duron's mandatory donation centers, had fought for me, bled for me the night I fled

Grey Oak. But they were rebels hiding in a hostile court, and I couldn't reach them. Not without starting a war with Callan.

I turned away, my mind racing. The torchlight cast dancing shadows on the walls, and I found myself staring at the fluid shapes they made.

"Nali," I whispered.

"What?"

I whirled. "Princess Naliadne of the river people. I met her at the party at Grey Oak." I thought of Nali's sea-green eyes, her enigmatic smile. I'd almost forgotten our brief exchange in the chaos of everything that had happened after. But now, the promise of an ally like her was a light in the darkness.

Rydian's brows drew together. "The river people have remained neutral for centuries. They don't involve themselves in court politics."

"She was willing to offer an alliance—as long as I wasn't allied with Autumn." I moved to the opposite side of the table, studying his maps for myself.

We'd have to navigate the Trolech and the Broadlands to get there, but—

"The naiad are lethal in the water, but they don't fight on land. And they've likely never even faced an Obsidian."

"Then I'll train them." I met his gaze across the table. "Or would you rather I hide here until Heliconia finds me?"

The door swung open before he could answer. Amanti strode in, her hair sticking to her neck, skin glistening. But she looked better today. Stronger.

She took one look at us—the tension thick enough to choke on—and raised an eyebrow. "Should I come back?"

"No," I said, at the same time Rydian said, "We're discussing strategy."

Amanti's lips quirked. "Is that what we're calling it?" She moved to the table, her keen eyes scanning the maps. "What's the plan?"

"Aurelia wants to seek an alliance with the river people," Rydian said, his tone carefully neutral.

"Patamoi's court?" Amanti looked intrigued. "That's... actually not terrible."

"Thank you," I said pointedly.

Rydian shot me a look. "I didn't say it was a bad idea."

"You didn't say it was a good one either."

"Children," Amanti interjected dryly. "Can we focus?" She tapped the map where the river territories wound like a ribbon, cutting between Summer and Autumn. "The naiad have stayed out of Heliconia's reach, which means they're one of the few courts she hasn't corrupted or manipulated. Their warriors are trained in water magic—defensive primarily, but it can be devastating in the right circumstances."

"Their princess was friendly to me when we met in Grey Oak," I told her. "I think the king might be open to working with us."

"And you trust her?" Rydian asked. "Based on one conversation?"

I thought about Nali's directness, the way she'd looked at me without artifice or agenda. "Yes," I said simply. "I do."

Amanti studied me for a long moment. "If you think the princess will listen, then it's worth pursuing." She glanced at Rydian. "We *do* need help. You know it as well as I do. If you're not going to let her open the gates, we'll have to look elsewhere."

Rydian's hands flattened on the table. I watched the battle play out across his features—the tactical mind weighing options against the protective instinct that wanted to keep me locked away from danger.

Finally, he exhaled.

"If we do this, we do it right," he said. "Crossing the Broadlands is risky enough without a bounty on our heads—"

"Wait. *Our* heads?" I interrupted.

He paused. "Callan banished me as well as you," he explained quietly.

"I didn't realize..." But of course he had. The black eye had been the evidence of his wrath against his brother. But he wouldn't have let it go at that.

"The point is," Rydian said when I remained quiet, "we need to stay on this side of the river, and we'll need to travel in two groups. A scouting party goes ahead at all times to scan for bounty hunters and Obsidians."

"Slade can shadow-walk ahead to scout," Amanti offered.

"Shadow-walk?" I echoed.

"Slade's gift allows him to slip between folds in the shadows of the world," Rydian explained.

My mouth fell open a little. "As in, he can teleport?"

"Not exactly." Rydian shook his head. "It involves a physical effort from one point to another, but it's incredibly fast, like stepping through folds of darkness."

"That's incredible," I said.

"It's also limited to darkness. And short distances. But it's useful," he admitted.

"Does this mean you're coming with me?" I asked.

His eyes found mine, and something in them made my pulse quicken. "There was never any scenario where I would have let you walk out that door without me, Furious."

His words, the utter conviction in them, sent shudders through me.

Amanti nodded approvingly. "When do we leave?"

"You're coming too?" I asked.

"It's Lesha," she said as if that explained everything.

For me, it did.

"At first light," Rydian said. "In the meantime, we'll gather supplies. And I'll send Shade and Thorne to scout ahead."

"What about horses?" I asked, remembering belatedly I had none of my own here—and I wasn't exactly interested in getting back in that carriage.

"I'll have Daegel and Keres bring horses up for all of us," Rydian said.

I wanted to ask *up* from where, but I swallowed the question. For now. At some point, I needed to learn all I could about the Midnight Court and its magically sealed gates. If Rydian thought I was going to simply bow under his command, he was going to be sorely disappointed.

"Horses will draw attention," Amanti warned him.

"Without them, we'll travel too slowly, and that makes us a target too," Rydian said. "We'll take the merchant road. It's less traveled and hopefully not being used by Heliconia's scouts."

The merchant road.

I'd used it often enough in the last seven years, mostly to sneak through the Broadlands in search of a way to break the curse. None of those trips had yielded anything remotely close to an answer—including the last one. The day I killed an Obsidian in a crumbling cabin. The day Rydian found me again.

He'd chased me right back into my engagement with Callan.

All along, I'd thought he hated me for breaking my word to his half-brother. But now I wondered if he'd only been testing me. To make me decide once and for all where I stood. Not just with Callan but with Heliconia. As the Chosen One of the realm.

The Furiosities' champion.

My father's daughter.

"Aurelia?" Amanti's voice pulled me back. "You good with that?"

"Yes." I forced the past aside. And did my best to ignore whatever feelings I still had for Rydian. He hadn't cared if I'd married Callan. I needed to remember that.

"Then I suggest we all get some rest." Amanti moved toward the door, then paused. "For what it's worth, I think this is the right call. The naiad have stayed neutral too long. It's time they fought for the fate of Menryth."

After she left, silence stretched between Rydian and me.

Outside, the late afternoon sun had already dipped behind the trees. Inside, the torches burned lower, casting longer shadows. I should have left too, should have retreated to my chambers to prepare. Instead, I found myself frozen, unable to look away from him.

"You were right," he said finally. "Earlier. I don't get to decide what you're ready for. That wasn't fair."

The admission surprised me, but I kept my arms crossed. "You're trying to protect me. I understand that."

"Understanding it doesn't make it acceptable." He moved around the table slowly, maintaining distance. "I sent you here because I thought I knew better. I thought I was protecting you. Instead, I just..." He stopped, jaw clenching. "I hurt you. And I've been trying to figure out how to navigate this ever since."

My throat tightened, but I forced the words out. "Navigate what, exactly? Because we haven't actually talked about any of it, have we? Not about you coming to my room that night in Grey Oak, sharing my bed.

Not about how you lied to me for seven years about who you really were that night or why you introduced yourself. Not about—" I stopped, hating how my voice wavered. "Not about you shoving me into that carriage."

The muscle in his jaw ticked. "You would have died if I hadn't."

"That was my choice to make." The anger felt good, safer than the confusion underneath it. "Just like it was my choice who I shared a bed with. Or it should have been. If I'd known the truth about who you were, what you wanted from me, I might have chosen differently."

"Aurelia—"

"Was I just a job?" The question burst out before I could stop it. "Track down the Chosen One, get her to trust you, open the gates to your precious kingdom? Was that all it was?"

Silence stretched between us, heavy and suffocating.

"At first?" His voice was rough. "Yes."

The honesty shouldn't have hurt as much as it did. I'd known, hadn't I? Deep down. From the moment he'd told me of their bargain with the gods.

"That night we met at the solstice celebration," he continued, "I came to see if you were worthy of your destiny. If the girl everyone whispered about could actually be what the prophecies claimed."

"And?" I prompted, anger heating my face. "What changed?"

"At first, nothing." His grey eyes met mine, unflinching. "You were a spoiled princess marrying a spoiled prince."

"As I recall, you seemed to have already made up your mind by the time you opened your mouth." I turned toward the door, done with this conversation.

"You asked me what changed."

I stopped but didn't turn around.

"I did," he said quietly. "Meeting you...what I felt... it has made me question everything I thought I knew about worthiness. About destiny. About what I was willing to sacrifice for duty."

"And yet you still lied."

"I couldn't have told you these truths if I wanted to. And gods, I wanted to."

The desperation in his tone made me study him.

"Koraz asked if I knew the truth," I said, remembering the way Duron's advisor had taunted Rydian that night in the garden. "He called Duron your master. What did he mean?"

I watched the shadows play across Rydian's face as he leaned against the war table, his fingers gripping the edge hard enough to turn his knuckles white.

"A blood oath," he said finally, each word dragged from somewhere deep. "To Duron."

"Like the one your people made with the Furiosities?"

He barked out a laugh, humorless and bleak. "No, this was nothing like that." His jaw tightened, but he went on quietly, and I waited, giving him space, "I made it when I was seventeen. An oath of loyalty, he called it. It prevented me from lying to him or raising a hand against him, no matter what he commanded."

"Sounds like enslavement."

"I did it willingly." The desolation in those words hollowed me out.

The air between us felt too thin. "Why would you—?"

"My mother." His jaw tightened. "Duron discovered her lineage. What she was. He would have used her, kept her locked away in Autumn as leverage against me forever." His eyes met mine, dark and raw to their depths. "The blood vow was the only way to keep her beyond his reach."

Rydian might have saved his mother from that abuse, but in doing so, he'd subjected himself. My heart broke for the seventeen-year-old who'd had to make that awful choice.

"Where is she now?" I asked.

Something shuttered in his expression, that familiar wall sliding back into place. He straightened, putting distance between us with nothing more than a shift in his posture. "She's safe."

"Rydian—"

"That's all you need to know." Not cruel but absolute.

The silence stretched between us like spider silk—fragile, nearly invisible, but there nonetheless. I could have pressed. Could have demanded more after everything he'd kept from me. But I recognized the fortress he'd built around this one thing, this one person he'd sacrificed everything to protect.

He'd wanted to protect me too. And the only way he knew how was to take the entire burden on his own shoulders. Even though I understood it now, I still couldn't let him think it was okay.

"I'm not her," I said as gently as I could.

His gaze whipped to mine.

"I am going to put myself in danger," I went on before he could argue. "And I'm asking you to stand beside me while I do it. To fight with me. Not fight in my place. And not send me away or arrange things behind my back."

He swallowed hard. "All right."

The words were raw but firm.

"And the oath you swore to Duron is broken now?"

"Yes." The word came out rough. He looked away, toward the darkened windows. "I'm free."

I wasn't sure if freedom was supposed to look so haunted. But I only looked at him, this warrior prince with shadows in his eyes and scars on his soul.

"And now?" I asked quietly. "Where do we go from here?"

"Now we go to the river people. We forge this alliance. We save Lesha."

"That's not what I meant."

"I know." He sighed. "But it's the only answer I can give you." Something dark flickered in his eyes. More secrets, I realized.

No matter how many truths he gave me, there were still more he kept for himself. The fact was, I trusted Rydian Nytherra with my life—but I couldn't trust him with my heart.

"I should prepare for tomorrow," I said, my voice flat. "Good night."

I turned to go.

"Aurelia." My name was rough in his throat. "We're going to save her. Lesha, your people, all of them. I swear it."

I nodded once, not trusting myself to speak. Despite everything—despite the betrayal and the hurt and the complicated mess between us—I believed him. Maybe that made me a fool.

I made it to the door before his voice stopped me one more time.

"You weren't just a job," he said hoarsely. "Not for a long time."

I didn't look back. Didn't let him see how those words affected me. "See you in the morning."

I slipped into the corridor before he could say anything else. Before I could do something stupid like ask him to define "a long time." Before I could forget that I had bigger things to focus on than whatever this thing between us was or wasn't.

Tomorrow, we'd go to the river people.

Tonight, I'd remind myself that hope was dangerous. Especially when it came to males who dealt in shadows and secrets.

THE
LOVERS

Chapter Thirteen
Aurelia

The mountain wind smelled of frost and pine sap, the cold sharp enough to sting my lungs when I breathed. The sun hadn't yet cleared the peaks by the time I'd gathered my things and emerged from the cabin, but its soft light caught on the edges of the valley below—casting the world in soft gold that made the haze-wrapped Midnight Court look deceptively peaceful.

I joined Amanti near the stone circle, my swords strapped to my back—both returned to me this morning by Daegel—and a small pack of supplies in each hand.

"Did you get any sleep?" I asked her, noting the dark circles.

"Some."

"I dreamt about Lesha," I admitted.

"As did I."

Worry coiled inside me. I shoved it away.

"Where are the others?" I asked.

I'd wondered if they would even join us. Keres and Thorne, especially. But every single one had heard our plans and jumped right in with their own preparations. No one had blinked an eye or bothered to make a pronouncement; they'd just jumped into action. Like a unit. Like there was never any question that where one went, the rest followed.

"Thorne and Slade rode ahead to scout the way," Amanti told me. "The rest are—"

"Here." Rydian rounded the corner, leading a saddled horse in each hand. Daegel followed with two of his own, and Keres brought up the rear, already mounted astride a beast of her own.

I noted the double blades strapped to her back and the bow stowed with her saddlebags. She caught my eye and dipped her chin in greeting, then halted at the edge of the path, waiting.

"This one's yours." Rydian handed me the reins of a black mare that I was fairly sure had participated in my kidnapping from Grey Oak.

"What's her name?" I asked, noting the way her coat gleamed like midnight itself. Her coloring reminded me of Shadow, the horse I'd ridden to the Autumn Court alongside Callan.

"Mouse," Rydian said.

I snorted, but when he didn't react, I stared at him. "You're serious."

Daegel grinned as he passed and handed Amanti the reins to a spotted grey. "Dove is all yours, Aunt," he told her.

"Thank you, Daegel." Amanti swung up into the saddle with all the ease of someone who'd done it a thousand times before, though I couldn't remember ever seeing her on horseback in my life.

I glanced at her damaged wings, my heart panging for what she'd lost. What had been taken from her.

A Brindalorn.

Was the South still somehow full of all the things we once thought were mere myths?

Everything except the Verdant.

Rydian took my packs and strapped them to Mouse for me.

I stared up at the cabin, noting the last trace of hearth smoke curling from the chimney. Frithhold was already half-swallowed by fog, its memory dissolving into the cold.

Directly ahead, the Trolech Forest spread out of sight where I knew it would eventually give way to the vast, barren wastes of the Broadlands. From there, our journey stretched all the way to the Osphanis, the winding river that cut through the land like a silver scar. It would take at least four days to reach it, and that was if we made it unscathed through whatever lurked in these lands.

To my right, the Concordian Mountains stood tall and snow-capped in the lightening dawn. I looked out over it all, watching the horizon swallow the last stars, and wondered if Lesha could see those same stars now. The thought made my chest tighten, made the furyfire beneath my skin pulse with a heat that was both comfort and threat.

Control it. Always control it.

"Ready?" Rydian's voice came from beside me, low and careful.

I turned to face him. He was dressed for travel in dark leather and worn cloth that seemed to drink the shadows, his sword strapped across his back with the ease of long practice. The morning light caught the sharp angles of his face, and I noticed—not for the first time but with fresh awareness—how he looked at me. Like I was something precious and dangerous in equal measure.

The Chosen One, I reminded myself. The savior of the realm. That look had nothing to do with his own personal feelings.

"As ready as I'll ever be," I said.

Amanti approached, her scarred wings tucked tight against her back, a posture I'd learned signaled determination. "We all know the Broadlands are no gentle crossing," she said, her warrior's pragmatism cutting through any false comfort. "Stay close. Stay alert. These borderlands belong to no one, which means anything can claim what's inside them."

"They're welcome to try," Daegel said cheerily.

"We go slow and keep alert," Rydian said quietly.

The others nodded.

I shook off my own dark mood and let him help me into the saddle. Touching him was completely normal, I told myself. A friend helping a friend mount a horse. Nothing more. But my hand tingled with awareness even after I'd let him go.

Daegel and Rydian both mounted, and we fell into line; Daegel at the front with Rydian following. Then Amanti and I, with Keres bringing up the rear.

Our processional remained silent for the first few hours. Slade and Thorne didn't appear, nor did they signal danger ahead, so we plodded onward, down the mountainside to the Trolech Forest's floor.

Every now and then, I caught the glint of Rydian's eyes when he looked my way. I pretended not to notice.

I wanted to hate him. Gods knew I had every reason to. But I understood him now in a way that scared me. His silence wasn't arrogance. It was armor. And I knew what it was to wear that kind of shield—to fear what might break through.

The trail narrowed to a pass where the mountain wall rose sharply on one side and dropped steeply on the other. Rydian slowed, allowing his horse to pick the best footing, and I followed his lead, bracing my hand against the rock that rose up beside me. A few paces ahead, Daegel muttered something about mountain goats, and Rydian's low laugh rolled like smoke in the cold.

The sound of it hit something traitorous in me.

I wanted to hear it again. To cause it. To call it mine.

When the path leveled out, I kept my gaze fixed ahead, counting the crunch of gravel under Mouse's hooves, the hiss of wind between stones. Anything to ignore how my pulse changed when Rydian drew closer.

By midday, the mountains fell away behind us, though the trees remained. The air turned warmer, heavy with the scent of damp earth and fallen leaves.

We stopped only when Rydian called for it, his voice cutting through the silence. "We'll rest here."

Daegel shrugged off his pack and began clearing a space for a small fire. I knelt to help Amanti unfasten the straps on her own pack. Her fingers were stiff from the cold, but she brushed mine away.

"I'm not helpless," she said.

"I know," I said, smiling faintly. "You'd probably stab me if I treated you like you were."

"I would never," she said, lips twitching.

It was a small thing, that exchange, but it felt like something loosening between us—some old thread of loyalty pulled taut with her admission about being Rydian's aunt now mending again.

An hour later, we resumed our trek, and the day passed quietly.

By nightfall, the world had quieted to only the sigh of wind through the trees. Daegel took first watch. On my left, Amanti cupped a mug of tea, staring into nothing with a look that hollowed me out. On my right,

Keres sat, sharpening her blade with slow, deliberate strokes, the rasp of steel against stone steady as a heartbeat.

Rydian sat across from me on his bedroll. His limp had improved, but I could tell from the way he sat that his hip still twinged, thanks to the injury Koraz had given him.

We couldn't risk a fire, but the moonlight was more than bright enough to see him watching me. I tried not to notice the way the starlight caught in his dark hair. The strong line of his throat. The capable hands that had killed for me, protected me, betrayed me.

"Tell me about the naiad," I said, desperate for distraction.

Amanti looked up from the tea Keres had forced on her. "They're a kingdom made of old magic. Older than the courts."

"Tyrion never could get them to agree to help us," I said.

"They still consider themselves outsiders in Menryth," Amanti said.

"They've been here for a thousand years," I said.

"For some, a thousand years is not long at all," Keres said quietly.

"Maybe for the gods," I snorted.

"It's not just that," Rydian said. "They consider Beneath a different realm. One not subject to the same threats as Above."

"They must know by now that Heliconia will not allow them to remain neutral," I said.

"Patamoi is no fool," Amanti said. "But he is no pushover either."

Rydian shifted, and I felt his gaze like a physical touch. "We'll need to prove ourselves worthy allies. Show him our strength."

"I'm good at strength. It's control that's the problem," I muttered.

No one else said anything.

Rydian frowned. Silence stretched between us, thick and heavy.

"Aurelia—"

Amanti's snarl was the only warning before chaos erupted.

One moment, we were sitting alone in the forest. The next, darkness itself erupted from the ground—shapes made of writhing shadow and malice, with eyes like dying stars and claws that gleamed like obsidian.

Heliconia's soldiers.

I scrambled to my feet as an Obsidian launched itself at me. My hand went to my back before I remembered I'd tucked my swords beneath the tree on the other side of my bedroll. Too far away now. I scrambled for my belt, for the knife Daegel had given me when he'd handed over my swords, but the creature moved faster—

Steel flashed. Rydian was there, his sword cleaving through the Obsidian's torso in a spray of dark ichor. The creature dissolved into smoke and screaming.

I dashed to my swords, snatching them up.

"Behind you!" Amanti's shout spun me around.

Another Obsidian. Larger. Its claws reached for my throat.

Dorcha sang as I unsheathed her, the dark metal humming to life. I pivoted, the edge of my blade catching the creature across the ribs in a burst of black ichor that splattered the earth.

It staggered and fell.

I spun, swinging Latha with my other hand. The twin blades gleamed—one dark as void, the other rippling with light—and when I crossed them, their hums resonated like the echo of thunder.

The next Obsidian lunged. I met it head-on, steel flashing as I slashed its throat and kicked it backward. Its scream came out wet and wrong, lifeless as it hit the ground.

Around me, chaos reigned.

Rydian's shadows coiled through the trees, strangling creatures mid-charge. Amanti moved like liquid lightning, wings flaring despite their damage, blades carving clean lines of silver through the dark. Daegel's sword work was heavy, methodical. Twice, he beat back the enemy with a shield made from shadows. Keres's arrows sang past my ear, precise and merciless. But the Obsidians kept coming—clawing from the soil itself, a tide of pale skin and inky eyes.

One leapt from the right, another from behind. I ducked beneath the first swipe, slashing upward, severing its arm. Spun. Latha buried itself in the second's chest, light flaring as it burned straight through the creature's ribcage.

Still more.

I could feel their life forces fading around me, three or four at a time. And something inside me, something quieter and more subtle than my furyfire, stirred.

A hunger.

Their life force could be mine if only I deigned to sip from it.

"Back-to-back!" Rydian's voice cut through the din.

I fell into position without thinking, the heat of him at my spine grounding me even as the air burned with magic. His shadows met my flames, colliding and curling into each other. The creatures hesitated, wary now—but not for long.

One screamed and dove at us. I met it midair, blades crossing. Dorcha sliced through its jaw while Latha split the air with light, severing its head. The body crumpled, dissolving into a pool of oily vapor.

No life force left in that one.

Another darted low, fast as a snake. I jumped, landed hard on its shoulders, drove Dorcha down through its skull. My boots hit the dirt, ichor splattering my legs.

A claw caught my arm, tearing through leather and causing me to drop my blade. I hissed and turned, fire instinctively flaring at my fingertips. A ball of furyfire shot out, catching the Obsidian square in the chest. It shrieked, flesh burning straight through to bone.

But the fire didn't stop there. It spread—too fast—licking up the trees, searing the grass.

"Get clear!" Rydian shouted, and the others scrambled back.

I jerked my hand, cutting off the flame before it could touch him. The sudden stillness left me shaking. The ground steamed where it had hit. I'd nearly—

No. Focus.

I plunged back into the fight. The air reeked of ash and blood and smoke. My arms screamed from the weight of my blades as I picked up the one I'd dropped, but I kept swinging—strike, parry, turn, stab. Dorcha drank their screams; Latha silenced them. Each kill came faster, more desperate.

A screech split the night. A larger Obsidian, twice the height of the others, barreled from the trees, claws like hooked scythes. I charged, ducked beneath a swipe that shattered a boulder beside me, and rammed both blades through its gut. It caught me in its massive fist before it died, flinging me backward.

Pain exploded as I hit the ground and rolled. My swords scattered—Latha near a tree, Dorcha in the dirt beside an Obsidian corpse. Three more loomed over in the darkness, lips peeled back in smiles too wide to be mortal.

I hesitated, not daring to unleash my furyfire again. Not after nearly burning the forest down around us. Out of the corner of my eye, I saw Rydian—surrounded and fighting. Keres was nowhere to be seen. Amanti and Daegel were busy cutting through their own swath of monsters.

I lunged for my blades, rolled as one of the creatures' claws struck where I'd been. I came up slashing, twin arcs of death. The first fell, head severed. The second, I impaled and shoved off the blade with a boot. The third grabbed me, claws raking across my ribs.

Pain ignited my furyfire. I let it rise this time, just enough. Flame roared from my skin, catching the creature's arm. It screamed, tried to hold on, and burned for it. The fire consumed its face, its chest, until there was nothing but dust.

I gasped, pulling the fire back before it could spread, chest heaving. The night rang with silence—echoing and eerie. Then I realized: The other Obsidians had stopped.

Rydian stood, blood streaking his bruised cheek, his shadows still writhing. Daegel and Keres held the perimeter, Amanti at their flank. The remaining Obsidians circled, cautious now.

I raised my blades. "Come on, then," I hissed. "Who's next?"

They didn't charge.

Instead, one tilted its head, its onyx eyes reflecting me in miniature. "The Chosen," it rasped, voice like breaking glass. "The master will be pleased to find you at last."

A growl rose from Rydian's chest. "Come near her, and I'll paint the ground with your rotten blood."

The Obsidians hissed, then—as one—slid back into the shadows, dissolving into smoke and ash.

The forest fell quiet again. Too quiet.

I stayed in my stance, blades dripping black blood, my breath ragged. "Why are they—"

"Retreating?" Slade's voice came from the trees, ragged.

He and Thorne stepped into the clearing a moment later, covered in black blood and gods knew what else. Thorne's tunic was torn open, a bloodied slash running across his torso. But they were alive.

"They're reporting back," Slade finished grimly.

I sheathed Dorcha and Latha slowly, heart still hammering. "To Heliconia."

Rydian's expression was grim. "She knows where you are now. And she'll send everything she has against you."

The silence that followed was worse than the battle.

Daegel came forward, his hand landing on my shoulder. I winced at the wet coating I felt on his palm. "You all right?" he asked me quietly.

I nodded. "You?"

"Fine," he assured me. "I'm going to check the horses."

I watched as Keres approached Thorne and led him to her healing supplies. The others remained standing among the fallen Obsidians, all of us trying to process what had happened.

"We spotted them an hour ago," Slade explained, "heading in the other direction. We thought we were clear, but their scout circled the flank and spotted your tracks. We tried to get back here, but they cut us off."

"Killed two dozen more of those assholes in the woods just there," Thorne added, pointing in the direction they'd come from.

Rydian cursed.

"How long you think we have?" Slade asked him. "Before they bring reinforcements."

"Days. Maybe less." Rydian's gaze found mine across the ruined camp. "We need to move. Now."

But he didn't move to pack up. Instead, he crossed to me in three long strides. His hands framed my face, tilting it up to the moonlight. Those storm-colored eyes searched mine with an intensity that stole my breath.

"Are you hurt?" His voice was rough, almost broken.

"I'm fine." The words nearly stuck in my throat.

"You're bleeding."

I blinked, looking down and noting the gash along my ribs where an Obsidian's claw had apparently torn through a gap in my armor. "It's a scratch."

"Keres will patch you up." His thumb brushed my cheekbone, and the tenderness in the gesture nearly undid me. "You're alive. That's all that matters."

Wrong. We both knew that was wrong. If I'd used my furyfire to its fullest, those Obsidians wouldn't have escaped. And doomed us all to whatever army Heliconia would send next.

But standing there with his hands on my face and his body close enough to feel his heartbeat against mine, all I could think was how badly I wanted to close the distance between us. To press my mouth to his and forget everything else—the prophecy, the uncertainty, the impossible choices that lay ahead.

His gaze dropped to my lips. Heat flared in his eyes, dark and wanting.

I swayed forward, gravity and desire pulling me toward him.

"Hate to interrupt." Slade's voice shattered the tension like a bucket of ice water. "But we should probably leave before more of those assholes show up for round two."

Rydian dropped his hand. The loss of contact felt like a physical wound.

"Right." I stepped back and wrapped my arms around myself. "We should go."

His jaw worked, but he nodded. "Pack up. We leave in five minutes."

THE
LOVERS

Chapter Fourteen
Rydian

The Broadlands stretched before us like an open wound, all sun-scorched grass and drought-baked earth. It had been three days since the Obsidians had found us. Three days of hard riding, rationed water, and the knowledge that, somewhere behind us, survivors carried word of Aurelia's location to the Winter queen.

I watched Aurelia from the corner of my eye as we rode. Always watching. Always aware of the precise distance between us—close enough to reach her if something emerged from the sparse scrub, far enough that I couldn't see the exact shade of gold in her hair where the sun hit it.

Far enough that I couldn't do something stupid.

She sat her horse better now than she had at the beginning of our journey. Back straight, hips moving with the animal's gait in a way that made my cock twitch as I imagined those hips moving against mine. I forced my gaze forward, jaw tight.

This was torture of my own design.

You sent her away, I reminded myself. *You lied to her then, and you're lying to her now.*

Every hour that passed without telling her the truth about who I was—what I was—drove the blade deeper.

"You're brooding again," Amanti said, drawing her horse alongside mine. My aunt looked as tired as I felt, dark circles under her eyes, but her spine remained iron-straight.

"No, I'm not," I protested.

"Your face gets this particular thundercloud quality."

"I'm thinking."

She smirked. "Same thing." She glanced back at Aurelia, then at me. "You should tell her now. On your terms. It'll go better coming from you."

I shook my head. "Not yet."

"Your funeral." But her voice held something softer beneath the words. Sympathy, maybe. Before she'd left for the Aine, Amanti had watched me grow up, had trained me to fight, had kept my secrets for years. She knew better than most what those secrets cost.

We made camp that night under a scatter of scrub oaks where the ground rose into a knoll high enough to break the wind and still give us sightlines. A fire was out of the question, so we stuck to cold rations, finishing up the last of the bread and meat.

Across from me, Amanti lay back with one wing half-open while Keres rubbed salve on it. I watched as my aunt pretended not to wince. Beside them, Aurelia sat, staring up at the stars like she could force them to tell her what came next.

She'd barely spoken all day. Ever since the attack, something had shuttered behind her eyes. I'd seen her hands shake when she thought no one was looking, seen the way she stared at her palms as if searching for bloodstains only she could see.

I wanted to go to her. Wanted to pull her against me and swear I'd never let her face that fear alone. Wanted to kiss her the way I'd almost kissed her three days ago, before Slade's interruption saved us both from my catastrophically poor judgment.

Instead, I watched her until she caught me staring. Our eyes held across the space. Something electric snapped in the air between us, hot and hungry and dangerous.

She looked away first.

I felt the loss like a punch to the chest.

"Get some sleep," I said to no one in particular. "Long day tomorrow."

Aurelia took my advice and retreated to her bedroll. It didn't take long for her breaths to even out as sleep claimed her. Amanti and Keres followed soon after, leaving Slade and me.

Thorne had taken first watch. Daegel was already snoring soundly and had been for an hour. The tough bastard could sleep anywhere, anytime.

Slade waited until the others' breathing had evened into sleep before speaking. "We going to talk about it?"

"About what?"

"About the fact that you're one bad day away from doing something truly stupid where she's concerned." He nodded toward Aurelia's sleeping form.

I reached into my pack and pulled out a skin of whiskey, drinking deeply. "I'm handling it."

"Handling it," Slade repeated. "Is that what we're calling the longing looks and the general aura of sexual frustration you've been projecting for the past week?"

"Fuck off."

He grinned, unrepentant. "At least, your face is healed. Though I can't say it's improved any without the rainbow of colors."

"It's better than your ugly mug," I told him.

He laughed.

"Your mother's going to be disappointed," he said after a moment, sobering. "That you didn't stay long enough to let her meet Aurelia properly."

My shoulders tensed. "Keres said she chose not to."

"You and I both know she was only waiting for you to return first."

I didn't bother to argue. My mother's belief in me was a tired subject. "It's better this way. For now."

"Better for who?"

"Everyone." I looked out into the dark, not meeting his eyes.

Slade was quiet for a long moment. "You're going to have to tell her eventually."

"I *know.*" The words came out sharper than I intended. I forced myself to breathe, to unclench my jaw. "After we secure this alliance."

If we secured this alliance. The doubt sat heavy in my gut.

Slade must have read something in my expression because he leaned forward, elbows on his knees. "What is it?"

I glanced at Aurelia again, making sure she was truly asleep. Then I said quietly, "The river people hate us."

Slade frowned. "You think they'll refuse the alliance because of old history?"

"You were there the last time we attempted to negotiate with them. You saw what they did to that Midnight fae soldier." I stared into the dark, but I was seeing something else. Somewhere else.

He grunted. "Does Aurelia know?"

I shook my head. "I don't want to disappoint her. She's put so much hope into this alliance."

Slade snorted.

"What?" I asked.

"The princess is a big girl. I'd say she's earned the right to process her own disappointments. And the sooner you figure that out, the sooner you stop making a mess of this whole damned thing."

I watched Aurelia turn in her sleep, hair sliding over her cheek, fierce even there.

Slade followed my gaze. "She'll ask you again how to open the gates. To let her try."

"I know."

"You'll say no."

"Until it won't kill her." The word *kill* was a foreign body in my throat. I forced it out anyway. "Until then, I keep her alive even if she hates me for it."

~

The following day, before the sun had hit its midpoint, a tributary of the Osphanis revealed itself with the arrogance of old power—broad and bright and slow at the surface, deceivingly serene until it was far too late. Underneath the surface, I knew, monsters lurked. Lights moved like eyes opening far down in the green murk.

We stopped at a bend where the bank rose into a little tongue of clay and root. From the looks of it, someone had camped there recently and left nothing but the remains of a small fire and the way the reeds leaned like they remembered a weight.

I said, "No closer."

The others halted.

"What is it?" Aurelia asked.

"A traveler moving on," Daegel said.

"Or a meal dragged Beneath," Slade added.

Aurelia blinked, considering.

"From here, we let them come to us," I said. "Aunt?"

Amanti stepped to the edge, tested the clay, and let out three sharp notes. They knifed through the lapping of water at the bank; a signal. I watched the ripples carry the sound and wondered which kind of predator would come to answer it.

Aurelia's fingers flexed at her sides, not a trace of furyfire beneath her skin. I stood where the bank gave me the best angle to intercept anything coming out of the water. Slade shifted to take our rear, eyes on the reeds. We didn't draw steel; that would be read as rudeness, or worse, war. But my shadows loosened of their own accord, uncoiling along the ground like patient snakes.

"Whatever happens," I said, without looking at her, "you let Amanti speak first."

"I'm not an idiot," Aurelia muttered.

I looked down at the water, at our reflections broken in the ripples.

The reedbed to our right shivered. Not wind. Rhythm. Something reverberating from Beneath.

I stepped half in front of Aurelia before I could stop myself.

"I don't need a shield," she said softly.

"I know," I said. "You have one anyway."

Behind us, the horses stamped the ground. Likely, they sensed something coming, as did I.

A moment later, shapes broke the surface: dark hair slicked flat to skulls, skin with a moon's hue to it, eyes too clear and opaque to be anything of the surface. The first naiad rose to her shoulders, naked, and set her hands on the bank like she meant to pull the land closer. Water slid from her knuckles in threads.

"Amanti of the Aine," she said. A voice like a current at the bottom of a pool. "You took your time returning to us."

"Has Patamoi passed his crown, then?" Amanti said, and there was fondness in the name. "Or are you the royal welcoming party?"

A smile showed small, pointed teeth. "He sent me to decide if you've brought him a flood or a drought." Her gaze slid to me. The current darkened. "Shadow-bearer. I'm surprised you would dare to return to these banks."

I kept my hands visible and empty of any weapons, including my shadows. "Princess," I said, bowing my head in respect.

The royal naiad's eyes cut to Aurelia last. The river stilled like a held breath. "Summer's secret," she said, but she said it like it was a title as much as any insult.

Aurelia didn't flinch. "Your Highness."

The naiad's smile widened.

Farther out, three more heads surfaced, each watching me and the Midnight fae that lined the ridge over my shoulder. Behind them, the current swirled in on itself.

Amanti stepped forward, wings tucked, and showed her empty hands. "We're here to ask an audience with your king. We come with news and a debt he may wish to collect."

"Your debt," said the naiad, "is overdue." She tilted her head toward me. "You shouldn't have come."

"The Winter queen seeks to detain us," I said. "We wish you no harm, I swear it on my own blood and that of the gods. Will you grant us passage?"

The naiad princess lifted her hand and flicked water from her sharp-nailed fingers. The naiad watching her back perked up.

"Follow," she said. "If you can keep up."

She vanished. The others slipped under with her, leaving only rings chasing rings across the surface of the water. Slowly, those rings became a tunnel. The water slid away from them, creating a hollowed path into the depths.

Amanti glanced at me. It was dangerous, letting her venture Beneath, considering the debt she owed. I knew better than to talk her out of it.

I stepped to the lip of the bank and held my arm out to Aurelia.

"I don't need—"

"I know," I said. "But the naiad should see you are not unprotected."

This time, she didn't argue. She took my wrist, warm and alive, her touch heating my skin in a way that had nothing to do with furyfire, and we moved together as the river opened and decided—for the moment—not to drown us.

THE
LOVERS

Chapter Fifteen
Callan

Winter had claimed the northern borderlands. From my horse, the world looked like glass; fields encased in silver, rivers frozen mid-current, trees split under their own ice. The villages of the northern reach had once been bright with harvest banners and the scent of mulled cider. Now their windows—what windows were left standing—gaped black, their wells frozen solid. Despite the ice, the air stank of death.

Another village destroyed by Winter's wrath. We'd put out the fires that morning. They still smoldered beneath the freshly fallen snow.

I dismounted in silence, boots clanging against brittle ground. Even with a layer of snow, the earth here was hard—stubborn, dying, unwilling to thaw. My breath puffed in clouds. The wind howled through the skeletal orchards like it was grieving.

My men waited beyond the ruins, camped in a valley that should have been high with corn. The tents gleamed dull gold beneath the pale sun, but nothing alive stirred. No birds. No insects. Not even the sound of water rushing through the streams.

A voice broke the silence behind me. "Majesty?"

It was Holt, shivering in his armor, his breath white in the air. "What are your orders, sire?"

"We'll return to camp," I said.

"Your Majesty." He swallowed. "We can't hold the line another night. The men—"

"The men will hold," I said, willing it to be true. "Reinforcements will be here in three days, and more rations to go with it."

He hesitated. "I don't know if they have three days."

I swung my gaze to him sharply.

"Their morale is weaker than their swords, Your Majesty," he was quick to add.

"I'll speak to them," I said, turning my horse away from the razed village. "Let them rally behind their love for their kingdom."

It was all we had left.

My tent stood apart from the rest, large enough to remind everyone who I was supposed to be. The canvas was embroidered with the crest of Autumn—a stag crowned in gold leaf, though the threads had dulled, brittle with cold. Inside, a fire warmed the space, but it did nothing to chase away the Winter queen's brutal bite.

I sat at my campaign desk, staring at a map of what used to be our northern provinces. Every mountainside village below the Concordian Ridge was marked in red. Every line of defense already gone.

All we had was this camp. At least until the new additions arrived in a few more days. More Autumn soldiers; our strongest fae. The legions who hadn't yet been required to donate their power to my father's vanity. And The Withered. Or a small contingent of them, anyway. The few who had agreed to work with me toward our common goal, though its outcome remained to be seen. As did our fragile alliance.

Even Lemuel did not know of that partnership.

"Majesty?"

The flap opened, letting in a gust of snow, and a soldier bent nearly double with it. His armor was rimed with frost. His cheeks were flushed pink with windburn.

"Report," I said.

"An emissary arrived from the north."

"The north?" I echoed, frowning.

"The queen requests an audience."

I looked up. "Heliconia?"

The man nodded once. "At the ridge. Alone."

The word *alone* carried no comfort. Heliconia didn't need an army to make a point.

I stood, brushing frost from my cloak. "Ready my horse."

The soldier bowed low and hurried stiffly out.

The ridge overlooked what used to be farmland—now a wasteland of cracked ice and shattered fences. She was waiting there, as promised, at the center of it all.

I'd seen her once before. Years ago, when she'd come to my father's court. To woo him to her side. His ego hadn't allowed a true alliance. I'd glimpsed her then. Young, vibrant, eyes glinting with a hunger that might have been mistaken for passion or even kindness. But that version of her was gone.

Now, Heliconia stood in a furred cloak the color of a winter storm, her skin pale as carved marble. Thick brown hair hung loose and wild where the wind caught it. She was attractive, but not beautiful. Not with such a hard mouth and eyes that stayed half-narrowed, as if everything she saw disappointed her. Too much cruelty had carved itself into her face, and the rest of her seemed to wear it like a crown.

Frost curled outward from her boots, spreading across the frozen ground in delicate veins. Something in me recoiled at the power that rolled off her.

Like one of the gods.

I batted the thought away.

She was mortal, same as all of us.

"Your Majesty," she said as I approached. Her smile was thin, sweet, sharp. "I wasn't sure you'd come."

"This was my land before your frost touched it," I said, dismounting. "I'll see what's left with my own eyes."

"The view is more than adequate." Her hardened gaze drifted past me to the horizon, where smoke still rose from a ruined village. "Autumn is where it will remain. Frozen in its destruction."

"You will go no farther," I said.

"You intend to stop me."

"My army will prove itself. We fight for the love of our land. Yours fights because you pull their hollow strings."

Her lips twitched as if she found this all amusing. "You cannot hold it forever."

I circled her slowly, the crunch of snow loud in the silence. "You asked for this meeting. Speak your purpose."

"I offer peace," she said simply, eyes glittering like diamonds. "And a future."

"Peace. I'm not sure you and I define that word the same."

"Then I'll use a different word. Compromise, darling." Her eyes caught the light—silver, endless. "Marry me."

I frowned, unsurprised by the trap she'd laid.

She smiled wider at my silence. "You have a kingdom on its knees. I have the power to keep it from shattering. Together, we could rule both realms. I only want to share your seat—what do you call it? The Harvest Throne?"

My throat tightened. "You'd share it. Equally."

"For now."

Her honesty chilled me more than any lie would have.

"And if I refuse?"

Her expression softened, pitying. "Then I will take it anyway, Prince. Piece by piece. You've seen how easily Winter spreads."

"I don't bow to threats."

"No," she said, almost fond. "You bow to ghosts. To a father who left you nothing but a broken crown. To a woman who left you nothing but regret."

I stiffened. "You presume much."

"I *know* much." She stepped closer, and the frost reached for my boots, curling around the leather. "You're still trying to prove you're more than a boy pretending to be king."

"Careful," I warned. "You stand on my soil."

She smiled. "This will all be mine soon. And you will bow. One way or another."

The wind shifted. The ice crackled beneath us like the earth itself was listening.

"I'll give you time to think on it," Heliconia murmured. "But not much. I have a war to win after all. A throne to claim."

"I won't say yes," I said. "Not now. Not ever."

"Then you'll watch your realm die. Just as she did."

"Her realm isn't dead," I said, knowing it was a useless barb. "They live."

"They sleep," she snapped, eyes narrowing. "And they remain lifeless and cursed. Dead in all the ways that matter."

An easily struck nerve, then.

"And you?" I asked, cocking my head, seeing past all the cold cruelty. "What did that curse cost you, I wonder? It's been seven years, after all, since the realm has seen you march your abominations to another court's doorstep to demand respect with violence. Did it really take you so long to recover from your wasted efforts?"

She laughed once—a sound like ice snapping.

"You mistake patience for price," Heliconia purred. Her voice was a cool blade drawn across silk. "I did not *lose* years. I learned how to wait until others exhausted themselves. I let harvest rot, and I let men like your father thin their own ranks, thanks to their greed and cruelty."

She stepped closer, a soft smile on her mouth. "These years have been much like your Autumn Court. I trimmed and pruned and stored. And now, we reap what we have sown."

I swallowed. "And now you come offering a fool's bargain. My crown for your hand. And you call it compromise." The words tasted bitter.

She cocked her head, eyes narrowing. "I offer survival. You, of all people, should know the difference. You are your father's son after all."

"And what if I am my own sort of king?"

Her smile sharpened as if she'd seen straight through my words to the lie. "Decide, Prince of Autumn. Marry and keep what remains, or refuse and watch what you would have ruled turn to a frozen memory. I do not threaten in anger, for you do not mean enough to me to stir it; I state what is inevitable. For you and all of Menryth."

The frost at our boots creaked, the land listening.

"You will not set foot any farther into my kingdom," I said with a snarl, more to keep my voice from breaking than from confidence.

She inclined her head as if obligingly amused. "Oh, I will set foot where it pleases me. But I will not dirty my soles where I can take the floor by breaking it beneath you. Think on that while your men shiver and starve, Callan. I will send for your answer soon enough."

I watched her go until the ridge swallowed the last of her. The silence she left in her wake was a new kind of cold.

I stood there long after the snow coated her footprints, staring at the horizon. The fields were white for miles beneath the moon's reflection, the sky dark and still.

Behind me, the campfires sputtered and died one by one.

When I turned for home, I could almost hear my father's voice again: *Rule, boy. Even if you have to lie to yourself to do it.* But I was done lying. Maybe not to my enemies—survival was cutthroat and required cunning—but I wouldn't lie ever again to myself.

THE
LOVERS

Chapter Sixteen

Aurelia

The tunnel stretched ahead like hollowed-out glass. I half expected the weight of the river to crash down on us, but the current curved around the passage—smooth, seamless, full of a magic I'd never witnessed before.

The naiad princess, whom I could only assume was one of Naliadne's sisters, didn't reappear. I hesitated, staring into the murky descent of the tunnel, trying to see the end of it. But it went on and on, deeper into the river's depths—beckoning for us to follow its trail.

The others crowded in behind, but no one volunteered to go first. Even Amanti hung back, waiting. For me to lead, I realized. As if he'd read my thoughts, Rydian nudged me to start moving, and we stepped inside.

The air shifted immediately—humid and dense as it pressed in around us. Beneath my boots, the ground looked like sand trapped in amber. The light that came through the walls wasn't sunlight anymore but something stranger: diffused, green-gold, and rippling, like the shimmer off fish scales.

Behind us, the crash of water rang out like a deafening roar. I turned just in time to see the river close over the tunnel's entrance, the surface smoothing itself until there was no tunnel at our backs; no sign we'd ever been there at all.

Rydian tightened his arm around me, pulling me in closer to his side as we walked. "An intimidation tactic," he whispered.

"Effective," I couldn't help but admit.

He grinned, and I caught a glimpse of the confident prince, the one drunk on his own ego but also obsessed with using it to impress me. For some reason, it reminded me of Callan.

"Don't tell me you're worried about a little water?" he teased.

"I'm more worried about the king whose will it bends to."

"Patamoi won't kill us without looking us in the eye first."

"That's so comforting," I said wryly. "And his half-naked daughter, whom you seemed to know quite well?"

He smirked. "Jealous, Furious?"

"Hardly. But to know you is to want to kill you, and I think that is the kind of information I deserve to hear before I visit her home, don't you?"

He laughed—a rough, low sound that made me forget for a moment that we were walking straight into mortal danger.

At least, the horses would be safe; at least, according to Daegel, who'd woven a shadow-shield around them before Thorne had whispered some kind of spell work in their ear that had sent them trotting for Frithhold.

"In that case," Rydian said, "Her name is Cerynth, and she was just as warm and friendly the first time we met as she is today."

Slade snorted.

Ahead, the tunnel sloped downward. The deeper we went, the more pressure I felt. I kept glancing up, half expecting cracks or leaks in the walls as the water pressed in, but the magic held.

Eventually, light glimmered ahead until we turned a corner—and the world opened.

The first glimpse of the naiad kingdom stole my breath.

The tunnel emptied into an expanse of light and color that shouldn't have existed this far below the surface. A city suspended beneath the river, alive and glowing. Coral towers rose in spirals, latticed with pearlescent bridges. Bioluminescent plants pulsed soft light in hues of blue and pink.

Naiad swam through open arches and across glowing currents that flowed like streets, their long tails flashing green or blue or silver. Mer-children darted along, laughing as their tails flashed, reflecting the light off their scales.

Slade muttered a curse at my back. "Look alive," he warned.

I scanned until I spotted the wide platform just ahead where a dozen naiad guards stood. Two legs had replaced each of their tails, and while their hair still dripped with water, the air around them was dry as they waited for us inside the tunnel's walls. Their armor was made of shell and light, their spears and tridents gleaming like shards of the moon.

Cerynth appeared on the other side of the tunnel. Her bared skin was covered in scales, and her hair floated eerily around her face in the still water. With a small motion of her hand, she beckoned us toward the platform.

"Welcome Beneath," she said. Her voice vibrated through the tunnel's walls, only slightly muffled as it reached us on the other side. "The king is expecting you."

We climbed up onto the platform, crowding the small space. Above, the roof of the cavern shimmered like an inverted lake reflecting sunlight.

Guards collected our weapons at the entryway. I set Dorcha and Latha carefully on the offered stand, the hilts catching the light and setting the gemstones ablaze.

My palms itched to reclaim them the second I let go.

One by one, the others handed their weapons over. Keres was the least willing, scowling and glaring at the naiad soldier as she produced blade after hidden blade.

"Gods Above," one of the soldiers muttered. "How many does she have?"

Keres shot him an acidic glare. "You better not lose a single one of these," she warned.

"You'll get them back when you leave," he said.

Keres huffed.

We were escorted along a path made of translucent stone. Everywhere I looked, I saw motion: naiad gliding through the currents beside us, markets suspended in bubbles of air, the faint thrum of music that felt like a heartbeat vibrating up from my feet.

Rydian walked beside me, quiet but watchful. The naiad looked at him the way people look at approaching storms—fascinated, wary, waiting for lightning. It made me wonder what had happened during Rydian's first visit here. Then again, if he'd wanted me to know, he would have already told me about it. Maybe I'd corner Slade later and force it out of him.

At the top of a steep staircase, the corridor widened into a great hall that felt both impossibly grand and ancient. The walls breathed light, ripples of blue moving through them like slow currents.

At the far end sat King Patamoi.

He was larger than any fae I'd met—broad-shouldered, skin the color of pale bronze, hair white as salt. No crown. He didn't need one. The current itself circled him, ribbons of water that moved like living serpents, coiling and uncoiling around his throne. His head. His biceps. Like the water itself was a living, breathing army of sentinels constantly on guard.

At Cerynth's direction, the others halted several yards behind us. Keres and Slade, especially, looking more than fine with that. Rydian, Amanti, and I stepped forward, the object of Patamoi's scrutiny.

When he looked at us, I understood why even Amanti's shoulders squared. His eyes were the river itself—clear, endless, old, sharp as a tooth ready to rip out our throats.

"Amanti of the Aine," he said. His voice wasn't loud but filled the room, echoing off the cavern's walls. "You owe me a life debt."

Surprise jolted me. A *life* debt? She'd failed to mention that particular detail. I could only hope Patamoi wouldn't demand flesh for flesh.

"I do," she said evenly. "I've come to pay it."

He studied her for a long moment, then shifted his gaze to me. The water around his arms flexed tighter. "And you are Aurelia, the daughter of Tyrion & Celeste. Summer's flame. The one who burned a king."

I held his stare. "I burned an enemy who sought to steal my power and use me for his own gain."

"Hmm," Patamoi hummed. "And now you stand before me with my enemy at your side."

I tensed.

His enemy? I slanted a glance at Rydian. "Maybe you should have waited with the horses," I whispered.

He winked, which only irritated me.

Patamoi seemed impatient, so I bit my tongue and faced the river king. "Whatever is between you and my companion is in the past. I've come to speak of the future."

"You've come to ask for something," Patamoi said with a disdainful sniff.

I pretended not to notice. "An alliance just as my father, Tyrion, proposed to you before. A united and formidable army against the threat of Heliconia."

Patamoi leaned forward slightly. The water curled closer to him, like an animal guarding its master. "My kingdom does not involve itself in land wars. The river follows its own tide."

"Heliconia's taken Concordia and uses it to build an army that will destroy everything in its path. Winter is spreading south into Autumn already. She'll come for your rivers next. Either invade them or freeze them into a block of ice."

Some of the naiad in the room gasped. A few murmurs went up.

I kept my gaze on Patamoi.

Something flickered in his expression—an almost-smile that wasn't kind. "You speak like your father, spreading fear and panic."

"Maybe you should've listened to him," I said before I could stop myself.

The room went so quiet I could hear the low hum of the currents shifting.

Patamoi's eyes narrowed. "Your father came to me once, asking for an alliance. He left with empty hands and an enemy at his back that called itself his friend."

"What enemy?" I asked, suddenly unsure. I'd never heard of anyone else—

He glared at Rydian again.

"The dark fae of the Great War have long been liars who care only of their own kingdom."

I blinked at that, ignoring the way Patamoi spat the words in Rydian's direction. Had Tyrion managed to ally with the Midnight fae after all?

"The Summer fae were fools to think they could be trusted," Patamoi finished. "Nevertheless, your father made his choice, and I, in turn, made mine. As it seems you have also made yours."

Rydian tried to pull his arm out of mine, but I held tight, keeping my gaze fastened on the river king.

"What can I do to earn your trust?" I asked.

"There is only one way to ally with us," he said, still glaring at the prince beside me. "Renounce the Midnight Court. Only then will I consider your request."

"You're serious?"

"I do not joke about such matters."

Rydian's entire body tightened, and I knew he was fighting for control to keep quiet. What the seven Hels had happened when he'd come here before?

"Neither do I," I said, my mind racing to catch up to what was going on beneath the surface.

Slade, Keres, Thorne, Daegel—they all shifted nervously now. Like they were ready to bolt. Or to fight.

Amanti wouldn't meet my eyes, and I realized I was the only one of us who didn't know what was happening and why. My own temper coursed through me, heating me until my furyfire rose to the surface. I shoved it down again.

Patamoi's eyes flashed. "And will you?" he demanded.

Rydian's gaze flicked toward me. His face stayed still, but I felt the tension radiate off him like a held breath.

Amanti stepped forward. "Patamoi—"

He silenced her with a gesture. "If you would have my rivers at your back, Summer's child, then you must prove your allegiance belongs to no shadow."

I could feel every eye in the chamber on me. My pulse thudded in my ears.

Rydian said quietly, "You don't have to—"

"I won't," I interrupted, keeping my voice steady. "The Midnight Court has already proven to me that they will fight for me and for all fae. The river people have done nothing to prove their loyalty."

"Loyalty is earned, girl—"

"This isn't about loyalty. And I am not a girl."

My magic flashed through me. Not flame. But something like a surge. It shoved at the edges of my skin, and I watched Patamoi blink in surprise. He'd felt it too.

A murmur rippled through the hall.

Patamoi's expression didn't change, but the currents around him slowed.

"You speak boldly," he said. "Perhaps unwisely."

"I've learned polite words don't change minds," I said. "You said I'm my father's daughter. Then you already know I'm stubborn as hell."

That earned a small sound—almost amusement—from the naiad.

Patamoi leaned back, his gaze moving over our group like a tide measuring the shore. Finally, he said, "You may think on who your true allies are. We will speak again when the moon rises."

He turned to Amanti. "Your debt will be measured before the next tide."

Amanti inclined her head. "As you wish, Your Majesty."

Patamoi's attention came back to me one last time. "You and your companions are invited to dine in my hall tonight."

"That's generous," I said, my tone slightly sharper than I'd intended.

He smiled then, faint but not even remotely nice. "The river's hospitality is both brutal and bountiful in the same turn." He looked to someone over my shoulder. "Daughter, show them to their rooms."

Cerynth approached wordlessly, this time on two legs and wearing a slip of a gown over her pale skin. Her eyes bore holes in me as she motioned for us to follow her out.

The meeting was over. Patamoi had already gone back to his conversation with his advisors and court. The guards moved in silent coordination, ushering us out of the chamber.

I shook the tension from my shoulders only once we were clear of the hall. None of the others said a word as we all fell into step behind

Cerynth. She led us through a series of hallways, never speaking a word to us or any naiad she passed.

Amanti caught my arm as the others moved ahead. "You did well," she said quietly. "Patamoi isn't easily swayed. But you showed him strength. He respects that."

"Respect doesn't win wars."

"No," she agreed. "But it keeps you alive long enough to fight them."

We exited the palace and headed across a narrow bridge. Beneath us, the currents of Osphanis glowed brighter as night began to settle above the river.

For a moment, I stopped and looked down. The naiad moved through the light like pieces of sea glass. Beautiful, distant, untouchable.

Rydian came up beside me. "You handled yourself well."

"That sounded almost like approval."

"It was."

I studied his face, the half-light making it hard to tell what he was thinking. "You didn't like being used as a bargaining chip."

"I've been called worse things than shadow."

"Mostly by me."

He glanced over, eyes dark and unreadable. "I deserved it."

Something in my chest tightened. I looked away first.

On the other side of the bridge, we entered another building. Or maybe it was another wing of the same palace. I couldn't be sure with the way the walls rose up, disappearing into the opaque waters above.

Ahead, Cerynth and her guards turned down another hallway. As we followed, faint music drifted from below—notes that rose and fell like a tide itself. The notes were beautiful.

If I closed my eyes, I could almost forget why we were here. Or what waited out there. Almost.

We were shown to a suite of rooms that looked out over the glowing city. Beds carved from coral, linens soft as river silk. On the dresser, a basin of clear water that refilled itself each time we drew from it.

When the guards left, I sank onto the edge of the bed in the room I'd claimed and let out a slow breath. The events of the last few days pressed in all at once—the journey, the court, the way Patamoi's eyes had cut straight through me.

Rydian stood in the doorway, arms folded, expression unreadable. The others were gone, probably prowling through their own rooms, hoping for a hot shower.

"He's testing you," he said.

"I gathered."

"The dinner will be another test. He'll wait to see if you'll cast me aside."

"Then he'll know my answer won't change."

Rydian looked at me for a long moment. "Stubborn. As you said."

"Don't start liking that about me now."

His eyes softened, and he started to speak, then seemed to think better of it. "Rest," he said instead. "You'll need to be sharp for tonight."

"What happened when you were here last time?" I asked. "Why does he hate you so much?"

"You mean other than the fact that the Midnight fae fought against the naiad in the Great War?"

"Yes. Other than that."

He sighed. "We came here once before. Years ago. Our mission was to request an alliance with a kingdom that would be willing to fight for our freedom until our own gates were unlocked and we were free to do the same."

"And Patamoi refused?"

"We never made it that far. His soldiers came to greet us. Words were exchanged. One of our men was killed."

"I'm sorry. That sounds awful."

"Patamoi has carried a grudge against the Midnight fae since the Great War."

"Why didn't you tell me?"

"I didn't want you to lose hope in your plan."

"Naivete and ignorance are not prerequisites for hope, Rydian."

"No," he said quietly, "You're right. Now you know."

I wasn't sure that was true, but I left it alone. "What about his comments about Midnight allying with Summer? Was that true?"

"If it is, I didn't know."

"And Amanti's life debt?" I asked.

"The story she told me is that Patamoi saved the life of one of the Aine at her behest. She owes him a debt."

"Whose life?" I asked.

He shook his head. "That's all I know."

When he was gone, the silence stayed behind.

Outside the window, the city pulsed with light and movement, all of it framed by the dark weight of the river pressing down from above. For the first time since we'd entered the tunnel that led Beneath, I let myself feel the ache under my ribs—the mix of exhaustion and hope and the thin, sharp edge of fear that never quite left.

Patamoi's words echoed in my head. *The river follows its own tide.* Maybe so. But tides changed. And I intended to make this one turn.

THE
LOVERS

Chapter Seventeen
Aurelia

The guest suite was carved into the side of a coral bluff—rounded walls, a window like an eyeless lid that looked out over the glowing underwater streets. I sat on the edge of the bed and made a list in my head of what we needed and how little time we had to get it: passage upriver, a way into the camp, a way out again with Lesha alive. Every minute we spent here was another minute she remained in Heliconia's hands. I could feel the clock ticking behind my ribs.

A knock sounded—four notes, rhythmic and light. Not a guard's rap. I stood and palmed a conch shell displayed on the dressing table.

"Come," I said.

The door opened without a sound.

Princess Naliadne stepped in.

Her dark blue hair rippled like water where it fell over one shoulder and hung to her waist. Iridescent scales glittered faintly along her temple and the line of her collarbones when she moved, catching the light the way fish did before they darted away. Her eyes were sea-deep and knowing. When she smiled, it was with small, sharp teeth she didn't bother to hide behind her full lips.

Three males trailed her, perfect and varied in a way that said she'd chosen them carefully: one tall and ash-blond with shoulders built for throwing spears; one with copper skin and a mouth made for trouble; the third dark-eyed and quiet, the kind who noticed every exit in a room. He reminded me of Rydian somehow.

They fanned out without being told—one at the door, one at the window, one setting a lacquered trunk on the low bench at the foot of the bed.

"Nali," I said, genuine warmth filling my voice as she strode toward me.

Her smile lit the room. "Aurelia," she said. Her voice was sultry and melodic—made for singing an unsuspecting fool closer to the water's edge. "It's been too long."

I couldn't help but laugh at that. "It's been at least a week," I said, taking her offered hands in mine and letting her press an air-kiss along my cheek.

She spotted me setting the shell aside and gave me a knowing look.

"Beneath, we find that time stretches differently," she said. "But need does not." Her gaze flicked over my travel-worn clothes. "And you, I think, have need. Specifically for something to wear to dinner."

"Among other things." I looked at the trunk. "Is that a bribe or a gift?"

"Both? Though, not from my father." She nodded to the dark-haired male, who flipped the clasps and opened the lid. Inside lay silk and river-linen, pearl hooks, bands of nacre, colors like deep night and bright reef and the inside of a conch shell.

"Nali," I breathed. "It's beautiful."

"You will be expected to dress for court," she said. "We take beauty seriously here. I took the liberty of sending suitable options to your friends."

I reached in and touched the edge of a gown the green of riverweed at dusk. The fabric slid between my fingers like silk. I tried not to like it, but gods, it was lovely.

"That color is perfect for you," Nali said. "Oh, and I saved the best for last."

Her guard lifted a second, smaller trunk onto the table and snapped it open: jewelry—thin chains, delicate hairpins, a set of pearl-studded combs shaped like waves.

"I think it's only fair that I ask what you want in return," I said. "Beyond making sure we don't embarrass you at dinner."

Nali crossed the room, letting her fingers trail along the carved coral as she went. She took up the window's view, all glowing lights and flitting mer-tails.

"My father sees hospitality as a tool," she said.

"This is a test," I offered, quoting Rydian.

She turned back to me, nodding. "A two-part test, I think. First, he seeks to gauge your mettle."

"I've fought more enemies than he has in the last seven years," I said.

"And he fought in the Great War."

I blinked. "Impossible. Fae don't live that long anymore."

"Naiad do." She flicked a glance at me, adding, "Not many of us. But some. My father remembers what it was like, the bloodshed, the loss. He does not march into that again lightly."

"And the second test?" I asked.

"He wants to see if you respect our values." She bit her lip before adding, "What he does not value are shadow fae."

I sighed. "I see your message is your father's even if the clothes are not."

"They are all my doing, I swear it. But you should know he will not ally with you while you stand with him," she said, her voice becoming earnest, her eyes pleading. "Send the shadow prince away."

"I've given my answer, and it won't change," I told her as gently as I could.

"You must be very sure about him," she said, studying me.

"I am." I met her gaze. "He's not like Callan."

Her expression shifted—curious, then faintly amused. "No," she said. "No, he's not." The tip of her tongue touched the back of her teeth. "Callan was a polished blade. Your shadow prince is a knife you sharpen yourself."

She pinned me with a look that seemed to see right through to my soul. "I imagine you've come away with a few cuts from that knife yourself, haven't you?" she murmured.

I looked away, refusing to let her see the truth of it. "Rydian has saved my life countless times. I cannot—will not—turn my back on a friend like that. Besides, he is no longer a prince. Not since Callan banished him."

"I don't speak of his Autumn blood," Nali said, gentle but pointed.

I didn't move. Didn't blink. "I don't know what you mean."

Naliadne's smile turned sympathetic the way a predator looks "sorry" for a smaller animal that hasn't recognized the danger. "You do," she said softly. "You're not a fool. He is not some soldier without a court, Aurelia. Honor runs in his bones just as surely as it runs through a crown. He is an heir, same as you."

My heart slammed against my ribs. I'd suspected it but told myself it wasn't true. It couldn't be. Not just because of, well, logistics—how had Duron allowed him to live if that were true—but because he wouldn't keep that from me... would he?

I lifted my chin. "And if I sent him away, would your father give me what I asked for?"

"Perhaps," she said.

I studied her, seeing more truth brimming in her enigmatic eyes. My shoulders slumped. "You don't believe he'll agree no matter what I do."

"I didn't say that." A delicate shrug, but not careless. "My father does not move for those who cannot move themselves."

"Then why ask me to cut off my own arm for nothing?"

"Because he will demand it," she said simply. "And because it's in your best interest to not refuse him in front of our entire court." She paused. "Our people are... fond of games at another's expense."

"What kind of games, exactly?"

"They like a drama. A prince who swore himself to Summer's flame before she sent him away to please our king? It sings." Her gaze softened the smallest amount. "But singing doesn't save your friend. And I think you came for her more than for songs."

"Lesha," I said because speaking her name out loud helped keep me pointed in the right direction. "She is being held prisoner by Heliconia."

Nali nodded gravely. "We know where she is."

I stepped closer without meaning to, desperation making my voice rough. "How do you know?"

"Just because we have not pledged our swords to this war does not mean we have buried our heads in the sea," she said. "The river people know everything that happens in their waters and on their banks. Your friend is being held at a camp tucked into the Concordian side of the river, just above the north fork, in the shadow of Nygard."

Nygard Peak was the tallest point in the Concordian Mountains. It sat on the bank of the Osphanis far to the north, the center point that divided the southern regions of Autumn and the Broadlands.

"Is there a way in? From the river, I mean."

She inclined her head. "There is a sluice there. Our currents touch it."

"How close?"

"Close enough to get in," she said. "Not close enough to get out again. I've seen what Heliconia has bred there."

"Obsidians."

"Yes, and other creatures far worse than those. But it won't matter. You'd never get that far without my father's blessing for passage. Nor would your fae lungs survive it without his help."

My shoulders fell.

She was right; we'd need naiad magic for that. And without Patamoi's blessing, we had nothing.

"Thank you," I told her quietly. "For giving me this information, for the clothes, for your friendship. Especially after everything that happened in Grey Oak. The danger I ended up putting you in. I am in your debt for all you're doing for me and my friends."

"It is what friends do." She stepped closer, enough that the scales along her throat caught the light like a net. "Be careful, Aurelia. The naiad play games. Our smiles hide our teeth." Her voice softened at the edges. "And our teeth are very sharp."

I shuddered.

But she was smiling again, the foreboding gone from her otherworldly eyes. She nodded at the dress again. The green one. Of course.

Her guard had already untied the laces and unhooked the shoulder fastens. "I had it cut to your measurements."

"My measurements," I repeated, arching a brow. "From our first meeting in Grey Oak?"

"From when you walked past one of our mirrors on the way in," she said, unabashed as she smiled sensually at her guards. "We like to keep track of our favorites, don't we, darling?"

I pretended that didn't make my cheeks flush with heat and went behind the screen to change.

The dress slid on like water. It left my shoulders bare and fell straight to the floor, heavier than it looked, with slits I could move in and seams that didn't stretch when I reached for an imaginary blade.

If only I had one to reach for.

When I stepped out, Naliadne's smile turned brilliant. "Yes," she said, satisfied. "If my father refuses you, it will not be because you were dressed like a beggar."

"That's almost a compliment."

"How's this for a compliment: You look more radiant now than you did for a single second on the Autumn prince's arm."

My teasing vanished at the mention of Callan. I swallowed hard, unsure how to ask it. "About that. Did he... when you met him, he shook your hand."

Her brows knitted. "Did he? I don't remember."

"Afterward, did you feel different? Did you warm to him? See him as an ally?"

Her expression hardened. "The Autumn prince does not spark a single ember of warmth for me. Nor do I consider him an ally of the naiad."

I exhaled, relieved to hear it. "As it is for me too," I assured her.

"We'll leave you to prepare. Good luck tonight. And if you feel the current turn cold—leave."

She left with her men moving around her like a current, the door shutting behind them quiet as a ripple in the sea.

Keres arrived as I finished pinning my hair with the combs. She wore a gown so dark blue it rippled with hints of black and purple. The color of the Deep. Mysterious. Ancient. Deadly. It suited her perfectly. She'd let her hair down so that it hung thick over her shoulders in soft waves.

The softness changed her, and I had to do a double-take to even recognize her. Her scars were unchanged, but they were no longer the defining feature. Her scowl, however, remained.

"You look stunning," I told her.

"I feel like a prized calf on parade."

I snorted. "That's probably accurate for what awaits us tonight."

"Here." She held out a thin blade that looked a lot like a shard of coral filed down.

"Where did you get this?" I hissed.

She smirked. "Let's just say the bed frame is a little lighter."

"Keres," I admonished.

"It's coral," she said. "It'll grow back. They'll never know."

"Unless you use it to stab someone tonight," I muttered.

Keres merely smiled like a cat.

I hurried back to the trunk that held the hairpins and jewelry, digging through until I found something to serve as a holster. We went to work fastening the straps, tying them off, and finally strapping our blades to our thighs.

"Can I ask you something?"

Keres looked up as she lowered her skirt. "Sure."

"What happened when you came here the first time?"

"What did Rydian say?"

"Only that they killed a Midnight fae."

Her expression hardened, but she nodded. "Back then, I was a runner. Delivered messages, did the grunt work no one else wanted. I was barely out of training. I think they only sent me because I didn't seem threatening at the time and they wanted to make a friendly impression."

I wanted to argue that I suspected there had never been a time Keres wasn't threatening. But I kept my mouth shut and let her talk.

"Our orders were to propose an alliance, but when we arrived and made our request, their soldiers laughed, called us demon savages. Said we deserved everything Heliconia did to us for running them out of Vorinthia. Our captain hit him. He hit back. It ended with a body in the water and the rest of us escorted out with spears in our backs."

"Gods," I breathed.

A knock came so suddenly that I jolted.

Amanti poked her head in. "Am I interrupting?"

I noted Keres' hand retracted from where she'd gone for her hidden blade.

"No, come in," I said.

Amanti stepped into the room, and I noted the flowing cape and pantsuit she wore. It was the color of stormwater, churned and spit out again, beautiful but destructive. The shade perfectly complemented her gray eyes.

"You look gorgeous," I told her, noting the fabric even had a sleeve sewn like a sling for her injured arm. Nali had outdone herself.

"As do both of you," Amanti said. "You've clearly made a friend in Nali."

"I hope she still sees me that way after tonight," I murmured.

A soft two-tone chime rang from the corridor—music that meant the hour turned.

Our summoning.

My questions about Amanti's life debt would have to wait.

We checked each other like soldiers before parade—laces, seams, hidden blades. Amanti reached for my hand the way she used to when I was small and afraid.

"We go together," she said.

"We come back together," Keres added.

"And we find a way to make them like us," I put in.

Keres's mouth quirked. "That's quite the strategic plan."

We stepped into the hall. Two naiad waited there in livery the deep blue of Naliadne's hair. They dipped their heads and led the way without a word.

As we followed, I thought of what Nali had called Rydian. The words kept catching at the edges of my breath. I hadn't let myself think on it before, but now it was an alarm ringing in my head.

An heir.

A shadow prince.

It fit Rydian in a way that made too much sense. Not because of the power. Because of how he carried it. How he carried himself. Not like a bastard-born second son. Like an heir to a kingdom all his own.

A Midnight prince.

He'd kept it from me. Even with Patamoi staring him down, king to future king, he'd let me think he was nothing more than a soldier fighting for his people. A lie that might cost me this alliance.

I set my jaw, fury clawing through me.

He didn't get to keep secrets from me. Not anymore.

The corridor opened. Music drifted toward me, richer than it had any right to be this far under the surface. The smell of salt and citrus and something sweet I couldn't place washed over us. Bubbles floated by, each holding a pocket of air and a set of lights that bobbed like captured stars. Naiad laughed and moved and shimmered on two legs through the dry hall.

I felt the urgency rise under my ribs again—Lesha's face, her pure and joyful heart, the way she'd held my world together with her laughter all those years. I didn't know how long we had until Heliconia snuffed those things out. I just knew it wasn't enough.

THE
LOVERS

Chapter Eighteen
Rydian

The hall opened like a bowl cut into the cavern's side, every rounded edge rimmed in light. Floating orbs drifted in slow patterns above—glass bubbles with captured flame inside, swaying as if by some current. Tables curved in crescents, tier by tier, all pointed toward the high dais where Patamoi sat on a massive throne carved from coral and shell. He didn't look at me, not directly. He didn't have to. His guards did it for him.

I'd hoped our arrival would be met with more openness, but it appeared the years since my last visit hadn't been enough to lessen his ire. And yet, Aurelia had stood with me.

I didn't deserve that loyalty from her. Not after everything. But I would earn it starting now.

Our table stood alone on the first tier where everyone could watch us eat. Not an honor. A pen without bars.

Slade stopped beside me, his suit tailored perfectly, as was my own. Naliadne's note that had accompanied the gifts made it clear that to refuse them would have been an insult. And we couldn't afford any more of those. Besides, it was a rare sight to see my second looking so formal. I planned to never let him live it down.

Slade let out a low whistle. "The naiad know how to party. This place is huge. Why the lifted tiers?"

"It's an arena," I said. "They prefer their enemies where they can see them."

"Not like we have anywhere to run." He snorted. "Or swim."

I didn't let myself think too hard about that fact.

The floor was polished sea glass that gleamed in the lights. Music drifted out from farther inside—strings, low drums, something like a flute but deeper. The smell was salt and citrus and spiced fish. But most of my attention remained fixed on the naiad in attendance. Guests wore shimmery gowns and barely-there coverings made from seaweed silk. Servants wore simple garments in greens and blues that carried just a hint of algae.

"This way, Your Highness," a female naiad in a blue-gray jacket murmured, leading the way.

Slade and I followed, noting the eyes that tracked us as we walked.

Daegel and Thorne were already at the table, pretending to look bored. Daegel had chosen the seat that kept his back to a pillar and his view on the floor; Thorne had done the same on the opposite side.

"Front row," Thorne said, not bothering to hide the edge in his tone. "We must be special."

"We are," Daegel said. He gestured with his drink to the dais. "Special enough to be the only ones the king can easily toss a trident at if he feels like it."

Slade took a chair beside Daegel with a grin that didn't reach his eyes. "I'll catch it for you, brother."

"Appreciated," Daegel said. "I'd rather not be a shish kebab before dessert."

Around us, conversation dipped and shifted, and the hall turned its attention to the archway at my back. Aurelia stepped through with Amanti and Keres, and for a second, the room went soft around the edges.

Aurelia wore a green dress—deep, river-dark, cut to move like a second skin. It bared her shoulders and cut gracefully across her breasts, the fabric catching light along seams that reminded me of scales. Her hair was pulled back from her face, held fast by combs the color of sea pearls. It was the only jewelry she wore. No crown. No gems. She didn't need it. Every inch of her commanded attention, and not just my own, if the hush in the room was any indication.

On her left, Keres wore deep ocean blue, laced up her sides like armor. Amanti's suit was storm-gray, a cape rippling like schools of fish as she moved.

They looked like what they were: royalty fit for the naiads' halls.

Aurelia's gaze found mine. Something like fury flashed in her, and then her eyes lowered, and she strode into the room, shoulders back.

I stood as they reached us and pulled her chair out.

She sat, careful not to brush my arm. Up close, I could feel it—the dark, stubborn spark she carried. Fire banked, sitting in a river's hall and refusing to be smothered.

She'd gone three days without so much as a tinge of smoke, and now her power felt close, burning beneath the surface of her skin. It made me wonder what had happened since we last spoke.

Keres and Amanti sat.

Drinks were served. Then food.

Still, with one eye on the king, we did not eat. Not when he'd yet to touch his own plate. Another reminder of who he was—and where we stood in the hierarchy of this place. Beneath the surface and beneath him. We'd eat when he told us to.

Slade muttered his opinions of that, and Keres shushed him.

"You look beautiful tonight," he told her.

"You look like a jester," she told him.

Daegel belly-laughed.

"I found out something about Lesha," Aurelia said quietly.

Everyone turned to look at her.

She kept her expression neutral and her voice low. "Nali told me she's being held at a camp just north of Nygard Peak."

"Do you believe her?" Thorne asked warily.

"Yes," Aurelia admitted. "Not that it does us any good without a way in."

"There are reports of a war camp on the northern border," Slade said. "It's her base camp for the attacks she's led on the Autumn villages."

"What attacks?" Aurelia asked.

"Utter destruction," Slade said grimly. "She's locking folks inside their homes and burning whole villages to the ground. No prisoners. No survivors. And then winter spreads to freeze it all over. Like a memory of death—preserved."

"Seven Hels," Thorne muttered.

"Gods," Aurelia breathed. "That's awful."

I wondered if she was thinking of what she'd done to Duron. My hand reached for hers before I thought better of it and tucked it away again.

Finally, up on the dais, Patamoi lifted a hand. The music dimmed. "Osphanis welcomes those who travel far to ask and farther still to swallow their pride," he said. The words were smooth. The current under them was not. Bastard. "Eat. Drink. Tonight, we honor our guests."

He lifted his own glass and drank.

The crowd did the same.

The king sat, at last taking a bite of his food. The crowd cheered as music resumed and the party officially began.

Servants came in quiet waves. Fish with skin crisped. Fruit jeweled with salt. Bread that cracked open and steamed. I didn't touch the wine. None of us did.

I watched more than I ate. The guards. The guests. It was all an elaborate distraction for the real risk: we were trapped with nowhere to go and no weapons to defend. None save our magic.

Slade leaned back in his chair, nodding toward a female naiad across the room who hadn't stopped watching him. "I'd like to state, for the record, that I am happy to do my part in furthering our goodwill with the river people."

Daegel snorted. "And when she drowns you in your sleep?"

"Worth it," Slade said, grinning.

Keres snorted her distaste and went back to watching the room. She hadn't eaten a crumb.

"You should at least pretend to eat," I told her quietly.

"Why?" she challenged.

"Manners."

"Was it manners when they executed Brigham six years ago?" she shot back.

I sighed. "Brigham started it, remember?"

"We should have finished it," she said.

"Who was Brigham?" Aurelia asked.

I glared at Keres. It was an old argument, but not one to have in this particular room.

"Ask me later." I pushed my chair back, letting it scrape as I stood. Aurelia looked up sharply, and I met her gaze evenly.

"Will you dance with me?" I asked.

"Is that wise?" she asked, glancing toward Patamoi.

"He wants us where he can see us." I shrugged. "I'd think us being in the center of the room offers him the best view of all."

I took her hand. Warm. Sure.

We stepped onto the floor. I felt the naiad watching us, but I no longer cared; all my attention was for her now.

I kept my palm at the small of her back and felt the small, deliberate push of her spine into it. Not an accident. An answer. An invitation.

Or maybe I was losing my mind down here.

We moved slowly. A rhythm in a foreign tongue; a feeling that had been building since a summer rooftop party more than seven years ago. When she looked at me, the lights swayed and threw a ripple across her cheekbone. Fire under skin that had nothing to do with a gods-given power and everything to do with want. Need.

"Your hip seems to be better," she said.

"It's healed," I agreed, wondering at how she'd picked up on the slight injury when none of the others had.

"Tell me about your shadows," she said quietly. Casual on the surface, but underneath, not casual at all. "When you call them… what do they feel like to you?"

I considered the question.

"They're not so much a call," I said. "More like… opening a door that's been there all along."

"A part of you."

"Yes."

"Did they come from your mother's side then?"

"They are a gift of Midnight."

"And is she... like you?"

"Stronger," I said, which was true, and left out everything that wasn't mine to say. "Smarter. Meaner when she has to be."

Her brow lifted at that, but she only said, "She's behind the wall, isn't she?" I hesitated. "That's why you didn't want to tell me about her. Before. Because you hadn't told me about the gates."

"Yes."

"You must miss her."

"Sometimes." I let the memory in for a breath and then set it back where it belonged.

"Do you speak to her? Is that possible with the locked gate?"

"There are ways of sending messages through. Shadow-guards who pass messages. But... she keeps her own counsel lately."

Aurelia held my gaze a second too long. The music shifted, and the floating lights swung low, their glow washing the floor in pale gold. She looked like something carved from that light.

A ray of sunshine that had somehow penetrated the depths.

We spun again, letting the music wash over us. The line of her throat was a temptation I chose not to think about. And then there was the tattoo. A wink from her father as if he, too, was watching this dance.

"Tell me something true," she said softly.

"I have," I said.

"Tell me something you haven't yet."

I looked at her mouth. "If I start with you, I won't stop."

Her breath hitched. She covered it by shifting closer, our bodies fitting in a way that was too easy. Her next words skimmed my jaw. "Maybe I'm not asking you to."

The room faded to edges—the guards, the dais, the way Patamoi's eyes tracked our every move. None of it mattered for two heartbeats when she tipped her chin and our mouths almost brushed. The space between her lips and mine was a coin's width, maybe less.

I could feel the heat of her.

It should have been wrong, flaunting what I felt for her in front of a king who despised me, but I couldn't bring myself to care what anyone thought but her.

The spell between us shattered as a distinctive tremor passed through the floor. Aurelia's steps faltered. The orbs overhead swayed, one bumping another and sending a scatter of gold across the crowd. A few guests laughed, thinking it a party trick—until the second vibration hit harder. Plates rattled.

Somewhere, a servant screamed.

Dishes crashed.

The walls groaned as if something enormous had shoved at them.

Aurelia's hand stiffened in mine. "Did you feel that?"

"Stay close."

The third shockwave cracked through the hall, and every light snuffed out at once.

For half a breath, there was nothing but the dark and the sound of the sea pressing at the walls. Then a single shape drifted out of it.

A naiad. Or what had been one.

Her skin was marble white, veins blackened like cracks in ice. Eyes hollow, mouth full of razor-sharp teeth. When she moved, she *jerked*, as if dragged forward by a force that was not her own.

Gasps echoed around us.

Patamoi rose halfway from his throne, trident in hand. "Guards—"

The creature shrieked, the sound vibrating through the space until my skull rang.

The naiad struck first.

The nearest guard went down in a swirl of black water; his armor turned brittle and split apart like eggshell. The infection spread through him before he hit the floor.

Keres's voice snapped through the din: "Daegel!"

His shadow shield expanded like a dome, pushing civilians back. Thorne waded into the chaos, hauling people behind pillars. But the naiad ignored the fleeing guests, its eyes fixed on Aurelia.

Her hand tore free of mine, furyfire flaring from her palms in a burst of magic. The flames rolled off her, lighting the entire hall in flickering darkness.

"Don't—" I started.

Too late.

The creature dove at her.

I met it mid-lunge, shadows slamming it against the far wall. It screamed again, body convulsing, obsidian shards shredding free from its skin and spinning like shrapnel.

Aurelia lifted her palm. Fire and shadow collided. The impact blew the air from my lungs, boiling the moisture coating the walls to steam.

When the haze cleared, the naiad hung there—half ash, half bone—still moving.

Then it laughed.

Not a naiad's laugh. This one was colder, silkier, threaded with malice that didn't belong here.

"Still playing at diplomacy, little flame?"

The voice filled the hall—Heliconia's, unmistakable. I felt Aurelia freeze beside me.

"Did you think the river would wash you clean? That you could make friends with the fish and forget what you left rotting on land?"

"You have no real power here," Aurelia told her coldly.

"And you do? Tell me, what has the river king promised you? Friendship? An army? Or the remnants of a grudge that will keep him Beneath until it's nothing more than his watery grave?"

Patamoi roared at that, lunging off his throne as sharpened ice spears shot toward the naiad. One of them buried itself deep in the naiad's chest, drawing ochre blood.

"Demon," Patamoi screamed. "You disrespect the very power you've stolen."

The naiad choked, its chest rattling with the effort. But still, Heliconia's voice rang out. "Lesha sings for me now." Hate laced her words. "She dreams in ice and wakes whispering your name. You should hear the things she says when I peel back her skin."

Aurelia's skin heated, and I knew she was fighting to hold herself together.

"Burn it," I told her.

Her eyes met mine, bright and furious. "Together."

I opened my hand, letting the darkness flood outward. Her furyfire met it mid-current. For a heartbeat, everything froze—the entire hall suspended in fiery darkness—then the creature disintegrated.

Ash drifted like snowfall.

Only the hiss of cooling stone rang out in the silence.

When I looked up, Patamoi stood on his dais, trident lowered, the expression on his face unreadable. Around him, his court stared as if they'd witnessed a sacrilege instead of a thwarted attempt at assassination.

Aurelia's fire winked out. My shadows coiled back to nothing. The smell of scorched salt lingered.

The king's gaze settled on us—first her, then me. The weight of it pressed harder than the sea itself. "What abomination have you brought into my waters?"

THE
LOVERS

Chapter Nineteen
Aurelia

The room was utterly silent, stripped bare of music and laughter. Only the scorch marks remained—dark streaks across coral tile and the faint shimmer of ash caught in the orbed light.

Patamoi hadn't dismissed us, but the nobles and guests had gone, along with the servants. All that remained were the king's personal guard—a number at least three times what he'd surrounded himself with at the beginning of the evening—and his daughters, Nali and Cerynth.

Rydian stood a few paces off, shadows reined in tight. The strain of the threat still clung to him, dimming only when he glanced at me. Keres, Amanti, Daegel, Slade, and Thorne gathered close, forming an instinctive circle without needing to be told. Even without an enemy in sight, they looked ready for war.

Unfortunately, war was a distinct possibility, judging from the look in Patamoi's opaque eyes.

The river king rose from his coral throne, the trident in his hand catching the reflection of the floating lights. Beside him, Nali stood expressionless. For once, her harem of males wasn't with her, and the look on her face wasn't friendly.

"You lured a monster into my waters." Patamoi's voice rolled through the chamber, ancient and heavy. "And my people suffered for it."

Amanti stepped forward, chin high. "My king, they—"

"Don't speak for them," he cut in sharply. "Not until your debt is paid to me."

"Consider it paid tonight," she said. "With our help, your people remain safe, despite your refusal to join this war."

Patamoi's eyes glinted. "And yet a war found us."

Daegel shifted beside me as if readying his shield. Out of the corner of my eye, I watched as Thorne scanned the empty alcoves for signs of another attack. Keres stood rigid behind Rydian, glaring outright at the king.

I ignored them all and stepped forward. "Your Majesty, you saw what happened tonight. You heard Heliconia's voice as she spoke through one of your own people. A naiad she corrupted before we ever arrived Beneath."

Patamoi's expression hardened. "She sent a parasite. Nothing more. My realm has endured worse things than the Ice Queen's tantrums."

"She's not throwing tantrums," I said, my patience a fraying thread. "She's amassing power, building armies, infiltrating our courts."

He descended from the dais, trident dragging faintly across the glass floor. The scrape echoed. "You speak as if you fear her."

"If you don't fear what she could become, you should."

A flicker of movement—Amanti's hand pressed warningly to my arm.

Patamoi stood before me. "You presume much, flame-born."

His word struck me, and I realized belatedly that he'd seen my fury-fire firsthand tonight. That meant he'd likely sensed its source—and knew it hadn't come from Summer's magic.

Nothing to be done about it now.

"I only ask that you protect your people," I said, lowering my voice. "You think the depths make you safe? They only make you isolated."

For a long moment, no one spoke.

Nali broke the silence. "Father—"

"Enough." His tone cracked through the chamber.

She fell silent, jaw tight.

Patamoi's gaze returned to me. "Tell me, flame-born, where does your power come from? It is not mortal craft. No fae magic burns so bright."

I hesitated only a breath. Lying to him felt pointless. "It's a gift," I said. "From the gods."

A ripple went through the guards. Even my friends went still. Rydian included. The tattoo on my throat practically pulsed with awareness now.

Patamoi's brows lifted. "So the stories are true. Your gods still meddle in our affairs, hoping we'll aid them in their own power struggles." He looked to Rydian then, eyes narrowing. "Do they still favor your kingdom to the destruction of all others?"

"I can't speak for the gods," Rydian told him quietly. "But my kingdom stands with yours. If you'll do the same."

The king studied him for a beat longer, expression shifting from curiosity to recognition—the kind that made my stomach knot.

Finally, he turned back to me. "A match forged of darkness and destruction," he murmured. "A dangerous balance to bring beneath my waves. Perhaps the gods think themselves clever."

"I don't presume to know what the gods think," I told him honestly.

"Wise of you." He leaned on his trident, gaze sharp as the tide. "Their games often end in ruin for the players."

Amanti stepped forward again. "We ask only for a clear path as we leave you in peace."

Patamoi's gaze snapped to her. "You will not leave."

Every muscle in me went cold. "Excuse me?"

"The rest of you may go." His trident struck the floor, the sound like a deep bell tolling. "But the Aine's debt remains unpaid."

"That's not fair," I said. "She helped save your people tonight."

"The debt between us is not to my people," he said. "It is to me. I spared her sister once. Now she will serve me as her king until the scales are even."

My eyes widened. I stepped toward him before I could think better of it. "You can't keep her here. She's injured. She needs healing after what she faced in the south." My voice sharpened. "Or don't you believe in Brindalorns anymore either?"

Patamoi's expression faltered for the first time, the weight of the name catching him off guard. "They were thought to be extinct."

"Apparently not," Amanti said softly.

He regarded her for a long moment, and for the first time, his anger seemed to ebb. "The Calidium Empire once held a great many wonders," he murmured.

Amanti nodded at him. "Selene willing, it will hold a great many again someday."

He blinked at that. Then he straightened, returning to his full height. "You will be safe Beneath, Aine. But your debt demands service. You will tend my court until I release you. A true Aine serving a kingdom of Menryth once again."

I took a step forward, fury rising again. "You can't—"

Amanti touched my wrist, her grip gentle. "It's all right."

"No, it isn't," I hissed. "You don't owe him this."

She smiled faintly. "I owe him my sister's life. I would do this and more for my family. And for you."

Her words left no room for argument.

Patamoi tapped his trident against the dais. "Then it is settled."

Rydian's hand brushed mine, a subtle warning, quiet understanding. We couldn't afford to start another fight.

I swallowed the protest on my tongue and met Amanti's gaze one last time. "We will see each other again."

"I know," she said simply. "But for now, this is how it must be."

Patamoi turned back to his throne, the conversation apparently over. "You will leave Osphanis by dawn. I will grant safe passage upstream. The old currents will carry you far from here, unseen by the Frost Queen's spies."

Patamoi's gaze lingered on Rydian one last time, and something like understanding passed between them. His mouth curved in a faint, humorless smile. "Prince," he said softly—too quiet for the guards, but I heard it all the same. "May your companion never regret the shadow Fate chose for her."

We left before the city woke, Cerynth waiting outside our rooms to escort us back to the platform where we'd first arrived. The halls of the palace were hushed, light still low through the corridors. Our weapons had been returned—cleaned, polished, laid out on coral slabs like offerings. Nali waited beside them, pale in the torchlight, her expression softer than it had been last night.

"Your blades," she said. She nodded at the packs, one for each of us. "And rations for a week."

"Thank you," I told her.

"Thank my sister," she said, flashing a grin at the silent princess. "I wanted to fill your packs with those beautiful clothes. She pointed out that having food to eat might be more important... to anyone else but me."

"Thank you," I told Cerynth.

The pale princess merely dipped her head.

"I don't know," Slade announced slyly. "I would almost go hungry for the sight of Keres in a dress one more time."

"Mention it again and see how fast I cut the grin off your face," she said, voice deceptively casual as she went to work strapping weapons to nearly every inch of her body.

Thorne elbowed Daegel lightly. "Ten gold coins say she does it before we reach the surface."

"Twenty says she starts with his tongue," Daegel said with a snort.

Rydian ignored them all, fastening his sword to his hip with deliberate, quiet movements. His shadows curled faintly around his wrists, restless, like they didn't trust the stillness here any more than I did. Not after last night.

Amanti lingered near the doorway, watching us all prepare. Her expression was contemplative. I broke away from the others and went to her.

"Does Patamoi know?" I asked quietly.

"Know what?" she asked.

"That you are related to the heir of—"

"Hush." She leaned in, lowering her voice to nothing more than a breath. "No. And he won't."

A beat of silence passed between us. Secrets brimmed in her eyes. Much like in her nephew's. But now wasn't the time.

"I hate to leave you here," I told her.

She touched my cheek. "I will be fine. And so will you." Her gaze flicked to someone over my shoulder, her lips quirking in the ghost of a smile. "And when I'm done here, we'll talk about what's between you and my nephew."

My face heated, but she only patted my cheek knowingly.

"Go," she insisted. "Keep them all in line."

I nodded. I didn't have words for the ache clawing up my throat. Nali must have seen it because she came over and squeezed my hands.

"We'll take care of her," Nali told me gently.

"There could be more among you like the Obsidian last night," I warned her.

"We'll be ready," she assured me.

There was a glint in her beautiful eye that told me she was more capable than she seemed.

"I'm sorry I can't do more for your friend," she added. "But I have no doubt you'll figure it out."

I didn't tell her I wasn't nearly as sure of it as she was.

Keres stepped up quietly and pressed a small glass vial into Amanti's palm. "Salve," she said gruffly. "For your wings. Use it daily, or the threads will stiffen."

Amanti huffed a soft laugh. "Bossy as ever."

Keres merely glanced at Nali and said, "She's a terrible patient."

Nali laughed and took the salve. "Challenge accepted." And then in a conspiratorial whisper, she added, "I'm a terrible nurse. But I am sure one of my companions would be happy to massage her daily."

Amanti flushed at that, which almost made this whole situation worth it. Clearly ready to change the subject, she looked at Rydian and said, "A moment?"

He crossed to her without hesitation, shadows fading from his hands as he led her a few steps away. Whatever they said was too quiet to catch, but I saw the way her shoulders eased, the way his did not.

When they stepped back, he bowed his head to her—a warrior's goodbye.

Nali reached for my hand. "I'm glad to have seen you again," she said. "And for what you did—for my people—I owe you more than thanks. You could've let the creature kill more of us. You didn't."

"I couldn't."

"You could have," she said simply. "But you didn't. I'll remember that." She hesitated, then added, "I'll look after her. You have my word."

"Thank you," I said, grateful.

She hugged me and let me go quickly.

Behind her, guards began to move the coral doors aside. The current stirred with the motion, revealing a narrow passage disappearing into darkness.

The tunnel up.

"My father has kept his word," Nali said. "No escort will follow." She lowered her voice, adding, "And I've done a bit more than that. When the tunnel ends, you'll surface far to the north. The tunnel's currents will know where to take you. It's the closest I can put you to your destination."

"Thank you," I told her gratefully.

"Ready?" Rydian asked, rejoining us.

"Let's do it," Keres said.

"You know," Slade said, eyeing the tunnel like he might size up an enemy, "I was just thinking I haven't nearly drowned yet today."

Keres gave him a look that could have frozen steam.

"Time to go," Daegel chirped.

Thorne was already moving.

We entered the passage single file—Rydian first, shadows brushing the walls like they recognized the stone. I went after him. Keres followed, then Daegel, Thorne, and Slade trailing last with a muttered, "If I drown, tell the naiad from last night that I love her."

Keres snickered.

With one last look behind me at the three figures standing on the platform, I left the river court and Amanti behind.

An hour passed. Then two.

Slade and Thorne told stories, recounting parts of the party the previous night. Daegel went on about the city we'd seen outside the palace walls. The naiad metropolis that no other fae had ever seen before. Keres let them chatter, clearly uninterested in anything to do with the river kingdom.

Rydian's hand brushed mine as he pressed in beside me.

"She'll be all right," he said quietly.

I nodded, not sure my words would reflect agreement.

"We're almost there," he added.

"How do you know?" I asked.

"Light." He pointed upward, and I squinted, noting the watery light that shone through from far above us.

I exhaled in relief.

Up ahead, Slade yelled out, "Something's happening."

The tunnel walls narrowed, the water on both sides beginning to shrink in around us. The tunnel darkened, the river on either side rippling past like predators. From the sandy floor, water began to rise, covering my boots, then rising quickly to my knees.

"What in the Seven Hels," Keres breathed.

Daegel's shadow shield flared, encompassing us all, but it couldn't do anything against the element of water. From beneath our feet, the river continued to rise, bringing with it a strong current.

The current caught my legs and pulled, light at first, then stronger. My boots were swept off the ground.

"Don't fight it," Rydian said, whipping along in front of me.

"I don't think I can," I said, breathless as the cold water soaked me and pulled me onward.

Slade called out, and Keres flailed her arms, trying in vain to shove against the water's strength. The pull quickened, swirling, roaring. My hair whipped around my face. Thorne swore behind me. Slade whooped like a man on a death ride.

Then everything tilted. The river-floor vanished. The world inverted, and water rushed in to meet me.

I was falling—no, *rising*—the current pushing me up so violently it ripped the breath from my lungs. I flailed blindly and caught Rydian's hand just before light exploded.

I broke the surface gasping.

The air on my face was bitterly cold, the water even colder. Light streaked weakly across the sky. For a second, I just treaded water, dizzy with the sudden weight of gravity.

Rydian swam to the shore first, boots dragging through mud as he hauled himself onto solid ground. I followed, shivering and forcing my limbs to move. The others climbed out one by one around me, coughing and swearing and blinking through the morning mist.

Keres looked back toward the river, whose surface rippled innocently enough. "Next time, we're taking a boat."

"Next time?" Slade echoed, shaking out his hair. "So, you're saying you'd go back?"

"Not if your life depended on it," she told him.

Daegel collapsed onto the bank, dripping and grim. "I hate the river."

Thorne smirked. "That's rich, coming from a man who bathes more than any of us."

"That's not saying much in this group," Daegel told him, and Slade hooted.

The banter eased something tight in my chest.

Then I saw movement ahead.

Figures emerging from the mist. Half a dozen at first, then more. Heavily cloaked, utterly silent. Weapons at their sides.

Thorne's hand went to his sword. Keres mirrored him instantly.

"Hold," Rydian said sharply.

The strangers didn't raise their blades. The one in front lowered her hood.

My breath caught. "Vanya?"

The Autumn fae maid smiled—familiar, warm, and, as always, polite. "My lady." She dipped into a curtsy.

I didn't think. I just ran across the muddy bank and hugged her, waterlogged limbs and all.

"I thought I wouldn't see you again," I said against her shoulder.

"As did I," she said, hugging me quickly before stepping back with flushed cheeks.

Behind her, more of them appeared—pale, gray-cloaked, faces I half-recognized from my short time in Grey Oak. Not enemies. Not a trap. For once, something *good.*

Rydian shook hands with a few of the men. So did Daegel and Slade, and I realized these men had served together, worked together. These were true allies.

"How did you know we'd be here?" Rydian asked.

Vanya's smile dimmed. "We heard the Winter Queen had gathered forces along her borders. We guessed you'd follow."

Keres lowered her weapon but didn't sheathe it. "Guessing's a dangerous habit. Then again, these are dangerous times."

The air shifted again before I could answer. A shadow detached from the Withered's ranks and stepped forward. Gold embroidery on forest-green. A familiar face, eyes ringed in dark circles.

Callan.

The others reacted instantly—swords half-drawn, Keres already moving to block my side. Daegel cast a shadow-shield.

Thorne palmed a throwing knife, arm cocked back.

"Your Highness," Callan called out, his eyes glittering as he took me in. "Here you are at last."

I glanced at Rydian. His expression didn't change, but the temperature around us did. Even the mist seemed to pause as the prince's shadows became nearly solid between us and the Autumn king.

"At my brother's side, no less," Callan added, tossing a fleetingly charming smile at Rydian. The expression dripped with a hollow disdain.

My heart thudded.

So much for the easy part.

THE
LOVERS

Chapter Twenty
Aurelia

The Autumn king stood before us, looking like nothing more than a rumpled courtier—crownless, sleepless if the dark circles around his eyes were any indication, the green of his wrinkled coat dulled to the color of moss after rain. His golden eyes caught the first light like blades, bright and too sharp for a casual meeting.

He looked desperate, though I wasn't sure what for.

The Withered rebels remained still at the sight of him, which meant they'd known he was here. Maybe even let him follow them all the way from Grey Oak. I could only assume it was for good reason.

Around us, the autumnal air moved like a slow breath. Mist curling between the trees, the scent of river water and wet earth thick in my nose. Rydian's shadows coiled like smoke around our feet, restless and on guard. Even Daegel's shadow shield seemed thicker than usual.

If Callan was concerned about standing between two groups of fae who wouldn't bat an eye at royal bloodshed, he didn't show it. Then again, between us, I was the wanted criminal. And currently standing on the soil I'd been forbidden to revisit on the threat of death.

Keres stepped up to my other side, sword drawn. "Tell me that's not who I think it is."

"Unfortunately," I murmured. "It is."

Callan's gaze swept over the group, lingering on each of them like he was cataloguing their usefulness. Then he stopped on me, and the mocking calm in his eyes flickered—just once.

In that glimpse, I saw pain. And fear. Then the cool mask returned.

"So, the rumors are true," he said. "The traitor has begun gathering her army."

Keres snarled at the sarcasm in his tone.

"I believe Keres here needs someone to do her laundry if you're feeling left out and want to join," I said.

Callan's gaze flicked to Keres. "A new addition to the cadre, brother?" he drawled. "This one looks like she's been in a skirmish or two already."

Keres didn't blink. "Draw your sword," she said, voice flat as a whetstone, "and I'll show you how it went for the other party."

Callan's smile sharpened. "Another time, perhaps."

Rydian's tone was flat. "What do you want, Callan?"

Finally, Callan's gaze snicked to his brother. "I was going to ask you the same question. You're standing on Autumn soil after I explicitly told you never to return. And your companion"—his eyes found me again—"is wanted for high treason and regicide. Hardly a smart choice to wash up on these shores."

"Then arrest me," I said.

His smirk deepened. "Restraints. Tempting offer."

Rydian snarled.

Keres took a small step forward.

Callan lifted a gloved hand. "For the moment, I'd rather talk. In private. My tent is just there."

The Withered behind him stepped back, parting to reveal a small camp just barely visible inside the trees—tents, horses, the faint shimmer of a campfire's flame.

Rydian's hand brushed my arm, a silent warning.

Callan caught the motion. "You'll be safe enough," he said smoothly. "Unless you intend to start a war in what's left of my kingdom."

What's left?

"And your companions are welcome to refreshment and a warm seat beside our fires."

"I don't take orders from you," Rydian said.

"No," Callan agreed, "but I think we both know Aurelia makes her own decisions. I only ask for a conversation with her."

The tension between them didn't diminish in the ensuing silence. I glanced at the Withered gathered behind Callan. He must have promised them something in exchange for their help. Or, more accurately, in exchange for his own life. Whatever it was, they stood with him now. That meant something. At least until I knew what he'd promised them.

I exhaled. "Fine. You have five minutes."

Rydian turned to me sharply. "That's not wise."

"It's necessary."

His jaw tightened. I expected him to argue, but he only said, "We'll be close. Checking the perimeter for any kind of trap."

"Of course you will," Callan said dryly. "It's what you're good at—lurking on the edges of what's mine."

I glared at Callan. "Don't push it."

"Say the word, and he'll have a scar across that mouth to match my own," Keres murmured.

I shuddered at the utter conviction in her voice.

"That won't be necessary," I assured her.

She scowled and stalked off toward the fire.

Callan led me through the rows of tents, the Withered soldiers watching from beneath their hoods. Some bowed as we passed, but most just stared, their faces pale and wrinkled.

Vanya walked just behind me. An escort. A maid again. Or just a friend. Either way, I could think only of those last days in Grey Oak—when she'd been forced to report to the donation center. To give what should have been hers by right. Magic. Life force.

All of them forced to donate themselves.

My heart hurt for what Duron had taken from them. How Callan could walk among them now with his head up only fueled my anger on their behalf.

Callan's tent stood at the center of the camp, larger than the rest, its canopy stitched with the golden stag of Autumn. Inside, warmth bled from a brazier that made me grateful and hungry for the heat it offered. My wet clothes were beginning to chill me to the bone though I refused to acknowledge it. The interior smelled faintly of mint and herbs, but it was different somehow than the scent that had always clung to Callan before.

He gestured to a chair. "Sit."

"I'll stand."

"Suit yourself."

He poured hot tea, the gesture smooth, habitual. Then he held it out to me. "Here. Drink."

I hesitated.

He sighed then took a sip.

"See?" he said, holding it out a second time. "It's not poisoned. Now, drink it. You look like a drowned rat."

I took the tea with a scowl, but the warmth of the mug against my hands was an instant balm.

"You wanted to talk," I said. "So, talk."

He set his own glass down untouched. "Heliconia sent an offer."

I folded my arms. "Let me guess. Marriage."

He smiled faintly. "You're still quick to recognize politics."

"I'm still sane enough to see through her games. Why tell me?"

His amusement vanished, replaced by a darkening cloud behind his gaze. "Because if I refuse, she marches on the Autumn Court. She's already taken villages on the northern border—frosted fields, frozen bodies. I've seen the destruction, and…" He swallowed hard, his gaze suddenly not quite meeting my own. "I can't stop her alone."

"I'm sorry, can you say that last part again?" I asked sweetly.

"Don't be immature about this."

"It's my ears. There's so much water in them I didn't hear you."

He groaned. "I don't know why I expected more of you than this."

I set the tea aside, embracing the chill. "Considering you used persuasion to manipulate me into agreeing to marry you when you had every intention of draining me of my magic in order to make your crops grow, I can't imagine why you'd think I'd make anything easy for you ever again."

"Look, we both want the same thing—"

"I'm not sure we do, Callan." I took a step toward him. "You want to rule a realm that will bow and kneel and praise your greatness. Heliconia stands in the way of that, and that makes her your enemy. But if she had never set her sights on your kingdom, would you still be here in this tent, asking for my help in stopping her? Or would you do what your father did, turning a blind eye to everything that didn't impact him directly?"

His jaw hardened, a muscle working back and forth as he stared me down. Part of me wondered if he'd throw me out. Or arrest me. Though I wasn't sure the Withered would obey that order. Instead, he sighed and slumped into the chair next to the brazier. "I don't want to be my father," he said, "But I'm not sure who I do want to be, either."

I studied him, again noticing the dark circles. The fact that he'd lost weight. "Honesty is a good place to start," I said at last.

His gaze darted to mine again, hope written clearly there.

"Why do you think I can help you?" I asked. "As you can see, my army isn't exactly vast."

"Is that why you went to see King Patamoi? For soldiers? And did he offer his naiad army to the Chosen One?"

I didn't answer, and Callan seemed to realize pressing me wouldn't work.

Instead, he said, "I met with Heliconia."

I blinked. "You saw her? When?"

"Two nights ago. At a village near the Concordian Mountains—or what's left of it. She made me an offer."

"I can't believe she wants to wed you."

His brow rose. "Apparently, you're the only one who finds that idea repulsive."

"I meant, why bother with diplomacy?" I said wryly. "You said she has an army ready to invade your kingdom. She's already proven they can defeat you and that she prefers violence over peace. It doesn't make sense."

"When she proposed it the first time, my father said she wanted to use marriage to legitimize her title with the other courts."

"But why would she care what they think when she plans to invade and destroy them too?"

He frowned. "What do you know about the Harvest Throne?"

"The seat itself?" I asked. "It was fashioned from an ancient oak tree taken from Vorinthia and fused with the horn of a Vorinthian stag," I said, trying to recall what my tutors had told me so many years ago. "Why?"

"Do you know of any magic imbued into it?"

"Do you?"

He hesitated but then shook his head. "No. But Heliconia specifically mentioned wanting a seat on the harvest throne as my queen. I've wondered..." He trailed off and looked at me again.

"Do you think she knows something about your throne you don't?" I asked.

"I plan to look into it when I return home," he said quietly. "But she will send for an answer soon, and I wanted to speak with you first. To see if we might come to an arrangement. Like before."

I met his gaze as his meaning dawned. "You're asking me to marry you again."

"I'm asking you to save what's left of this realm." His voice softened, genuine for once. "You said once that I couldn't see beyond my father's shadow. Maybe you were right. But now the shadow is all that's left. If I join Heliconia, Autumn survives as her puppet. If I stand against her alone, my kingdom will fall. I need another way."

"I will not be made a pawn again, Callan. You'll have to find a bride elsewhere."

He flinched—then hardened. "Marry me, and I'll pardon you for killing my father."

"At least, now you aren't pretending to care for me."

"I do care for you."

"You never wanted me, Callan. You wanted the version of me that would make you into a great king."

His eyes narrowed, but he only continued to negotiate. "I could give you an army."

"If you were not your father's protégé after all, you would offer them to me freely."

"You still plan to fight her," he said as if only now realizing it.

"My birthright has always been that of a warrior. It's time I acted like it."

"To face her alone would be fatal," he said.

"I am not alone."

"You think a handful of Midnight fae—"

Furyfire sparked, landing on the rug at his feet before fizzling out. He fell silent, our gazes locked.

I smirked, choosing one of his expressions. "Reminds you of old times, doesn't it?" He said nothing. "Those Midnight fae are braver warriors than you could ever hope to be. And when I leave here, it will be with them and the Withered you have so graciously brought me. But don't forget that I am not Summer's daughter, submissive and sparkling beneath your thumb. I am Hel's heir, and I have furyfire in my veins and vengeance in my heart."

Callan's mouth tightened, but I didn't wait for a response. This meeting was over.

I started for the door.

Callan's words stopped me. "Is that why you chose him over me? A warrior at your side instead of a prince?"

Slowly, I turned. "You think I chose Rydian over you? I chose myself, Callan. I encourage you to do the same."

THE
LOVERS

Chapter Twenty-One
Aurelia

By the time the morning mist began to lift, Callan and his men had ridden out. Vanya ushered Keres and me into her tent where we changed into dry clothes and then dried our hair by the cooking fire.

Rydian returned an hour later and didn't ask where his half-brother had gone. I suspected he'd tracked the Autumn king himself just to make sure there wasn't a trap laid in his wake.

After a brief meal of stew and hot tea, we gathered in what had been Callan's command tent, a structure of green and gold canvas sagging slightly from the damp. Someone had stoked the brazier in the corner, but the heat did little against the chill that crept through the seams.

The Withered army waited outside, their voices muted beneath the hush of wind through the trees. At my insistence, Vanya had joined us. She stood quiet as a mouse near the door like she might bolt at any moment. She'd already asked me three times if I needed anything.

Rydian stood near the table where maps were spread open, his shadows curling faintly in the low light. Keres stood on the table's other side, arms crossed, looking ready to stab anyone who spoke out of turn. Daegel and Thorne sat opposite each other, a mug of ale in their hands. Slade sprawled in a chair, eyes half-lidded but alert. They'd all found dry clothes somehow, but the contents of our packs—the food Nali had given us when we'd left—were ruined.

And then there was Eirnan.

Clearly a leader among the Withered here, he entered without announcement, tall and spare as a winter pine. His hair was streaked silver, his skin pale, his cheeks and nose bright pink from the cold, but there was something unbroken in the way he moved. Soldier. Survivor. From the looks of his weathered body, his magic was nearly gone, but he held himself as proud as any fae warrior.

"Your Highness," he said to me with a bow so crisp it belonged to another era. "If titles still mean anything, that is."

"They don't," I said, though part of me still felt the weight of it. "Not out here, anyway. Aurelia will do."

He nodded once and looked to Rydian. "And you, my Prince?"

I tried not to react to the reference, knowing full well Eirnan meant it for Rydian's Autumn roots.

"I've never liked that title either," Rydian told him kindly.

Eirnan smiled faintly. "Good. Then we may speak as soldiers."

"Please," Rydian said, gesturing. "You have the floor. Tell us what you know."

Eirnan approached the table, spreading out a crude parchment map of the northern reaches—one clearly drawn from memory. "Heliconia's army holds the ridge along the Concordian border. Her troops have doubled in the past month, and every village in their path has been leveled to complete destruction."

"She's done licking her wounds," I murmured.

Eirnan nodded. "There's more than simply war. The ground freezes where her soldiers march. Snow falls, enough to bury home and hearth. Rivers have frozen over. Game has migrated south or succumbed to the frigid temperatures."

"Winter magic is spreading," Daegel muttered.

"The rumors are true, then." Rydian's gaze flicked to mine. "She's recovered at last."

"Our scouts overheard her soldiers talking. They say her strength has been renewed. That the curse she cast on Summer nearly killed her, but she's come back even stronger. They believe she's drawing from something ancient."

"Something more than the power she stole from the gods?" Keres asked.

"We don't know," Eirnan said.

The tent fell silent except for the hiss of the brazier. I traced the jagged line of the mountains on the map. "And she plans to use that power against the Autumn Court?"

Eirnan inclined his head. "Her soldiers speak freely of it—how their queen will make an example of King Callan for trying to take a traitor queen."

Keres' gaze sharpened on me. "Wow, she really is obsessed with you."

Slade snorted.

"Heliconia proposed to him," I said. "Again."

"What?" Keres' eyes widened.

Slade sat up straighter. "I heard she did once before. Back before he announced his engagement with you."

"Apparently, I was his loophole so he didn't have to outright refuse her," I said.

"And now?" Keres asked, brow lifted as if she'd already guessed Callan had come here to try that same loophole again.

"She offered him mercy in exchange for his throne," I said, unable to keep the bitterness from my tone. "If he refuses, she marches on his kingdom."

Thorne leaned forward, brow furrowed. "And will he? Refuse?"

I hesitated. "I don't know."

Rydian's scowl deepened. He said nothing, but his silence was loud enough to fill the tent.

Slade cleared his throat. "In light of this new information, do we continue on our own course?" he asked pointedly. "Or offer our aid to Autumn?"

He shot a look at Eirnan and Vanya.

I turned to them both, explaining, "We came north because Heliconia has my friend Lesha, one of the Aine, as a prisoner in her camp. We intend to free her."

Vanya's eyes widened.

Eirnan studied me thoughtfully. "You'd risk all your lives against an entire Obsidian army for one friend?"

"Yes," I told him simply.

He looked from me to the others, one by one, and something behind his eyes clicked. "Then we march at your side."

"I can't ask you to do that. But if you can point the way."

Eirnan shook his head. "Not much in the way of cover stands between you and the Winter army. The moment we take a step north, we'll be seen."

"Then we find another way in," Keres said, but I could see the bleakness in her eyes. The naiad had refused us, so the river was out. And now, a land approach was out too.

"There is another way," Eirnan said. "Old tunnels under the mountains—traders and smugglers alike have used them for centuries to avoid the snowstorms rolling off the mountains. I worked those routes as a trader before..." His mouth tightened. "Before everything."

"And you can find them again?" Rydian asked.

"I can."

I studied him. "What's the catch?"

"Only that the tunnels aren't stable," he said. "Parts have collapsed, and there are creatures living deep inside those caves that would make an Obsidian look friendly. But if you want to reach the war camp unseen, it's the only way."

Keres rubbed her temple. "Collapsed tunnels full of monsters. Perfect."

Slade smirked. "You're not afraid of a little dirt and a few bats, are you?"

"Dirt doesn't scare me," she said. "Idiots do."

Daegel grinned. "Then you've been terrified since you met Slade."

The faint ripple of laughter broke through the heaviness for a heartbeat. Even Rydian's mouth twitched before his attention returned to the map.

"We'd do well with a day's rest before we continue on," Rydian said.

Eirnan nodded. "I'll see to it. And when the time comes, we'll march with you to rescue your friend."

"I can't ask—"

"We will fight beside you, Aurelia of Sevanwinds. We remember what loyalty once meant."

"You already fought for me once," I told him quietly. "I owe you a debt for it."

"We fought for ourselves that night as much as for anyone else," he said. "And we walk free now. The debt is paid."

"Even so, I won't ask you to die for me."

He smiled sadly. "We've been dying for kings who didn't deserve us for centuries. Let us die for something better."

Something in my chest tightened. "Thank you."

Rydian rolled the map closed and handed it to Eirnan. "Send your scouts. We move at dawn."

The meeting dissolved after that, everyone filtering out. Keres and Slade bickered their way toward the campfires. Daegel lingered just long enough to mutter something about rechecking our supplies. Thorne followed with a whistle that couldn't quite mask his weariness.

Eirnan paused at the exit, meeting my gaze once more. "I am glad our paths have crossed again, my lady."

"Is that why you traveled with the king?" I asked. "To find me?"

"It's he who asked to travel with us."

"And why did you?" I asked.

"He vowed to be a better king than his father."

"And has he been?" I asked. "So far, I mean."

"The donations ended. The centers are closed." His eyes sparkled with grief and hope. "It's a start."

"It's a start," I agreed, surprised and relieved to hear Callan had done so.

He dipped his chin. "We have you to thank for it all. You'll have our blades, my lady. And whatever magic we have left."

THE
LOVERS

Chapter Twenty-Two
Rydian

Night settled over the Withered camp like a slow bruise. The air was colder here than it should have been, even this far north, thin with frost and laced with a magic that was all wrong for the autumn kingdom. Beyond the trees, the river whispered as the current ran—a sound I was beginning to hate after our visit with Patamoi. Or maybe it wasn't the river's whispers but the voices in my own head that tortured me now.

Every time I closed my eyes, I saw *her* standing before me, flames burning beneath her skin like defiance given form. And every time she looked at me, there was a question in her eyes that I was terrified of having to answer.

I sat alone by the dying fire, Callan's map unrolled across my knees. My mind should have been on strategy—on Heliconia's army, on the tunnels Eirnan promised would get us into the Concordian war camp—but every thought circled back to Aurelia.

To the way she'd disappeared inside Callan's tent. To the private moments they'd shared. To the moment she said she didn't know if he'd accept Heliconia's offer.

Would she care if Callan married another?

The thought made something inside me snap taut, irrational and sharp. I told myself it was worry. It wasn't.

By the time I realized I'd stood, my feet were already moving.

The camp was quiet, the Withered sleeping in tents pitched in uneven rows. Their campfires were nothing but embers now, a symbol of the powerful fae they'd once been. I moved through them like a ghost, following the tug in my chest I'd long since stopped pretending to understand.

I found her at the edge of the clearing. She stood on a rise above the camp, the wind teasing strands of her hair free of its braid. The moonlight turned her into something almost divine—half sunlit honey, half frost, all untouchable.

"You should be asleep," she said without turning.

"So should you," I answered.

Her shoulders tensed, then eased. "You're restless to get moving again too."

"Something like that."

Silence stretched between us, filled with the soft creak of branches and the faint hum of her power beneath her skin. I could feel it even from here—warmth against the cold, life against the ruin of this place.

She finally looked at me. "What is it?"

"Callan."

Her expression shuttered. "What about him?"

"He asked you to marry him again." It wasn't a question.

She didn't bother denying it. "He did."

"And what did you say?"

Her brow rose. "What do you think I said?"

"I don't know," I said honestly. "You have a tendency to surprise me."

"I said no."

Relief, bright and foolish, flashed through me before I could stop it. I masked it with a low sound that might have been a laugh. "Good."

Her brow arched. "Good? Is that all?"

"He doesn't deserve you."

"And you do?"

The directness in her gaze squeezed my chest. She was daring me to declare myself.

"Not me," I said, stepping closer despite my words. "But that doesn't stop me from wanting you."

Her breath caught. The space between us felt suddenly fragile. "What if I don't want you to stop?"

I could have kissed her then. I *wanted* to. Every inch of restraint I'd built around myself cracked under the weight of wanting to. Her eyes searched mine, daring me, pleading, burning.

I gave in.

Her mouth met mine, and the world stopped. Fire and shadow collided, the kind of kiss that rewrote every oath I'd ever sworn. Her fingers found the collar of my jacket, gripping like she meant to anchor herself to me. On her lips, I tasted flame and sunshine and everything I wasn't supposed to want.

When we broke apart, we were both breathing hard. The night felt different now—alive, trembling.

"Rydian," she whispered, and I knew what she was asking. Knew it and hated myself for the answer.

I touched my forehead to hers, eyes closing. "I can't."

Her hands tightened. "Why not?"

"Because I'm not a match for you."

She drew back enough to look at me. "I don't care what anyone thinks. The courts—"

"It's not about them," I said. "It's about me. About what I am meant for."

Her eyes softened, confusion threading through the hurt. "You think being the Midnight heir makes you somehow unworthy?"

I blinked, stunned.

Her mouth curved. "Your secrets are unraveling faster than you think, Your Highness."

"When did you know?"

"I suspected at the cabin, but our visit Beneath confirmed it. Why didn't you just tell me?"

"It's complicated."

"You'd rather the realm believes you're a second-born prince of

Autumn than the heir to the Onyx Throne. I expect your reasons must be complicated, if not well thought out, to choose to hide. Something you once accused me of doing, if you remember."

"The Midnight fae have lived one purpose these last years, and that is to wait and fight for the Chosen One."

"And your crown? What is the purpose of hiding that?"

"Duron would have killed me had he even the slightest inkling."

Her brows lifted. "You mean he didn't know?"

"And neither does Callan," I said.

She stared at me, eyes wide. "To protect your people," she murmured.

I nodded. "And to protect you." At her furrowed brow, I went on, "The oath I swore to fight at your side came before anything else, even my own title or crown. If I'd been found out and killed or imprisoned for it, I would have failed you before we'd even begun."

"And now? Here we are. Fighting together. Allies. Friends. And something more?"

I shook my head. "Nothing more than that. For your own sake."

"After everything, you refuse to let me decide what's best for me."

I swallowed hard. "Your father already did."

She blinked. "My father—?"

"I promised him," I said quietly. "The night I took the oath."

"Wait. You took the oath from my father? From Ire himself?"

"Yes."

"I thought— All this time, I just assumed it was a figurative oath. One passed down from your queen." Her eyes widened. "Your mother, I guess," she murmured as if realization had dawned. She shook it off. "But you saw him. Spoke to him."

"Bled for him," I added quietly.

She stared at me.

I swallowed hard, forcing the words out before I could think better of it. "I swore that, when the time came, as he had foreseen that it would, I would die for you."

The color drained from her face. "No."

"I was meant to be your shield, Aurelia. Not your equal. Not your choice. It's why I was gifted this power. Why my people were preserved, protected. Set aside for the time you would need us all. Your father saw it and made provisions so that you might live."

She shook her head, stepping back. "You can't mean that. That's not fate—that's madness."

"Before we met, I might have agreed. But now… it will be my honor to trade my life for yours should the Fates demand it."

Her voice broke. "And what if I refuse to let you?"

"You are becoming more powerful than any fae to walk Menryth in a thousand years," I said, unable to quell the sadness in my soul. "But even you cannot stop Fate's wheel from turning."

I watched as she fought for control, refusing to accept what I'd told her.

"Do you remember that Obsidian, the one in that farmhouse in the Broadlands? He said Heliconia sees what she fears most. The prince and I united—to her destruction. I thought it was Callan, but…"

I didn't respond.

"You knew it wasn't him," she finished.

"I thought, if you found a way to unite with Callan, the worst might be avoided," I admitted.

"I can't imagine what it's like for you, wondering if and when the time will come. I'm sorry—for my parents' mess becoming your problem, for my father—for Ire—asking this of you."

"Do not apologize. I can never regret knowing you."

Her eyes brimmed with tears that she refused to let fall. "A spoiled brat, like me? You sure?" she teased. "And you're willing to fight beside me anyway?"

"I'll fight for you," I said, voice rough. "I'll be your blade, Aurelia. Point me where you need me. Wield me against every enemy that stands in your path. Until my last breath."

Her eyes shone, fury and grief warring in them. "Don't say that."

"It's the truth."

"I don't want your death, Rydian. I only want your love."

"I refuse to hurt you by giving you both."

Silence. The kind that hurt like an arrow in the chest.

I brushed my thumb along her jaw, memorizing the shape of her.

"You were born to end a war. I was born to end with you. For me, it will be enough."

And before she could speak, before she could make me refuse her again, I kissed her once more—soft this time, final—and turned away.

Her voice followed me, quiet and breaking. "Rydian—"

But I didn't look back.

The shadows welcomed me like an old friend, like I knew they would in the end.

THE
LOVERS

Chapter Twenty-Three
Aurelia

I didn't move for a long time, just stood there with the brittle wind on my face and the taste of him still on my lips. I thought I knew pain—war, loss, exile—but heartbreak had its own kind of cruelty. It lingered. It burned without flame or smoke.

Rydian's words spun through me on a loop I couldn't silence. *I was meant to be your shield. Not your equal. Not your choice.*

The gods had made him into my weapon, and me the reason he would fall. How could the Fates be so merciless as to weave love into a prophecy designed for ruin? Then again, it hadn't been the Fates at all. It had been my father. The Furiosities. Hel's gods *meddling*, as Patamoi had put it. I was starting to agree.

I thought I'd guessed Rydian's secret. The heir to the Onyx Throne. But there had been a much heavier burden behind it. One he carried on shoulders made of steel, it seemed.

When he'd walked away, the shadows had swallowed him whole, as if the realm itself had conspired to swallow him up. Maybe it had. Maybe it would before everything was over.

I didn't sleep that night. I tried—gods, I tried—but every time I closed my eyes, I saw him walking away again, saw the resignation in his face when he said it would be his honor to die for me.

No one should ever look so beautiful while saying something so tragic.

By the time dawn broke, I'd buried what was left of my heart beneath the same armor I'd worn since the night my own court had been cursed to sleep. And I swore to use the jagged pieces of my broken heart to cut them all down before I was done.

Beneath my skin, my furyfire burned and burned. It had been growing ever since the night I'd used it on Duron. As if doing so had unleashed some torrent I hadn't known before. Whatever well of magic I'd felt these last years, it was suddenly much deeper.

I'd woken a beast—and that beast was me.

I had a feeling, when I was ready to unleash it, the destruction would be absolute. So, for now, I left it sleeping, waiting in a sort of hibernation that only stoked the embers hotter for the moment I'd let it come alive once more.

The air outside the tent was crisp, laced with pine and decaying leaves, the ground covered in frost. The camp slept—tents still and quiet in the pre-dawn. I went to work, stoking the fire and setting out water to boil for coffee and tea.

Keres slipped out of the tent behind me, dressed in fighting leathers and a thick cloak that one of the Withered had gifted her. Her hair was braided and coiled at the nape of her neck. She sat near the fire pit, sharpening her blades in slow, deliberate strokes. The sound of steel on stone broke the stillness like a heartbeat.

"You're up early," she said without looking at me.

"So are you," I replied.

She studied me over the edge of her dagger, eyes and scars half-hidden beneath the fall of her hair. "You look terrible."

I snorted. "Thanks. I didn't sleep much," I admitted.

"I didn't think you would," she said, turning back to her blade. Her tone wasn't cruel. Just knowing. Of course she knew. Rydian's biggest secret, the one they'd all been waiting for him to tell me.

The fire crackled and sputtered, throwing a spark of orange between us. For a moment, her expression softened. "You don't have to carry all of it alone, you know. The rest of us are here too."

"I know."

She looked up sharply. "Do you? Because I know I can be..."

"Scary?"

"Unapproachable," she said, glaring.

I grinned. "Go on."

"We all understand what's at stake. We've always understood," she added in a low voice. "But you're just now finding out. It makes sense that you need some time to process. So, I'm here if you want to talk."

I swallowed. "I'm not great at that—talking, I mean. But I'm working on it."

That earned a faint smirk. "Probably for the best. Slade talks enough for all of us combined."

I almost smiled. "He does, doesn't he?"

She sheathed her dagger and stood, brushing dirt from her trousers. "Eirnan's men will be back soon. If the tunnels are what he said, we'll need to be ready to move. Tonight's frost will likely be a freeze, and we'd do better inside a cave."

A freeze. The phrase landed like an omen. Each one carried Heliconia closer.

I nodded. "Let's hope he's found us a way in."

Keres hesitated, then said more quietly, "This thing weighing on you... set it down before we march. There's too much at stake to fight yourself and her at the same time."

I looked at her, surprised by the softness in her voice. "I'll try."

She gave a curt nod, the moment gone as quickly as it came, and stalked off toward the supply tents where a couple of Withered had begun gathering items for breakfast.

I stayed where I was, watching the sun creep through the trees. Frost glittered on every branch, turning the world into a prism of glass. The light didn't melt anything—it only made the cold beautiful.

Around camp, more of the Withered were stirring, their murmurs rising like a prayer. Rydian did not emerge from his tent. I wondered if he ever returned to it last night.

Vanya brought me a bowl of stew, steaming and deliciously warm in my palms. She ushered me into the war tent, insisting I stay warm while I filled my belly.

"Thank you," I told her gratefully. "This is delicious."

She dipped her chin.

"You never told me what happened to you," I said between bites. "The night I left Grey Oak, I mean."

"After I delivered your note to Eirnan, I waited in the forest outside the city until after the attack," she said. "Any Withered who made it to the meeting point joined us and fled. The ones who were lost... It was terrible leaving them behind, but we had no choice."

"I'm sorry for those losses," I said and meant it.

She shook her head. "Don't be. You gave us the chance to stand up against what was done to us. And now we are free."

I ate quickly, grateful for Vanya's company.

Eirnan arrived as I finished up, bringing two scouts with him, their cloaks rimmed with frost. Their faces were gaunt, but their eyes were bright as Vanya waved them into the tent.

"We found the tunnels," one of them said without preamble. "Hidden beneath the north face of Nygard Peak. Collapsed in parts, but passable if we dig. We saw smoke on the ridge too—Heliconia's army is close. We can only pray the gods keep us from their notice before we can get to the opening."

The others had arrived by then—Thorne and Daegel, Keres joining us with her usual scowl. The fire crackled between us, painting our faces gold and shadow.

"She looks ready to mobilize them," Eirnan's scout said grimly.

He'd thrown his cloak back to reveal a youthful face at odds with the lines and wrinkles etched into it. My heart ached for him.

"She's moving faster than we thought," Thorne said.

"No, she was always moving toward this; she was just doing it quietly for a time," I replied. "She wasn't only licking her wounds in Concordia after casting the curse. She was creating this army. Training them. We're only just catching up."

Daegel leaned over the map, tracing the path north with one gloved finger. "If we go through the tunnels, we'll come out behind the war camp. Strategically, that will likely put us closer to the prisoner, but it's less defensible as an escape."

"Which means we'll have to fight our way back through once we find Lesha," Keres said.

I shook my head. "Not if we don't give them the chance."

"You have a plan," Slade said.

"We'll go in quietly. Daegel can use his shadows to shield us." Daegel nodded. "The rest of us will focus on taking out the eyes and ears—sentries, scouts, anyone who might raise the alarm. We'll get Lesha before they know we're there. Once we have her, we have to assume they'll have found us out. So, we go out with a bang."

Slade cleared his throat. "And by a bang, you mean—"

"Furyfire," I said, flames licking inside my veins at the permission it'd heard me give it.

They all studied me, nodding as if they'd noted the power I intended to unleash and found it acceptable.

"Your flame will only alert them to your identity, Your Highness," Eirnan warned. "The army will turn its full force on hunting us down."

"I don't intend for there to be an army left when I'm done."

He bowed his head slightly. "Then we'll follow your command, Aurelia of Sevanwinds. Until the end."

His words sank like a stone in my chest. Until the end. The same phrase Rydian had used hours ago, his voice breaking under the weight of it.

I forced myself to meet Eirnan's gaze. "Let's make sure it isn't our end."

The meeting ended, and the others began to file out.

I caught Slade before he could follow.

"Have you seen Rydian?" I asked.

"He took the night watch guarding the perimeter," Slade said. "Should be back soon to break camp with us. Don't know when the bastard ever sleeps."

He shook his head as he strode out.

I followed and saw that the camp had come alive—tents disassembled, ropes loosened, supplies packed; the muted rhythm of purpose. The frost had begun to melt, but even underneath the watery autumn sun, a distinct trace of winter swept down from the mountains.

I turned northward, toward the horizon where the peaks gleamed white in the distance. Nygard Peak rose from among them, taller than the rest. Somewhere beyond it, Lesha waited. On its ridge, Heliconia's army was gathering, her power growing stronger with every heartbeat.

My hands curled into fists. For the first time since the curse, I wasn't afraid of what I was going to face. Rydian was right; I'd been gifted the power to claim this realm as my own. It sang in my blood. Whispered in my heart. Clung to the fabric of my soul.

So, I would use it. For the survival of the fae of this realm, not the victory of a war between the Fates and Furiosities. The gods could write whatever ending they wanted. I would be the one to set the page on fire.

THE
LOVERS

Chapter Twenty-Four
Rydian

The northern half of Autumn was dying. Not the slow death of the season for which it was named. The kind that spread like ice across a poisoned lake, a disease for which there was no cure. I could smell it in the air—cold and rot, pine needles gone brittle, frost creeping down the trunks of trees like veins of glass. We marched through it anyway. Step after step, breath after ghosted breath, the land surrendered a little more to Heliconia's brutal influence.

By the time we'd reached the foothills of the Concordian Mountains, even the birds had stopped singing. The silence made every creak of armor, every boot against half-frozen soil, sound like a horn announcing our presence.

Slade walked beside me, his cloak snapping at his heels. He wasn't quiet often, but this morning he'd managed nearly half an hour without a word. I should've known it wouldn't last.

"So," he started, tone casual as he adjusted his crossbow strap, "you told her."

I didn't look at him. "Told her what?"

He scoffed. "Don't play dumb, Shadow Prince. The secret you've been brooding over since we left Grey Oak. She knows now, doesn't she?"

I kept my eyes on the path ahead. Frost crunched underfoot. "She knows both of them."

He faltered. "You told her about the oath?"

"I did."

"And?"

"And what?"

"Come on." He kicked a stone into the ditch. "Did she throw you into a firepit? Curse your bloodline? Try to kill you with her bare hands?"

"No."

Slade gave an exaggerated groan. "Gods, you're impossible. Fine, I'll guess. She doesn't hate you. You were terrified she would, and instead, it had the opposite effect. Am I close?"

I didn't answer, which was answer enough.

He grinned, sharp and knowing. "See? Not so bad, then."

"Doesn't change anything," I said quietly.

Slade studied me sidelong. "Sure it does. She knows what you are and still looks at you like you hung the stars."

"She shouldn't."

He snorted. "Tell that to her face. Or better yet, keep pretending it doesn't matter. I'll enjoy watching you both unravel."

I gave him a look that should've shut him up for good. He just smirked and jogged ahead to bother Daegel instead.

The frost thickened as the day dragged on. Patches of white spread between the roots of trees that hadn't known winter in centuries.

Legends claimed all of Menryth bore changing seasons up until the moon split. I suspected the change had more to do with the gods' negotiation for power than it did the moon itself. Now, if Heliconia had her way, the entire continent would be buried beneath winter's weight forever. I refused to imagine a world like that, mostly because it suggested we had failed entirely.

Eirnan's scouts returned every few hours with grim updates—the ice was spreading faster than Autumn's fading magic could stop it. A curse made visible, crawling south like a living thing.

Aurelia took the news with a sort of grim determination. Her hood remained down despite the cold, sunlight glancing off the streaks of gold in her hair. Every now and then, when she brushed her hand against the trees, the frost melted. Leaves turned gold where her fingers trailed, the ground thawing faintly in her wake.

I wondered if she even knew she was doing it. Or if it wasn't simply an expending of her magic but the land itself reaching—and taking what it needed to heal.

I kept my distance, though I caught myself watching more than I should—how she moved, how she carried herself as if the weight of the prophecy didn't crush her with every step. She'd buried her grief somewhere deep, beneath armor and fury. But it was there. I could feel it humming through her like a blade held too tight, her gaze always carefully averted from mine.

By afternoon, we reached the scorched remains of another village. The smell of ash still lingered despite the winds attempting to carry it off. Blackened rafters stuck out of the ground like ribs. No bodies left—Heliconia's army didn't leave corpses behind. Fire took them, same as it took everything else.

Heliconia wanted Aurelia to see destruction caused by her own gift.

Eirnan halted near what had once been a well. He crouched, touching the rim, then the ice that had filled it solid. "Why bother expelling so much power to freeze it all when her soldiers have already destroyed the life here?"

Aurelia joined him, crouching beside the frozen stone. The surface shimmered faintly under her reflection. She pressed her palm to the ice, and I watched as it gave way slowly to liquid. "She wants us to know how powerful she is."

Eirnan nodded grimly. His skin was pale as bone, eyes sunk deep from years of magic starvation. "This is why she waited years to come for us. She was gathering more power."

I didn't miss the way Aurelia's jaw tightened. She straightened, her breath rising in pale curls. "Let's refill our water supply here. Then we find the tunnels before her soldiers find us. I don't want her knowing we're coming until we get there."

We drank, refilled, and moved on. The mountains loomed closer with each hour—great white spines tearing at the clouds.

Later, when we stopped to rest for lunch, Keres challenged Aurelia to spar. I was surprised by it but glad. Keres had been the least convinced of us that Aurelia would be what we needed. I still wasn't entirely sure what had transpired between them at the cabin, but every day since, Keres had warmed a little more.

I wondered if Aurelia knew a challenge like this one meant acceptance—and respect. Keres only challenged those she considered a worthy opponent. Or a true ally.

The clearing rang with the clash of steel, the crackle of Aurelia's faint heat against Keres's shadow-threaded strikes.

I watched from a distance, arms folded, pretending disinterest.

Aurelia moved like flame given form—grace and precision and fury all at once. Every swing of her sword was measured, deliberate. She had Aine training to thank for it. But Keres was relentless, driving Aurelia back until sparks scattered in the frost. Aurelia laughed once, sharp and breathless. It was the first real sound of enjoyment I'd heard from her in ages.

When she disarmed Keres with a twist of her wrist, I couldn't stop the surge of pride. Or wanting.

"You're staring again," Slade muttered beside me. I hadn't heard him approach.

"I'm watching my commander," I said flatly.

He smirked. "Sure you are."

Before I could respond, a low whistle came from the edge of camp. Eirnan's scouts were back, cloaks heavy with snow. One of them—Leif, the younger—hesitated before stepping forward. Vanya appeared almost instantly at his side, handing him water but lingering a heartbeat too long. Leif flushed red to the tips of his pointed ears at her attention.

Slade leaned closer, elbowing me. "Young love. Isn't it adorable?"

I ignored him as Leif and Eirnan approached us. Aurelia and Keres followed, all of us forming a loose circle.

Eirnan nodded at us then gestured for Leif to speak.

"The base of Nygard is another few hours' march, but the way looks clear. If we keep moving, we'll make it before nightfall."

"You'll continue to scout ahead," Aurelia said to him. She glanced at me before adding, "We can't afford to be spotted."

"Of course, Your Highness," Leif said, offering a slight bow.

"Thank you," she said. "Please rest and eat something before you head back out."

Leif bowed again and then headed for the fire where Vanya was already heating food for the scouts. Eirnan followed them. Keres and Slade walked off, both heading for the bank of trees where I knew Thorne and Daegel were keeping watch at our backs.

Aurelia remained, though she looked like she'd rather be anywhere else.

"I'm going to—" she began.

"What changed?" I asked.

"What do you mean?"

"Last night, I told you... You seem different after our conversation. Not what I expected."

Her brow lifted. "Did you think I'd be heartbroken and crying? Too devastated to remember what we marched for today?"

I felt a flush creeping up my throat. "Of course not. But I thought—"

"You thought I'd fall apart," she said quietly. "That's why you refused to tell me before. You didn't want to hurt me."

There was no anger in her words, but guilt tugged at me nonetheless. "I underestimated you."

"Maybe not," she admitted. "I think if you'd told me when you found me in the Broadlands weeks ago, you would have been right. Certainly, seven years ago..." She swallowed, looking south and east as if gazing toward home. "My feelings for you haven't changed, Rydian. But my commitment to my purpose has."

I didn't know what to say. I couldn't let myself respond to that. Not when I'd already told her those feelings couldn't matter. But her purpose was the same as mine. And I refused to let her shoulder that alone.

"I hope you'll allow me to share the burden of that purpose," I said.

"Yes, I've been thinking about that. Out of the both of us, you're the one with the battle experience. It only makes sense that we use it to our best advantage."

"What do you need of me?"

Her gaze heated, and I knew we were both thinking of many

answers to that question, none of which had anything to do with battle or Obsidian armies.

"I'd like to have your input concerning what comes next," she said slowly.

"With the rescue?" I asked.

"With all of it. Lesha's rescue. Our exit strategy. The war that has already begun and will inevitably only get worse. For us, for Grey Oak, for Menryth. You make a much better general than I do."

I blinked. "You want me to lead your army?"

"I want you to lead your army," she said pointedly. "The Withered are Autumn fae, which are your people. And when I inevitably open the gate to your kingdom," she smirked, "that army is your people too."

Her smirk vanished. "Once, I had hoped my purpose would involve me leading an army to fight for my people, but I see now what my purpose truly is. And I'm beginning to realize it will take all I have to fulfill it. I can't do this alone."

"You will never have to."

Her smile was forced, but I could see relief in the way her expression relaxed at the edges. "Thank you."

A beat of silence passed.

"I'm going to get some air," she said, turning away.

I lingered a moment longer, watching her as she walked the camp's edge. And still, I couldn't make myself go to her. To take down the wall I'd erected between us. Because every time I looked at Aurelia, I remembered what I'd promised her father. And every time I heard her laugh, I wondered how long before I'd have to die for that promise. I would allow her to lose her general. I couldn't allow her to lose her mate.

THE
LOVERS

Chapter Twenty-Five
Callan

Grey Oak slept under a blanket of thick clouds; its streets shrouded in mist that swirled like a nightmare's thin veneer. Few lanterns still glowed in windows. Even the drunkards kept to themselves at this late hour. I preferred the solitude. It was better than the constant murmurs during the day. The king was dead, and the new one was worse—or so they whispered.

Maybe they were right.

Every day, our lands grew colder. More frozen. Crops had died. So had the sick and weak. The Withered, especially, were too frail to withstand the plunging temperatures. At least, Heliconia's frost hadn't reached the city yet. I prayed to the gods that it never would. But I knew I couldn't count on the gods. Not anymore. Nor could I count on Aurelia, their Chosen One.

It was up to me to protect my people. To save them.

I was sure my father would have groaned in his grave to know that. Maybe that's why I'd already cast aside every possibility the old bastard would have considered viable. And now, here I was, doing the last thing he ever would.

Alone, I moved through the back alleys with my hood pulled low, the cold gnawing at my knuckles. Above me, the great stag banners of

Autumn hung limp, their golden embroidery dull in the moonless night. Fitting, when I knew the once-great magic of the Autumn fae had long since dulled to match.

I'd stopped the donations on the same day I'd held my father's funeral. It had felt righteous in the moment. Noble. Now, walking the empty streets of my starving capital, I wondered if it was too little too late. At least, with the donations, they'd been given coin so they could eat.

The oracle's shop was tucked in a narrow lane behind the apothecaries' square. The symbol of an open eye marked it, but I'd known it anyway—and had avoided it until now. I was surprised to find the door unlocked and was instantly wary of it.

The bell chimed once as I entered.

The air smelled of crushed herbs and burnt honey. Shelves crowded every wall, stacked with vials of dust and bone, fragments of quartz still humming faintly with captured light. Above my head, candles floated midair, their flames flickering as I passed below.

Seated at a small table tucked against one wall was a woman with hair the color of clouded moonlight and weathered hands. Meerdra, I'd heard she was called. She didn't look up from the rune stone she was carving.

"I wondered how long it would take you," she said. Her voice was soft and sharp at once, like silk wrapped around glass.

"You knew I'd come?"

She glanced up then. Her face was lined with wrinkles, but her moss-colored eyes were all-seeing; the kind of ageless that spoke of magic alongside the many years. "Everyone comes eventually, Your Majesty."

The title scraped, but I didn't bother to deny it.

I pulled my hood back and met her gaze. "Then you know why I'm here."

"Of course. The Harvest Throne has awakened, and you don't want it to fall into the wrong hands."

That startled me. "What do you know of my throne?"

"Maybe the question you should ask is why you, its king, did not know?"

I frowned.

"Then again, I learned of the history of the thrones before your bloodline became kings," she said, returning her attention to the rune stone. "And I've watched those same kings starve their people on altars to gods they don't understand. So, is it any wonder that I didn't share what I knew with your kind?"

Her words stung. "My father—"

"Was a fool," she finished. "And you are trying very hard not to be. So, tell me, Callan of Grey Oak, do you want to preserve or simply to control?"

I hesitated. "I want to save my land. And its people."

"We cannot always have both, as your father well knew."

I exhaled slowly, refusing to acknowledge that or believe it. "You said the throne is awake. What does that mean?"

She finally set down the carving tool. Her cloak shifted as she moved, and faint runes glimmered along the hem—old, curved symbols that tugged at my memory. I'd seen them before. Or something like them.

"Verdant," I murmured. "I've seen markings like those before... on Aurelia's neck."

Her gaze flicked to me, unreadable. "You notice more than most."

"Then you are truly descended from the Verdant tribe?"

A small smile. "A line that yet lives even if a home for us does not."

I blinked, stunned.

Aurelia had asked me to bring her to see the oracle. She'd suspected there would be clues to breaking Summer's curse buried in the Verdant's history. Its old magic. Its healing. And I'd ignored her. Assumed the Verdant had vanished long ago, along with the rest of the Calidium empire.

Aurelia had been right.

I'd been a fool.

"Wait. You've met Aurelia, then?"

The old woman's eyes sparked. "More than most, indeed."

"What did you tell her?" I asked.

Meerdra continued carving. "What she needed to know. As I may offer you, if we agree."

"You demand a price for your information," I said.

"As you demanded a price of her," she pointed out.

I tried hard not to scowl. "What do you want?"

She motioned to the empty chair across from hers. "Sit."

I did as she asked, impatient.

She leaned closer until the scent of sage enveloped me. "A promise," she said softly. "When the time comes, protect the Marble Throne. Heliconia must never touch it. Not even if it costs you your own."

The Marble Throne. The Calidium throne, far in the south. But it was long-abandoned. Empty now. As it had been for centuries since the war.

"Why the Marble Throne?" I asked.

"It is the heart of Vorinthia," she murmured. "And the only throne that remembers the balance."

I had no idea what that meant. And what she was asking—to protect another throne above my own. It was the opposite reason I'd come in the first place.

"Give me your hand."

I hesitated then offered it. The oracle took it and spread my palm open, shoving up my sleeve to reveal my wrist. She pressed her thumb to my vein, and I felt the faint hum of old power beneath her skin. "You seek to be a better man than your father," she said. "So be one. Do not seek to rule. Seek to restore. Only then can you keep my promise and fulfill the one to your people."

I swallowed hard. "All right. I will protect the Marble Throne from Heliconia even over my own if it comes to it."

Meerdra nodded gravely, and magic slammed into me. I tried to pull my arm away, but she held it fast, her grip impossibly strong. Pain lanced my arm, burrowing into my bones. I gritted my teeth, holding myself to the chair despite the urge to kick and scream.

As quickly as it had come, the pain vanished, and Meerdra released me. I yanked my arm back and noted a small rune inked into my skin.

"The bargain is sealed," she said and sat back.

My heart pounded, but I forced my breaths even. "And the answers I seek?"

She picked up the stone and the small blade beside it and went back to carving. "When the moon split an age ago, even the gods knew the balance of their own power had shifted irrevocably. They fought and negotiated for their grip on this realm, but they each knew there would be no going back. They must make room for one another in order for each to enjoy the flow of life and magic in these lands. And so the thrones were fashioned. Each one a living conduit to what the gods had imbued to sustain us. Together, they kept Menryth breathing. But power is greedy. The more your ancestors took, the more the thrones gave. Until their magic belonged not to the gods but to kings."

Magic. There was living magic in the throne itself?

"And Heliconia?" I asked. "Why does she want access to my throne? What will she gain from it?"

Meerdra's eyes darkened. "What she always wanted—more. The Ice Throne bends to her will now. But she's drinking from a well that cannot refill itself. The frost you see crawling down your borders is her hunger, not her strength. She wants to drink from Autumn's throne. To drain it. To take it into herself."

"Is that what she wanted from the Summer Court? To drain the Whitestone thrones? Take their magic for herself?"

"The power in those thrones...two rather than one. It would have made her unstoppable. Instead, Tyrion and Celeste made sure the thrones were able to strike back at her. It's why her curse failed."

I rubbed a hand over my jaw, the weight of it all pressing like stone. "Then maybe I can use mine. If it's a conduit, I can draw from it, replenish what we've lost. Fight her."

"You can use it to replenish your land, or you can use it to fight off Heliconia. You cannot do both. Your father knew that. He chose the land. He chose his own ego so that others would think him great. So that others would fight for him. He was a coward."

"If I use it to fight her, will it be enough?"

"I cannot say." She stopped carving, her gaze faraway. "Taking from the thrones would require a sacrifice. There will always be consequences when you steal from the gods."

I laughed once, hollow. "We're already living the consequences. I have dying crops, razed villages, and a withered kingdom. The only thing left is for Heliconia to storm my gates and take the throne by force."

"It is never the only thing."

"If there is another way, I would like to know it."

"That is not for me to tell."

"Then what the Seven Hels am I doing here?" I snapped.

"You are asking for help," she said, eyes flashing. "But that is not the same as someone else doing it for you."

"So fucking cryptic," I muttered, sitting back. Of course she would go this far and then refuse to give me anything actionable.

Meerdra tilted her head. "The gods are watching you closely, Autumn. You stand at the threshold of legacy or ruin. And I fear both roads will feel the same beneath your feet."

This was nonsense. A lecture disguised as wisdom.

I shoved back my chair and stood. But one last question held me still.

"And if I fail?" I asked quietly, bracing myself for the answer.

Her smile didn't reach her eyes. "Then I'll see your bloodline again in the next life. Kings always come back."

Outside, I pulled my hood up and started toward the castle, Meerdra's words echoing like the wind itself. *You stand at the threshold of legacy or ruin.*

I had a rune etched on my arm to prove it.

I'd wanted to believe I could save my realm with a throne's power. Now, I wasn't sure if that same power might destroy it in the end. But one thing was certain: If Heliconia thought she could claim every throne in Menryth, she'd have to go through me first. I now had two thrones to protect.

THE
LOVERS

Chapter Twenty-Six
Aurelia

The air in the tunnels was still and heavy. It pressed against my ears like the walls were closing in, reminding me far too much of the silence I'd endured inside the walls of my own castle.

I thought I'd left that kind of silence behind. Finding it here, now, left me gritting my teeth as I followed Eirnan and then Rydian deeper into the network of caves that led straight through Nygard Peak. We'd only been walking for an hour, having broken camp just inside the tunnel's entrance at first light this morning.

I dreaded to think about how many hours we had left in the close stillness. Most of us carried torches, chasing the darkness away. I opted to use my own flame if necessary and keep my hands free to grab a weapon should I need one.

It felt good to expend some of the power that built up inside me. A sleeping beast that grew every day, though I'd yet to mention it to the others.

We moved in a narrow line, torches flickering against the rock walls. The flamelight carved our shadows into twisted shapes, tall and crooked, across the stone. Every sound—every step, every scrape of a sword hilt against armor—echoed back a thousand times over, like the mountain was whispering our progress to itself. Or to whoever else might be listening.

The path had a noticeable descent. The deeper we went, the more the world above felt like a dream I'd once had and forgotten. It was warmer here, and while I'd been grateful for it at first, it soon became a stagnant sort of warmth that left a sheen of sweat on my brow.

Just ahead of me, Rydian's shadows curled along his boots, testing the path ahead in a way his torchlight couldn't. Keres followed close behind me, her daggers drawn. Behind her, Daegel and Thorne carried torches, along with half the Withered soldiers who brought up the rear. We'd left several of our ranks back at camp, including Vanya and those like her who could not fight. She'd been teary-eyed at our parting. I'd sworn to see her again soon, a promise I intended to keep.

The walls glistened where the torchlight hit them—black rock shot through with veins of quartz that caught the flame and held it like trapped stars. In places, the ground shimmered faintly. More quartz. Or something like it.

"It feels so old in here," Keres said softly.

"And crowded," Slade muttered.

Eirnan's voice drifted back. "These tunnels were carved long before the courts," he said. "The legends say smugglers used them during the Calidium wars. They say you could travel all the way from the Concordian Mountains to the Vorinthian border and never see daylight."

"They go that far south?" I asked. "But the mountains end here in Autumn."

"The tunnels burrow beneath the land. Below the Osphanis itself. They say there's a place near Rosewood where you can glimpse the caves above ground."

Rosewood.

I could almost smell it—the riverbanks blooming with lilies in spring, my mother's roses climbing the palace walls, the markets loud with laughter. All of that life gone now; cursed into sleep.

A lump rose in my throat, but I swallowed it down. "I remember those caves," I managed to say.

We walked in silence for what felt like hours.

The air grew colder, the stone narrowing around us until my cloak brushed the walls. My flame pulsed beneath my skin, a quiet warmth I didn't dare unleash in a space so tight.

When the sound came, it was faint. A whisper of stone shifting against stone.

Keres froze mid-step. "Did you hear that?"

Everyone stopped. The tunnel filled with the soft crackle of torchlight, the hush of breathing.

Then the ground trembled.

Just once, like something massive had shifted beneath it.

Daegel raised his torch higher. "What in the—"

Something erupted from the darkness ahead—its massive body slick and gleaming like obsidian. It struck so fast that Einan and Rydian barely dove aside before it slammed into the spot where they'd just stood.

A pair of gleaming yellow eyes, larger than I'd ever seen, stared straight into mine.

For a moment, everything stopped.

Then it opened its mouth, and a roar shook the air, deep and guttural, echoing down every corridor.

"Get clear," Rydian barked, shadows flaring from his hands.

I retreated along with the others, drawing Dorcha as I went.

From the looming darkness ahead, the rest of the creature burst through the rock—a worm-like monstrosity thick as a tree, its scales black and glassy, its body ridged with spines that pulsed faintly with blue light. Its mouth gaped open, a ring of fangs glistening with frost.

Soldiers began yelling as the creature's tail lashed across the tunnel, sending two Withered flying into the wall.

"Back," I shouted, raising my sword.

I lunged, slicing into its side. The blade barely cut through the glassy scales before the creature reared back and slammed its body into the rock wall, trying to crush me against it. Thorne shoved me aside, hard enough that I hit the wall with a pained grunt.

"Thanks," I managed.

Thorne was already moving, trying to put himself between the creature and whoever it chose next. The serpent whirled, far quicker than

Thorne or anyone else could move, and snatched a Withered soldier with its maw, impaling him on its fangs.

The soldier screamed—and then abruptly fell silent.

The creature dumped him aside and then turned for its next victim, its jaws snapping inches from my face. I rolled, furyfire bursting from my palm. The blast hit its flank, searing through the first layer of armor. The air filled with the smell of burnt carcass.

The serpent shrieked, a sound that echoed inside my skull.

Daegel said something to Slade, and they began inching around, trying to sneak up from the creature's rear. Rydian's shadows coiled up the serpent's body, wrapping around its neck like chains. He yanked hard, forcing its head back, then drove a second wave of darkness straight down its throat. The creature convulsed, shrieking as its breath was cut off.

The serpent thrashed, slamming its body into the walls so hard the tunnel shook. Shards of rock rained down. One caught my shoulder with enough force to make me stagger.

"Now," Rydian shouted, voice rough with strain. His shadows bit deeper, even as the serpent choked and thrashed.

Keres darted in, daggers flashing, driving one into the seam beneath a scale. The monster jerked hard. Its armor split, leaking black ichor that hissed against the hot stone.

I stepped in to finish it, furyfire blooming along my blade. Pain stabbed through my arm as I swung, and Dorcha slipped from my grasp.

The creature saw the weakness.

It lunged.

Thorne caught me around the waist and spun us both out of reach. The creature's fangs scraped the wall where my head had been an instant before. Its breath hit us, a blast of cold so sharp it burned. More ichor sizzled along the stone where it dripped from the creature's pointed fangs.

Poison venom.

Rydian roared. His shadows speared forward, plunging into the beast's open eye. It screamed—a high, piercing sound that made every torch gutter. Then the darkness erupted outward, bursting through its skull and severing the scaled creature from itself.

Its head hit the ground with a wet, final thud.

I slumped against the wall, clutching my shoulder. My fingers came away slick with my own blood. The wound burned, cold seeping inward.

"Don't touch it," Thorne said, waving Keres over. "Looks like poison."

"It was just a falling rock," I said, but he ignored me.

Keres was already there, tucking her blades away, eyes narrowed at the torn flesh. "Hold still." She reached for her salves, shadows gathering at her fingertips to pull the toxin free.

The world tilted. A deeper cold crawled up my arm, and my knees nearly buckled.

Rydian's arm braced my back, steadying me. "Easy."

Black ichor pooled beneath the creature's severed head, viscous and smoking in the torchlight. The remnant of power inside it whispered—cold, wrong, barely alive. Something in me answered before I could think better of it.

Heat flared from the rune at my throat—then raced down my arm, through my veins, white-gold and furious. The pain vanished. Flesh knit beneath Keres's hovering hands, the torn edges drawing closed as if stitched by invisible thread. Strength flooded my limbs so sharply I gasped.

Rydian jerked back in shock. "Aurelia—"

"I'm fine," I said, though my voice came out strange, layered with a hum that wasn't mine.

Keres stared, then grabbed my wrist and turned my arm to the light. The wound was gone—only clean skin and faint smudges where poison had touched. Her expression shifted from suspicion to something like wary respect. "Well. That's new."

Daegel held up a jagged spine with the tip of his sword, black ichor dripping. "It was poison," he confirmed before glancing at my now-healed arm.

I pushed to my feet, breath steadying. The heat beneath my tattoo cooled; the hum faded. But the memory of that power lingered—wild, ancient, and hungry for more.

"You have the power to heal yourself," Leif said, his voice hushed with awe.

I glanced at him then away again, unease filtering through me as I noted all of the Withered watching me with that same reverent expression. Even Einan was slack-jawed.

I found Rydian's gaze, and in it, no trace of damnation.

"It's called Makarios," I told them. "A gift from the Furiosities."

A few of the Withered gasped at that.

"They are not what we think," I added, my voice only trembling slightly.

Keres' expression was hard, but her eyes glittered with appreciation. Slade and Thorne said nothing. But Daegel nodded at me.

"They want to defeat Heliconia too," I said. "They are the reason I was Chosen. Their gifts…"

I trailed off. If the Withered rejected me because of the gods who'd gifted me this power, I needed to let it happen now. Before any more of them died for me.

"The Fates are of the light. They alone bestow gifts to chase away the darkness," someone said.

"The Fates have vanished," I said, impatience creeping in. More than anyone else, I knew the frustration of the Fates' abandonment. I'd watched Sonoma and the others try for years to call their masters—to no avail.

"They have left this realm and us," I went on. "We must fight with what we can in order to save ourselves."

A few murmured, but no one argued.

"We've all learned the hard way that our leaders were not who we thought they were," Einan said into the silence. "Our minds are open to new allies, lest we find ourselves with no one beside us at all."

Leif looked at the elder Withered and nodded.

A few of the others made quiet signs against ill fortune, while others murmured their support. It was better than outright rejection. Or hostility.

Keres snapped her kit closed and straightened. "Whatever it was, it saved us time and a good deal of pain. Can you walk?"

"I can."

"Good," she said briskly, already shifting back to business. "Because we shouldn't linger."

Her abrupt words seemed to break whatever spell the others had fallen under. They began to move, to gather their weapons and supplies and murmur amongst themselves.

I exhaled, glad for the reprieve.

Still, Rydian remained at my side, and I was glad for that too. For however long it lasted.

Daegel glanced between us. "Orders? Burn the carcass?"

"Leave two to set it alight once we're clear," Rydian said. "Eirnan, you said there's a place to rest ahead?"

"A cavern not far," Eirnan answered, torch lifting. "It will provide cover against anything else lurking here."

Rydian nodded. "Let's move."

Even after Einan strode away, Rydian lingered. I looked up and found myself held still by his gaze. Too close. He was standing way too close. With an arm around my waist. When had that happened? And the way he was looking at me—I'd rather be poisoned again than resist that look.

He reached up and brushed his knuckles along my cheek. "I thought —" His voice frayed, then hardened.

He shut his eyes. When he opened them again, I glimpsed true fear. Only for a moment before it was gone again. Not gone, I realized. Hidden. Tucked away so no one else saw it. Or to pretend he hadn't felt it himself.

"I'm fine," I assured him again, gentler this time.

He nodded as if he didn't quite believe it. "Stay close."

"I intend to," I said, thinking of the Withered who'd looked at me like I was a demon.

He stepped away to confer with Daegel and Eirnan, shoulders squared, shadows still moving restlessly around his boots.

I inhaled, feeling the serpent's life force thrumming faintly under my skin. Then I sheathed Dorcha, drew a steadying breath, and fell in with the others as we pressed deeper into the dark.

THE
LOVERS

Chapter Twenty-Seven
Rydian

We camped in the belly of the mountain, beneath a ceiling so high even our torchlight couldn't find it. The air still smelled of smoke and ichor. The creature's carcass was burning somewhere behind us, its poison turned to smoke that clung to the passages. The stench clung to everything—metal, skin, memory.

The Withered made their camp in a shallow alcove off the main tunnel. The fire they built was small, the flames flickering unsteadily in the stuffy air. Too many of them were whispering. I could hear the words even when they tried to be quiet—*Makarios. Demon-blessed. Hel's flame.*

They'd seen her power. The way the rune on her throat had glowed like something divine—and dark. The way the poison had fled her veins when she drank the serpent's lifeforce into her own.

I'd felt it in my bones—the depth of her power. The breadth of it, how many other gifts were still dormant and had yet to emerge. I'd underestimated her back at the mountain cabin. When she'd asked to open the gates to the Midnight Court, and I'd ruled it out as far too dangerous. Decided she was too weak to handle it. Maybe I'd been wrong. Then again, a maybe was still not enough to change my mind. But today had proven she would be ready—and soon.

Even my shadows had winced at the dark magic inside that serpent beast. But Aurelia had drunk it in like it was nothing more than a refreshing sip of water. She'd alchemized its darkness into healing.

She truly was the gods' Chosen. The hope of the realm.

While we made camp, Aurelia had gone with Keres to wash off the blood in a side cavern where an underground stream pooled. I could still sense her flame faintly through the stone—warmth that anchored me even from a distance.

Slade sat across from me near the fire, whittling at a piece of wood he'd fashioned into a glimfang. I wondered if Keres had seen it. If he'd made it for her. He'd never once spoken of feelings for the female warrior, but sometimes his flirting bordered on something more. I wondered if she'd gut him if she knew he cared that way.

While he worked, his eyes flicked toward the group of Withered soldiers clustered on the other side of the space.

"They've been muttering since we arrived," he murmured. "Some of them don't know what to make of her."

"I hear them," I said, following his gaze.

Eirnan was among them, standing with his usual calm authority, but two of his soldiers—Taron and Brist—were the ones doing most of the talking. Brist's voice scraped like gravel, thanks to the magic Autumn had drained from him. But I'd heard enough of his words to know there was anger in him. Fueled by fear. And that made him dangerous.

"You saw what she did," Brist was saying. "Duron at least needed machines and priestess-witches to take our magic. She could drink our magic with a snap of her fingers."

Eirnan kept his voice steady. "And instead, she saved your life. She saved all of ours."

Taron spat into the dirt. "For now. But what happens when she decides we've outlived our use? She'll drain us next, same as that monster."

The murmurs grew louder. A few of the Withered nodded, uncertainty rippling through the camp like an infection.

I rose before I could talk myself out of it. "Enough."

Every head turned. Shadows stretched long and thin around my boots as I crossed to them. The air tightened, thick with their unease.

"She didn't drain it because she wanted to," I said, voice calm, deliberate. "She did it because it was that or succumb to its poison. Because she chose to live and to lead you, despite every reason not to trust anyone with the knowledge of what she's been gifted."

Brist met my gaze, jaw tight. "You'd defend her even if she were one of Hel's own creatures, wouldn't you?"

"She isn't," I said flatly. "Aurelia of Sevanwinds carries the light of the gods themselves. All of them," I added emphatically. "It's why Heliconia couldn't kill her seven years ago. She's the only reason this realm still has hope."

Taron laughed, the sound humorless. "Hope's what our last king promised before he demanded we relinquish every last drop of our own life force. I don't fight for liars and tyrants anymore."

Eirnan stepped forward, cutting him a sharp look. "You'll hold your tongue. She might not be our queen, but she's the only ruler who gave us the opportunity to fight back."

"And when she decides we're no longer useful?" Brist countered. "When she needs an antidote to poison again and we're the ones standing closest to her? Will you still defend her then?"

"You forget your place, soldier," I warned him.

He shoved to his feet, Taron alongside him, both facing off with me.

"You forget yours," Brist snarled.

A snarled curse ripped from me then.

A few hands drifted toward weapons.

I felt the shadows stir in answer to my heartbeat. Reaching for their throats, more than happy to make my point for me. I leashed them but barely.

"If any of you so much as raise a blade toward her," I said quietly, "you will feel that same blade buried in your own chest before you can utter a word."

My shadows lashed out, clouding the fire until it was nearly smothered.

They froze.

Eirnan bowed his head slightly to me. "We remain your allies, Your Highness."

But the others said nothing.

After a long moment, Brist looked away. "We're only saying what everyone's thinking. The Furiosities are a darkness none wish to provoke."

"Heliconia has already done that. And now, the Furiosities are the only gods left to protect us. They chose her."

"They don't choose for me," he sneered, and I considered letting my shadows loose after all.

Eirnan snapped an order for him to walk away, and Brist reluctantly obeyed, muttering something under his breath about demons and fools. The rest of the men dispersed in his wake, the tension bleeding into the shadows.

Slade rose as I stalked back to my own fire.

"Well," he said quietly, "that went better than I thought. No bloodshed. Barely even yelling. Proud of you."

"Keep an eye on them," I said. "If they start whispering again, I want to know."

"On it," Slade said. "You want Daegel with me?"

I nodded. "His shadows will keep you out of sight while you listen."

Slade grinned. "And he's less likely to kill one of these fools for insulting our queen."

Our queen.

I jolted at that.

Slade winked knowingly. Then he clapped my shoulder and wandered off.

I turned to Thorne, who'd been keeping his distance, sharpening a blade but not missing a word, where he leaned against the stone wall. He was stronger here, closer to the land and its powerful ley lines. That strength was what we needed now.

"Stay close to Aurelia the next few days," I said. "Don't tell her about this—not yet."

He nodded once. "If they try anything?"

"They won't." I met his eyes. "But if they do, better you stop them before I do."

He inclined his head and disappeared down the passage.

I stayed where I was, watching the shadows shift and breathe around the firelight. My pulse still hadn't slowed.

I'd nearly lost her once today—saw the blood on her arm, the way her knees buckled when the poison hit. For a heartbeat, I'd believed she was dying, and it had hollowed me out.

Then I'd felt her take in the life force of the dying serpent, healing her wounds in the process. And all I could feel was relief. Relief that she was alive, that her gods-given power had saved her when mine hadn't been quick enough.

The Withered saw darkness in her. I saw the only light left in this realm.

The flames guttered, shrinking low. I stared into them and whispered to the fire, to the gods, to whoever might still be listening.

"Let them doubt her," I murmured. "But if they touch her, I'll kill them all."

The shadows around me shifted, almost like an answer.

And somewhere in the distance, I felt her flame pulse—warm and steady as a heartbeat.

THE
LOVERS

Chapter Twenty-Eight
Aurelia

The fresh spring was small, hidden behind a split in the rock that most of the others had passed without noticing. I'd only found it because I'd gone looking for a discreet place to relieve myself. Instead, I'd found a rounded pool big enough for two, filled with crystal clear water.

Keres stood behind me, torchlight painting her in amber. "Do we need to worry about serpents?"

"I think it's safe to say it's just us," I said. "Look. You can see all the way to the bottom."

She pressed in close beside me. "And the steam? Is that your addition?"

She glanced at my hand, but I held my empty palms up. "Nope. Must be a hot spring."

She hesitated, still wary. "How hot?"

I bent down and put my hand in. Sighing, I said, "Perfect for sore muscles." I pushed to my feet and started stripping out of my clothes. "Now, come on. You smell like blood and guts."

"I could say the same," she muttered, but her mouth tipped up in a smirk. "You first."

I stripped off my armor piece by piece, setting each beside my swords. The heat wrapped around me as I sank into the water, sighing as I sank to my shoulders. The grime, the blood, the serpent's ichor—all of it washed away in streaks that clouded the water for a heartbeat before the spring cleared itself.

Keres followed, wincing at the heat before easing in across from me. The torch she'd set into a crevice burned low, its light refracting across the rippling surface.

For a while, we just sat there. Letting the silence stretch.

Finally, Keres said, "So. That's two gifts from the gods."

I huffed out a laugh. "You're counting?"

"Your tattoo glowed," she said. "Hard not to notice there are three stars. What's the third?"

"I don't know yet," I admitted. "So far, there's only been the fury-fire and the death magic."

Her brow lifted. "Is that what you call it?"

I shrugged. "It's what Sonoma—my mother—called it. The oracle called it Makarios. The gift of life."

"In the old language, we would call it *ἀθανασία*."

"What does it mean?"

"Athanasia. Immortal."

I looked away. The oracle had said as much, but I'd been categorically ignoring that fact ever since she'd told me.

"The Withered nearly pissed themselves watching it happen," Keres added, clearly entertained by it.

I dragged a hand through my tangled hair, water dripping down my arms. "Do you think they'll change their minds about helping us?"

"If they do, they are fools."

I didn't answer. I appreciated her support, but I couldn't expect the entire realm to share her open-minded acceptance. Not when they'd been raised to believe the Fates were good and the Furiosities were evil.

Ironically, only the Midnight Court—a kingdom I'd once believed was filled with horrible monsters—understood that darkness didn't equal evil.

I looked up and found Keres studying me.

"What?" I asked warily.

She tilted her head. "What did it feel like? Taking the serpent's life force?"

"Like... a drink of water after a week in the desert," I admitted. "Like every cell in my body was being rewritten. And when it was over, I wasn't sure if I'd done something right or something unforgivable."

"Did it hurt?"

"Not exactly. It was more like... remembering something I shouldn't know. Something old." I met her eyes across the water. "It doesn't feel like my furyfire. It was colder. Sharper. It felt alive."

She nodded slowly.

"They're afraid," she said simply. "Afraid of what they don't understand. You didn't ask for this. You're just using what you've got to keep us alive. That makes it a weapon, not a curse."

"A weapon forged by gods who delight in ruin."

Even if those gods were my blood relatives.

"Maybe." She shrugged. "But ruin can be useful, depending on where you point it."

For some reason, her words made me think of what Rydian had said to me. *I am a weapon aimed at your enemies. Wield me how you see fit.*

I sank deeper into the water, letting her words settle. "You really don't think it's evil?"

"I think good and evil are stories we tell ourselves to sleep better at night," she said. "What you did back there was survival. And survival's not evil—it's necessary."

I studied her in the steam. "Spoken like a fellow survivor."

Her expression flickered. For a moment, I thought she'd deflect. But she surprised me.

"I was born outside the wall," she said. "Midnight's borderlands. My parents were scouts—hunters, really. We lived close enough to Concordia that we could taste the frost in the air. One night, two Obsidians attacked our home. I was six."

Her tone was flat, like she was reciting from a history book instead of her own life. "Back then, we didn't even know what they were. Or how to kill them. My father tried to fight. My mother hid me in a hollow under the floorboards. I heard them die. It wasn't quick."

My heart ached as she went on.

"After they left, a snowstorm blew in, and early the next morning, the roof collapsed. Snow came down, and I couldn't dig out. I remember thinking, *so this is what it feels like to die a slow death.*"

"Keres..."

She shook her head, not looking at me. "I managed to dig myself closer to the surface before I passed out from dehydration. A pack of glimfangs found me. Thought I was an easy meal at first. Then I bit one back, so they decided I was worth keeping."

I blinked. "You *bit* a Glimfang?"

"They were going to eat me," she said dryly. "It was self-defense."

Despite the story, I smiled. "So, what, they took you in as one of their own?"

"For a while. Two years, maybe. They're smarter than people think. Pack creatures. They fed me, protected me, taught me how to hunt. The only threat they feared was Obsidians, and the mountains were crawling with them by then. We migrated south into the Trolech, but eventually even that became overrun. The pack was attacked and forced to split up as we fled. I never found them again. Then Daegel found me."

She went quiet.

"He brought you back to the cabin," I guessed.

"Dragged me, more like. I was feral. Didn't speak for weeks. The others didn't know what to do with me. Thorne was the first one I trusted. Taught me how to speak properly again." She smirked faintly. "He's been regretting it ever since."

"Is that how you got the scars? From the pack?"

"They taught me to fight like one of them," she said. "And don't worry, I gave as good as I got."

I smiled, but it faded quickly. "You lost everything. And you still chose to fight for this realm."

She shrugged. "What else am I going to do? Sit around, waiting for the world to fix itself? People like us don't get to be soft. We just keep moving."

"You make it sound simple."

"It's the only way I know."

The steam curled between us, hazing her scars until they almost disappeared.

"Sometimes I worry they're not wrong," I said quietly.

"Who?"

"The Withered. The ones who look at me and see something monstrous."

Keres arched a brow. "You *are* monstrous. All great leaders are. The difference is what you do with it."

I laughed under my breath. "Comforting."

"You won't get comfort from me, but if that's what you seek, I have an idea where you can get it." She smirked.

I scowled. "Shut up."

She snickered.

The warmth seeped into my bones, loosening the ache in my chest that hadn't eased since that moment I'd scorched Duron to dust. When I knew the rest of the realm would hear of it and know exactly what I was.

The steam shimmered between us, turning gold in the torchlight.

I leaned my head back against the stone. "You know, I never really had any real friends growing up. This is nice."

"Just don't start braiding my hair or talking about feelings, and we'll be fine."

"Is that why you chose all those males to be friends with?"

"I wish. You'd be surprised how many feelings they have."

I laughed at that.

For a moment, it almost felt normal—two women soaking sore muscles, trading stories, pretending the world outside didn't exist. The laughter faded, but the quiet that followed wasn't heavy.

It was... easy.

Keres pushed out of the water first, steam rolling off her as she reached for her cloak. "We should get back. Rydian gets cranky when he worries."

I nodded, standing and wading out after her. The air bit colder on my wet skin, but it felt good. Alive.

We dressed quickly.

Keres strapped her daggers back into place, watching me with that measuring look of hers. "You know they'll keep whispering about you," she said.

"I know."

"Let them. They'll see soon enough what you are."

"And what's that?"

Her smirk turned wolfish. "The thing of Heliconia's nightmares."

I didn't have an answer for that, but the fire inside me stirred at her words. It wanted to prove them right.

When we stepped back into the tunnels, my chest felt lighter. For the first time in a long while, I wasn't just fighting for the realm or for prophecy. I was fighting alongside someone who saw me—not the curse, not the chosen one—just *me.* Rydian had made me feel seen too, but he'd always wanted something in return. Keres didn't want anything from me except equal treatment as friends. And gods help anyone who'd try to take that from either of us.

THE
LOVERS

Chapter Twenty-Nine
Aurelia

The tunnels widened the farther north we went. The walls that had once felt close enough to suffocate now arched high above our heads, forming a vast corridor of black stone veined with white and green. Every sound—the scrape of boots, the soft hiss of torches—echoed like the mountain was listening.

We'd been marching for hours already today, each turn and descent taking us deeper. I wasn't sure how far we'd come anymore. Time lost meaning down here. There was no sun, no wind, no scent of open air. Only the steady rhythm of our steps and the whisper of magic in the rock around us.

I'd begun to feel it more strongly the longer we walked—a subtle pulse beneath the stone, like a heartbeat. I thought maybe it was the rune on my throat responding to whatever ancient power lived in these caverns. Or maybe it was just my imagination feeding on exhaustion.

Late in the afternoon, Daegel halted suddenly, lifting a hand. "Look here," he said. His voice carried low but clear through the tunnel.

We gathered around him. The light from our torches flared across the wall ahead—and revealed what had caught his attention.

Symbols.

Dozens of them, carved deep into the rock, spiraling outward from a central point like constellations etched into the earth. They shimmered faintly, reflecting the light in shades of green and gold.

I stepped closer, brushing my fingers along one of the grooves. The stone was smooth, the carvings worn down by time but still sharp enough to catch at my skin.

Eirnan came closer and lowered his torch, the light rippling across his weathered face. "They've been here since my people first found these tunnels," he said quietly. "No one knows who carved them. Or why."

"They're not natural," Keres said. "Too deliberate."

Daegel crouched beside her, squinting at the nearest markings. "Could be an old trade route message. A warning, maybe."

"They're not warnings." The voice came from Thorne, who stood a few paces back, the torchlight catching in his pale hair. His tone was steady, certain.

Eirnan turned. "You know this script?"

Thorne stepped forward, eyes scanning the wall. "Some of it. The center symbol—the one shaped like an inverted crescent—that's the Verdant mark for *throne.*"

I frowned. "Verdant runes? Here?"

But now that he mentioned it, I did notice the familiar curves and lines.

Thorne nodded. "After the Great War, the Verdant were driven out, scattered to the four corners just like all fae were."

"Except they never formed a new court like the other fae tribes did," I said, thinking of Meerdra, the oracle from Grey Oak. For seven years, I'd searched the lands surrounding Sevanwinds for some trace of the Verdant healers; our only hope of breaking Heliconia's curse on the Summer Court. But none had been found. Not alive. They'd been scattered and then lost.

Had they come this way?

Deep beneath the Concordian Mountains?

Keres straightened. "If their runes are here, that means so were they."

"What does the rest of it say?" I asked.

Thorne traced a hand over the next few runes. "Summer, Winter,

Autumn, Midnight, Spring." Thorne pointed. "This one here—see how it intersects the others? It's not just a word. It's a number."

Rydian moved closer, his shadows flickering across the markings. "What number?"

"Seven."

A low murmur passed through the group.

"But there are only five courts," Keres said.

"Six if you count Calidium," Thorne explained. "Look, this rune is for the Marble Throne."

"Six courts," Keres said, "So, what's with the seven?"

"Seven thrones," I said softly, looking at Thorne. "Summer has two thrones."

Thorne nodded. "That would be my guess. The Verdant used numeric sequences to represent governance—their structure, their power hierarchy."

"But the Verdant ruled at a time when there was only one throne," I said. "The Marble Throne that ruled the Calidium Empire. Back then, there were no other courts in Menryth. No other thrones."

"That's true," Thorne admitted.

"So, how are the other six thrones depicted here?"

"Look." Keres had drifted further along the wall. Now, she pointed at a set of runes larger than the others. Their position represented a point earlier in the story, if this was truly meant to be carved in a specific order.

"What does this one mean?" Daegel asked.

Thorne met my gaze then turned to the others.

It was the rune from the book I'd chosen in the cabin's library. The one Thorne had warned me about then let me keep. I'd paged through it and noted these exact runes inside. But I hadn't been able to read the inscriptions.

"Life," Thorne said quietly. "But not a mortal life, the Source that all life comes from."

"A god," Daegel said.

"Not just one." Keres pointed. "Six total. Three Fates, three Furiosities."

I stared at the carvings. Six courts. Six gods. Seven thrones imbued with Life.

A shiver ran down my spine.

Rydian's voice found me through the haze. "What are you thinking?"

I hesitated. The Withered were all listening now, their gaunt faces lit by torchlight, hungry for answers.

"Just that the Verdant left more behind than we thought," I said carefully. "They somehow knew the continent would scatter into all these new courts and kingdoms. Their Seers were incredibly gifted, not to mention their connection to the gods. They clearly knew more than we did."

"You think these thrones mean something?" Rydian pressed.

"I think they represent a power that we shouldn't ignore."

One of the Withered, Brist, snorted under his breath. "And you'd know that, would you? From all your time sitting on a throne of your own?"

Eirnan turned sharply. "Enough."

Brist lifted his chin, defiant. "You saw what she did to that creature. Drank its life like a leech. Now she's down here in the dark, talking about ancient thrones and gods' power. How long before she decides we're next?"

The Withered beside him murmured his agreement.

Rydian stepped forward, shadows curling at his feet like smoke ready to burn. "Watch your mouth."

Brist's hand went to his blade. "Or what, Prince?"

Shadows leaked from Rydian's hands. "Or you'll lose your tongue."

"Rydian," I warned, but he didn't take his eyes off the Withered who'd spoken out.

The shadows thickened, stretching toward the two dissenters like serpents testing the air. They didn't flinch, but I saw their throats work as the dark tendrils coiled closer.

Eirnan moved to intervene, but Rydian's power lashed out faster than any of us could stop it. The shadows struck, forcing their way down the men's throats in a blur of black mist.

They gagged, choking.

"Stop!" I shouted.

Rydian's jaw was clenched, eyes burning like twin storms.

"Rydian, that's enough!"

Still nothing.

I stepped forward, furyfire sparking beneath my skin. "That's a command," I said, my voice sharper than steel.

The shadows froze mid-motion then recoiled like wounded things, ripping back into the dark around his boots.

The two Withered collapsed, gasping, coughing up black smoke. They were alive, barely.

The silence that followed was absolute.

Rydian turned away first, his face unreadable. The air still trembled with leftover magic.

I knelt beside the men. "You're all right," I said, though I wasn't sure I believed it.

Brist looked up at me with eyes that burned—not with gratitude but resentment. "You order him around like a trained hound. Is that supposed to make us feel safer?"

"Safer than you deserve," Rydian muttered.

"Rydian," I said again, lower this time.

He said nothing, only stared into the dark, his shadows curling restlessly.

Eirnan helped the men to their feet, but his expression was tense. "Get to the back of the line, and stay there."

They staggered off without another word, their glares lingering on me before they disappeared down the tunnel.

When they were gone, I exhaled slowly. Keres, Slade, Daegel, and Thorne stood nearby. Not a single one of them had moved to stop what had happened.

"What in the gods' names was that?" I hissed.

"They threatened you," Rydian said flatly.

"They spoke out of fear," I said. "That's not the same as drawing steel."

"They would have. Eventually."

I stared at him. "You don't get to decide that."

His jaw flexed. "I won't stand by while someone plots against you."

"I'm not asking you to stand by," I said. "But I *am* asking you to trust me to fight my own battles."

His gaze met mine then, sharp and unyielding.

Finally, he turned away, muttering something to Daegel about scouting the next passage. Shadows trailed after him like the tail of a storm.

The rest of us stood there in uneasy quiet.

Keres sheathed her daggers with a faint metallic sigh. "He's not wrong," she said. "But he's not right either."

I looked at her. "Meaning?"

"Meaning people like them will always look for someone to blame when they're scared. If it isn't you, it'll be him. Or me. The trick is to make sure they stay more afraid of the enemy outside than the one beside them."

I frowned. "That's not exactly the kind of leadership I was going for."

She shrugged. "It's the kind that works."

Eirnan cleared his throat. "We should move," he said. "If my memory serves, we're not far from the exit now."

I nodded. "Let's go."

But as I turned to follow him, my gaze caught on one of the throne runes. The lines of it seemed to pulse with awareness. A memory stirred —Callan in his tent, his eyes dark and tired as he said, *Heliconia wants my throne.* The pieces were starting to fit together, and I didn't like the picture they made.

Rydian's voice came from somewhere ahead, distant but clear. "Aurelia."

I tore my eyes from the glowing mark and followed the sound.

The tunnel narrowed again, forcing us into a single line. The quiet stretched, broken only by the drip of water and the scrape of boots against stone.

No one spoke. Even Slade kept his jokes to himself. The tension hung too heavy for levity.

When we reached the next junction, Thorne found me. "You were right to stop him," he said quietly. "But it won't be the last time you have to. Not with how determined those soldiers are to stir trouble."

I sighed. "I know."

He hesitated, then added, "The others won't say it, but what you did back there—the serpent, the healing—some of them see it as proof of what you are. Not a curse. A sign."

"Of what?"

"That the gods haven't abandoned us after all."

I didn't know what to say to that.

We left the chamber behind, but I couldn't shake the feeling that the mountain was watching us. That the runes weren't relics at all, but eyes—old, patient, and very much awake.

THE
LOVERS

Chapter Thirty
Rydian

We'd been walking for what felt like forever; hours stretched into an eternity of stone walls and the steady drip of unseen water. Then, suddenly, the air changed. Colder. Thinner. The scent of fresh pine bleeding through the cracks ahead.

Eirnan raised a hand. We stopped. The faintest thread of moonlight filtered through a fissure in the rock wall, illuminating his gaunt face as he turned to me.

"We're here," he whispered.

Through the split, I could see a valley below, washed in silver light. Heliconia's army spread across it like a plague.

The war camp was vast—tents in rows that went on forever, where they vanished into the darkness, the faint glint of frost-coated armor crawling along the perimeter. The ground itself was layered with snow and ice—a blanket of frozen death if one stayed too long.

Then there was the wind. It whistled keenly through the fissure, whipping through the pines that dotted the hillside.

"Gods," Slade murmured behind me. "There must be thousands down there."

"Closer to five," Eirnan said grimly. "And that's just the front lines.

Who knows how many more monsters she has stashed in those mountains?"

The sight of it stole my breath. I'd known. After years of skirmishes along the Autumn border, the raids along trade routes, the intel from our scouts, I'd known she was building a vast force. But seeing it with my own eyes—here, on the edge of Autumn's doorstep—was enough to make me pause.

Aurelia stepped forward to see for herself. The moonlight caught the gold in her hair, turning her into something too bright for this cursed place. I wanted to pull her back into the shadows, out of sight, out of danger. But that would be a fool's move. One I'd already made too many times.

Aurelia was born to march into that nightmare, not hide from it.

And I was born to march beside her.

Her voice was steady as she surveyed the Obsidian ranks. "The barracks in the northeast corner are more heavily guarded than the rest. Do you think that's where they're keeping Lesha?"

I scanned until I found the structure in question, noted the posted guards, all armed despite being inside the safety of the camp.

"Or it's Heliconia's private quarters," I said.

"Wouldn't it make more sense to have hers at the center there?" Slade put in.

Sure enough, in the center of the camp stood a massive tent with guards posted. Same as the tent on the outskirts.

"We need to get closer," Aurelia said. "To know for sure."

"I'm not sure that's wise," Eirnan warned.

She turned to him. "How close can we get before exiting the caves?"

"See that lower ridge?" He pointed to a spot far below us. It was a lot closer to the edge of the camp, but not on the same side as the tent in question. "We'll exit there. Any further and the tunnels are blocked from rock slides."

"That's where we'll have to reach when we leave," Keres pointed out.

I mentally clocked the time it would take to get in, gauging the difference between the Aine prisoner being in the outer tent versus the one in the center. We'd likely have to split up to search them both. A doable strategy for infiltration. Getting out would be a different story. It might not have been impossible if there weren't five thousand Obsidians between us and a safe retreat.

Aurelia didn't answer, just kept watching the valley, jaw tight.

I knew that look. The calm before her power tore something apart.

We retreated deeper into the cave, far enough that the light dimmed to nothing but what our torches allowed. Eirnan found a sharpened stone and used it to draw a crude map into the dirt.

"This is the valley," he said, drawing a boundary. "Their command tents are set here, near the ridge."

"How do you know that?" Aurelia asked.

"More soldiers in and out of there than anywhere else," he said with a shrug. "That's likely where the prisoners are kept. They'd want her within reach of any orders received from their masters."

Aurelia's throat worked once before she nodded. "Then that's where we'll strike." She looked at me. "Right?"

I looked down at the map, considering all options. "We want to disrupt their organization, especially for our retreat, so yes, it's the best place to strike."

She leaned over the map, her hair falling forward in loose strands. I watched the flicker of torchlight paint her features—focused, resolute, beautiful. My chest tightened at what I could never have.

Eirnan looked at me. "Your shadows could cover the approach."

I forced myself to focus. "Yes. But they won't mask sound. We'll need to move in small groups. Slade, how many do you think you could take with you on a jump?"

"Two, maybe three," he said.

"All the way to the center?" I asked.

"Sure. But not out again. Not if I'm bringing friends."

"We'll help you get out," Aurelia told him.

"Three teams then," Thorne said. "One to breach the prison and extract the captive. One to hit their communications. And one to check the center tent."

"No," Aurelia said.

"We need to hit their supply lines. Burn everything that slows them down."

"Thorne and I can take the supplies," Keres said. "We're quieter."

Slade smirked. "You? Quiet? That'll be the day."

Her dagger hit the dirt beside his boot with a solid *thunk.*

"I'm seeing it now," he said cheerfully. "Very stealthy."

Aurelia lifted her gaze from the map. "Slade, you and Thorne shadow-walk to the center tent. Just in case Lesha is there."

"And if Heliconia is inside?" Slade asked.

Aurelia hesitated, and I could see the indecision weighing on her.

I cleared my throat. "Then you get the Hel out of there. We can't afford a direct altercation. Not until Lesha is safe."

He nodded.

Aurelia didn't argue.

"Daegel, take Keres and a small contingent to the barracks on the outskirts," I told them. "Once you secure the Aine, do what you can against their communications tent, but the priority is getting everyone out safely."

"Will do," Daegel said.

Keres studied Aurelia. "You sure?" Keres asked her.

Aurelia nodded. "I'm sure. If Lesha's there..."

"We'll get her out," Keres finished for her.

Aurelia looked at me, swallowing hard, and I knew it was killing her not to be the one rescuing her friend. But I saw it now—what she intended.

"I'm going with you," I said.

She nodded. "All right."

"We all meet back at the cave entrance," I said, though the words tasted wrong. Setting our rendezvous point implied we'd all live long enough to get there.

The others moved off and began preparing—checking blades, restringing bows, murmuring in low voices that didn't quite mask their nerves.

Eirnan lingered near me. "They're scared," he said quietly.

"They should be."

He gave a tired half-smile. "So are you."

I didn't deny it.

The truth was, I wasn't sure what I feared more—the Obsidian soldiers we'd face or the discord in our own ranks. The Withered had been fractured too long, their loyalty cracked and patched over by desperation. The argument yesterday still echoed in the camp's whispers. Even now, I could feel their unease pressing at the edges of their resolve.

They would fight, yes. But would they hold the line when Obsidians came for us in legions? When it was their lives or Aurelia's?

I'd seen what happened to armies that didn't.

Aurelia must have felt it too. I found her still sitting in the dirt, staring at the map Eirnan had drawn. Her power hummed faintly under her skin, leaking through the cracks of her restraint. It had been doing that for days now, though she hadn't brought it up.

I sat beside her. "You should rest."

She didn't look at me. "Plenty of time for that when I'm in my father's kingdom."

Hel. The afterlife.

I exhaled through my nose. "We've been through worse."

"Have we?" she asked softly.

I didn't answer, but I thought of that rooftop seven years ago. The crack and boom of world-ending magic. The sick belief that she'd been killed.

Her eyes flicked up to meet mine. "They don't trust me."

"Some don't," I admitted. "Most do."

"That's not good enough."

"They'll follow when it matters."

She studied me, like she could read the things I wasn't saying. "And if they don't?"

I hesitated. "Then I'll make them."

Her brow furrowed. "By force?"

"If necessary."

"I don't want that."

"I don't either," I said quietly. "But I'll do whatever it takes to get you out of here alive."

Her jaw tightened. "It's not about me."

"It will never not be about you," I said. "Not for me."

Our gazes held. In her eyes, I saw it. A different future. One where we gave in to the moments we had left. Where we lived as long as possible for our own happiness. Our own hearts. Even if that time would be unbearably short.

It never would have been enough.

Even a thousand years would have been only the beginning of what I felt for her.

Maybe it was useless to try to pretend anything else. Maybe—

Eirnan cleared his throat then.

I looked away.

"My men have their orders. We'll be ready to move in the hour before sunrise."

"Thank you," Aurelia told him. "I know this can't be an easy request to make. Once the army realizes what's happening, they'll send everything they have."

"We'll be gone before they can," Eirnan said with more conviction than I knew any of us felt.

Aurelia looked at him like she wanted to believe it. Maybe she did.

With a nod, he left us alone again.

We sat together, both of us studying the map. Neither one talking about what we intended to do to the enemy camp drawn roughly before us. Or what might be done to us if we failed.

Eventually, the others quieted as soldiers found their bedrolls.

"If something happens to me," Aurelia began.

"Then it will happen to me too," I finished.

She didn't argue. Only nodded and rose.

"Good night, Rydian."

"Good night, Furious."

When she was gone, I looked toward the tunnel mouth where a sliver of stars was just barely visible through the crack.

Tomorrow, the valley below would burn.

And whether it was Heliconia's army or the princess asleep in this cave that struck the match, I knew one truth with terrible clarity: If she fell, I'd burn with her. There'd be nothing left for me in this realm without her in it.

THE
LOVERS

Chapter Thirty-One
Callan

I sat on the Harvest Throne, sprawled in what I hoped looked like careless confidence, one leg draped over the armrest. My father's crown glinted dully on the table beside me. I didn't wear it unless I had to. It was heavy and had a phantom scent of blood no one had ever managed to wash away.

Reports lay scattered across the table at the base of the steps—lists of troop movements, dwindling supplies, villages lost to ice and flame. I'd read them all twice. The numbers didn't change. No matter how many soldiers I sent north, Heliconia's destruction crept farther south each night.

I leaned back, studying the vaulted ceiling. Dust motes floated through the shafts of afternoon light slanting across the chamber. It should have been beautiful. Instead, it just looked old and worn.

"Majesty."

Lemuel's voice cut through the silence like a chisel through stone. The elder advisor appeared in the doorway, robes the color of old parchment, eyes sharp and humorless.

Despite his irritating demeanor, he'd proven useful in the short time I'd been crowned. I'd dismissed the others when I'd realized their loyalty to my father had made them too eager to backstab me.

"What is it?" I asked.

"The queen of Winter has arrived."

"Already?"

"You requested she be admitted the moment she arrived."

"Yes, well." I rose, smoothing the wrinkles from my coat. "That was before I remembered she's likely come to freeze me to death."

"Majesty," Lemuel said in that disapproving tone that suggested I was twelve again. "It would serve you to take this seriously."

"Oh, I take it very seriously," I said, flashing him a grin I didn't feel. "I'm simply choosing not to cower in the face of my death."

He sighed, muttered something that sounded like a prayer to whatever gods still tolerated me, and stepped aside.

The great hall's doors creaked open. Cold wind rushed in first—sharp, metallic, laced with the scent of frostbitten pine. Then came Heliconia.

The temperature in the room dropped a full ten degrees as she strode in.

She was draped in white fur with silver trim as she'd been the night we'd last met, her dark hair pinned with shards of ice that didn't melt even under the glow of the braziers. Her beauty wasn't the kind that invited warmth—it was the sort that warned you away from the edge of a cliff even as you leaned closer to peer over its deadly edge.

"Your Majesty," she said, her voice smooth and cold as a winter stream.

"Conqueror," I said, mocking a bow as if it were a title equal to my own.

She let it roll off. "When you failed to answer my letter, I was worried some ill had befallen you, but you look well."

"I thought I'd offer some build-up," I said.

"And, in turn, I allowed you more than ample time to consider my offer."

"Oh, do you mean the offer to spare my kingdom if I agreed to a lifetime of marital bliss? What's to consider?"

A faint smile curved her lips, more animal than fae. "And yet you delayed your answer."

"I wanted to think on it."

"Think?" Her tone sharpened, still soft but cutting all the same. "That's not a habit I associate with the Autumn kings."

I forced a laugh. "Perhaps that's why the last one's dead."

Her eyes gleamed like shards of polished ice. "You're smarter than he was."

"Or more desperate."

"It can be both." She moved closer, and the cold rolled off her in waves. "Have you come to a decision, Prince Callan?"

At her disrespect, my carefully-hewn façade threatened to slip.

Instead of letting it, I gestured lazily toward the throne beside mine —identical in shape, carved of marble and oak, veined with silver instead of a stag's horn.

"I had something made for you. A gift. Should we come to an agreement on a union?"

"What is that?" she asked, her own good humor giving way to wary disgust.

"A throne, of course. One matching my own."

"It is no match for the Harvest Throne," she said.

"It is what I'm offering my queen," I told her quietly. "My only offer."

Her hand lashed out before I could blink. Power cracked through the air, white and violent, and slammed into my chest like a blow from a god. I stumbled back, my breaths sharp against my ribs.

"Careful," I managed, forcing a grin through the pain. "You'll bruise the merchandise."

"You dare toy with me." Frost crept across the floor, veins of ice spidering outward from her feet. "Do you know how many worthless fae I've buried beneath my snow, boy?"

"Dozens, I'm sure," I rasped. "But none of them looked half as good as me."

Her fury rolled off her in waves, but there was a flicker—admiration, maybe—that kept her from ending me outright. "You truly believe arrogance can mask fear."

"So far, it's worked wonders."

She shoved me aside with one hand, the force sending me staggering down the dais. Her attention turned to the Harvest Throne. The power in the room shifted.

"Don't touch it," I warned.

She ignored me, mounting the steps like a queen ascending to her altar. When she reached the throne, she trailed her fingers over its armrest. Gold veins shimmered faintly beneath her touch.

Then she sat.

The sound that followed wasn't just silence—it was *absence.*

Nothing happened.

Her posture stiffened. Frost flared along the marble, trying to take root, but the veins of gold refused her. The throne remained inert, defiant.

A slow, awful realization spread across her face.

Then she turned that look on me.

"What have you done?" she demanded.

I straightened my coat, schooling my features into innocence. "What do you mean?"

"Don't play games with me, Autumn." The temperature plunged, the braziers flickering out one by one. "Where is the real throne?"

I blinked at her. "How do you know this isn't it?"

"Because this," she hissed, rising to her feet, "is a *dead chair.*"

"Fascinating," I murmured. "Perhaps it simply doesn't like you."

She shot to her feet.

Her power flared again, wild and biting, shards of ice cracking through the floor and up the columns. The palace groaned under the weight of her fury. "Tell me what you've done with its power."

"I've done nothing," I said.

The air around us shimmered with frost as she stalked toward me. The crown on the table froze solid. "You will tell me, or you will die."

"If I die, then you'll never know," I said.

Frost slithered up the walls behind her, leaving hairline cracks in its wake. Behind me, the door banged open as two guards rushed in.

"Your Majesty, are you—"

Ice shards flew like spears, embedding deep in their chests. Both guards staggered and fell. More would come. It was only a matter of time before Lemuel sent for an entire legion. And Heliconia would fell them all.

I had to stop this.

I softened my tone, taking a careful step toward her. "Darling."

She turned, eyes bright as broken stars.

"Rule *with* me," I said. "We can still have peace. No more ice. No more blood. Just... two thrones, side by side."

For a heartbeat, her fury flickered. Her head tilted as I leaned closer.

My voice dropped, low and coaxing. "You don't have to destroy everything in order to win."

Her expression shifted, her breath catching just slightly as I closed the distance. Slowly, I reached out. The heat of my skin met the cold of hers. She didn't pull away.

I brushed my thumb along her cheekbone, felt the shiver that might have been pleasure. "You're tired of fighting," I murmured. "I can give you something better. Stay."

The warmth of my persuasion unfurled between us—soft, honeyed threads of power sinking into her skin. I felt it take hold, that subtle give as her mind leaned toward mine. Her lashes lowered. Her lips parted.

Then she laughed.

The sound was wrong. Beautiful, yes, but hollow.

She leaned in, her lips near my ear. "How adorable," she whispered.

The charm shattered like glass.

I staggered back a step, breath catching. "You—"

"I am immune to mortal persuasion," she said lightly. "Did I forget to mention that? A pity. You might have saved us both some time."

My pulse roared in my ears. The only weapon I had and it was useless. So, I did what I had not done seven years ago. I stood and defied her. "I'll never give you this throne."

She shrugged. "Then you and your people will die."

The silence stretched. Farther out, I could hear shouts sounding. Soldiers would come. They would fight for me. And they would die. And Heliconia would still walk out of here, undeterred. And someday, no matter how long it took, she would find the throne I'd hidden in the bowels of this castle.

It would all be for nothing; the lives lost. The soldiers who fought.

We'd lose in the end.

My shoulders sagged as I said, "Fine."

Her head tilted.

"You win. Congratulations, Your Majesty. You get your alliance. And your throne."

"Where—"

"Not today. Consider it a wedding present when we take our vows." I forced a grin that felt like swallowing glass. "When do we wed?"

Her eyes glittered. "Soon."

She withdrew her power pressing in on me, the frost receding like breath on glass. "You'll announce it tomorrow."

"To whom?"

"To the kingdom that still dares call itself yours."

I clenched my fists to keep from shaking. "And when they ask why I would tie myself to my enemy?"

She shrugged. "Tell them the truth."

"Which is?"

"That you've chosen survival. Just as your father did."

She turned to leave, the air warming slightly in her wake. At the doorway, she glanced back, a cruel kind of softness in her expression. "I'll see you soon, husband."

When the doors shut behind her, I waited until the sound of her footsteps had faded. Then, I let myself out through the small door in a hidden corner of the room.

Lemuel would be beside himself searching for me, but he would have to wait.

Down the stairs that spiraled deep beneath the castle, I went quickly enough that sweat dotted my brow by the time I'd reached the bottom. The air was stale here, unmoved for the centuries Grey Oak had stood carved around it.

In the small room at the back of the passage stood the true Harvest Throne. It had taken half a dozen soldiers and a pulley to lower it here. My compulsion had helped them forget what they'd seen and done. And now, only I knew where the true throne was hidden.

Breathless, I approached it and slid into its seat.

The stag's horn inlaid felt warm. Too warm. Like it recognized what had just happened and was deciding what to think of it all.

I pressed a hand to the armrest, trying to still the tremor in my fingers. "You and me both," I muttered to the throne.

The veins of gold pulsed once beneath my palm, like a heartbeat answering mine. For a moment, I swore I heard it whisper—soft, almost kind. Almost relieved. *You made your choice.*

I closed my eyes. "Gods help me. I hope it's the right one."

THE
LOVERS

Chapter Thirty-Two
Aurelia

Cold air hit my face, thin and sharp, and the world opened from a slit in the rock to a silver-washed valley of Obsidian soldiers. I didn't let myself look there too long. Instead, I watched as Slade, Eirnan, and Thorne slipped away, there and gone in an instant as Slade shadow-walked them down the rocky path toward the camp's edge and then straight into its wicked heart.

Then it was Daegel's turn.

Keres stood with half the Withered soldiers, their breaths puffing out in hot clouds as they waited for their camouflage to envelop them. Daegel's shadows were a dark ward around them, different from Slade's murky portals, but just as effective, and soon, they were invisible, lost among the last dregs of darkness.

I watched them all go, my heart in my throat, and sent a prayer to whatever gods might still listen to keep them safe.

My thoughts drifted to Sonoma. And Ire.

Protect them, I pleaded.

The wind whipped in response; an assurance or a refusal, I couldn't be sure which.

Rydian crouched beside me in the mouth of the fissure, our backs pressed to stone slick with condensation. He'd woken me a half hour earlier and hadn't said more than necessary since. Neither one of us seemed interested in goodbyes.

When the others had gone, I shifted my weight, anxious to move.

He lifted two fingers. *Wait.*

His shadows rose—quiet, obedient smoke—then spilled over us both like a second skin. The torch behind me guttered as if suddenly choked for air.

Wrapped in that shadow, I tasted metal on my tongue. Fear. Steel. The promise of a fight. Remnants of a dream filled my mind. Ash and smoke and scorched earth—the whole valley burnt to a crisp. A dream or a nightmare.

Dorcha and Latha were strapped to my back. My hair was braided tightly, and my Aine leathers were soft against my skin, cold in the damp morning air. I didn't feel the chill, though. Not when the flames beneath my skin heated me from the inside—ready to consume everything it touched. But it was the hunger stirring in my belly that I leashed most tightly, my nerves dancing alongside that gnawing desire.

Makarios was a weapon I'd yet to master, but I would wield it just the same. Today, I would drain them all or burn them to ash. No more hesitation or being ashamed of what the gods had gifted me. Not if it brought Lesha home. Not if it made Menryth safe.

"On me," Rydian whispered, pushing to his feet.

I nodded, and together, we slipped from the cave lip, moving down the slope like shadows of the night.

The ground crunched faintly with frost where there should have been dew and wild thyme. To my left, a thin ribbon of black water threaded the camp's far edge. The sight of it made me think of Nali. And Amanti.

I turned away from those thoughts, focusing on our path ahead as the rocky descent leveled out into a more open ground packed hard by the frigid temperatures.

Rydian's shadow curtain flexed with us—thicker when we crossed open ground, thinner when we hugged boulders and dead brush. My body whispered its training: Keep low, keep loose, keep moving. My power whispered something else: destroy. Burn. Protect.

Soon, the camp resolved into detail—rows of tents edged in frost, guy lines sparkling with ice crystals. The cooking fires were banked low to spare the smoke. Onyx-eyed horses stood tethered between posts, their coats too still, manes unmoving even when the wind cut through camp. Obsidian eyes. No whites. No shine. A wrongness forced into the shape of a horse and then broken into lifeless obedience.

It was the same with the soldiers.

But I saw more than Obsidians standing watch or huddled around a fire, and the sight of what else Heliconia had wrought spread through me like a poisoned dread. A cluster of figures in white leather and woven bone; when they turned, there was nothing where faces should be. Masks strapped to emptiness.

I stumbled, momentarily enthralled.

Rydian gripped my elbow, steadying me. I tore my gaze from the camp's creatures and anchored myself in his gray-brown eyes. He didn't speak, but I found steadiness in the way he looked at me. Like he was just as horrified as I. And just as determined to destroy them all.

We kept moving.

The ground near the outer tents was dead—the frost there not a film but a deep layer of frozen earth, scorched with the burn of ice. I was careful to step without slipping on the slick patches.

We rounded a thick hedge of briars, and Rydian raised his palm.

Two sentries moved along the outside perimeter, their patrol unhurried, spears tipped in ice-burnished metal. Their helmets were smooth—no ornament, only efficiency. The nearer one turned his head, and I caught the glint of eyes like polished coal.

Obsidian.

His pointed ears and male frame marked him as fae. Or former fae. Now, he was only an empty shell. A Made thing. Soulless and utterly loyal to its master.

"Left," Rydian mouthed.

His shadows pulled across us like a curtain. Ten steps. Twenty. My heartbeat was a drum beating too fast. One of the sentries paused, head lifting slightly as if scenting.

We stilled.

He turned toward us.

Rydian breathed out, barely more than a thought, and darkness lifted from the ground to swath the sentry's helmet.

"What are you…?" I watched, confused at the way the shadows merely hovered rather than struck a blow.

"An illusion," Rydian whispered. "He'll see us as fellow soldiers. Nothing more."

The sentry stepped closer. The illusion stretched to accommodate him. His weapon lowered a fraction as if to accept us as his own.

Then the shadows parted, and his gaze snagged on the exposed mark inked on my throat.

Something flickered behind those obsidian eyes.

"Ident—" he began.

Rydian was already moving. His hand clamped the sentry's jaw, shadows knifing between the helmet and skin. The Obsidian's body went slack in a single, horrible sigh. Rydian lowered him without sound.

The second sentry came rushing; I was already there. Dorcha slid under ribs where armor parted for movement. The Obsidian's breath whooshed out as his knees buckled. I caught his weight and lowered him to the frost-coated ground.

We dragged both bodies into the briars and kept going.

Faster now.

Past the outer line, where I scented animal, sweat, boiled meat. Rydian steered us toward a line of heavy canvas structures near the northern quadrant where supply wagons sat: coils of rope piled beside crates, racks of barbed grapnels gleaming in the fading moonlight, stacked barrels that stunk of sour ale.

Somewhere on the other side of it, a guard sneezed.

We froze and let a patrol pass so close I could count the smudges on their boots.

Rydian's shadows held. Then we were moving again.

We found gaps, slipped through them, became the night. My mouth was dry with fear that, at any moment, we'd be spotted and it would all come crashing down. I swallowed back the fear and pointed to the largest of the tents in this section.

The hub of supplies.

Hopefully, food stores or even weapons.

Either way, if that tent caught fire, the rest would burn with it. They stood too close not to catch on one another.

It was perfect.

My palms warmed at the idea of igniting this camp. The sleeping beast inside me that was my newfound well of power purred in a slow awakening. It was nearly time.

Rydian led the way, both of us keeping low despite the shadows shrouding us from view.

When we reached the tent, he slid the flap aside with gloved fingers, enough to slip under one at a time. Pressing in close at his back, I stepped through and was greeted by a wall of cold air, more frigid inside than out. Cold storage, maybe.

But it smelled wrong for any kind of food stores.

Instead, beneath the chill, I scented disinfectant—and blood.

Rydian stepped aside, and I glimpsed what we'd found. Cots. Rows of them, most empty, but a few of them with bodies wrapped in blankets. On the bedsides, lanterns burned low.

A medic ward.

I noted onyx-eyed soldiers staring unseeing at the tent ceiling. They showed no signs of life. A few others lay on their backs, bandages soaked through, breaths shallow. All of them past the point of caring at the sight of us.

One cot sat apart from the others. On its bedside were instruments laid out on trays: a bone saw, various blades, an iron hook. On the floor, a long, thick length of chains lay coiled. There was nothing healing about any of it. Only torture and suffering.

My pulse stuttered once, hard, and then recovered. Rydian's fingers brushed my wrist, and I knew it was a warning. A reminder that we weren't here for injured Obsidians.

And then I heard it. A raw, small exhale with just enough voice that I recognize it instantly.

I turned back to the cot and looked closer at the frail form lying wrapped in a thin blanket. Cheekbones like knives. Lips chapped and split.

"Lesha," I breathe. Her name tasted like salt in my mouth.

Something in her eyes shifted.

She was alive, thank the gods.

"Lesha, can you hear me?" I whispered, voice cracking.

She blinked slowly, staring through me, then at me as if she had to practice the steps of remembering how to do it.

"Auri," she whispered like it hurt to speak. Hearing her use my childhood nickname almost broke me.

"Yes." I bent over her, fingers ghosting over her face, afraid to touch, more afraid not to. "It's me."

Rydian's head snapped to the door. He inhaled, cocking his head, listening. "Two coming."

"Please," Lesha begged. It was hardly sound.

"We have you," I told her, and I meant it with every piece of power in me. "We're taking you home."

I slid an arm beneath her shoulders, and the heat of fever scorched my forearm. She'd gone so slight. Rage vented through me like a fault line letting off steam. Furyfire licked through my veins, fully awake, aching to free itself, but I banked it. There would be no wrecking their supplies or scorching their camp.

All that mattered was getting Lesha out.

Rydian appeared at the cot's far side. He gathered Lesha into his arms with a practice that betrayed how many bodies he'd carried for Autumn over the years. Her lips made a shape that might once have been a protest but now was only breath.

He looked at me. "My shadows will do their best, but the sun will be up soon. You'll clear our path?"

I nodded, Dorcha already loose in my hand.

We moved. The smell of cauterized flesh followed us all the way to the exit. I held the flap to let them pass then followed them out. The cold night air was both balm and blade. The moon was gone, offering a darkness that was already lightening toward dawn.

A quartet of Obsidian soldiers rounded the medic tent from the left, armor chittering like teeth. The nearest spotted me just as Rydian's shadows swallowed him up, undoubtedly morphing our faces into something that resembled allies.

The soldier faltered, yawned, and kept walking.

We hurried the other way, but it wasn't the same path as the one we'd come in on. I had no idea if the twists and turns I was taking now would lead to an exit point or if we'd find ourselves surrounded after each new bend.

Twice, we flattened against the side of carts or tents as patrols passed. Once, we pressed into the space between a supply cart and a meat rack while an officer checked the hitching posts. Through all of it, Lesha was nothing more than a silent wraith in Rydian's arms.

At a fork in the path, I held up a fist. Rydian paused. A sentry in a cowl stood with his back to us, head turned toward the central pavilion. Beyond his post, the outskirts of camp gave way to a clear path back into the wilderness of the valley. To our escape.

I switched Dorcha to my other hand and quietly pulled a small blade free from where I'd hidden it in my boot. Rydian didn't say a word as his shadows pulled and twisted around me, beckoning me forward to do what I must.

Barely breathing, I moved.

One step.

Two.

The knife was in and out of his neck before the sentry realized what had happened. He folded soundlessly. I caught and lowered him, dark blood leaking from his opened throat.

Then we were moving again, low and quick as we ducked behind a line of carts. I could already see the brush beckoning us. The hillside sloping up and away.

A figure stepped from between the last two carts. Not Obsidian. Fae. Gray cloak. Hood pulled low. But I caught sight of the face inside it and froze.

Taron.

"What are you doing?" I hissed.

His attention flicked to Lesha. "You found her."

Rydian snarled softly. "Eirnan sent you?"

The Withered's gaze ticked to me, to the shadows, to the way Rydian held Lesha like breakable glass. Something ugly curled at the corner of his mouth in a shape that had nothing to do with triumph. "I don't serve Eirnan."

His words sent a shudder through me.

"Move," I told him softly.

For a breath, he only stared at me, the gaunt, hollow look in his eye now filled with something deep and treacherous. Then he stepped aside.

I didn't turn my back on him as we passed. Rydian didn't either. When we were clear of him, I marked the most direct line to take us back up to the cave's entrance.

From around the brush, two Obsidian soldiers appeared. Rydian's shadows coated us and, for a breath, the soldiers' helmets angled as if they accepted us as part of the retreating night.

Then one straightened. "Identify."

My hand tightened around Dorcha.

The Obsidian's neck broke backward like a reed in winter wind. Rydian's shadows went through the second helmet as gently as smoke and retreated in a mist of darkened blood.

My sword hung at my side as I stared at Rydian. His stoic expression was unwavering as his stormy eyes met mine.

The thing nightmares fear.

I'd never realized what he was truly capable of. What my father had gifted him when he'd vowed to protect me. But there was no time to process it now.

"Come," he said, and we resumed our retreat.

Above us, the sky was lightening. Rydian's shadows would be no use now.

The stream was just ahead. A thin ribbon of murky water between us and the path that led to the caves. The current was slow, the bank on the far side a dark smear. Beyond that, a stand of bracken. Good cover for our ascent straight up to the cave's mouth.

"Almost there," I urged.

If we jumped, we could make it without getting our boots wet.

The sound was small. A single whistle—three rising notes—carrying from the high ridge. A scout's signal. One of ours. Except it wasn't.

My gut dropped.

"Rydian."

He'd already whipped his head to the ridge. A figure stood there, barely a silhouette against moonlight. Gray cloak. Hood low. Withered.

He should have been signaling our teams' safe return—one whistle for Slade's team, two whistles for Daegel's, three for Rydian and me. Instead, the three short whistles were followed by a lantern being lifted in his hand. The shutters flew back. Light spilled wild and bright in the graying morning.

He swung it overhead.

Once.

Twice.

Thrice.

I felt sick.

All along the edge of camp, Obsidian helmets snapped toward it like a field of flowers turning to the sun.

The cloaked figure on the ridge held the lantern high, illuminating his face. I was close enough to see it all. The hard set of his aged jaw. The hate glittering in his hollow eyes. Brist.

I watched as he angled the lantern toward the valley, low and left, as if pointing at us.

Horns split the night.

At our backs, the sentries we'd evaded erupted in shouts.

And from the ridge, the traitor's lantern burned steady as a small, treacherous sun.

THE
LOVERS

Chapter Thirty-Three
Rydian

Lesha's body was all bone and torn flesh, wrapped in rags that smelled of sweat and rot. Her back was bandaged, thick with dried blood where her wings had once been. Every breath shuddered through her like it might be her last. She weighed almost nothing, especially compared to the dread that filled me as I watched Brist betray us all.

"We have to move," I said.

"What about the others?" Aurelia asked, stricken.

I knew the horrible fear that gripped her because it gripped me too. Slade, Thorne, Keres, Daegel. My family. They'd never make it out in time.

At our backs, a group of sentries approached—a trio of Obsidians and a trio of... something else. They wore white leather armor, reinforced with straps of bone and plates of ice that didn't melt under the torchlight. Masks of carved ice-bone covered where faces should have been—smooth, featureless ovals strapped to emptiness. Nothing moved beneath those masks. No breath, no flicker of eyes. Just a hollow cold that rolled ahead of them.

Frostwights.

I'd heard stories, mostly scary tales told to children to keep them from venturing too far into the northern mountains. But even those stories hadn't conveyed the true horror of seeing the creatures advancing toward us now.

The air dropped ten degrees in an instant.

Aurelia stilled. I felt her power bunch beneath the surface of her skin, ready to explode.

I stepped in front of her and let my shadows swell. Let the nightmarish illusion take the place of our true faces. Let them see what they wanted to see. Two fellow soldiers, also relieved of our fae souls and made into something enslaved to Heliconia's darkness.

"Soldier," one of the soldiers barked. "Report. Have you found the traitors we were warned about?"

"Not yet," I said, pitching my voice low and dull. "We were ordered to sweep the hillside."

One of the Frostwights tilted its mask as if smelling the air. Frost smoke drifted from the seams in its armor. For a heartbeat, I thought we might slip past. Then the Frostwight's head snapped toward Aurelia.

The hollowness behind that mask *noticed* her.

A hiss of cold rushed through the tent-rows. The Frostwight raised its hand, fingers gnarled into icicles.

My shadows tore under the pressure of that ancient, unnatural cold. The illusion faltered.

"It isss her," the Frostwight hissed. "The traitor. We mussst kill her."

"Run," I snarled—and dropped the illusion.

The closest Obsidian reached for his horn.

I didn't give him the chance to sound it. A blade of shadow shoved through his ribs, cracking bone, slamming into his heart. I ripped it free and turned, but the second soldier was already raising his axe.

Aurelia moved faster.

Furyfire erupted from her palm, bright and wild, engulfing the soldier. His scream was brief. When the fire died, only blackened armor and smoking bone remained.

The Frostwight did not scream.

Flames licked across its armor and guttered. Frost crawled over the fire, devouring it, leaving scorched ice in its wake. The thing kept coming.

"What in the—" Aurelia began.

"Frostwight," I snapped. "It's made of bone, which won't burn. Don't let it touch you—"

It lunged.

Cold like a god's last breath slammed into me. I twisted, throwing myself sideways with Lesha clutched tight to my chest. The blast hit the thick brush behind us. Thorny branches froze solid, then shattered into a rain of frozen shards.

Aurelia didn't flinch away.

She moved through it.

Flame roared out of her, the heat singeing the hairs on my hands. The Frostwight met it head-on. Ice and fire collided, power shrieking, throwing sparks and shards across the frozen ground.

Her rune flared, bright as a brand at the hollow of her throat. I felt the pulse of it from where I stood—old, deep, dangerous.

The Frostwight's armor began to melt.

Not from heat.

From a draining of whatever magic held it together.

Furyfire climbed its body, but beneath the snapping bone and cracking ice, something else was happening. I felt it like a current in the air. A pull. A siphon.

Life force—whatever Heliconia had tethered inside that corpse of bones—ripped free.

The Frostwight staggered, knees buckling. Frosted smoke poured out from the seams in its leather armor, racing toward Aurelia, drawn like breath to her mark. Her eyes widened. For a second, she looked like she might push it away.

Instead, she took it in.

The last of the light in the Frostwight's body went out. Its armor crumpled in on itself, collapsing like an empty shell. Aurelia's breath caught, shoulders jerking as warmth flooded her skin. The exhaustion in her gaze cleared like fog burned away at dawn.

She hadn't just burned it.

She'd *drained* it.

Drank it in and let it strengthen her.

Makarios.

The word thudded through me like a warning. Suddenly, I wondered if it wasn't such a good thing after all. If she took too much, like the gates to the Midnight Court—

"Aurelia."

Her head snapped toward me. For a terrifying heartbeat, her eyes were wrong—the blue too bright, pupils blown wide, something ancient and hungry looking out through her face.

Then she blinked, and the woman I knew was back.

"I'm fine," she said, voice rough. "Get Lesha to the cave. Now."

We ran.

Lesha's body was a dead weight against my chest, but I held her like she was made of glass. Aurelia kept pace, flames low now but ready, a barely-contained inferno under her skin.

We made it across the river and onto the far bank when the camp erupted behind us. From the far side, a plume of fire and smoke shot into the sky—their communications tent, by the looks of it, going up in a controlled explosion.

Thorne and Slade.

I felt the pulse of Slade's shadow-walking tug, distant but unmistakable, as he blinked someone—several someones—out of that firestorm. Relief slammed into me as hard as fear.

They were alive.

For now.

"Keep going," Aurelia said. "We can't help them if we get ambushed on this hill."

I kept running, uphill, zigzagging around the thick brush that blocked a straight ascent.

We were almost to the far slope.

Another horn blared, ahead of us, not behind.

"Patrol on the outer ring," Aurelia said. "We're going to run through them."

Lesha stirred weakly in my arms, a faint sound scraping from her throat.

"Almost there," I murmured to her. "Stay with us."

We slid through a narrow opening in the brush—and nearly collided with a wall of pale leather and ice.

A line of Frostwights, moving in eerie, perfect unison. White armor, masks like featureless moons, blades of blue-white ice burning in their hands. Behind them, a handful of Obsidians stood, eyes black and eager for our deaths. Thanks to Brist, they'd likely been waiting for us here all along.

One of the Frostwights lifted its arm, pulling its ice-spear back and aiming its sharpened tip at us.

"Get down," I called.

I dropped, twisting my body to shield Lesha as a spear of ice screamed through the space where our heads had been.

It landed impaled in the hardened ground behind us.

Aurelia rolled away, coming up on one knee. Flame spiraled from her hand, flaring into a wide arc that forced the nearest Frostwights to halt. The fire didn't burn as quickly as it should have—it clung to their armor, eating at it slowly, hungrily.

Her mark flared bright, pulling.

I felt it again.

"Leave them!" I shouted. "We don't have time—"

A Frostwight stepped through the fire.

It reached for her.

I surged to my feet, shadows whipping out like chains. They wrapped around the thing's arm, trying to pull it off course, but the cold that met my power was like nothing I'd felt before. It crawled up my shadows, burning them away in shards of frozen darkness.

"Rydian." Aurelia's voice snapped through my head like a whip. "Go! Get her to the cave. I'll hold them."

I looked at the slope, at the line of Frostwights, at the obsidian-eyed soldiers moving in a tightening circle.

Leaving her here went against every instinct I had.

"I won't—"

She turned on me, furyfire roaring up her arms, eyes gone molten. "Go," she growled. "I'll be right behind you."

Our gazes locked.

She'd accused me of not believing in her once before.

I wouldn't make that same mistake again.

"Don't die," I said.

Her mouth curved; not quite a smile, too feral for that. "I wouldn't dream of it."

Then she turned back to the Frostwights and unleashed Hel.

In one hand, she swung her sword, its metal gleaming in the light of dawn. From her other hand, flame poured out in waves—onyx-black and inferno-hot, rolling up and down the slope, devouring Obsidian soldiers in its path.

Frostwights cracked and screamed. The air became a living furnace, heat slamming into my face even as I turned away.

Even as I ran.

The climb to the cave mouth felt like scaling the side of a nightmare. The slope was slick beneath my boots, patches of ice hidden under loose rock. I used my shadows to steady my footing, focusing every shred of attention I had on staying upright, on not dropping the fragile life I carried.

Two Withered soldiers pounded up the hill, breath rasping, faces drawn and determined. I recognized them from Slade's hunting party. They bypassed the cave's mouth, going higher still, and I knew they had their orders from Slade.

Get to Brist.

End him.

Whatever death he met today wouldn't be merciful enough.

The cave mouth loomed ahead—a jagged crack in the cliffside, dark as a swallow of midnight. Obsidian soldiers swarmed it, each one knocked back by a Withered soldier's sword.

As I got closer, Daegel appeared beside the opening, shadows up like a wall, deflecting a rain of ice shards that hammered down from somewhere below.

His eyes widened when he saw me, then again when he noticed what I carried. "The Aine?"

"Alive," I said, staggering the last few steps. "For now. And Slade?"

"He's gone back for the others," he said. "Keres and Thorne among them."

I turned off the fear that wanted to grip me, to distract me.

He reached for her. I hesitated a fraction of a second, then surrendered her into his arms. She looked even smaller there.

"Get her inside," I ordered. "Take whatever soldiers we can spare and retreat. Somewhere they can't reach with frost or fire."

Daegel nodded, his usual sarcasm gone. "She'll be safe with me." His gaze flicked over my face. "You're going back down."

"Yes."

He didn't try to stop me. Just shifted Lesha's weight gently, then jerked his chin at the Withered clustering near the entrance. "You heard him. We hold this tunnel, or we all die."

They let out a battle cry, their swords swinging with renewed fervor.

As Daegel turned, Lesha's eyes slit open, hazy and unfocused. Her cracked lips shaped a word that might have been Aurelia's name.

I didn't stay to hear it.

I spun back toward the hillside.

Flame rolled below us, painting the golden dawn in black and blue. Smoke rolled thick. Screams rose through it—Obsidian, Frostwight, maybe some of our own. Down below, the camp itself was beginning to burn—tents catching, supply wagons roaring, smoke clawing up toward the sunrise.

Somewhere between me and that inferno, Aurelia was still fighting.

I took one step—

A shout cut through the chaos.

"Rydian!"

Keres.

I snapped my head toward the sound.

She stood halfway down the slope to my left, one arm bloody, daggers coated black with Obsidian ichor. A cluster of Withered held the line beside her, blades up, magic flickering. Behind them, a gap in the flames opened for the span of a breath, revealing movement just across the river at the camp's edge.

An explosion ripped through the tents.

A ball of orange flames swallowed a cluster of canvas, blooming up like a poisonous flower. The force of the explosion hit a moment later, a hot wind that knocked several soldiers to their knees. For an instant, I saw silhouettes framed in the fire—Slade dragging someone away,

Thorne's broad shoulders turning as he hurled a knife that glowed white-hot.

Then the smoke swallowed them.

My heart stuttered at what they'd managed to do. But it wouldn't matter if they didn't get themselves clear of the blast.

"Aurelia!" Keres' scream tore through the din, raw and furious. I couldn't see what she saw from this angle.

All I could see was a wall of furyfire, and I ran toward it.

Black flame curled up the slope, faster than it should have. It clung to the ground like liquid, licking at rock and frost alike. Furyfire, but unleashed now, not contained to Aurelia's will.

Spreading fast up the dry hillside. Straight toward Keres.

"Keres," I shouted, breaking into a run.

Her figure vanished in the wall of flame.

Heat slammed into me hard enough to throw me back. I hit the ground, rolled, threw my shadows up in a desperate shield. For a second, the fire hit the darkness and held there, pressing, testing.

Once, back in Grey Oak, Aurelia had used her dark flame on me. It had been such a small thing then, a kernel of what she had now. Back then, I'd withstood it easily. Now? It would consume me.

My power buckled.

I gritted my teeth, bearing down on my own strength as I shoved at it. If that wave reached the cave, everyone inside would burn. Withered. Lesha. Daegel.

I shoved my power forward, shadows stacking on shadows, a wall of smothering smoke against flame. The fire snarled back, hungry, ancient, as if it remembered its true master: a god of Hel itself. As if it remembered nothing in Menryth could stop it.

I poured everything I had into the shield, feeling my magic strain and tear at the edges. Shadows screamed as the furyfire clawed through them, burning away layers of dark, inch by inch.

"Rydian," someone called.

I didn't look. Couldn't look.

If I let go now, that wave would hit the mouth of the cave like a hammer.

Flame licked around the edges of my shield. My skin burned, the heat searing exposed flesh. My lungs felt like I was inhaling knives.

Still, the fire climbed.

My knees buckled. I dropped to one hand, gritting my teeth as the slope rolled under me. The river roared somewhere to my right—a dim, distant sound under the thunder of blood in my ears.

I thought, for a moment, that this might be it. The way I would die. Not on some glorious battlefield. Not on the day we vanquished Heliconia. Not protecting Aurelia from another's cutting blade. Just here, on a hillside, holding back the fire of the woman I loved long enough for her to live and fight without me.

I could make peace with that.

I started to let go.

A hand closed on my ankle.

I barely had time to register the grip—cold, strong, wet, like water given form—before the ground vanished beneath me.

The world turned sideways.

I slid down the slope, shadows ripping free of the furyfire as my concentration shattered. The furywave roared overhead, devouring the space where I'd been standing a heartbeat before.

Ice-cold liquid swallowed me.

The river's cold embrace gripped my bones as it sucked me below its surface.

I thrashed, instincts screaming as my body plunged into black water so cold it stole my breath. The current seized me, dragging me down, spinning me end over end. The roar and crackle of the fire vanished above, replaced by the dull rush of water against stone.

Hands pulled me down.

Not one. Several.

They gripped my arms, my shoulders, my coat, dragging me deeper, away from the burning sky. I caught a glimpse of pale faces—eyes that glowed faintly in the dark, hair streaming like riverweed, webbed fingers tight around my wrists.

Naiad.

I tried to speak, to beg, to demand they save Aurelia—but river water surged into my mouth, stealing the words. Stealing my breath. My life.

Cold carved its way into my bones. The last of my air tore free in a stream of bubbles that spiraled upward, toward the distant smear of gold that was the surface.

"Aurelia," I thought, as the dark closed in.

Then even thought was sucked away, and there was nothing left but water and hands and the relentless pull of Beneath.

THE
LOVERS

Chapter Thirty-Four
Aurelia

The world was burning, and I was the spark that had ignited it.

Fire roared up the hillside in a black-gold wave, devouring frost, tents, and soldiers alike. The air was so hot it scorched the breath from my lungs. My mark blazed at my throat, furyfire pouring out of me faster than thought.

At my back, Rydian had vanished into the smoke. Gone to deliver Lesha to safety. It had been the only option, but I'd never felt more alone without him beside me in this fight.

Frostwights appeared through the haze of smoke. More than I could count. Unlike the Obsidians, who still possessed mortal fae bodies, these undead monsters were unaffected by thick plumes of smoke that left the other soldiers coughing and doubling over.

The nearest Frostwight raised a blade of blue-white ice, and the cold coming off it was so sharp it made my teeth ache. Behind its bone mask, nothing breathed. Nothing blinked. Just that hollow, waiting hunger.

Hunger. Not unlike my own.

The Frostwight lunged.

I met it head-on.

Furyfire clawed down my arms, splitting into two streams that slammed into its chest. Heat exploded across its armor. Frost shrieked as it met my fire, ice turning to steam.

The creature staggered, but didn't fall.

I drank in what was left of its life force, draining it dry until it was only a husk of bones and ice.

My furyfire surged, stronger than ever.

Behind it, three more Frostwights advanced. Around them, Obsidian soldiers fanned out, black-eyed and eager, their blades gleaming dully in the smoke-choked dawn.

"Come on, then," I muttered, raising Dorcha. "Let's see what Hel's gifts are really worth."

I lunged.

Metal met ice. The impact jarred to my shoulder, but the blade bit into the seam between plates of bone. I twisted and felt something crack.

The Frostwight's free hand clamped around my wrist.

Cold rushed through me like an avalanche.

For a heartbeat, the world went soundless and white. My muscles locked; my breath froze in my chest. Frost crawled up my arm in delicate patterns, burning as it went.

My mark flared.

The rune at my throat blazed so hot it hurt. Something inside me—something deeper than furyfire, older than the Fates, older than this realm—stirred and bared its teeth.

Mine, a voice whispered.

The next breath I took ripped down my throat like I'd been drowning.

Power surged up from the mark, racing down my veins, crashing into the Frostwight's touch. For a second, the two magics tangled—Winter and Hel's own darkness, ice and fire—and then the connection flipped.

The cold stopped pouring into me.

I started pulling it out.

The thing convulsed. Its hand spasmed around my wrist, bones creaking. Frost smoke poured out of the seams in its armor, streaming toward me. The world sharpened, every color too bright, every heartbeat too loud. The roar of battle drew into piercing focus—the clash of steel, the crack of exploding tents, the distant boom of something Slade and Thorne had set off.

I drank in the Frostwight's life force like a drowning woman gulping air.

It didn't have a heartbeat. It didn't have blood flowing in its veins. Whatever magic had animated it was older and stranger than mortal flesh—a knot of foreign magic and bone-deep cold. It slashed at me, trying to break contact, but every second our skin touched, more of its life force ripped free.

Its armor dimmed. The ice in its blade cracked. The hollow behind the mask went thinner and thinner until the thing was just a cage of bone, its movements failing.

Then it wasn't anything at all.

I didn't stop with just one.

With my next inhale, the rest were consumed. Their life forces sucked down my throat and soaked into my veins. Magic soared, my vision going white as the realm itself breathed through me for a fleeting, uncontainable moment. In that space, I was nothing. I was everything. I was Menryth itself. Something More than the gods had intended. A kernel of Life itself.

When I blinked, reality resumed.

The smoke, the advancing army, the burning tents.

As one, the Frostwights crumpled, collapsing into blackened ice and splintered leather at my feet. Whatever Heliconia had bound inside them came pouring out in a last rush—a torrent of icy magic that streaked for my mark like it had always belonged there.

Then, the Obsidians fell with them.

Then their horses.

The sheer volume of what I took from them nearly broke me then.

I staggered.

Heat flooded me, wild and intoxicating. The ache in my sword-hand vanished. The bruises along my ribs smoothed out, pain receding as if it had only ever been a dream. Power crawled over my skin, beneath it, through it. I felt every heartbeat in the valley as my own. Every breath. Every life.

Makarios.

I could feel the war camp like it was an extension of my own body. The paths between the tents. The river curling along its edge, thin and dark and glinting in the light of burning canvas. The line of horses tied near the outer ring, their panic thrumming against my skin.

And the lives.

So many lives.

Thousands of them, bright and hot and sharp. Obsidian soldiers whose mortality still beat in their chests, even if their souls had been given a slow death. Scath wolves whose magic Heliconia had twisted until they bowed to her as their master. Frostwights stitched from stolen pieces of the dead. A handful of Autumn fae pressed into service, hearts beating too fast.

And my own people—Withered, Midnight, Lesha.

Distantly, another explosion shook the valley. A blossom of fire flared in the center of the camp.

Slade and Thorne.

The sound of it rolled up the slope. Some of the soldiers turned back to look. Some ran toward the chaos. I reached for my fire to rip a path straight through them. But my magic moved first. It flooded my limbs, reckless and wild.

"Aurelia," someone called.

It might have been Keres. It might have been the god who'd branded my throat.

Too late.

Fire tore out of me.

It wasn't the controlled arc I'd been throwing. It wasn't even the roaring wave I'd sent down the slope earlier. This was... everything. All at once. Furyfire and Makarios entwined, pouring through nerves and bones and out into the world like the cracking of a dam.

It flew down the hillside, an onyx tide edged in the white of consumed souls. It hit the nearest line of Frostwights and pulled their life from their bones even as it cooked their armor from the inside out. It slammed into the ranks of Obsidians behind them, ripping the magic from their veins and setting their bodies alight.

They screamed.

They fell.

The fire didn't stop.

It rushed down into the valley, catching the first row of tents like dry kindling. Canvas bloomed into flame, ropes snapped, poles fell. The heat spiraled upward, slamming into the shield spells netted over the camp. They crackled, tried to hold, then shattered like glass.

The river steamed.

The world below became a writhing mass of shadows and fire.

"Aurelia!" Keres shouted again, closer now. A gloved hand seized my arm. "You need to pull back—"

"I'm trying," I gasped.

I was. I tried to pull the fire back into myself, to shut it off, to dam it somehow. But the Makarios gift had tasted the army. It had tasted the sheer volume of life and death and magic packed into that valley, and it had decided it wanted more.

The more it took, the stronger I felt.

The stronger I felt, the easier it was to take more. To use more.

It became a vicious circle—fire feeding off power feeding off fire.

Below, figures ran like shadows over a burning map. Some tried to form ranks, shouting orders that vanished in the roar. Others broke and fled. Frostwights leaped through the chaos, trying to reach higher ground, only to buckle as their animating force drained into the inferno.

The life pouring into me turned everything sharp.

I barely needed the torches or the dawn. I could see in the dark through the eyes of a hundred dying soldiers. I could feel their panic. Smell their fear. Hear their pleading, whether or not they spoke it aloud.

Make it stop—

Spare me—

Forgive—

No.

My grip on my own mind slipped.

A flash of movement caught my eye—shadows straining against a wall of fire. Rydian, shoving every ounce of his power against my flames, fighting to get to me even though coming closer risked burning him alive.

"Stop," I whispered.

My fire didn't listen.

It surged higher, up the slope, licking at the rocks. The heat struck my face like a slap. Somewhere in that glare, I thought I saw Keres' silhouette vanish into the blaze.

Gods.

Rydian.

I tried again. This time, I didn't reach for the fire. I reached for the mark. For the source.

Hel's rune seared. A sound tore from my throat, half snarl, half scream. The influx of stolen power slammed against whatever limit was left in me.

Too much.

It was all too much.

The ground shifted under my boots. The air warped, thinner, crueler.

Something deep in the mountain groaned.

"Aurelia!" Slade's voice cut through the din from somewhere off to the right. "You're going to bring the whole gods-damned peak down—"

I turned. Or thought I did. My vision tunneled. The world narrowed to fire and gravel and the feeling of the realm itself shuddering around me.

A fissure cracked across the slope above the cave, splitting stone like dry bark. Ice that had crept into every crevice from Heliconia's arrival met the white-hot heat of my power. Water flashed to steam inside the rock.

The mountain exploded.

A thunderclap tore through the hillside. Boulders sheared free, tumbling down in an avalanche of stone and ice. The entrance to the cave disappeared behind a choking cloud of dust and debris.

My knees hit the ground.

The fire kept going, burning through the last of the enemy's camp. Then, like a candle snuffed by a giant's fingers, it went out.

THE
LOVERS

Chapter Thirty-Five

Aurelia

I surfaced to pain, a dull, heavy ache that seemed to weigh down every limb. My throat was raw, my lungs scraped clean. I might have been lying on snow or stone or the back of a Brindalorn; I couldn't tell.

Something cool brushed my forehead.

"Thank the gods," a familiar voice muttered. And then louder, "She's waking up." Murmured replies sounded, and then the voice added, "I was starting to think I'd have to haul your soul back myself. And I really don't want to go to Hel today."

I pried my eyes open.

Keres' scarred face hung over mine, pale in the torchlight. A thin thread of shadow still ran from her fingers into my chest where she worked her healing gifts on me. The ceiling above her was jagged rock, slick with condensation. I'd made it back to the cave.

"Did we win?" I croaked.

Keres' mouth twitched. "That's one word for it."

A face appeared over her shoulder. Slade's hair was singed, one eyebrow missing, soot smeared across his jaw. His smile was fuzzy with barely contained adrenaline.

"You scorched the entire fucking valley," he said cheerfully. "Took out half the army. Very dramatic. Ten out of ten for spectacle. Zero for self-preservation."

I tried to sit up. My body protested, every muscle trembling. Keres' hand shifted to my shoulder, pushing me back to the bedroll I was lying on.

"Slow down," she said. "You burned yourself out. Makarios or no, your body's still fae and very much mortal."

I didn't have the energy to argue, which likely proved her point. Already, exhaustion tugged at me, trying to pull me under, and I knew I wouldn't be able to resist it for long.

"Lesha?" I rasped.

"Alive," Slade said. "Barely."

My eyes went wide. Panic spiked.

"I'm already working on her," Keres assured me.

I looked around but didn't see anyone else.

"Daegel's with her farther in," Slade said. "We've set up as far from the collapse as we can without getting lost in this gods-cursed maze."

Lost? Where was Eirnan? Or the rest of the Withered?

"What... happened?" I asked.

Pieces returned in jagged flashes. The Frostwights. The surge of power. The valley burning like a sacrificial pyre.

"Your gifts happened," Keres said dryly. "You pulled enough life out of that camp to live for a thousand years. Then your Furyfire did the rest."

I swallowed hard. "The camp—"

"Gone," Slade said. "What's left is a scorch mark big enough to see from the moon."

I closed my eyes, seeing again the way the flames spread faster than I'd meant them to. The sound of screaming. The pull of all those lives ending, ripping through me like I was a conduit carved just for that purpose.

"What about our people?" I whispered.

Silence.

It stretched long enough that I forced my eyes open again.

Keres' jaw was tight. "Many made it into the tunnels," she said. "Some didn't. We're still counting."

"And Rydian?" The name tore itself from my throat before I could shape anything more neutral.

They traded a look.

Panic slammed into me, hard enough that I shoved at Keres' hand and lurched upright. The world reeled; my vision went black at the edges. Slade caught my elbow, bracing me.

"Aurelia," he said quietly. "Let us explain before you set something on fire in here too."

I grabbed his sleeve. "Where is he?"

Keres scrubbed a hand down her face, leaving a streak of soot on her cheek. "I was midway down the slope when your power went wild," she said. "I saw him at the ridge, holding back the worst of it so the cave entrance wouldn't burn."

I remembered the glimpse. Shadows stacked like walls against my fire. A figure silhouetted in the blaze.

"I tried to get to him," she went on. "Then the furyfire hit. You... you weren't you anymore. It was like the god behind your mark took over. The hillside went up. I lost sight of him. The next thing I saw, he was gone."

Gone.

The word hollowed my chest.

Slade shook his head quickly. "Not dead."

I latched onto that. "Then where—"

"The river," she said. "Something or someone pulled him under."

Naiad.

The realization hit with the force of a blow. I'd begged Naliadne to watch the river borders, to help us if she could. If she'd seen that fire...

"They took him Beneath," I whispered.

"Seems that way," Keres said. "Better than burning. But it means he's out of our reach. For now."

I sagged, the tension in my muscles turning from rigid to liquid. The cold cavern felt suddenly too small, the air too thin.

Alive. He was alive. Drowned or half-drowned or furious with me somewhere under the river, but alive.

The relief hurt almost as much as the fear.

"I need to go back," I said. "We have to get out, find another path down, reach the river—"

"You're not going anywhere," Keres snapped. "Besides, that entrance is gone."

Slade nodded grimly. "She's right. The rockfall buried it. We tried clearing some of it while you were unconscious. Every stone we moved brought more down. If we keep going, we'll bring the whole tunnel on our heads."

"You can shadow-walk," I insisted, looking at Slade.

"You're in no shape," Keres said sternly.

I started to argue, but Slade cut in. "Keres is right. We got lucky that Heliconia wasn't at that camp, or we never would have been able to escape with your friend. Or our lives. But the minute she finds out her camp's gone, she'll know who did it."

"And she'll figure out how we got in," Keres added grimly.

Slade nodded sadly. "The cave mouth will be the first place they look."

My chest tightened. "So we're trapped."

"No, we're taking the only way out we have now." Slade crouched beside me, resting his folded arms on his knees.

Back through the tunnels.

The idea of spending days and days in the dark was its own anguish.

Keres spoke, reading my distress. "Eirnan says there are other exits. We can take Lesha and whoever's left of the Withered and get them away from here before Heliconia regroups."

Eirnan.

The knot in my stomach twisted. "Is he...?"

"Alive," Keres said quietly. "But hurt. He won't be leading anyone on his own two feet anytime soon. He pushed too far, trying to get his people back here before the fire..."

The memory of the dissenters' faces flashed across my mind. Fear. Disgust. The way they'd called me demon-touched.

"Do they still want to follow me?" I asked.

Keres' mouth twisted. "Most saw the Obsidian camp burn and decided they don't care what gifts you carry so long as they're pointed in the right direction."

"And Brist?" I asked, rage burning hot in my gut.

"Dealt with," Keres said quietly.

"Taron too," Slade said. "A shame. If we'd had more time, I would have made it last. A quick death is more than they deserved."

"After their brothers' betrayal, I don't think the others will be eager to confront you again," Keres added.

That should have made me feel better.

It didn't.

"I lost control," I said slowly.

Slade tilted his head. "You unleashed the kind of power that levels armies. That tends to be messy."

I pressed a hand to my throat. The skin around the rune was tender, as if it had been burned from the inside out. "I didn't choose how far it went. Or who it took. I was... feeding, and the magic just kept pulling and pulling. If I hadn't burned out—"

"You'd have taken more," Keres finished. "Maybe all of it. Maybe us."

Her honesty cut—but I needed it.

"And this is why Rydian doesn't want you opening the gate just yet," Slade added. "Not because he thinks you're weak. Because he knows you're strong enough to break everything if you're not careful. Including yourself."

The thought of the Midnight gate—of that much power crashing up against the thing I'd just felt in the camp—made my stomach turn.

Whatever else I'd felt out there. The voice that had whispered through me, claiming all those lives, all that power, it wasn't my own. And it wasn't a part of my furyfire or my Makarios gifts. I wasn't sure I was ready to know what else had risen in me. A third gift, though it felt much heavier—like a curse. One I hadn't been able to control in the end.

Rydian had been right about me.

I dragged in a breath, forcing my pulse to slow.

"All right," I said. "We'll find our way back through the tunnels. And get Lesha and Eirnan somewhere they can recover."

Slade nodded once, relief flickering in his eyes like he'd been bracing for me to say something far more reckless. "Music to my ears, Princess."

Keres pushed to her feet, flexing stiff fingers. Shadows flickered faintly around them, thin as smoke. "I'm going to check Eirnan's bandages before we move. He'll want to speak to you before we go deeper."

When she went to tend the others, Slade stayed, watching me with that annoying, perceptive gaze that meant he knew too much and said too little.

"You should hate me," I said quietly.

He blinked. "For what?"

"For burning half a valley. For almost destroying our only way out. For…" My chest tightened. "For maybe getting your prince killed."

Slade shrugged. "To be fair, he made that a group effort. And you didn't kill him. Your friendship with the naiad saved him." He paused. "Also, Aurelia? You just crippled Heliconia's army. That's the kind of thing bards are going to sing about for centuries, assuming there's any courts left to sing in."

"It still doesn't free my court," I said. "Or stop her."

"One battle was never going to fix any of this," he said. "Or one girl. Even if she happens to fight like a demon-god's daughter." His mouth quirked. "This?" He gestured to the cave, to us. "This was a start."

A start that had nearly ended us.

But he was right about one thing—we had hurt Heliconia. Badly. She'd poured power and soldiers and Scath wolves and whatever abomination the Frostwights were into that camp, confident no one would dare strike it.

And I had.

Me. The girl she'd cursed. The princess she'd tried hard to keep sleeping forever. Let her feel that when she looked at the ashes. Let her know it was me who burned it all to the ground.

THE
LOVERS

Chapter Thirty-Six
Aurelia

I woke in a different place but on the same bedroll, the cave lit by a torch. Exhaustion still clung to every part of me, but I forced myself to sit up. A cask of water sat nearby. I drank deeply, noting the cavern where I slept had a lower ceiling than before. The air was humid, stale, unmoving.

Farther down the narrow tunnel, more torches flickered. I could hear voices murmuring quietly. The only other bedroll beside mine was empty.

Shoving aside the temptation to sleep again, I pushed to my feet.

My legs shook, but they held. Slowly, I made my way down the tunnel, my head nearly brushing the ceiling above me. Around the bend, the path opened, widening into a rough chamber where the others had gathered.

Faint torchlight illuminated the faces of the survivors.

Withered, hollow-eyed but alive. There were far fewer now than we'd brought with us. A dozen at most. They regarded me warily but without the hostility of Brist and Taron. Eirnan was seated against the wall, one leg splinted, cloak torn and blood-streaked, gaze steady and watchful. Beyond him, on a pallet of cloaks, Lesha lay motionless, wings nothing but blood-stiff bandages. Keres bent over her, tending her wounds, and my heart squeezed at the sight of them all.

My people. My responsibility. My war.

I stepped toward them, pressing a hand to the rock for balance.

"Your Highness," Eirnan greeted. "It's good to see you up and about."

Leif appeared, taking my elbow and offering support. I leaned on him gratefully and let him lead me over to where Keres hovered over Lesha.

"What are you doing up?" Keres demanded.

"How long was I out?" I asked.

No one answered.

I glared at Keres. "How long?"

"Two days, Your Highness," Leif answered quietly.

Two days.

I tried not to think of everything that might have happened in the world during those two precious days. Instead, I looked down at Lesha. Her chest barely moved with her small breaths.

Fear twisted inside me.

"How is she?" I whispered.

"She's weak," Keres admitted. "Hasn't woken for more than a few minutes at a time. Thorne and Daegel have taken turns carrying her."

I looked over at where the two warriors stood watching us. "Thank you," I told them. They dipped their chins. I looked back at Keres. "Will she recover?"

"I don't know," Keres admitted quietly. "There are broken bones and wounds that healed over, only to be inflicted again."

Torture.

"But the loss of her wings is the most concerning," Keres went on.

I swallowed, eyeing the bandages. "They cut them off."

"They ripped them. Slowly, piece by piece. For maximum suffering, I think."

Eirnan loosed a string of curses.

"To what end?" I asked bleakly. "Did she have information they wanted?"

"They must have thought so," Keres said, and I knew the look she wore could only mean one thing.

"Me," I said grimly. "They wanted information about me. My whereabouts. My plans."

"Your magic," Eirnan said pointedly.

I swallowed, a weight pressing down on me at the thought of Lesha enduring such a horrific nightmare because of me.

"Then they were disappointed," Slade said. "You hardly have any plans at all."

I shot him a flat look.

He held up both hands. "I mean that in the nicest, 'you keep improvising and almost dying' sort of way."

A faint sound came from the pallet.

It was small. Broken. But it was a sound.

I bent closer. "Lesha?"

Her eyes opened, clouded and unfocused at first, then clearing as they found my face. For a heartbeat, she just stared at me, like she wasn't sure I was real. Finally, her cracked lips curved.

"You... look terrible," she whispered.

Relief hit so hard my vision blurred. I huffed out a laugh that sounded suspiciously close to a sob. "You're one to talk."

Her gaze drifted past my shoulder, taking in the cave, the others, the dim torchlight. Confusion creased her brow. "Am I...?"

"Safe," I said quickly. "You're with us. We got you out."

"Took you long enough," she murmured, but even that hint of her old spark was a ghost of what it had been.

Keres slipped a hand under Lesha's shoulders, easing her up enough to sip from a waterskin. "Small sips," she warned.

Lesha obeyed. Every swallow looked like it cost her just as much as it gave.

I waited until she slumped back against the makeshift pillow, eyes half-lidded, then said quietly, "I'm sorry."

"For what?" she managed.

"For not getting to you sooner," I said. "For not being there. For... this." I glanced at the bandages. My throat tightened. "They hurt you because of me."

"Nonsense," she rasped. "They hurt me because Heliconia is a monster."

Her gaze sharpened slightly. Her fingers twitched toward mine. I took her hand, careful not to grip too hard. Her fingernails were broken, peeled down to the beds on some fingers. I hated imagining that happening to her. The pain—

"Aurelia," she whispered. "There isn't much time."

Panic sparked. "You're not dying," I said. "Keres says—"

"I'm not dying," Lesha cut in, a shadow of her usual impatience. "But I'm drained—utterly and maybe in a way that cannot be repaired."

"Don't say that—"

"Hush now. I need to get this out before I'm too tired for it." She swallowed. Her eyes found mine, and in them I saw the weight she carried—the knowledge she'd held alone all this time. "Heliconia nearly died when she cast that curse on our people seven years ago. The drain on her power nearly ended her then and there. What she took from your father was not enough to sustain her. But she found something else to take from. To revive herself. To build this army."

"What?" I asked, even though the word whispered through me already.

"The Ice Throne," Lesha said, "contained the power of the gods, left behind in this realm when they were cast out of it after the Great War. Heliconia found out. And she drained it."

Lesha squeezed my hand, desperation and urgency swimming in her murky gaze. "She cannot be allowed to claim another throne. Do you understand?"

"Because of the power in them," I said. "The oracle hinted in Rosewood, but she was vague."

"You saw Meerdra," Lesha said, and there was relief in her.

I decided not to mention that I'd granted the old Verdant fae a favor. Marked myself to seal the bargain. Instead, I merely nodded and said, "She told me about my gifts. Said I was the gods' champion, that I am to fight for Menryth."

"Heliconia has made herself a champion now too. A contender for ruler of Menryth—a fate that will be sealed if she drinks from the other thrones."

"What's inside them?" I asked.

"Kernels of the gods' power," Lesha said softly. "The pieces of themselves the gods left behind when they agreed to the treaty between them."

"The treaty my parents broke," I said quietly.

"Yes. And the balance must be righted, or we will all be destroyed."

The cavern went still. Even Slade didn't have a quip for that.

"She wants the others," I said slowly. "Not just Concordia. All six."

"Five," Eirnan corrected. "The Verdant court has no throne anymore. If the legends are to be believed."

"Yes, but the Summer Court has two." The two Whitestone thrones at Sevanwinds. The Harvest Throne in Grey Oak. The Onyx Throne behind the walls of Midnight. The Coral Throne Beneath the Osphanis. The Ivy Throne in Lightshore. "Each one a piece of what the gods left behind."

"And if she gets them all," Lesha whispered, "she won't need armies anymore. She'll be something else. Something the realm can't survive."

Lesha was right. She'd be a god herself.

My thoughts flew, unbidden, to Callan.

To the way his eyes had gone distant and wary when he'd mentioned Heliconia wanting a seat beside him on his. Wanting legitimacy. Wanting access. But mostly, wanting his throne for herself.

My fingers curled into the rough fabric of Lesha's pallet. "Callan was right; the Harvest Throne really is her next target."

"She'll kill him the moment he gives her what she wants," Keres said. "Or even if he doesn't."

"Not without an army," Slade pointed out.

"She won't need them," I said, the shape of Heliconia's plan snapping into place with cold clarity. "She'll marry him. Or pretend to. Get close. Get onto that throne. And drain it from the inside out before anyone realizes what she's done."

"With Concordia's stolen power backing her," Slade said. "Clever bitch."

Lesha's fingers tightened weakly around mine. "You can't let her sit on another throne, Auri. Not Autumn. Not any of them. The more she takes, the harder it will be to stop her. If you wait... there will be nothing left for you to save."

Her words landed like stones in my gut. The weight of it all... not just my court's curse. Not just my parents' bargain. The whole realm. The thrones. The magic that held all of Menryth together. It was all hanging in the balance now.

"I thought all I needed was an army," I whispered. "To break my curse. To face her on a battlefield and win." I shook my head. "But armies won't be enough, will they?"

"You'll need the thrones," Lesha said. "Or at least, you'll need to keep them out of her hands. Meerdra told you that, didn't she?"

"She gave me riddles and headaches," I muttered. Then softer, "She warned me. I just didn't understand how bad it could be."

Lesha's gaze met mine, soft and clear. "I have missed you."

"I'm sorry," I whispered, tears burning my eyes. "I'm here now."

Her eyes drifted shut, her breaths going shallow again. Panic flared in my chest.

"Rest," Keres murmured, gently easing Lesha's hand from mine to tuck the blankets higher. "She's done more than enough for one day."

I sat there a moment longer, watching the rise and fall of Lesha's chest.

Callan's face flashed across my thoughts again. His fear. His arrogance. The way he'd said he didn't want to be his father—and how easy it would be for Heliconia to make him into something worse than Duron ever was.

If she claimed his throne, Autumn would fall. And with it, every fragile hope we had of stopping her before she came for the rest.

I pushed to my feet.

The cave swayed then steadied as I fought off my own lingering exhaustion. Leif's hand hovered near my elbow as if he wasn't entirely sure I wouldn't topple over.

I looked at Eirnan.

He watched me like he already knew what I was going to say.

"How long," I asked hoarsely, "until we reach Autumn?"

THE
LOVERS

Chapter Thirty-Seven
Rydian

I woke to the sound of leaves rustling softly. Not dripping water, not the roar of a river or the crackle of fire in a stateroom inside Patamoi's castle Beneath—just the soft, constant hush of wind threading through branches. For a second, my half-conscious mind insisted it was some new form of drowning, the world reduced to one endless, rushing.

Then I realized I was breathing.

Air, not water.

I dragged in another lungful, greedy and sharp. It tasted like earth and sap and sunlight. My chest hurt with the stretch of it, ribs bruised but intact.

I opened my eyes.

A tent roof hung above me, canvas dyed a deep, moss-green. Light bled through it in shifting patterns, as if the whole thing was tucked under a canopy of leaves. The air was warmer here than it had any right to be after what I remembered last—the frozen valley burning, furyfire rolling uphill, the river's black mouth opening under my feet.

I was on my back on a narrow cot, boots off, armor gone, stripped to a plain linen shirt and trousers. Flexing my fingers, I patted my body, seeking the familiar weight of swords, daggers, anything.

Nothing.

Panic flared.

I shoved myself upright.

The world tilted sharply. My head spun. My stomach roiled. I braced my elbows on my knees and stayed very, very still until everything stopped pitching like a ship in a storm.

"I was beginning to wonder if you were intending to sleep until winter ended. Which, granted, would be a statement in itself, given current politics."

I looked up.

Talthis Knuhina stood just inside the tent flap, holding it open with one olive-skinned hand. Sun-dappled forest framed him—towering trunks, sprays of emerald leaves, shafts of light spearing through the canopy.

He wore Lightshore green, but not the formal silks he'd shown off at Aurelia's almost-wedding when I'd last seen him. We hadn't spoken that night, but I wondered if he realized I'd seen right through the ridiculous glamour he'd worn to disguise himself. A shifter indeed. His clothes had been far too soft and expensive for anyone to believe it. Least of all my shadows.

This was a soldier's traveling gear. Dark leathers softened with wear, a light breastplate of overlapping bronze leaves. A cloak the color of new moss hung from his broad, lean shoulders. His eyes were the same as before, though—bright, calculating, amused at everything and everyone, including himself.

"Talthis," I said, voice rough.

"Rydian, you old, crusty shadow. Good to see you up and breathing."

"What are you doing here?" I grunted.

"The real question is, what are *you* doing here, my friend?"

"Feel free to answer either one."

His gaze swept over me, quick and assessing. "How do you feel?"

"Like I lost a fight with the river and then got trampled by a pack of Obsidian horses," I said. "Where am I?"

"A very long way from where you nearly died," another voice answered.

Princess Naliadne slipped past Talthis into the tent, her bare feet silent on the packed earth floor. Her dark blue hair hung in wet ropes down her back, dripping onto a simple shift the color of riverstone. Her skin still held the faint, pearly sheen of the river's magic, eyes a shade too bright to belong to anything wholly mortal. Or wholly fae.

The naiad had dragged me under. Apparently, they'd decided not to keep me.

"You brought me here," I said.

"Beneath didn't suit you," she said, glancing at my body currently wrapped in a thin blanket. "Too much shadow. Not enough scales." She looked at Talthis, a playful grin on her lips. "Besides, Talthis made me an offer I couldn't refuse."

I looked between them, trying to figure them out. "I hadn't realized you two were... friends."

"It's more of a partnership," Talthis said.

Nali's gaze glittered at that, and I decided not to ask for details of this so-called partnership. Instead, I tried to piece together what led me here.

I remembered hands on my ankles, my wrists. A pale face underwater, blue hair fanning around it like ink, eyes luminous in the dark. A pressure against my mouth that had tasted like cold lightning and let me breathe where no one should.

Then nothing.

"How long?" I asked. "How long since you pulled me under?"

Talthis and Naliadne exchanged a look.

"Two days," Talthis said.

My heart lurched. "Two—"

"Your lungs were full of smoke," Naliadne said. "Your skin was half-cooked. Your shadows were... tangled." She tilted her head. "You should be grateful you woke at all."

I wasn't feeling particularly grateful. Not with the image that slammed into me next: Aurelia on that hillside, surrounded by Frost-wights and Obsidians. Her mark blazing. Power pouring out of her like a god had taken her over.

"What happened?" I demanded. "Aurelia—"

"Is alive," Naliadne said before the panic could finish carving its way through me. "My scouts saw her reach the caves. Your friends dragged her into the mountain before the fire could eat her as well."

Some of the tightness in my chest eased. Not much. Enough.

"Then we need to go," I said. "If they're in the tunnels—"

Talthis made a quiet sound, somewhere between a sigh and a laugh. "You're in the Emerald Forest, Prince, smack in the center of Menryth. Four days' ride from the Concordian border if your horse doesn't break a leg in the foothills. And that's if you had the strength to remain in the saddle—or a horse, which you don't."

I stared at him. Then at the tent walls. Then at the trees beyond his shoulder. "The river dragged me this far?"

"It might have dragged you much farther," Nali said pointedly. "And deeper had my father gotten wind of your presence. Instead, I remembered my partnership with Talthis. One where I deliver messages regarding various news of the realm." Her mouth curved faintly. "Consider yourself one of those messages."

I studied Talthis with more wariness. "And what are you doing on this side of the realm?"

"Certain developments of late have required me to maintain a post closer to our allies."

I eyed him, remembering the adamant claims Autumn's emissaries had returned with from every trip. "I thought you had no allies."

His smile sharpened. "We have no allies in Autumn," he corrected.

I shook my head. "You were always a smug bastard."

"In this case, it's earned. Lightshore has more eyes in Menryth than most assume. Some of them have legs."

"And some of them have fins," Naliadne added with a wink.

"You've been using the naiad as spies. Patamoi agreed to this?"

"This has nothing to do with my father," Nali said quietly. "But I won't sit by while my friends are at war."

I shook my head. Patamoi would lose his mind if he found out. The river god did not enjoy being circumvented.

"Talthis has been meeting with us for years," she said. "He brings us word from Spring. We bring him news from the rivers. Between us, we've been trying to slow the bleeding while your kings bicker and your queens plan weddings."

My jaw clenched.

"And now?" I asked, glaring at the Spring fae male. "Do you plan to remain on the sidelines, observing like this is all some sort of game for your entertainment? Or do you plan to fight?"

"That depends on your savior," Talthis said.

"Do not mock Aurelia, or you might find yourself at the pointed end of her wrath. And mine."

His gaze sharpened on my face. "You're sure she's the one, then."

"She's the Chosen One," I said.

"That's prophecy." He waved it aside. "I'm asking if she's the leader you thought she'd be. Before you drove yourself half to death, trying to keep her alive."

Images slammed through me: Aurelia in the garden with Duron, scorching him to ash with a flick of her hand. The way she'd sent me to deliver the Aine to safety—like all that mattered was the one life against her own. The hillside below Nygard, burning with her furyfire, her control gone. Her power unstoppable.

"She is," I said quietly. "And she's more dangerous than any of us realized."

Talthis studied me for a long moment, then nodded once. "Good. That's what I told my queen."

"You spoke to her of what happened at the war camp?" I asked.

"I told her what Nali's scouts reported."

"Which is?"

"Half the army in that camp—scorched to ash."

I blinked. Half? Aurelia had destroyed more than two thousand Obsidians. It was...too vast a number to go unnoticed. And when Heliconia found out, she would rain fury down on us all.

"And what does your queen intend to do about it?" I asked. "To keep dithering while the rest of us bleed?"

He didn't bristle. I'd give him that.

"My queen said that, if the Chosen One could strike Heliconia's army and live, Lightshore would consider offering aid."

My hands curled into fists. "So she sat in her gilded tree while the rest of us fought and bled."

"Kings and queens have been doing that since we learned to put crowns on heads," Talthis said. There was no heat in it. Just bitter humor. "You should be familiar with the pattern by now."

I thought of Duron.

Point taken.

Still, the thought of some Spring council weighing Aurelia's life like a gamble on a board made something ugly twist in my gut.

I looked at Nali. "Do you know where she's headed?"

"They remain on a return through the caves," she said. "When they emerge, our scouts will know their direction."

I rubbed my hands over my face, fingers scraping over stubble. "How long until I can at least hold a sword without my arms shaking?"

Talthis glanced at the light filtering through the tent flap. "Give it a couple of days," he said.

Silence settled between us, threaded with the distant murmur of the forest outside. Birds called somewhere high in the canopy. A breeze shifted the tent walls, carrying the cool, green smell of the Emerald Forest inside.

"Fine," I said. "I'll stay. I'll wait for word." I pointed a finger at Talthis. "But I want to know everything your scouts report. The minute they emerge from those caves, I want her location."

"Done," Talthis said easily.

"What do you want in return?" I asked warily. With Talthis, there was always a favor traded.

"We are, in fact, short on soldiers who have actually seen Heliconia's army up close. Consider yourself conscripted."

Naliadne grinned. "Careful, Prince, he's already the general of the Chosen One's army.

"How do you know that?" I asked.

She winked. "A good spy doesn't reveal her secrets."

I glared.

"Rest now," she said. "I'll send word to your aunt that you're awake."

"She's here?"

Naliadne softened. "She is on an errand for my father and not permitted to travel with me. But I will get her a message. It will please her to know you are well."

"Thanks," I told her.

When they were gone, I slumped back against the pillow. Aurelia was alive. Trapped once again in those blasted caves. But alive.

I was useless for the moment—but not for long.

Heliconia had lost half her camp.

And somewhere in Lightshore, a queen was weighing lives and deciding whether to risk hers to save theirs.

I stared at the tent roof until it blurred.

THE
LOVERS

Chapter Thirty-Eight
Callan

The palace had never felt so small. Not when I was a boy hiding from my father's rages. Not when I was a young prince expected to smile at foreign dignitaries while my father threatened their emissaries behind closed doors. Not even seven years ago, when Aurelia had broken our engagement and I'd returned home without a bride or the promise of another kingdom to rule over. But today? Today, the marble halls of Grey Oak felt like a coffin built expressly for me.

I stood at the balcony overlooking the courtyard as soldiers—*her* soldiers—marched beneath me in orderly rows. Obsidian helmets glinted like beetle shells in the thin autumn light.

The air smelled faintly of frost.

In the palace garden, decorations for the celebration were underway despite Heliconia not setting a date yet. White roses in full bloom. Ice sculptures in the shape of Aqras and other mystical creatures. The obsidian stonework was a lovely touch. Really warmed the soul. I gripped the railing until my knuckles bleached white, trying not to think about what would come after I spoke my vows. If I'd even live long enough to attend the party in the garden or if I'd already be dead then.

Farther out near the stables, a few Autumn soldiers caught my eye. They steered clear of the Obsidians, huddling with one another as if there would be any strength in numbers. A couple of them stole glances up at me, their faces pale with fear. I forced a smile. Lifted a hand in a small, confident wave. The Autumn king, unbothered, unconcerned, unshaken.

Inside, I was shaking hard enough to rattle bones.

"You should not be out in the open," Lemuel said sharply behind me. "Any one of her soldiers could decide to make themselves king with a single arrow."

"Ah, Lemuel," I sighed. "Must you always ruin a perfectly good panic attack?"

He stepped beside me, arms folded. His robe sleeves frayed where he'd tugged them raw over the years. "I ruin nothing. You stand in full view where a single shot could end both your rule and your life."

"That's the point," I said lightly. "If they see me, they assume I am powerful enough to be unconcerned with the risk."

He paused, looking visibly shaken at my words. "And are you?"

"Unconcerned with risk?" I flashed him a grin. "Always."

His lips compressed into a thin line. "You played a dangerous game with her yesterday."

Played. Past tense. As if the game had ended. Heliconia likely thought it had. Likely thought she'd won.

Lemuel lowered his voice. "Majesty, the real throne cannot stay hidden indefinitely. If she discovers where you moved it—"

"She won't."

"I hope you're right," Lemuel said. "There are a lot of lives counting on you."

"Maybe they shouldn't," I said. Lemuel's brow went up. "The Autumn fae counted on my father, and look where it got them. Drained and halfway to the Afterlife."

"Your father made many mistakes," Lemuel said. "I hope you do not repeat them."

"My dear Lemuel," I murmured, "my father would never have survived the day Heliconia walked into his hall."

"Survival is not victory."

I opened my mouth, some witty retort half-formed—when the temperature dropped. A suffocating chill slid around my throat like a gloved hand. The air turned brittle, crystalline. Frost spidered along the marble railing beneath my fingers.

She was here.

I didn't turn. I did not give her the satisfaction. "Your Majesty," I called over my shoulder. "Isn't it bad luck for me to see the bride before the wedding?"

Heliconia's voice drifted from behind us, smooth and deadly as a drawn blade. "I'd wager your luck has run out, whether you look at me or not."

I turned then.

Her gown today was a sheet of winter—white, silver, and crystalline layers that rippled like snowdrifts. Her hair fell like a spill of ink against all that white. Her eyes were pale and sharp, glinting like frost-rimmed glass.

She looked... amused.

Which was probably not quite as bad as if she were angry, but it felt dangerously close.

"You look radiant," I said, sweeping an exaggerated bow. "Frostbite truly brings out the glow in your complexion."

Her lips curved faintly, but her words dripped with acid. "Charming until the end."

Lemuel stepped between us. "Your Majesty, might I remind you—"

Magic struck Lemuel, knocking him clean off his feet. His knees hit the marble with a sound that made me flinch. Frost rimmed the stone beneath him, spreading like veins, creeping toward his body.

"No!" I called. "Heliconia—"

She lifted one pale hand, stopping me mid-step with a ripple of cold. "He forgets his place."

"He was only—"

"Afraid," she finished. "And rightfully so."

Lemuel struggled to sit up, breath frosting into the air. "Your Majesty," he rasped to me, not her. "Do not—bend."

Heliconia's gaze sharpened. "Bend?"

She drifted forward. Like mist over ice.

"How about *break*?" she purred.

Lemuel scrambled backward until his spine hit the stone pillar. But the ice reached him. Touched his hand. Raced up his arm.

His scream was thin and small.

I lurched forward. "He's harmless."

"On the contrary." Her voice was almost kind. "Loyal men are always the most dangerous. They make kings believe they have something worth fighting for."

She held out her palm and blew. A puff of icy air shot straight into his face.

The frost took him instantly.

A single, awful crunch as his entire body froze.

Then silence.

My breath hitched. Something in me twisted.

Heliconia stepped over his frozen body like it was a stray log in her path. She touched my cheek. Her fingers were so cold they burned. "You look pale, Callan. I do hope you find some color before our big day."

"And what day is that? I have an opening in my schedule a week from tomorrow—"

"Sunset tomorrow," she said, tone sharpening. "You will stand beside me as we are bound before your people. And then I will be crowned and set upon the Harvest Throne."

"Tomorrow?" I repeated, incredulous. "Bit rushed, isn't it?"

"We do not have the luxury of time," she said coldly.

"What could possibly—"

"That little bitch thinks she can burn my soldiers and get away with it," she said darkly. "But I will show her just what her little trick will cost her in the end."

The blood drained from my face.

Aurelia.

She'd managed to get into the camp. Maybe even rescue her Aine friend. And now Heliconia would take out her wrath against my people.

I bowed, masking the tightening in my chest. "As you wish."

She studied me, her expression unreadable. "Remember this, Callan. When you stand beside me tomorrow, your realm survives.

Resist me…" Her gaze drifted to Lemuel's frozen body. "…and Autumn will fall before the moon has set on its lands."

Then she left.

A sweep of ice in her wake, a cold so deep the candles guttered.

When the doors shut behind her, I stood there, unmoving. Lemuel's cracked, iced-over face stared up at me from the marble. I swallowed the bile rising in my throat.

"You idiot," I whispered. "You should have kept your mouth shut."

But grief crept in anyway. Grief and guilt. He'd died trying to save me.

I crouched beside him. Reached out. My fingers hovered above the frost but didn't touch.

"Thank you," I whispered.

Then I stood. Steadied myself. Straightened my coat.

And walked away.

I didn't stop until I reached the hidden door in the back of the hall. Down the spiraling stairs. Into the cold, stale depths beneath the castle.

My footsteps echoed as I approached the small chamber.

And there it sat. The true Harvest Throne. Alive with power. Pulse slow and steady under the veined gold. I sat and rested my palm against its armrest. Warmth thrummed beneath my skin.

"Tell me how to stop her," I whispered. "Tell me how to save my people. Tell me how to be different than him."

A faint pulse answered.

Soft.

Warm.

Steady.

Not a promise. A reminder. *You already chose differently.*

I closed my eyes.

"I know," I breathed. "Now tell me what choice I make next."

No answer.

Because that was the cruelest truth of all. The throne could not rule for me. My father's crown could not protect me. Heliconia would not spare me. And Aurelia—the one person who might have stood with me—was gone.

Above, the palace groaned under the tightening grip of winter. And far north, the smoke of my own scorched army still curled into the sky.

THE
LOVERS

Chapter Thirty-Nine
Rydian

I lay on the cot Talthis's people had given me, staring at the roof of the tent while the sounds of the Lightshore camp slowly thinned. At first: low-voiced conversations, the clink of armor, someone laughing too loudly. Then: the occasional cough, the rustle of bedrolls. Eventually, only night remained—crickets, the distant rush of the river, the whisper of leaves.

My body was exhausted, but my mind refused to quiet.

Every time I closed my eyes, I saw the endless cascade of furyfire.

A valley turned to ash. Frostwights crumpling. Obsidians screaming. Aurelia, standing alone on that slope, her mark blazing like a dark star while the world burned around her.

And then nothing.

Smoke. River. Hands dragging me down.

I gritted my teeth against the fragmented memories. Nali and her people had saved my life. They'd done what Aurelia had asked and provided a safe retreat. Problem was, they'd also ripped me away from her.

I dragged a hand down my face and pushed up to sit. The tent Talthis had loaned me was large enough to stand in, but not by much. A single lantern swung from one of the center poles, its light turned down to a faint glow. My boots sat neatly beside the cot, cleaned and dried again by some Spring fae soldier with more patience than I had.

My sword leaned against the far wall.

The mark on my ribs burned.

A dark, angular rune inked into my skin years ago. The one that tied me to a vow I couldn't stop thinking about these last few weeks. One that was made of the same magic as Aurelia's. Gifted from the same dark god.

I promised him I'd die for her.

I'd meant it when I'd said the words all those years ago. I still meant them now.

What I hadn't anticipated was what it would feel like to love Aurelia and know every day brought me closer to the moment I'd lose her forever.

For all I knew, that moment could be happening right now. What if I wasn't there when she needed me? What if she burned herself out, alone in those mountains, while I lay in a pretty tent in the Emerald Forest, drinking spring wine and waiting for news?

I slid my boots on and rolled my shoulders, testing the stiffness in my muscles. The naiad's touch still lingered, a cold deep in my bones.

I buckled on my sword and turned the flame down on the lantern until it was nothing more than an ember. Then I loosened the tent flap and listened.

Silence.

Good.

I slipped out into the night.

The camp was a spill of low tents tucked beneath massive trees with a canopy that glowed faintly with filtered starlight. Ancient magic hummed in the roots and branches, a gentle, living thrum that made even the shadows feel softer than they should have. It was a comfort, knowing the magic of the Emerald Forest had not begun to fade as the rest of Sevanwinds had. Not yet at least.

At the perimeter, sentries stood, spears in hand. I recognized one or two from earlier—scouts who'd stared at me like they were still deciding whether I could be trusted.

Better they kept thinking about it.

I let my shadows loosen.

They slid from my feet like spilled ink, pooling across the ground, then crept outward. Not enough to be visible as anything but a deep patch of darkness. Enough to bend the edges of sight, nudging gazes away from where I moved.

They'd grown stronger these last weeks. Since I'd found Aurelia again. The way I'd used them to slide through those Obsidians' throats at the war camp; that had been new for me. Slade's shadow-walking, too, had grown stronger. He'd never carried anyone with him such a distance before. I wondered if he'd noticed the way his own gifts expanded in her presence. If Ire had done that or if it was something our own bond had brought.

One of the sentries glanced in my direction, blinked, and turned away.

Good.

I stole along the camp's edge, breath slow, steps careful. In another life, I might have slipped out of camp like this to meet some lover in the trees.

Now, I was going to pick a fight with a god.

The forest thickened as I left the last of the tents behind. Emerald leaves arched overhead, drinking in what moonlight it could find among the clouds. Moss muffled my footsteps. Somewhere in the distance, an owl called.

I walked until I'd left all trace of the camp behind. Where the trees grew older, wilder. Here, the air felt less curated. Less safe. A thin ribbon of the Osphanis whispered somewhere farther off. Hopefully, far enough to avoid its listening ears.

When I was sure I was out of range of the patrols, I stopped in a small clearing where the canopy opened just enough to show a slice of overcast sky.

I drew my sword.

Darkness rushed in, choking out the starlight.

For a long moment, I stood perfectly still, listening to my own pulse. The mark on my ribcage thrummed in time with it, hot and insistent. As if the god who'd imbued it already knew what I intended.

"Fine," I muttered. "Let's do this, then."

I unbuttoned my shirt and shoved the fabric aside, exposing the black-inked rune carved into my skin. The lines were sharp even after all these years, looping around my ribs like a brand. At the center of it, a small, circular knot of ink.

I pressed my thumb there.

Heat flared. The rest of the rune answered, coming alive under my skin like a nest of serpents stirring.

I turned the tip of my blade inward, and without giving myself time to think, I sliced the tip across the knot of ink.

Pain lanced, sharp and immediate.

Blood welled, dark in the night.

I pressed my palm to the cut, smearing my own blood across the rune. "Ire," I said, voice low but steady. "Get down here."

The forest held its breath.

Wind shifted, carrying the faint scent of brimstone and storm.

Shadows thickened around the edges of the clearing, pooling at the bases of trees, creeping inward. My own shadows twitched warily.

Then the night... bent.

A figure stepped out of nothing.

The youngest king of Hel looked exactly as he had the last time I saw him—tall, lean, dark hair falling in careless waves, eyes hard as iron. He wore no crown, no armor. Just a long, dark coat lined with starlight.

"Most mortals offer prayers," he said by way of greeting. "Or at least address me with more respect than my first name."

"Most mortals are afraid of you."

"And you're not?"

"I carry your mark on my body. I would think that makes us well enough acquainted for first names."

His mouth curved, not quite a smile. "Fair point." His gaze swept the clearing, then returned to me. "Traveling alone rather than at my daughter's side. You're far from your post, Shadow Prince. Lose your way?"

"You know exactly how we were separated."

"You say that as if I had some hand in it."

"You say it as if you don't have your hand in everything that happens in Menryth."

His expression hardened.

I sheathed my sword with deliberate calm. I wouldn't need it. If he wanted me dead, steel wouldn't make a difference.

He watched the motion, one brow lifting slightly. "You know what calling me like this costs."

"Usually," I said. "This time, I'm trying something different."

"Ah." He folded his arms, eyes gleaming. "You've come to bargain."

"I've come to break a bargain," I corrected.

Ire's attention sharpened. "Go on."

"The vow," I said. "The one I made to you. To die in her place when the Fates come to collect."

He nodded slowly. "I recall."

"I want it undone."

He tilted his head, studying me with the intense curiosity of a predator puzzling over an interesting new prey. "Regretting your heroics? I did not take you for a coward, Rydian Nytherra."

I met his gaze, biting back my own temper. Cursing a god would get me nowhere. Besides, he was already cursed to Hel. "I am only regretting that I might not be there when she needs me most. All because I thought martyrdom was the only way to save us all."

A flicker of something—amusement, maybe—passed through his eyes. "The boy grows into a man."

"Don't patronize me," I said evenly. "I knew what I was offering. I still do. But I swore that oath when Aurelia was an idea more than a person. A prophecy. A symbol." I stepped closer, ignoring the way the air around him felt thinner, hotter. "Now, I've bled beside her. Watched her wake up, cursed and alone, and still choose to fight. She doesn't deserve any more loss than she's already endured. We can find another way."

Ire watched me like he was reading every thought I tried not to show.

"You care for her."

I didn't flinch away. "Enough to do anything to keep from hurting her. As should you."

His eyes narrowed a fraction. "Do you think insulting me as a father will help your cause, Prince?"

"You and I want the same thing."

"Which is?"

"Her happiness."

"And you think you can be that?" he asked quietly.

"I intend to be," I said. "But I can't if this blood vow drags me into an early grave."

His gaze drifted once more to the rune on my ribs. Blood still trickled slowly from the cut, tracking along the lines of ink.

"You misunderstand the nature of the vow," he said at last.

"I understand it well enough," I countered. "Death comes for her; I die instead. So she can live to free the realm."

He shook his head. "The vow says that, if the Fates choose to claim her, my power will offer... an alternative. A trade. It will not force you into that grave. It will make you available to choose."

"Available." The word tasted bitter. "Like a weapon pulled off a rack."

"Like a king sent to the front line so his people might live," he said. "You didn't object to that part when you asked me for the strength to protect them. Or her."

"I didn't know her," I shot back.

"And now you do." His gaze softened in a way that wasn't comforting. Gods' pity never was. "That doesn't make the bargain invalid. It just makes it hurt."

I clenched my jaw. "Undo it. Find another way."

"I can't," he said simply.

Rage flared—hot, sharp, immediate. My shadows surged, twitching toward him before I yanked them back. "Won't, you mean."

"I mean *can't*," he said. "There are rules, Rydian. Even for me."

"You're a god. You make the rules."

"That was before. We tore this realm apart once, fighting over who got to move you all like pieces on a board. The Fates won that round. We ceded ground to keep the realm from collapsing entirely." He spread his hands. "I cannot unmake the treaty between us and them—not even if I wanted to. To do so would likely destroy this world. I can only craft my own bargains around it."

It wasn't the answer I wanted.

But there was something in it I hadn't heard the first time I stood before him all those years ago.

Limits.

"You're saying," I said slowly, "that you don't control this. Not fully."

A shadow of irritation crossed his face. "Careful."

"No," I said, stepping in until we were almost chest to chest. My shadows curled around my boots like loyal dogs. "You marked Aurelia. Branded her with your power. You locked my court up as leverage so you'd have a blade to point at her enemies. You made my life a weapon. And all this time, I thought you were the one holding the other end of that leash." I searched his eyes. "But you're not, are you? Not really. You're tied up in this as tightly as I am."

Lightning flashed faintly in his gaze.

"Watch your tone, mortal prince," he murmured.

"Or what?" I asked, voice low. "You'll kill me? Then you lose your blade entirely. Then you'd have to trust the Fates to save your daughter, and we both know how that ends."

For a heartbeat, neither of us moved.

Then Ire laughed.

It wasn't a pleasant sound. But it wasn't furious, either. More... grudging.

"There it is," he said. "The defiance I remember. The stubborn determination I chose you for in the first place."

Despite his laughter, there was a sharpness in his gaze now. A stillness to the air between us. And a power so great, it made my bones tremble. Like he wanted me to remember I stood before a Furiosity rather than a mortal.

I hadn't forgotten, but for good measure, I wisely kept my mouth shut.

His gaze swept over me again, slower this time. "You're right about one thing," he said. "My brothers and I are more bound than I want to be. The accords limit how overtly we can meddle. I cannot storm Heliconia's camp and drag her to Hel by her hair, tempting as that might be. I cannot snuff her like a candle. I cannot walk into Autumn and rip the Harvest throne from under that pretty boy brother of yours." His mouth curved even as his words jolted me with surprise. "And I cannot unmake the terms of your vow without unraveling the careful balance that keeps this realm from tearing itself apart."

"Then why answer my summons tonight?" I asked, irritated and impatient with this useless meeting. "Why come at all?"

"Because," he said simply, "you offered me your life for hers before you even knew her name. I was curious how you'd live with that."

I met his gaze. "And?"

"You didn't disappoint," he said. "You seldom do. Which is why I'll give you this much." He leaned in slightly. "Heliconia seeks the magic that sleeps within your brother's throne. And if she gets it, she will be more powerful than any mortal in Menryth."

"The Harvest throne contains magic?"

He inclined his head.

"She drained Winter's," I realized. "The Ice Throne is where she's been drinking from all these years. Where she recovered her strength after what she did to Summer."

His gaze flicked to the trees, as if he could see through the mountains and into the north. "She stole power from the throne, yes. And from other places where the old magic pooled when we stepped back. That power was meant to hold the realm together in our absence. She uses it to crack the seams instead."

"And Autumn is next," I said.

"Callan is a convenient key," Ire said.

My stomach turned. "That's why he came to us in the north."

"Even broken lines feel the pull of the current," he said.

I stared past Ire, into the dark, seeing Grey Oak Keep in my mind. The Harvest Throne sitting silent—but not empty.

"She already tasted what lies in Concordia. She will want more. All of them, if she can reach them. You've seen what happens when one falls."

Summer.

Aurelia's kingdom, cursed and asleep.

Winter, drained and dead.

"If she drains Harvest too…" I didn't finish the sentence.

"You won't have a realm left to save," Ire said. "Only a graveyard of frozen, empty thrones and the bones of fae who once knelt before them."

A muscle ticked in my jaw. "You telling me this is your way of helping?"

"My way of reminding you," he said, "You're not as unimportant as you might think to the fate of the realm. Aurelia can wield enough power to turn an army to ash, but she cannot stand in every city at once. She cannot guard every throne."

"And I'm what in this scenario?" I asked. "Her errand boy?"

His gaze burned. "You are the blade she can't afford to be. The one who goes where she can't, does what she shouldn't." He nodded east, in the direction of Grey Oak. "If you want to protect her, Shadow Prince, you will stand between Heliconia and that throne. Whether it kills you is beside the point."

"Not to her," I said quietly.

His expression softened again, that same not-comforting way. "You think she would thank me for undoing your vow?" he said. "She would not. She would waste years trying to spare you both fate's cruelty. Time you don't have." He spread his hands. "Better a blade that knows its edge than one constantly trying to dull itself."

"I'm not going to spend whatever time I have left waiting for some preordained moment to die," I said. "If the Fates want me, they can come and pry me out of Aurelia's hands."

His mouth quirked. "That would make for an awkward meeting, don't you think?"

I ignored that, buttoning my shirt over the dried blood still caked on my ribs. "You said you can't undo the vow. Fine. That doesn't mean I have to accept how it ends."

"Meaning?" he asked.

"Meaning I'm done imagining myself in a grave," I said. "If the Fates try to claim her, I'll be there. I'll make the choice then. But until that moment, I am not your sacrificial pawn. I'm her general. Her ally. Her equal. I'll bleed for her. Kill for her. And if I must, I'll die for her. But it will be *my* decision. Not yours. Not theirs."

Silence stretched.

Shadows coiled tighter around my boots, drawn by the iron in my voice. For once, the god of Hel didn't snap at me for my disrespect.

Finally, he said, "You mortals are always so dramatic."

"Comes from growing up in your shadow," I said.

He huffed a laugh. "Very well. I can't unmake what you swore. But I won't push you toward it either. I've seen too many heroes run headlong into their deaths because they thought it made them worthy." His gaze sharpened. "Don't be that stupid."

"I wasn't planning on it," I said dryly.

"Good." He stepped back, the clearing seeming to grow deeper around him. "Then go to Grey Oak. Play politics with your half-brother. Protect the throne he's too arrogant to fear properly. And when Aurelia arrives—and she will—try not to provoke Heliconia before you're both ready to face her."

I froze. "Aurelia's going to Grey Oak?"

He gave me a look that said I was being slow. "Where else would she go, once she learned what you just did? You think she'll let Heliconia take another throne without trying to stop it?"

The thought of her marching into Grey Oak alone—of her furyfire sparking too hot to be contained, of Heliconia turning the Ice Throne's power on her—made something inside me twist.

I looked back at Ire, unsure whether to thank him or curse him for his part in all this. The light around him dimmed, his shape already blurring at the edges.

"Rydian," he added.

I stiffened. "What?"

"When the moment comes," he said softly, "and the Fates offer you the trade you asked for... remember this night. Remember that it is *your* choice. Not theirs. Not mine. Not even hers."

Then he was gone.

Night rushed back in, too loud, too real.

I took a breath. Then another. My hand shook when I touched my side; the cut had stopped bleeding, sealed over by whatever lingering warmth Ire's presence had left in my veins.

The Emerald Forest watched as I walked back through its shadows, more awake than I'd been in days. My purpose felt like a blade newly sharpened—clear, bright, lethal. Grey Oak waited. Callan and his desperate grasp of a powerful throne. Heliconia with her cruelty and stolen magic.

Somewhere in the dark between us, Aurelia was marching toward them both. So, I picked up my sword and marched toward them all.

THE
LOVERS

Chapter Forty
Aurelia

In the graying light of dawn, I stood at the base of the foothills and watched Keres, Daegel, Vanya, and Lesha until they were nothing more than a speck on the horizon. After three days, we'd finally made it to the Autumn border. This morning, we said goodbye to the others and sent them on their way back across the Broadlands to Frith-hold. Lesha would be safe there. And, gods willing, Keres would find a way to heal the wounds on her body—and maybe even the wounds on her soul.

Leif stepped up next to Eirnan, jaw clenched, his hair still singed at the ends from where my furyfire had gotten too close. "We'll bring as many as we can," he said. "Just... don't do anything reckless before we get there, all right?"

Slade snorted. "When have we ever been reckless?"

Leif's mouth twitched—not quite a smile. More a grim acknowledgment that he had no doubt we would indeed be reckless before it was all over.

They weren't happy about splitting up, but we all understood what was at stake. Slade could carry only so many with him before it drained him dry. And if we had any hope of reaching Grey Oak before the wedding, we had no time to lose.

Eirnan leaned heavily on the crutch Daegel had made for him, but his voice was steady as he made his goodbye. "We'll spread word along the road."

"Carefully," I added. "Do not bring trouble or attention to yourselves."

"We have many friends along this route," he assured me. "And there are still Autumn fae who will fight for their own freedom if asked." His gaze held mine. "They'll fight for you."

"I'm not their queen," I said quietly.

"No," he agreed. "But you're fighting for them anyway."

I swallowed. "Thank you. Both of you."

Leif shifted awkwardly, rubbing the back of his neck. "Just… don't die. I'm tired of losing friends."

Friend. The word hit harder than I expected.

I hugged them both—Eirnan stiff but accepting, Leif clumsy and bright-eyed—and then Slade set his hand on my shoulder.

Thorne pressed in, a hand on Slade's shoulder, and murmured a low warning at me to "get ready."

And the world vanished.

Shadow-walking wasn't graceful. It wasn't like slipping through darkness or drifting like mist. It felt like being yanked through a crack in the world by something with claws. A cold rush, a stomach-lurching drop, a dizziness that made me scramble to know which way was up.

Now I understood why Thorne hadn't looked thrilled by the idea.

Slade exhaled sharply as the world blinked back into place—gray sky, tall pines, the tang of damp moss.

"Halfway," he said, already breathing harder than he wanted me to notice.

Halfway? That was it?

Thorne steadied me. "You good?"

I nodded, though my head was spinning. "You?"

"I've had worse," he said. "Being burned by furyfire, for example."

I snorted.

Slade flexed his fingers. Shadow leaked between them like smoke.

"You okay?" Thorne asked him.

"Just taking in the sights," Slade drawled.

He grabbed our arms again, shadows swallowed the world, and we lurched into another clearing. My stomach roiled, but I clamped down on the nausea, shut my eyes, and let the world shift to greet us.

By the third jump—shorter, rougher—Slade's knees buckled, and he dropped to all fours.

"That's it," he rasped. "Unless you want my corpse as a travel companion."

Thorne handed him a flask. "Tempting. But I think I'll pass. You'd stink, and I'm not carrying you."

Slade took the flask and drank.

When we'd all regained our balance, we set off on foot through the trees, the leaves drifting down in gold spirals. The air smelled like pine and early frost, and every mile closer to the palace felt like time slipping through my hands.

The others felt it too. Our steps were too quick. Our breaths too sharp.

Slade finally broke the silence.

"So... question."

"Seven Hels," Thorne muttered. "Here we go."

He ignored Thorne and nudged me. "Why the theatrics? Why bother with a wedding? If Heliconia wants Autumn, she could just kill Callan and take it."

"I wondered the same," I admitted.

Thorne answered first, voice low. "Maybe the throne won't unlock for her if she takes it through assassination."

I frowned, ignoring my own discomfort at the word. Technically, out of the pair of us, I was the assassin of kings—not her. "What do you mean?"

He shrugged. "Thrones are imbued with old magic gifted by the gods. And don't the gods all love their rules? The kind you don't break so much as work around."

"And marrying the king counts as working around?" Slade asked skeptically.

"If she's queen," Thorne said, "she sits beside him. Or on the throne when he's away. Maybe that's all she needs."

"Or," Slade said, "maybe Callan's harder to kill than we gave the brat credit for."

That made my throat tighten unexpectedly.

He *was* a brat. Spoiled, arrogant, manipulative. But he'd helped me. And he'd tried—tried not to be his father. Tried to stand between Heliconia and his throne.

More importantly, Heliconia didn't waste time on preserving a life if taking it was an option.

"Maybe," I said softly, "she needs him alive."

Slade's expression shifted—not joking now. "For what purpose?"

I shrugged. "The throne's magic. The courts' recognition of her as queen. Who knows?"

"Maybe she wants the wedding night experience," Slade said, and Thorne groaned.

"I'd rather not imagine that scenario, if you don't mind."

I couldn't help but make a face of disgust. "Agreed," I muttered.

"And if she gets the throne's power for herself?" Slade asked, serious again.

"Then Autumn falls," I said quietly. "And she moves on to the next throne."

A shiver ran through me.

The more thrones she drained, the more unstoppable she'd become.

My fingers brushed the rune at my throat. Tender. Sore. As if something ancient inside me had clawed to the surface that day. As if it wouldn't be buried any longer.

Thorne must have seen something in my face. "You're not alone in this."

I breathed slowly, trying desperately not to think about how Rydian wasn't here. Or that I had no idea where he was. Or if he was okay. "Feels like it sometimes."

"You're not," Slade said quietly. "Keres, Daegel, Eirnan, Lesha. Rydian. Us. You've got more people than you think."

It helped, those words. More than I expected.

We camped for an hour under a dense cluster of pine boughs while

Slade regained his strength. Somehow, I managed to doze off. Boots rustling jolted me awake. Slade stood over me, Thorne beside him.

"Ready?" Slade asked.

I nodded and let him pull me to my feet.

Thorne rolled his shoulders. "Let's go save your ex."

Slade grinned. "And ruin a wedding—again."

"And stop an unstoppable queen," I added.

"And not die," Thorne finished dryly.

Small goals.

Slade took our arms again.

Shadows surged.

The world folded.

We stepped out into the world again near the edge of the forest. And there, through the trees, stood the walls of Grey Oak. Tall. Weathered. And wrong. Ice veined the stones like frostbite, creeping outward from the highest tower like a beacon. A thin layer of snow coated rooftops.

My stomach hollowed.

"She's already here," I whispered.

Slade wiped his nose—blood streaking his thumb. "That's it for shadow-walking. I'm done."

Thorne scanned the tree line. "Her soldiers are patrolling the roads. We need a place to lie low."

"What about the townhouse?" I asked.

The two of them exchange a look. "We'll need to make sure she isn't recognized. But you and I should be safe enough," Slade said.

Thorne nodded. "We'll have to take the river path and come up from behind. Less visible."

The river path.

The last time I'd been on that path, it had been to attempt escape. Rydian had caught me. I'd been angry enough to blast him with my furyfire. He'd been immune to it then. But not to me. It had been the same night he'd come to my room through the secret passage. We'd shared a bed, and I'd officially lost my heart.

It had belonged to him ever since.

I forced the thought down before it could unravel me.

Focus. Survive. Stop Heliconia.

We crept closer through the underbrush, moving slowly so we wouldn't crunch dry leaves. My furyfire thrummed beneath my skin, but I didn't let even a spark escape.

Not here.

Not now.

The closer we moved, the more wrong the air felt. Heavy. Chilled. A kind of cold that didn't come from any season.

Heliconia's power was inside those walls.

For the first time since the valley, I felt something sharp and dangerous settle in my chest. Not fury. Not fear.

Resolve.

"I'm stopping that wedding," I said.

Slade cracked a wicked grin. "Well, you have experience with that."

"Let's hope, this time," Thorne said, "you don't burn the whole palace down."

My mark pulsed once—almost offended.

I squared my shoulders.

"Let's go," I said. "We don't have time to lose."

Because somewhere beyond those icy walls, a prince of Autumn was about to give away his throne. And somewhere beneath a river far behind me, the man I loved was fighting his way back to me.

I wouldn't let either of them down.

Not tonight.

Not ever.

THE
LOVERS

Chapter Forty-One
Aurelia

Even from a distance, I could tell the city wasn't itself. The streets bustled—banners fluttering in the wind, vendors calling out prices, fae dressed in their finest silks, hurrying toward the palace gates. It looked festive. Joyous.

But the joy felt... empty.

Every banner waving the goldleaf stag had frost creeping along its edges. And in between the bustling fae, Obsidian soldiers patrolled with hollow gazes and blood-crusted blades.

Slade stared at the city and let out a low whistle. "Callan really knows how to throw a party."

"It's not a party," Thorne muttered. "It's a funeral dressed as one."

He was right. Duron's. Callan's. The realm's.

I pulled my hood lower. I'd altered my appearance as much as I could—darkened hair with soot, sharp line of shadow smeared across my cheeks, cloak marred with road dust—but it wouldn't fool anyone who looked directly at me. Too many fae here had seen my face before. Not to mention the Obsidians who had my face imprinted in their mind's eye by their master.

"Let's move," I said quietly.

We slipped into the flow of bodies entering the city. Market stalls were crowded, fae buying ribbons and pastries and bottles of honey-spiced wine. Musicians played at the corner of Oak Square, cheerful and oblivious.

"Can't believe they're excited," Slade muttered. "What kind of idiot celebrates their king marrying the woman who froze half their kingdom and cursed another besides?"

"The kind who's been told it will save them," Thorne said.

He nodded at a pair of gossiping fae near a fruit cart.

"—Her Majesty brings peace—"

"—Our people will be protected—"

"—Winter will shield us from the curse—"

Propaganda. Crude but effective.

My stomach twisted. If Heliconia could convince an entire city she was salvation instead of ruin, what hope did the rest of Menryth have?

Cold prickled the back of my neck.

An Obsidian patrol turned the corner ahead of us—six armored soldiers with blackened eyes and ice-woven blades. They moved like a single living weapon.

Slade nudged me. "Stay behind Thorne."

I stepped behind them both, head down.

The patrol approached.

One of them paused—head tilting, inhaling sharply.

Slade dropped a pouch containing coins—loudly—and swore. "Perfect, just perfect. First day on leave and I'm already broke."

Three of the soldiers glanced at him.

Slade made a spectacle of scrambling after the rolling silver. "Fates above, I hate this city. Why are your streets uneven? Don't they know clumsy people exist? This is discrimination, that's what it is—"

Thorne rolled his eyes, annoyed at his fellow soldier.

The patrol lost interest.

They continued toward the palace gates.

Only when they were gone did my lungs loosen.

"Thank you," I murmured.

"You can name your firstborn after me," Slade said breezily.

Thorne made a sound like choking. "Absolutely not."

"She can put her own twist on it," Slade said as if that made it entirely better. "Preferably something handsome and heroic. 'Sladerius' has a ring to it."

I rolled my eyes as Thorne barked out a laugh.

We made our way through the city, keeping to the shadows. I saw frost creeping along windowsills, dead flowers wilting from planters, a thin glaze of ice forming on fountain water even in midday sun.

Heliconia's presence was everywhere.

By late afternoon, we reached the cheerful row of townhouses tucked behind the edge of downtown. My eyes landed on one of a dozen like it, but I recognized it immediately. My heart ached at the sight.

We snuck along the side to the back door. Thorne pushed it open with his boot. The hinges groaned. Dust motes swirled in the dim entryway.

I stepped inside the kitchen just as I'd done the first time. Rydian had been at my back then. He'd saved my life that day in the alley despite pretending to hate me through it all. That was the day he'd admitted what he really felt. And the day I learned who Callan truly was.

My chest tightened painfully.

Had it only been weeks since then?

Slade dropped his cloak on a hook. "I'm going to find out if we still get hot water."

"I'll see if there's anything to eat," Thorne said, turning for the pantry.

But I was already drawn toward the stairs.

Rydian's room was at the end of the hall—small, neat, sparsely furnished. A cot, a trunk, a weapons rack. A small wooden table. I didn't need to ask whether it was his. I knew it by the scent. Even now, after so much time away, it still lingered here. Woodsmoke and pine resin.

I sat on the edge of his bed.

It felt wrong to be here without him. But it was also a comfort.

On the table, half-hidden beneath a folded shirt, was a letter. The handwriting struck me instantly—sharp strokes, elegant flourishes, ink blotted once as if the pen had trembled. My gaze drew down to the signature line.

Cadira.

Rydian's mother. The queen of the Midnight Court, who had refused to meet me when I'd been all but on her doorstep.

My heart thudded.

I shouldn't read it.

But my fingers were already unfolding the parchment.

Rydian,

I prayed the Furiosities had turned their attention elsewhere and chosen another vessel to burden with such a sacrifice... but when have the gods ever been merciful?

If she truly carries the Chosen's power, then your path is already written. I cannot ask you to step off it. I cannot beg you to stay. So I will simply say this: I do not want to lose you. I do not want you to die for someone the gods chose without care for the ones left behind.

If there is another way—any other way—I will find it.

—Mother

My hand shook slightly.

She hadn't been cruel. She'd been terrified. Terrified of losing her son. Terrified of me taking him from her. A single line burned in my mind: *I do not want you to die.* Neither did I. But the gods didn't care what we wanted.

I folded the letter carefully and set it back.

I lay down on his bed, burying my face in his pillow. The faint scent of him on it made my throat ache.

Slade knocked on the doorframe, pushing open the door to peer in. "Thought I might find you here."

I pushed myself upright. "And the hot water?"

"Thank the Fates, yes." His eyes narrowed. "What is it?"

"Nothing. I'm fine."

"Liar." He pulled out the chair in the corner and sat, boots kicking up dust.

"I miss him," I said quietly.

Slade's smirk softened into something gentler. "He misses you too."

"He probably doesn't even know if I'm alive."

"He knows," Slade said firmly. "He always knows."

I swallowed. "I lost control in that valley, Slade. If he'd reached me—if he'd gotten closer—"

"You didn't hurt him," he said simply. "And you didn't lose yourself."

I shook my head. "He jumped straight into that fire for me. I saw it. Before the naiad pulled him into the river."

"He'd jump into a vat of acid for you," Slade said. "Doesn't mean you did anything wrong."

A faint, reluctant breath escaped me. "He shouldn't have to—"

"He's your equal," Slade cut in. "Not your shield. Stop treating him like one."

I stared at the floor.

He bumped my knee with his. "Also, I'm betting coin he's halfway here already."

"You're probably right," I admitted.

"Come downstairs when you've cleaned up," he said. "We need to plan."

We spread maps across the battered dining table. My full stomach grumbled in appreciation at the soup Thorne had managed to pull together from gods-knew-what he'd found in the pantry.

"This is delicious," I said.

"It's not as good as your usual," Slade put in.

"Your usual?" I echoed. "Is making soup yet another hidden hobby of yours?" I joked.

Slade snorted. "I'd say this soup is ranked far below his usual."

"I blame the ingredients at hand," Thorne said with a shrug. He turned to me. "I'm not hiding anything. I cook, so what? You didn't complain back at Frithhold."

"You cooked the meals at Frithhold?" Why hadn't I noticed? Oh yeah, I was too busy hating all of them for kidnapping me. "Including the bread?"

He smirked—just like he had the night he'd found me trying to read one of the books in his collection. I made a mental note to bring him on every mission forever if it meant eating this good. But after the comfort of the meal, it was time to focus on what came next.

Slade had slipped out earlier to gather news from the markets. The ceremony was at sunset two days from now. It would be private, mostly guards and a few nobles, followed immediately by Heliconia's ceremonial crowning. When Heliconia would be declared a queen of Autumn—and take her place on her new throne.

And once she sat upon it...

"We need to stop the ceremony before she gets anywhere near the throne," Thorne said, tapping the map of the castle's layout where the gardens were located. "Preferably before she gets near Callan."

"Without killing him," I said.

Slade sighed dramatically. "You're no fun."

"Slade," I warned.

"I'm kidding," he said. "Mostly."

"We might need him," Thorne added. "If our theory is correct, he's the only one the Harvest Throne will share its magic with."

"Fine," Slade pouted.

Thorne traced the route from the townhouse to the palace. "We go in hidden. Through the servants' quarter. Aurelia, you'll need a disguise."

"Heliconia will sense me no matter what I look like," I said.

"What if we could cloak your magic?" Thorne suggested.

"How would we do that?"

Thorne shrugged. "A spell or something. Maybe a witch—"

"There are no witches remotely powerful enough to fool Heliconia," Slade warned.

"So I don't bother hiding," I said. "We make a grand entrance."

"Dramatic," Slade said with a gleam. "I like it."

"How will we get past the guards?" Thorne asked.

Everyone was silent at that. But I couldn't let go of the idea that was forming.

"What if we could persuade them to let me through?" I asked, and now it was my turn to have a gleam in my eye.

"How?" Thorne asked.

"Callan."

We spent the next hour arguing about contingency plans—what if Heliconia sensed me, what if the Obsidian patrols spotted Slade, what if Callan refused to help, what if we all got killed before we got in the door...

We didn't have perfect answers.

But we had a plan.

A thin, reckless plan.

It would have to be enough.

THE
LOVERS

Chapter Forty-Two
Aurelia

The bell above the jewelry shop door didn't ring when I slipped inside. But I still heard it echo inside my head from the first time I'd come here. Then, it had been a friendly chime as Callan led me from glass case to glass case, hoping to impress me with the coin he'd spend on something shiny for his almost-bride. All while lying to me about how his father planned to bleed the entire court dry of their magic. Me included.

Tonight, the shop was dark. According to Slade, it had been closed since the day the Withered attacked us here. The bell had been silenced —just like the shop owner himself had been silenced on Callan's order.

My heart ached for the elderly fae who'd lost his life that day, likely for the simple crime of trying to warn me about what was really happening to Autumn citizens. Then, the Withered had attacked us.

Rydian had saved my life—again.

And everything had changed.

It seemed a fitting meeting place for tonight's subterfuge. Here I was, planning to stop a wedding. Again. At this rate, I was probably qualified enough to fall back on it as a career if being the Chosen One didn't work out.

Slade had picked the lock in about three heartbeats. Thorne had checked the alley twice. Now they waited outside, one at the front, one at the back, shadow and muscle guarding the exits while I stood surrounded by reminders of a life I'd narrowly escaped.

I ran a finger over the counter where Callan once told me to pick something—"anything you want, Princess"—like trinkets could make up for losing everyone I loved to a curse made of perpetual slumber.

"Are you sure he'll come?" Slade had asked me earlier, after convincing a courtier to carry the message into the castle.

Of course Callan would come.

His ego wouldn't allow him to ignore it.

I shifted my weight, listening to the muted sounds of Grey Oak at night—distant voices, a wagon wheel rattling over cobblestone, the faint clatter of a tavern somewhere down the lane. The city felt tense. Like it was holding its breath for tomorrow.

For the wedding.

For the moment their king publicly tied himself to the monster at their doorstep.

My fingers brushed the tattoo along my throat. The only way we'd stop Heliconia would be with the power imbued to me from this mark. And even then, only if I could control it. I hadn't been able to bring myself to admit that to Slade or Thorne. And neither one had asked.

The door latch clicked.

I went still.

No bell. No sound. Just a soft draft of cold air and the faint, familiar scent of expensive cologne.

"I have to say," Callan murmured, "your choice of location is almost romantic."

He stood just inside the door, unhooded, unguarded. No crown. No armor. Though, beneath his dark cloak, I glimpsed a tunic pressed and tailored within an inch of its life, as if he'd stepped out of a ball rather than skulked here alone in the middle of the night.

His gaze swept the shop before landing on me. For a heartbeat, his expression flickered.

"Hello, Aurelia."

"Callan."

He shut the door behind him and leaned against it like he owned the place. Which, knowing him, he probably did now.

"No entourage?" I asked.

"I travel light these days," he said. "Besides, according to your note, if anyone asks, I'm visiting the goddess' temple and praying to the Fates before the big day."

"Did you? Pray?"

He smirked. "The Fates aren't exactly my go-to deity these days. Nor, I suspect, are they yours. Even if they were reachable, they're a bit too sweet for what I want done."

"Maybe you won't need divine intervention," I said. "You do have a knack for scaring away your bride all on your own."

"Aren't we full of humor tonight?" He stepped closer, boots soundless on the floor. "So. You summoned me to a jewelry shop the night before my wedding. Either you're here to kill me, or you've finally come to your senses and want a ring from me after all."

He said it lightly, but there was something under the words. A question he wouldn't ask outright.

I ignored both. "I'm here because you're out of time."

His jaw flexed. "Yes, well, I did bring that to your attention back when we had a bit more of it."

"I know. And I'm sorry for not doing more to help."

The humor fell away like a cloak. I saw it then, the pain I'd caused by refusing him. The fear he was battling on his own.

"Tell me what you want," he said quietly.

I gestured to the back of the shop, where a curtain separated the front room from a narrow storage space. "Not here."

He glanced once at the door, as if reassuring himself no one had followed him, then moved past me. His shoulder brushed mine as he went by, and I couldn't help but flinch.

He stilled. "I'm not going to compel you."

"I know," I said even though I wasn't sure I believed it.

We ducked behind the curtain into a cramped room that smelled of metal polish and old wood. Shelves lined the walls, cluttered with small boxes and trays. A single high window let in a sliver of moonlight.

Thorne would be just beyond the rear door. Slade, a shadow near the front. We were as safe as we were going to get.

Callan turned to face me, back to the shelves, arms folding loosely across his chest. "You have my undivided attention."

I stared at him, at the dark circles ringing his eyes and the fine lines around his mouth that hadn't been there before. For all his bravado, he looked tired.

"You know why she wants you," I said.

"I assume you don't mean my devastating charm."

"The Harvest Throne."

His gaze intensified. "Go on."

"The power inside it. The gods' power left here after the Great War. She drained Concordia's throne to keep herself alive after she cursed my people. She wants yours next."

A muscle ticked in his jaw. "How do you know this?"

I swallowed past the lump in my throat. "Lesha."

"Your Aine friend."

I nodded. "She learned the information while she was Heliconia's prisoner."

His expression was grim, the gaunt look in his eyes like death.

"The last time we spoke," I added, "You knew Heliconia's interest in Autumn wasn't just about territory."

He huffed out a breath. "I suspected something. Since then, I've confirmed it. *She* confirmed it."

"She's not going to stop," I said. "Once she takes Autumn, she'll move on to the others. Midnight. Lightshore. The Coral Throne Beneath. If she drains them all…" I swallowed hard. "She won't need armies anymore."

"She'll be a god," Callan finished quietly.

We let that hang between us.

He broke the silence first. "So that's your grand plan? Come to Grey Oak, scare me with worst-case scenarios, and hope I'll call the whole thing off?"

"If you do," I said tightly, "she'll kill you and take it anyway."

"I was wondering when we'd get to the comforting part."

I bit back the instinctive retort. "I didn't come here to fight with you."

"Then why did you come, Aurelia?" The question had an edge to it. I couldn't blame him for it, but I refused to take the bait.

I lifted my chin. "I came to stop her."

"From where I'm standing," he said, "she's the one with five thousand soldiers and a kingdom of ice at her back. You brought..." His gaze flicked to the door, to the fae I knew he sensed there. "Two soldiers. And whatever wretched plan has you breaking into jewelry shops in the middle of the night."

"We have more than two soldiers," I said. "The Withered are on their way. Eirnan's gathering Autumn fae along the route, recruiting anyone willing to fight."

"Autumn?" His eyes flashed. "You're recruiting my soldiers into your army?"

"Your people, your army, Callan. They're doing what you can't do yourself, so be grateful for it. But they won't reach Grey Oak in time for the wedding. And we can't let her sit that throne. Not even once."

"So we stop the wedding," he said. "How? Convince her to call it off? I've been trying that for weeks. She doesn't take no for an answer."

"We interrupt it," I said. "In the throne room. In front of everyone."

He stared at me, then shook his head. "Of course you will."

"Slade's magic can get us inside."

"No," Callan said, already shaking his head. "Autumn is warded against unauthorized entry. My father made sure of it. After Heliconia's surprise arrival at our party those years ago."

Seven Hels.

"In that case, you'll have to make sure the guards let us through. No resistance. No alarms."

"And how exactly do you propose I do that?" he asked, though we both knew the answer.

"You use your gift," I said. "Your persuasion. Tell them to stand down. To let us pass."

"You're asking me to expose my ability—one that I've kept secret my entire life."

"I'm asking you to help me stop her from stealing your kingdom."

His jaw tightened. For a moment, he looked like his father. Then he shook it off, forcing a smile that didn't reach his eyes.

"And after I persuade the guards to let you in?" he asked. "What then? Do you actually think you can take her?"

I held his gaze. "Yes."

The word felt both too big and not big enough.

Callan lifted a brow. "Last I checked, she nearly killed you in Rosewood seven years ago."

I exhaled slowly. "In the valley," I said, "I burned her camp. Drained her Frostwights. Took the magic out of their bones and set fire to everything she'd built there."

He held still. "I heard a rumor," he admitted, "but I thought it was exaggerated. You're telling me that was really you?"

"Would I lie about something like that?" I asked.

"Absolutely," he said. "If you thought it would get you what you wanted."

Despite myself, a corner of my mouth twitched. "Fair enough. It was me."

For a moment, he just looked at me. Not like a king. Not like a boy who'd once thought he could buy my compliance with dresses and jewels and public adoration. Just like someone trying to reconcile the girl he'd tried to own with the woman capable of killing him where he stood.

"And you controlled it?" he asked quietly. "Your magic?"

I hesitated.

His gaze sharpened further. "Because I heard rumors about that too. A loss of control. A fire so brutal it burned friend and foe alike."

"I controlled it," I said.

"Aurelia," he warned. "Do not lie to me."

"I lost control at the end," I admitted. "The magic… it was too much. Too many lives. Too much power. It burned through me, and I couldn't shut it off." I met his eyes. "I nearly brought the mountain down on us."

He blew out a breath, running a hand through his hair. "Well, that's… encouraging."

"It won't happen again," I said.

"You don't know that."

"I won't *let* it happen again," I said, heat flashing in my chest. "I know the cost now. I know what it feels like when I'm close to losing control, and I know when to stop."

"And if you misjudge?" he pushed. "If you lose control in *my* court, in *my* home, with my people standing there?"

"Then Slade gets everyone out," I said sharply. "He's already promised. Once the fighting starts, he'll shadow-walk as many as he can away from the line of fire. I don't suppose the wards will prevent magic from leaving, will it?"

He shook his head.

"Good. Thorne will shield me from her first strike. I'll hit her as hard as I can, and if it goes sideways, we retreat."

"We run," he translated.

"Yes."

Silence settled between us, thick and tense.

"You really think you can win?" he said at last. "Even knowing what she took from the Ice Throne. Even knowing what she did to your court."

"I think," I said, "that if anyone has a chance, it's us. I'm the one the gods chose to stop her. I'm the one she failed to curse. And you're the one she keeps underestimating."

"And if you're not ready?" he asked, voice gone softer. "If your power eats you alive before you ever get close enough to touch her?"

"Then I die trying," I said simply. "Just like you were going to die slowly, in her bed or on your throne, while she hollowed you out and used your crown to legitimize her rule. At least, this way, we get to bloody her first."

He stared at me, all traces of humor gone. "I never wanted you to die," he said quietly.

"I know," I said. "You just wanted me safely out of the way."

His mouth tugged. "I wanted you safe. Full stop. Out of the worst of it. Away from the battlefield. Away from her. And him."

"By caging me," I said.

"To protect you," he insisted.

"You always wanted to hide me," I said, the realization settling like a stone. "Tucked away somewhere pretty where you could feel good about saving me while the rest of the realm fought for their own freedom."

His expression flickered. "Is that what you think?"

"It's what you showed me," I said. "Here. In Rosewood. In every conversation where you told me you wished I would just let someone else fix this."

"Because I didn't want you to die for a court that didn't deserve you," he snapped. Then softer, "I still don't."

"That's the difference between you," I said quietly. "You think safety is the same thing as freedom."

"Is he here?" Callan asked after a beat. "My brother?"

My throat tightened. "No."

"Where is he?"

"We got separated in the valley," I said. "The naiad pulled him under before the fire could reach him." I swallowed against the ache. "He's safe. Or safer than he would've been on that hillside."

Something like genuine relief flickered across Callan's features, quickly smoothed over with his usual arrogance. "I'm surprised he let you come here without him," he said. "Surprised he'd let you walk into this alone."

"He didn't 'let' me do anything," I said. "He trusts me to fight my own battles. Even when he's afraid of what it might cost."

"And I don't?" he challenged.

"You're here because you're afraid of what it will cost *you* if you don't help," I said. "That doesn't make you a coward. It just means you're not doing this for me."

He stared at me for a long moment, something like hurt moving behind his eyes. Then he blew out a breath and leaned back against the shelves, fingers drumming lightly on a wooden box.

Outside, a cart rattled past. Somewhere in the distance, a bell chimed the late hour.

"You know," he said finally, voice quiet, "in another life, I might've been good for you."

"In another life," I said, "you might've been good. Full stop."

He winced, but he didn't deny it. And I knew what he was thinking as sure as if he'd asked it aloud.

"I can't marry you," I said, softer now. "Not to stop her. Not to save you. Not for anything. If I tie myself to you, I become a tool all over again. For your court. For your council. For every fae who thinks a queen's power comes from who she stands beside instead of who she is."

"And Rydian?" he asked. "Is that different?"

"Yes," I said simply, ignoring the heartbreak in that one word.

It was absolutely different because with Rydian, I'd never be his.

Callan swallowed. Looked away. When he met my eyes again, his were bright, but his voice was steady.

"I'll make sure no one stops you from walking through."

"Thank you," I said.

"Don't thank me yet," he muttered. "If this goes poorly, we'll all be dead, and she'll make Frostwights out of our bones."

I didn't let myself picture that.

He stepped past me, toward the curtain, then paused. "Aurelia."

"Yes?"

"If you survive this," he said, "and if by some miracle I do too... what then?"

"Then we keep fighting," I said. "Until she's stopped. Until my people wake. Until this realm remembers what it is to be free."

"And us?" he asked, almost lightly. "Is there an 'us' in that future somewhere? Even as allies? As friends?"

I considered him.

The boy who'd tried to save me by caging me. The king now risking his crown to give me a shot at saving something bigger than both of us.

"There could be," I said honestly. "If you keep choosing the realm over your pride."

He huffed a quiet laugh. "That sounds exhausting."

"It will be," I said. "But you might start to like yourself before it's done."

He looked like he wanted to say something else. Instead, he nodded, squared his shoulders, and slipped back through the curtain.

THE
LOVERS

Chapter Forty-Three
Aurelia

We approached the palace with hoods pulled low against the swirling snow falling in thin, icy flakes. All around us were Autumn citizens headed for the castle, hoping to get a closer look at the royal wedding. I winced at the sight of a young Autumn fae girl clinging to her mother, both with wreath-crowns in their hair and bright smiles on their faces. If I lost control today, these fae would pay the cost.

I could not—would not—let that happen.

A layer of ice crept along the fountains and gutters we passed. The wind dug in through the holes of my cloak, wringing any warmth from my skin. But the crowd did not seem deterred by it. The mood was festive. Hopeful.

If only they knew their king did not share that hope.

I clung to mine like a precious thing.

"Final chance to back out," Slade murmured at my elbow as we walked. "No shame in fleeing. I hear Vorinthia has lovely beaches."

But beneath the humor, he was coiled, ready. Shadows clung to him like oil. Thorne walked on my other side, quiet strength radiating from him like a heartbeat.

I took a breath that did nothing to steady me.

Tomorrow wasn't promised. Tonight wasn't promised. I was about to come face-to-face with the woman who had cursed my kingdom, ripped wings from the backs of my friends, tortured a hundred others, and nearly killed me multiple times.

If I died today, it had to mean something.

"Slade," I said softly.

He turned, eyebrows lifting at the shift in my voice.

"If I don't make it out of this—"

"Stop." He lifted a hand.

"I need you to tell Rydian—"

"Nope. Absolutely not." His tone sharpened. "If you die, I'm dying too. Because Rydian will murder me for letting it happen. So really, it's in everyone's best interest that you stay alive."

"Slade—"

Thorne stepped closer, voice firm. "None of us is dying today."

I looked between them—the soldier who joked too much, the warrior who spoke too little. My friends, whether I'd meant to make them that or not.

"All right," I whispered, breath hitching. "Then let's crash a wedding."

Slade grinned. "Now *that's* the spirit."

We broke off from the crowd one at a time, converging at a servants' entrance Callan had described. Hidden beneath an archway of carved oak leaves, it looked innocuous—locked, unused. But when I pressed my palm against the etched wood, the latch clicked open.

He'd kept his promise.

Inside, the corridor was dim and narrow, the air heavy with wax and wine and a hush of anticipation from the grand halls above. The muffled sounds of a crowd drifted in from the back gardens.

Slade peeked around the corner. "So far, so good."

We moved fast.

Up a spiral staircase. Across a gallery lined with portraits of former kings. Through a narrow linen closet with a hidden second door that Callan had sworn would be unattended—and thankfully, it was. There was no time for nostalgia or memories, not even when I found myself noting familiar sights inside the secret passages or the main halls.

Twice, we were stopped by guards who demanded our business here. But when we pulled our hoods back to reveal our faces, they waved us on without delay.

The closer we got, the colder it grew.

My breath puffed out in white clouds as we reached the final corridor.

Slade lifted a hand, shadows coiling.

"No going back after this," Thorne said quietly.

But I'd long since passed the point of no return. For me, that day had come and gone seven years ago, when I'd stood on a Summer rooftop and watched everyone I loved be taken away from me.

I pressed my hand to the door. My heart hammered, my magic stirred restlessly, and the mark at my throat pulsed like it recognized its enemy beyond the threshold.

"Ready?" I whispered.

Two nods.

I pushed the door open.

The throne room blazed with light.

Goldleaf banners hung from the vaulted ceiling, though frost crawled along their edges. Dozens of fae lined the aisles in formal finery, whispering amongst themselves. At the far end, beneath a massive autumn-gold arch, with the Harvest Throne gleaming behind them, Heliconia stood with Callan.

She was dressed in winter-white, a gown that shimmered, not with silk but with frost. Her hair spilled in sleek dark waves, glittering with ice shards. A crown of frozen thorns rested atop her head.

Callan stood beside her in green and gold, coat immaculate, expression carved from stone. When his eyes met mine across the room, the tension in his shoulders loosened—not relief, not fear.

Acceptance.

He nodded, almost imperceptibly.

Now.

I threw my hood back and stepped into the aisle.

Gasps rippled across the room.

Heliconia's gaze snapped toward us.

The temperature plummeted.

"Ah," she said, glancing at Callan, her voice smooth as a blade through fresh snow. "You brought me a wedding present. Two potent vessels to drain."

The room gasped and murmured.

My heart thundered at the weight of this moment. Facing her again after all this time. My fingers itched to toss Hel's flame at her smug face.

"It's over, Heliconia."

Her attention whipped to me. "You look tired, child. Expending more power than you know how to wield must take quite a toll."

"I'm standing," I said. "That's more than your army can say."

A flicker of annoyance crossed her face—gone in an instant. "Lucky for me, I have many more legions of soldiers just like that one tucked away in my Winter court."

I blinked, unable to stop the weight of her words from settling around my shoulders. *Many more legions*. Of course she did. What we'd done would be a drop in the bucket. A mild inconvenience.

The only way to truly stop her was to end her now, today.

I called on my Makarios, letting that familiar hunger rise inside me until I felt it tugging at the life force energy of everyone in this room. But there was only one whose life I wanted to drain away. I found the thread that led to Heliconia and sipped from it.

Power slammed into me, so potent that my head swam and my knees threatened to buckle.

I let go of the power, sucking in a gulp of air.

Her laugh was soft. Beautiful. Deadly. "Little Summer ember. Still pretending you understand the first thing about a god's power."

Furyfire stirred in my veins.

Slade shifted to my left, Thorne to my right, both ready.

Callan exhaled slowly. "Heliconia," he said, voice low, persuasive magic lacing the words, "perhaps we should—"

Heliconia lifted her hand.

A cold wind slithered across the floor, coiling around my ankles like a serpent.

"Behold," she said, her voice carrying to every corner of the room, "the girl who thinks herself chosen. The girl who thinks draining an army makes her a god."

"I don't think I'm a god," I said. "I'm just here to make sure you don't become one either."

Her eyes flashed with a depthless, ancient rage. "You are nothing more than a vessel, child. And a fragile one at that. Your body is cracking under the weight of the magic you possess. The gods made a mistake choosing you. You were always meant to break."

"Maybe," I said. "But I'll break you first."

With a snarl, Heliconia stepped forward. The frost on the floor thickened, spreading in spiderweb cracks beneath her feet. Ice crawled up the pillars. Torches flickered, dimmed.

The room hummed with power.

Screamed with it.

Callan swallowed, stepping subtly aside—not openly aiding me, not openly defying her. The gathered courtiers shrank back, some ducking behind columns, others clutching loved ones, trembling.

Heliconia's voice went soft. Lethal. "And now, little Summer ember, your power is mine."

The thread sprang to life, only this time, my Makarios magic screamed in pain as that hunger was fed on. And the life force I'd so easily sipped from—now gave of my own to the monster on the other end.

My fire roared as I struggled to sever the connection. Furyfire dripped from my fingers, landing on the rug, sparking into embers that ate at the material. Sparks flew, landing on gowns, igniting cloaks.

Slade cursed and leaped into action, grabbing the closest fae and winking away on a trail of shadows.

Thorne's hand shot to his blade.

The life-thread Heliconia had gripped between us—thin as a spider's web seconds ago—snapped tight like a garrote. My magic bucked violently, clawing at the inside of my ribs.

No. No—stop—

Heliconia smiled, her teeth small and perfect and carved for cruelty. "Too late, little ember."

I gasped, collapsing onto one knee as the connection inverted again—her siphoning *me*, not the other way around. The Makarios part of me screamed in agony, yanked open like a wound as she pulled at the core of who I was.

My life force tore from me in hot, ripping surges.

My fire guttered.

My vision swam.

I heard Slade shouting something. All I could feel was the hollowing ache inside me as Heliconia fed.

Frost bloomed across the floor, reaching for my hands, my legs, my throat.

She's killing you.

The realization rang clear in that same whispered voice I'd heard back in the valley. Dully, I registered it as someone other than my own, even as the room spiraled wildly.

Heliconia's cruel smile swam in my vision.

I flung fire, anything, everything—

It met a wall of ice and vanished.

Snuffed out, absorbed into that impossible, stolen power she'd taken from Concordia's throne. She didn't even flinch. It was as if I'd thrown sparks at the sea.

Heliconia's fingers curled. The siphon tightened like a noose.

"You thought draining a camp of soulless pawns made you powerful?" she purred. "You drained bones. Dead things stitched together by my hand. What I took was a *god's essence.*"

I couldn't breathe.

She stepped closer, frost cracking beneath her feet like brittle bones.

My heart hammered once—twice—

Stuttered.

I reached for my power again, clawing for it desperately. Furyfire flared… flickered… died. My Makarios screamed but couldn't break free.

"Aurelia!" Thorne's voice cut through the chaos as he surged forward, ley-line magic flaring bright across his palms like veins. A shimmering barrier went up between Heliconia and us.

For two heartbeats, it held.

Heliconia's expression barely changed before she lifted one hand. Ice slammed into Thorne's shield with a thunderous crack. It shattered—exploding into a spray of glittering shards.

Thorne was thrown backward. He hit the marble wall so hard it spiderwebbed behind him.

"Thorne!" I choked out, trying to crawl toward him, but Heliconia yanked the thread again, and pain ripped through my lungs.

Slade flickered into existence a dozen yards away, dragging five terrified courtiers with him out of the path of her spreading frost.

"Aurelia!" he shouted, but I couldn't answer. His shadows reached for me—

Heliconia swatted them aside like smoke.

She was toying with us.

"Good," she said softly. "Bleed a little for me. Break a little. It makes the harvest that much sweeter."

My blood chilled.

Callan moved—not much, not fast—but enough that Heliconia's eyes flicked toward him.

"Stay," she commanded, and ice laced his boots to the dais.

She turned back to me, eyes alight. Hungry.

"You come into my court," she whispered, "my wedding, my throne room—and offer yourself up on your knees. What a beautiful sacrifice you've made. Unfortunately, a useless one."

"Go to Hel," I rasped.

She smiled. "Haven't you heard? Hel came to me. And I learned what it takes to become a god."

The thread pulsed.

My vision blurred.

The world dimmed at the edges.

My fire guttered out completely.

"Aurelia!" Slade roared—but it was distant.

Heliconia lifted her hand, fingers glowing with stolen power. "Goodnight, Summer ember."

This is it.

My consciousness slipped. The floor groaned beneath me as frost crept up my arms.

"Rydian," I breathed. Not a call, not a spell—just a thought. A prayer.

The pressure shifted.

The room filled with smoke.

No, not smoke at all. Shadow.

A cyclone of shadows ripped through the aisle, tearing apart Heliconia's frost as if it were made of vapor. Chandeliers overhead rattled violently. Courtiers screamed, hurling themselves against the walls.

Heliconia's siphon against me finally broke—violently—sending a backlash of power crashing through me like lightning. I choked, collapsing sideways.

Night pressed in from all angles, swallowing torchlight, swallowing sound.

A nightmare come to life.

And at its center, cloaked in shadows like a god of horrors—

Rydian.

Shadows burst from him in a violent shockwave, spiraling up columns, along the ceiling, ripping through frost and ice.

He moved before anyone could breathe.

In a single motion, he lunged, grabbed me by the waist, and yanked me backward into his shadows just as Heliconia's killing strike slammed into the marble where I'd been kneeling.

The floor exploded.

Heliconia screamed her frustration. More ice flew at us, but Rydian didn't stop. He wrapped me in his coat, pulling me against his chest. His heartbeat thundered against my cheek—alive, alive, ALIVE—and the room vanished behind swirling darkness.

We reformed ten yards away, halfway behind a pillar.

Air rushed back into my lungs in a violent gasp.

His shadows flared, roaring around us in a vortex that made silk banners tear free of their mounts.

He cupped the back of my head, forcing my face up. "Breathe."

"I—I can't—"

"Yes, you can." His voice was hard steel and rough edges. "Look at me."

I did.

His eyes were molten shadow—glowing with raw power, far more than he'd ever shown me. His hair was mussed like he'd run here through a storm. When he looked at me, it was like he could see every fracture, every scar, every place I'd given too much and didn't have enough left.

"Hello, Furious," he murmured. A ghost of a smirk touched his lips. "Did you miss me?"

"You're late," I whispered.

He grinned and kissed me.

THE
LOVERS

Chapter Forty-Four

Rydian

I pulled away from Aurelia, but only after promising myself there would be time for more of it later. There had to be. I was done denying us this, the realm and the gods be damned. We'd survive this day because we must. And then Aurelia and I would deal with what lay between us once and for all. Now, shadows collapsed back into me, snapping to heel like wolves, and the chaos of the throne room rushed into brutal clarity. Courtiers screamed as a wave of Obsidians surged through the northern doors—dark armor, black eyes, weapons already raised.

Heliconia's frost shot across the floor, icicles erupting like spikes.

Aurelia leaned against me only for a moment before straightening and standing tall. Fury lit her features—not the kind that burned out of control, but the kind that forged steel.

"Behind you!" I barked.

She spun right as an Obsidian soldier lunged. Her sword flashed, clean and lethal, carving through the space between them before his blade could fall. She slid under him, came back up hard, and drove Dorcha through his ribs.

Another soldier tried to flank her.

I was already moving.

Shadow leapt from my fingertips, slamming into his throat. The impact snapped his helm sideways, and he crumpled as my magic recoiled back to me in a rush of vapor.

More boots hit the marble, the throne room surging with Obsidian soldiers rushing in as the remaining guests tried to shove their way out.

Heliconia shrieked an order, her voice like cracking ice. "Kill the princess! Kill the shadow brutes! Bring me the traitor king alive!"

Her soldiers swarmed toward us, eager to do her bidding.

I glimpsed Callan near the front, fighting with a stolen Obsidian blade, then lost him again as more incoming Obsidian soldiers blocked my sight.

"Rydian." Slade's voice echoed from somewhere near the balustrade. "On your right!"

I spun, blocked a blade, shoved my sword through a gap in armor, ripped it free. Aurelia fought beside me—quick, terrifying, beautiful. Not a comet blazing out of control anymore. A blade honed to lethal purpose.

Watching her fight without her furyfire made my rib burn like someone had pressed a brand into it.

The Furiosity rune.

The warning of an early death.

I ground my teeth. "Not today."

Aurelia didn't hear me—she was already ducking under another swing. Her braid whipped past my cheek, lightning-fast. She twisted, drove a knife into the soldier's thigh, ripped it sideways, and took him down.

"Show-off," I muttered.

She kicked another soldier square in the chest, batting him away from my blind spot. "You're welcome."

I glanced toward the front again, to where I'd last seen Callan. Heliconia's power hissed as she advanced toward the Harvest Throne. Frost crawled up the dais like living vines. And Callan—idiot that he was—stood frozen there, jaw clenched, eyes darting between his throne and the monster he was supposed to hand it over to.

"Callan!" I shouted. "Move!"

He didn't.

Heliconia stretched out a hand. Frost curled around Callan's boots again. "Speak the words," she hissed. "Give me what you promised. Give me your throne."

Callan's face contorted. His mouth opened—against his will.

Aurelia faltered. "Callan—" she gasped.

I grabbed her arm. "Isn't dying on my watch."

We sprinted—cutting through the chaos, ducking between columns, weaving through clashing blades. Frost lashed out at us in jagged arcs. My shadows met them midair, cracking the ice apart before it touched her skin.

"Behind you!" Slade yelled again, flashing into existence for half a heartbeat to yank a terrified Autumn guard out of a frost wave.

Thorne held the southern end of the room, ley-line magic roaring beneath his skin like molten gold. He carved a barrier line across the floor, cutting off an entire swell of soldiers from reaching Aurelia's back. Each pulse of his ability made the stones glow.

Ahead, Heliconia was stepping toward Callan.

She lifted her hand. "Speak the vow. Name me your queen, and I will make your death quick."

Callan's throat seized. He tried to fight it—his jaw trembled, but frost tightened up his legs, his chest, his arms. His lips, already blue and trembling, shaped the first syllable.

Aurelia's breath stuttered.

"No!" she screamed and threw herself forward, but I got there first.

I slammed into Callan, tearing him sideways off the dais. Heliconia's magic screamed in fury as her grip on him shattered into ice shards.

Callan hit the floor with a grunt.

Aurelia was already between us and Heliconia, Dorcha raised, her stance low and deadly. Flames of furyfire licked across the marble at Heliconia's feet like predators scenting blood.

Heliconia's face twisted with the first true sign of fury I'd ever seen on her. "You insolent wretch," she spat at Callan.

"That's King Insolent Wretch," Callan wheezed behind me. "Show some respect—"

"Callan," I growled. "Shut. Up."

Aurelia didn't turn, but her voice clipped sharp as a blade. "She wants him to say the words. She can't take the throne without consent—"

"I know," I said.

Heliconia's eyes flared. "He *will* give it."

"Over my corpse," Callan muttered, dusting himself off.

"Not happening," Aurelia said.

She and I shared one look—one of those looks that lasted no longer than a blink but contained a thousand unspoken understandings.

We weren't winning this fight.

Not today.

Not like this.

I turned toward the shadows, toward the one person who could change everything in a heartbeat. Slade materialized out of the smoke at the far end of the room, dragging two terrified nobles behind him.

"Slade," I roared.

His head snapped toward me. I jerked my chin at Callan.

Slade's eyes widened. He understood.

He let the nobles go and dissolved into shadow so violently his form blurred.

Heliconia snapped her fingers.

Ice spears erupted from the ceiling. Twenty of them. Maybe thirty. All aimed at us as they fell.

"Aurelia," I yelled.

I seized her waist. Shadow roared beneath my skin.

Slade dropped into existence beside Callan in a spill of darkness, grabbed his arm—

And winked out.

Heliconia shrieked.

She pivoted toward us, eyes blazing with enough stolen power to crack the realm itself.

"Where is he?" she roared with enough power that the entire throne room trembled.

"Oh, she's pissed," Aurelia whispered, eyes bright with what we'd just done.

"Is she? I hadn't noticed," I said.

Heliconia threw up her palms. Frozen spears exploded outward. I shoved Aurelia behind a toppled pillar just as their pointed ends obliterated the marble where she'd been standing.

My shadows buckled under the impact.

"Now!" I yelled. "Slade—NOW!"

For an agonizing heartbeat, nothing happened.

Heliconia gathered power—far too much power—and flung it at us like a tidal wave of frozen death. Snow and ice so thick there was no seeing through it. No melting it. No stopping it.

Aurelia slammed into me. I wrapped both arms around her and spun, ready to take the hit—

Slade burst into existence behind us.

"Hold on," he warned, putting a hand on each of us.

The avalanche hit.

Or—it would have.

But we were gone.

The throne room snapped away in a violent crush of shadow and cold. My stomach twisted. The world folded, then unfolded in a blinding rush—

And light vanished.

Everything went dark.

Everything went still.

Aurelia's fingers dug into my coat.

My arms stayed locked around her.

I felt her breath against my neck—a small, ragged sound. *Alive. Alive.*

Slade swore behind us. "Someone tell me she didn't get a hit in before we blinked."

I exhaled once—shaking with relief and fury.

"She didn't," I said. "We're clear."

Aurelia's voice was a rasp. "Where's Callan?"

"Safe," Slade said and then added, "With Thorne. Probably complaining already."

Good. I didn't care where Slade had taken him. Not when Aurelia was in my arms and we were safe from death.

I didn't loosen my hold. Couldn't.

Aurelia finally lifted her head, eyes still dazed.

"Rydian," she whispered. "I couldn't do it. I failed."

"You survived," I corrected, brushing a thumb over her cheek without thinking. "We all did. And she didn't get the throne."

"She did, though. We left her in there with it."

"It doesn't belong to her," I said. "That's not a failure."

Her breath hitched. But I pulled her closer anyway—because I needed to feel her heartbeat, needed to know she was whole.

"We will finish this," I told her quietly. "We'll end her. But not today."

Her fingers curled into the front of my shirt.

"Not today," she echoed.

Slade's voice broke the moment. "So. Good news: We're alive. Bad news? Heliconia's about to tear the entire Autumn Court apart, trying to find us."

Aurelia sagged slightly in my arms. "Then we run."

"Where?" Slade asked.

"I know a place," I said, my voice low, certain, absolute.

They both looked at me, but all I saw was her.

Aurelia's throat bobbed as she swallowed. "You came for me."

I met her gaze, let her see the truth in it. "I would walk through Hel and back for you, Furious."

Her breath shivered.

Behind us, Slade groaned. "Gods above. If you two start kissing in front of me again, I'm shadow-walking myself into the nearest river."

Aurelia elbowed him weakly. "Just say you're still daydreaming about that naiad hottie."

"I don't know what you're talking about."

But there was a grin on his face.

And Aurelia was alive.

THE
LOVERS

Chapter Forty-Five

Aurelia

The road out of Grey Oak felt colder once Slade and Thorne vanished north.

A simple nod, a promise of, "See you soon," and then Slade took Thorne's arm, shadows curled around them, and they were gone. Headed north to intercept Eirnan and Leif and whatever Autumn army they'd managed to recruit. If they succeeded, the entire contingent would regroup in the caves to the north to await orders for our next move. If they were caught—

I didn't let myself think about it.

And now, without Slade or Thorne as a buffer, the three of us stood together in the moonlight far east of Grey Oak's city limits.

Rydian.

Callan.

And me.

Our long journey stretched before us, and I swallowed a groan at how awkward this was going to be.

"Let's get moving," I said, determined to get this over with as fast as possible.

Night draped itself across the land as we moved. Shadows pooled in the hollows of the hills, clung to the trees, and stretched long behind us like restless things. We kept off the main road, weaving through wooded paths and overgrown animal trails.

Callan led for a while, mostly because he didn't trust Rydian not to "accidentally" trip him into a ravine. Rydian walked close behind me, silent, shadows coiling at his heels out of habit. He hadn't said much since we'd left the throne room behind, but I had the distinct impression that something in him had changed. I didn't know what. Just that the air felt different around him. Charged. Alive in a way it hadn't been before.

Every time my gaze flicked back to him, he was already looking at me.

The first few times I caught him, I looked away. By the fifth, I didn't bother.

"Anything behind us?" I murmured.

"No," he said softly. "Not yet."

The way he said *yet* had a weight to it. Like he already knew, the moment danger appeared, he'd feel it first. Maybe he would. His body moved the same as always, precise and lethal, but his magic… it hummed under his skin as if something old had been awakened.

And then there were his eyes.

Every time light hit them, they flashed darker. Not like the void he'd shown as a prince of Midnight. This was deeper. Wilder. The kind of magic the Fates used to hide behind stories and warnings.

Callan noticed it too.

He kept glancing back at Rydian like he wasn't entirely convinced we hadn't brought a monster along with us.

I wasn't convinced either.

But mine was the opposite problem—I felt safer with him there.

We walked until the moon slid low between the branches. The forest thickened around us, shadows clustered beneath the trees. The air here smelled like moss and spring water and distant flowers that only bloomed at night.

"Keep moving," Rydian murmured softly behind me. "We still need to find shelter before the sun comes up."

"There's an estate not far from here," Callan began, but Rydian shook his head.

"Too risky. We can't afford anyone reporting back to Heliconia with our location."

"Well, it's not like we have supplies for tents," Callan said, clearly pouting at the idea of sleeping on the ground.

"We'll make do," Rydian said simply.

Callan muttered, "Lovely. A king reduced to sleeping in the bushes like a fugitive."

"Well, you are traveling with the two most wanted criminals in your lands," Rydian pointed out.

"Don't remind me," Callan snapped.

I didn't bother stepping between them. They'd bickered at least ten times since leaving Grey Oak. I knew them well enough by now to recognize Rydian's patience was paper-thin, and Callan's sarcasm was a defense mechanism. The exhaustion didn't help.

As dawn approached, Rydian directed us off the narrow hunting path and deeper into the brush where we'd have more cover. We skirted fallen logs slick with dew. The trees grew older here—massive trunks wide enough to hide a dozen fae behind. Strange fungi glowed faintly near their roots. The forest had always been beautiful, but tonight it watched us like an old creature taking stock of trespassers.

Eventually, Callan stumbled and caught himself on a tree.

"That's it," Rydian muttered. "We stop before His Majesty breaks a nail."

"I hate you," Callan said.

Rydian didn't even look back. "Excellent. I recommend the silent treatment."

I blew out a tired breath, noting the sky beginning to lighten. "We need shelter. Something hidden. Somewhere no one will look."

Rydian pointed east. "There used to be an old hunting cabin two miles that way. Half rotten. Probably crawling with spiders. Perfect for a groom on the run from his bride."

"She's not my bride," Callan muttered, and I noted the way his jaw tightened.

I caught his eye, but he only turned away, ducking his head as he went.

We trudged toward the direction Rydian indicated. My legs ached.

My ribs ached. My magic—it didn't ache so much as simmer uncomfortably under my skin, like it hadn't settled since the throne room. It had wanted me to unleash it so badly, and I'd held it back. Now, it had built into something like a pressure. Then there was the life force Heliconia had drained from me. It had left me empty. Tired to the bone.

But something else tugged at me too.

Rydian.

Every time he came close, I felt his presence like a magnet. And when he moved away, his absence was a loss.

After another hour of weaving between boulders and thick brush, we saw it: a small cabin half swallowed by overgrowth, with broken shutters and a roof patched with moss.

It was barely standing.

"Home sweet home," Rydian murmured.

Callan looked personally offended by it.

Inside, it smelled like damp wood and old leaves. But it was shelter. And no one sane would look for royalty here.

"Callan, take the cot," I said. "Rydian—"

"I'll take first watch."

Callan dropped onto the cot with a theatrical groan. Rydian nodded and stepped back outside, shadows curling protectively around him like a cloak.

Leaving Callan and me alone.

He sat slumped over, elbows on knees, staring at the floor.

I debated going to look for Rydian but decided against leaving Callan unsupervised.

"So," he said eventually. "We survived after all."

"Barely."

He lifted his brows. "Trying to diminish my gratitude?"

I snorted, sitting down opposite him on an overturned crate. "Gratitude? Is that what this is?"

He hesitated. And for once, Callan's humor fell away. "Yes," he said quietly. "Thank you."

I blinked, a little stunned by his earnest candor.

He rubbed his palms over his face. "Gods. I can never go home."

My chest ached. "We'll stop her. You'll get your throne back. Your court—"

He shook his head. "You don't understand. I surrendered it. Gave it up. I walked—no, ran—away from my throne to save myself, knowing full well what it meant. I fled like a coward."

"That isn't what you did."

"That's exactly what I did." He looked up, the look in his eyes bleak and full of self-condemnation. "Just like I tried to do seven years ago."

I swallowed. "Callan—"

"My people will never forgive me," he said hoarsely. "My own guards watched me let her try on my crown. Watched her take over my court even before we'd spoken our vows. Watched me do nothing. And then today, I relinquished Autumn to her in a heartbeat."

He looked at me then. Really looked at me. And he didn't look arrogant or amused or smug. He looked young. Afraid. Mortal.

"You've been given a second chance," I said softly. "What you do with it is what matters. The choices you make now will determine whether you were running from something... or toward something else."

He drew a breath that sounded like it hurt to take.

"What could I possibly be running *toward*?" he asked quietly.

"That," I said, "is up to you."

He sank back against the wall, eyes drifting shut like the weight of it all was finally hitting him. His breathing evened out slowly. His shoulders dropped.

I watched him for a long moment. This boy I'd nearly married. This king who'd already become something entirely different than the one before him. Then I lay down on a patch of old blankets and stared at the cracked ceiling.

I thought of Heliconia. Of Lesha. Of the thrones. Of the valley burning. And most of all...

I thought of Rydian.

The way his shadow-wrapped arms had closed around me when he'd pulled me to safety in that throne room. The way his kiss had felt like the first breath after drowning. The smile he'd worn like a secret promise he was saving for later.

Something had changed in him.

Something had changed in me.

I didn't know what it meant—not yet. But I was more than ready to find out.

I woke to a slant of afternoon light making dust motes dance in front of the broken window pane. Callan snored softly from where he'd sprawled on the cot. I sat up, wincing at the soreness in my hip from the hard wood floor.

Moving quietly, I slipped outside.

The sun had arced to the west, already beginning to dip toward the horizon. I was surprised to find I'd slept the day away. And Rydian had let me.

I wandered into the brush, looking for some sign of him. Maybe he'd fallen asleep too—

"Sleep well?"

His deep timbre startled me, and I whirled to see him standing before me. His hair had swept down over his forehead, his gaze dark and piercing as it held mine. Standing here among the soft Autumn woods, he looked like a dream come to life. Or maybe, for some, a nightmare.

"You startled me," I said.

"Apologies." He took a step toward me.

"Did you sleep at all?" I asked.

"No."

"You should have woken me. I would have taken a watch."

"You needed rest."

"So do you," I said pointedly.

"I'll sleep when we get there."

"Are we getting close?"

"If we move quickly, we'll arrive by midday tomorrow."

"Callan will complain," I said.

His gaze darkened. "Then he can find his own way."

"You don't mean that."

He glowered. "Sometimes, I wish I did."

My mouth curved. "You know, you're not as grumpy and scary as you pretend to be."

His eyes narrowed. "Is that so?"

Shadows leaked from his feet, crawling over the ground and whispering up my legs. Their touch felt like a second set of hands, trailing lightly up my body. I found myself leaning into it. Into him.

I watched as he took another step toward me. Then another. Until he was standing over me. His hands remained at his sides, but his shadows swirled and caressed me, leaving small, phantom strokes along my hips.

"What about now?" he asked in a low voice.

"I'm not scared of you," I whispered.

His eyes flashed. Not with fury. With desire. "Maybe you should be."

I swallowed hard as he leaned down until his mouth was only a breath from mine.

"And now?"

My heart stuttered, and I felt my own desire stir in every cell of my body.

"You two are nauseating."

Rydian's shadows abruptly vanished.

I whirled to find Callan, his lip curling in disgust, his eyes still lined with sleep.

"At least wait until we've had breakfast," he added before turning away and sauntering off behind a tree.

When I glanced back at Rydian, I expected him to be upset. Instead, his smirk was anything but.

"What is that look for?" I asked him.

"Soon, Furious."

"Soon what?" I asked, my breath suddenly short.

"We'll find somewhere with no interruptions." His voice dropped to barely a whisper. "And thick walls."

I swallowed hard, imagining it. Remembering the night we'd had in my room at Grey Oak. The way it had felt to have his hands on my body. And then the rejection of anything more. When he'd told me what vow he'd made to my father. That he refused to get involved when his time was so short.

"I don't understand. You said you didn't want to—"

"I changed my mind."

My heart leaped. "About what?"

I had to hear it. To know.

His gaze dipped to my mouth. "About everything. You're mine, Furious. Soon. And then forever."

THE
LOVERS

Chapter Forty-Six
Rydian

We moved through the forest as the light bled out of the sky. Callan kept up a steady stream of low-grade complaining —about the lack of horses, about the quality of our nonexistent food, about the injustice of his current wardrobe. Aurelia humored him with the occasional jab. I ignored them both and focused on the path only I could see.

The Emerald Forest wasn't just trees and dirt. It was layers—old roads buried under roots, streams diverted and remade by shifting magic, pockets of wild sorcery that didn't care whose banner flew on which castle.

The Spring Court had wrapped its camp in some of that wildness. I'd felt it when I'd woken there after Nali's naiad had pulled me from the river—half-conscious, half-drowned, more shadow than flesh.

We walked until my legs started to feel the weight of the last few days —a battle, a wedding crash, a god-summoning, almost dying—and then kept walking anyway. The moon slid lower between the branches. Shadows grew thicker. The Emerald Forest wrapped around us like a living thing.

In the deepest dark of the night, Callan's stomach growled—again.

When no one answered it, he made a disgusted noise. "Remind me again why I didn't go north with Slade to meet my own army?"

"Because Heliconia will look there first to find you," Aurelia said way more nicely than I would have.

Callan was not mollified. "This whole arrangement is deeply offensive."

"If you have enough energy to complain, you have enough energy to keep moving," I told him.

He scowled but did as I said.

Brat. I had no sympathy for him.

Heliconia was out there, sitting on the throne of her stolen court and dreaming of the god-magic imbued into that throne. She'd turn the realm upside-down for Callan. And if that didn't work, she'd set her sights on the next victim.

We had one shot to convince Spring not to be next.

I didn't care how badly that goal inconvenienced Callan.

By the time the first gray hint of dawn brushed the horizon, Aurelia was swaying on her feet. Callan's steps had lost their kingly swagger. Even my shadows dragged a little.

It hit me then—the exhaustion I'd been outrunning.

Not just in my muscles. In my bones. In the place beneath my ribs where the Furiosity rune burned low and steady, like banked coals waiting for a gust of wind.

I pressed my palm flat over it.

"Not today," I muttered.

The god who'd branded me didn't answer. He rarely did unless I forced him to.

I thought of the throne room. Of the moment Aurelia had gone to her knees, ice and death creeping over her skin. Of the sound her breath had made when Heliconia had started to siphon her power.

I'd moved before I'd thought.

Shadows, teeth, rage. The rest was blood and instinct.

Now, in the quiet of the dark woods, the memory crawled under my skin in a different way.

She could have died.

If I'd been one breath slower.

If the naiad hadn't dragged me from the river. If Talthis hadn't agreed to shelter me. If I hadn't gone to Ire, if he hadn't defied the rules of his treaty and told me what I'd needed to know about the thrones, about Aurelia's location.

Too many ifs.

I was done with ifs.

And I was done staying away from her.

We pushed deeper. The air cooled. The sounds of the forest changed —less underbrush rustle, more distant, crystalline notes like someone plucking glass strings.

We walked another twenty minutes before I felt it—the faint hum along my spine, the way the shadows around us sharpened, not mine this time but something older.

"Stop," I said.

Aurelia halted immediately. Callan did not. He took one more step, opened his mouth to say something snide, and ran headfirst into an invisible wall.

He bounced off it with a curse, stumbling backwards. "What in—"

"Ward line," I said. "I've been looking for it. Congratulations. You found it with your face."

Aurelia's mouth twitching told me she'd appreciated that more than she was letting on.

The forest went very still.

Not quiet. Just... listening.

Callan scowled but dropped his hand pointedly away from his dagger.

I stepped forward alone, stopping just shy of the unseen barrier, and let my shadows slip ahead. They touched the ward—recognizing the taste of it from before—and eased a thin opening.

"Rydian?" Aurelia murmured.

"We're here," I said.

Leaves rustled overhead. A soft, melodic whistle cut through the air, as if someone had plucked a note out of the breeze itself.

Then figures stepped out of the trees.

Spring guards, two of them, in green-and-gold leathers that seemed to grow from their bodies rather than be strapped onto them. Bows drawn, arrows nocked, aimed at our chests.

"Identify yourselves," the taller one said.

Aurelia looked at me uncertainly.

I nodded at her to go ahead.

"Aurelia Valeen, heir to the Summer Court," Aurelia called out.

The shorter guard's eyes widened. She lowered her bow.

"And the rest?" the taller one asked.

"Rydian of Midnight," I said.

The guard's eyes narrowed. Not at me.

"And him?" he asked, gesturing with his chin toward Callan.

My half-brother straightened instinctively, like his body couldn't help responding to being challenged.

"His Majesty King Callan of the Autumn Court," he said coolly.

The guards exchanged a look. Their magic rippled, conferring in a way words didn't. Finally, the shorter one lifted two fingers to her lips and let out a high, trilling whistle.

A minute passed.

Then the forest shifted.

Branches bent aside of their own accord. Roots drew back, revealing a faint path lit by a glow that came from nowhere obvious. The scent of jasmine thickened in the air.

Talthis stepped out of the green.

The Spring emissary looked fresh considering he was camped in the forest—braided hair threaded with new leaves, armor polished, eyes too knowing for someone who smiled as much as he did.

He wasn't smiling now.

"Talthis," Aurelia said.

"Aurelia." His gaze swept over her as he cut a short bow. "This is unexpected. We received word you were headed for Grey Oak."

His gaze flicked to me, his frown evident.

"We've just come from there," Aurelia told him. "Heliconia has taken control of the court."

"Yes, we felt the surge yesterday from here. Frost and... something older." His eyes flicked to me and lingered. "I see you survived it."

"Disappointed?" I asked.

"The opposite," he said mildly. "Come. We'll talk at camp."

The camp was just as hidden as before, half-grown, half-built. Tents stitched from living leaves. Platforms nestled in the branches above, vines woven into ladders. Lanterns glowed from high in the canopy. The ground itself felt softer underfoot, like a mossy rug, cozy and welcoming.

Spring soldiers watched us as we passed—bows lowered but not put away, hands near blades, expressions a mix of curiosity and suspicion.

One young woman near the center whispered Aurelia's name. I couldn't tell if it sounded more like a prayer or a curse. More than a few glared outright at Callan.

Talthis led us into a large tent where a low table had been set up, maps spread across its surface. A couple of his advisors followed us inside but remained silent near the tent wall. Nali was nowhere to be found.

Talthis turned, crossing his arms.

"All right," he said. "Tell me why Heliconia's curse bearer and Autumn's runaway king are standing in my camp."

I glanced at Aurelia.

She lifted her chin and spoke, laying out the facts with that calm, steady voice I'd come to recognize as the one she used when the ground was falling out from under her.

The war camp. The Frostwights. The valley burning. Lesha. The thrones. The wedding. Heliconia trying to use a marriage to take the throne's power for herself. Callan yielding his court to save his people.

By the time she finished, Talthis' expression was troubled.

He exhaled. "And you're certain," he said slowly, "that what she took from Concordia's throne could be taken from ours as well."

"Yes," Aurelia said.

I stepped in before he could argue. "She's not guessing," I said. "Whatever the gods left in that throne, Heliconia stole it. And now she wants more."

His gaze sharpened. "And you know this how?"

"Because I spoke with a Furiosity before I left this camp," I told him quietly. "And he confirmed it."

I could feel Aurelia's gaze burning into me, not to mention Callan's, but I didn't let myself look. Instead, I held the Spring fae's gaze while he studied me, considering it all.

"Assuming all of this is true..." Talthis rubbed his jawline thoughtfully.

"It is," I cut in.

He ignored me. "My queen is cautious. We protect our borders. Our people. Our throne. We do not go courting trouble."

"If you don't go to her," Aurelia said, "she'll come to you. That isn't a threat. It's just where the path leads once she fails to retrieve Callan."

Talthis stared at her a moment, then tilted his head. "And what exactly are you offering, besides warnings and doom, if my queen chooses to involve herself?"

I bit back a snarl at that. He was a diplomat, I reminded myself. He couldn't help it. Everything was a trade to him. A gain and a loss.

"An alliance," Aurelia said.

"With what army?" he asked, blunt now. "Summer is cursed and out of reach. Autumn has just lost its king but gained a usurping queen. Midnight is... whatever Midnight is these days." His eyes flicked between us. "You are three fugitives with no army and no allies."

Heat crawled up my spine. Not anger. Something colder. Sharper. And then the words were out before I could decide if it was wise to utter them.

"Three fugitives we may be," I said. "But we are also three crowns."

Talthis frowned. "I count two; am I wrong?"

Aurelia shot me a frantic look. She knew what I was about to do. Callan, on the other hand, stiffened at my side.

I met the emissary's gaze head-on.

"I am the son of King Duron of Autumn—and Queen Cadira of Midnight," I said. "Rightful heir to the Onyx Throne. And I pledge the full force of my armies to this fight."

Silence fell like a stone.

Talthis stared at me. Then at Aurelia. Then at Callan.

Callan's expression closed so fast it might've shattered something behind his eyes. "You're joking," he said flatly.

"I speak the truth," I told him.

"When," he asked, voice dropping, "were you planning to mention that little detail? Before or after we all spent our lifetime thinking we knew you at all?"

"I told Aurelia," I said. Not apologetic. Just honest.

"You told *her*," he said. "But not your own brother."

I met his anger without flinching. The old guilt was there, yes—but it had teeth now. I'd lived too long with secrets carved into my bones to pretend they hadn't kept me alive. That I wouldn't do it all again the same way. For the people who needed me.

"Duron cared only for the power he could gain from me," I said quietly. "Telling you would've painted a target on your back long before you were ready to see it."

He laughed once, harsh and humorless. "Don't act like you did this for me. If you had, you would have brought your army to fight with mine to keep Heliconia from getting as far as she did. Instead, you continue to protect your own kind while mine suffer."

"Enough," Aurelia said.

We both looked at her.

"This isn't about who should've told whom," she said. "The only thing that matters is this: Heliconia wants to drain every throne in this realm and remake herself into something we won't be able to kill. If we keep arguing, she'll get what she wants."

She turned back to Talthis. "You asked what you'd be getting," she said. "The answer is three courts who will stand with you when she comes for your throne. Summer, Autumn, Midnight. Autumn's army is gathering now under a shared banner between Callan and me." Callan huffed but didn't argue it, though I was sure it pained him. "They will march where we send them and fight bravely."

"And Midnight?" Callan pressed. "Will they march for anyone but themselves?"

"Yes," Aurelia said gravely before I could offer up any kind of answer. She met my gaze steadily. "Soon," she said, echoing my promise to her.

And I knew I would not be able to stop her from trying to open the gates. Not for much longer. The danger be damned.

Talthis studied her. Then studied me again, like my confession had rewritten some equation in his head.

"I will take this to my queen," he said.

He wasn't promising anything. But it was more than we'd had when we walked in.

"She doesn't have to pledge troops," Aurelia said. "Not yet. Just guard her throne. Use whatever magic she has to make sure Heliconia can't get near it. If that means closing borders, do it."

"And if it means painting a target on our backs because we chose a side?" Talthis asked softly.

"You already have a target," I said. "You just can't see it from inside your walls. Concordia didn't think they'd fall either. Ask them how that went."

Finally, he inclined his head. "You have given us much to think about. It will take some time for me to hear her answer, but you are welcome to remain while we wait for word."

"We're not staying," I said. "We're headed northeast."

His gaze flicked to the mark on Aurelia's throat, then back to mine. "To your court?"

"Until we know where we stand," I said.

Talthis dipped his head.

"Thank you," Aurelia told him.

He gave her a long look. "You're different than you were when we last met," he said quietly. "Your power has grown. I can feel it in the air."

"I am becoming more myself," she told him.

"Indeed." He glanced between us. "You're all welcome to take rest and refreshment before you depart."

"We could use both," she said.

Callan looked visibly relieved though he actively avoided looking at me as the guards led us to tents of our own. I didn't bother trying to speak to him again. Not when exhaustion left me without any words that would have changed things between us now. Instead, I slipped into the tent beside Aurelia's, shucked off my boots, and slept hard enough to forget this world.

THE
LOVERS

Chapter Forty-Seven
Aurelia

By the time the old hunting trail bent toward the foothills of Midnight territory, my entire body felt like it had been scraped hollow and stuffed with gravel. Four days of walking through the darkest hours of the night. Four days of hiding in bramble thickets during the day, buried under leaves so no Obsidian patrol would spot us. Four days of eating sun-dried rabbit and foraging for berries. Four days of Callan muttering complaints under his breath and Rydian pretending not to hear them.

And four days of... this thing simmering between Rydian and me.

A pull.

A magnet.

A hunger I refused to acknowledge out loud—but which deepened every time he looked at me with that new, shadow-drenched intensity.

We were nearly at the cabin when Callan tripped for the eighth time.

He caught himself on a tree and hissed, "Gods, I'm going to shatter my ankle before Heliconia ever finds us."

"A worthy sacrifice," Rydian said dryly from behind me.

"Stop, both of you," I muttered. "We're close."

Callan glanced up sharply. "You're sure?"

I lifted a hand toward the faint shimmer in the air ahead—barely visible between the trees. A subtle ripple. A whisper of magic. I recognized it now for what it was: protection wards.

My pulse sped at the thought of seeing Lesha. Or taking a hot bath. "Positive."

Callan straightened, combing leaves out of his hair as if he still cared what he looked like. "Well. Finally. We'll have food. And beds. Or gods forbid, hot water."

"I'll put in a good word with the master of the house," Rydian drawled.

We stepped through the shimmer and into the clearing.

And there it was.

Dark wood notched at the seams. Sloped roof. Smoke curling faintly from the chimney. A ring of protection stones half-buried beneath moss. A warding field humming like a heartbeat around it.

Frithhold.

For a strange moment, it felt almost like coming home.

The front door burst open.

Keres stood framed in the threshold, eyes wide. She wore a tunic and loose slacks, and her hair had been left in a long braid down her back. She looked more at ease than I'd ever seen.

"They're home," she called over her shoulder, her voice cracking.

Then Vanya peered around her. "Aurelia, Rydian," she called, smiling. Then she spotted Callan, gasped, and promptly dropped into a curtsy so deep her forehead nearly hit the floor.

"Your High—High—Highness," she stammered.

Behind her, Daegel leaned against a support beam, arms crossed, eyebrow raised. "Took you long enough."

I walked straight to Keres and threw my arms around her. She held me tight, her usual sharp sarcasm absent for once.

"It's good to see you," she whispered.

"And you," I whispered back, voice breaking.

Rydian stepped in behind me, and the air shifted again.

Shadow. Strength. Presence.

Keres looked over my shoulder and exhaled. "Glad to see you're not dead."

He inclined his head. "Not for lack of trying."

Callan cleared his throat pointedly.

"Your Majesty." Keres' voice was full of sarcasm. "What a surprise. Wish I could say it was pleasant." She shot me a pointed look full of questions.

"Callan's going to stay with us for a while," I said.

Her eyes narrowed. First on me, then on Rydian, and finally on Callan. "Couldn't we just get a puppy and be done with it?" she asked.

Callan looked offended.

Rydian snorted a laugh.

"Vanya," I said, "can you show Callan to a room?"

"Of course." She led the way into the house.

We all followed, the rest of us gathering in the great room while Callan disappeared down the hall with Vanya leading the way.

I turned to Daegel. "How's Lesha?"

His expression sobered instantly. "She's awake. Barely. But she asked for you."

My heart clenched. I followed him through the den and into the back room.

Lesha lay on her stomach, thin as reeds, wings nothing but bandaged scars. Her hair was matted. Her skin too pale. I didn't know what I'd expected. More healing than this; she looked just as frail as the day we'd rescued her.

"Auri," she whispered, voice rasping, breaking.

I dropped to my knees beside her bed and took her hand. "I'm here."

Her fingers squeezed weakly. "Good."

I bit my lip hard, trying not to cry. "How do you feel?"

"Like I lost a fight with a frost giant," she murmured.

A painful laugh burst from my chest.

"And you…" Her gaze softened. "You look different."

I froze. "Different how?"

"Stronger. Older." Her eyes flicked to my mark. "Brighter."

My throat tightened. I wanted to tell her everything—but she was already fading, her eyes closing as she slipped toward sleep.

"I'll stay," I whispered.

"No." Keres stepped forward, voice firm but soft. "Let her rest. She used too much strength today during our exercises. She'll sleep for hours."

Lesha's fingers went slack in mine.

I pressed a kiss to her knuckles before I stood.

Keres placed a hand on my shoulder. "Come on. You need sleep too."

"I'm fine," I said, waving off her concern.

"Really?" Her brow lifted. "Because you look like Hel."

"I missed your brutal honesty, you know that?"

She laughed. "You missed Thorne's home cooking, you mean."

"Are they back yet?" I asked.

"Here and gone a day ago," she said quietly. "They told us what happened in Grey Oak."

"The Withered made it back to the caves then?"

She nodded. "Along with the contingent they recruited."

I exhaled. "How many?"

"Not enough," she admitted regretfully. I'd known it wouldn't be. "But a start. Now, come on. I'll give you all the details later. You look asleep on your feet."

"I think Vanya gave my old room to Callan," I said, stifling a yawn. "But I don't mind the floor."

"You're not sleeping on the floor," Rydian said, stepping into our path.

My heart stuttered.

Keres arched a brow at him. "And where exactly do you suggest she sleep?"

Rydian's eyes met mine. "With me."

My breath caught. Heat curled low in my stomach.

Keres's brows shot up to her hairline. Daegel choked on his own spit behind us. From behind my old bedroom door came a faint, muffled, "Of course she does," from Callan, because apparently the gods hated me enough to give him perfect hearing.

I swallowed. "Rydian—"

He stepped toward me. Even tired, filthy, and half feral from sleepless travel, he looked like a nightmare carved into the shape of a male. A very handsome, very tempting male whose attention bordered on obsession just now.

Suddenly, Keres was gone, and we were standing alone in the hallway.

"Aurelia," he murmured in a voice that sent a shudder of pleasure through me, "Come to bed."

The way he said it, the question brimming in his depthless eyes—it felt like he was asking for so much more than one night. And I was more than willing to grant it.

Rydian extended his hand.

I took it.

The decision settled between us like gravity—inevitable, certain, ancient.

"Come," he said softly. "Sleep. Before your legs give out."

He tugged me toward the door to his room.

My pulse thundered as we reached it.

Inside, the room was dimly lit. Clean. Familiar in a way that made something in my chest ache. A heavy bed. A small table. A single candle flickering.

I stepped inside.

Rydian closed the door behind us with a soft click.

Shadows curled around his feet as he leaned back against it—watching me in a way that made every inch of my skin feel too tight.

And then he said, voice like velvet dragged over stone, "Come here, Furious."

My breath hitched.

And I did.

THE
LOVERS

Chapter Forty-Eight

Rydian

She stood before me, shoulders rising and falling like she'd just run a mile instead of crossing a cabin. Sunlight cut across her profile from the window, catching the smudge of travel-dust on her cheek, the shadows under her eyes, the stubborn tilt to her chin. The need to touch every inch of her had driven me across the realm just as powerfully as the need to make her safe again.

And now, finally, we were alone.

For the first time in too long, there were no obsidian-eyed soldiers, no naiad judging my worth. No thrones. No gods. No blood vows. No Heliconia.

Just her. Standing before me like some kind of holy offering.

I took a step toward her, then another.

A pulse of nerves flickered across her face, quickly masked.

"Don't," I said quietly.

"Don't what?"

"Second-guess this. Or me."

"You were very clear before. About not letting this happen ever again."

"I see things differently now."

"Is that so?"

I hummed. "Almost losing you—twice—helped to clarify what matters."

I lifted my hand. Shadows crawled up the log walls at my gesture, darkening every knot and seam. A second curl of power slid under the door and along the cracks in the floorboards, sealing every gap with thick, velvety darkness.

The sounds of the cabin—murmurs of Keres and Vanya in the kitchen, Callan's movements in the far room—muffled, then vanished altogether. The air went soft. Close.

Aurelia glanced around, eyes narrowing. "What did you do?"

"Soundproofed us." I let my shadows settle like a curtain around the room, coating the window, masking everything that existed outside these walls. "No one hears anything that happens in here unless I allow it."

She swallowed. I watched the movement of her throat like I'd been starved for it.

"Do you expect there to be a lot of noise?" she asked.

I stepped into her space, close enough to feel the heat of her body through my shirt. My hand braced against the doorframe beside her head, caging her in without touching her. And I let my lips curve into the smile that conveyed the depth of my intentions as I said, "I certainly hope so."

She shivered, and the sight of it only fed my hunger for her.

My gaze dropped to her mouth, then back. "I'm going to spend the rest of the night coaxing every noise you're capable of making from that pretty little mouth of yours."

Her hand curled in the fabric of my shirt, pulling me closer, but I stepped back.

"Bath first," I cut in gently.

She blinked. "What?"

"We've been walking for days. Your shoulders are one big knot. There's dirt in your hair." I let my fingers hover near a streak of dirt along her collarbone, not quite touching. Her breath hitched anyway. "I'm going to take care of you tonight. All of you. Starting with that bath."

Suspicion warred with desire in her eyes. "You just want to undress me."

"Obviously," I said. "I'm not a saint, Princess." I leaned in, my mouth brushing the shell of her ear. "But I intend to enjoy every step of the process. And so will you."

A shiver rippled down her spine. Her grip on my shirt tightened—this time, dragging me closer. "Bossy."

I smirked. "Get used to it. I'm the heir to a throne, too, after all."

I pulled back and let my hand fall from the door. For a second, she stayed pressed where she was, as if testing whether I'd keep her pinned there. Tempting. Very tempting. But tonight was about drawing this out, not slamming her against the wood and losing my mind.

Later, maybe.

I turned toward the adjoining bathing chamber instead. The cabin was simple, but we'd stocked it well. A copper tub sat near the window, empty, waiting. I flicked my shadows toward the ceiling, banked them, and reached for the lever.

The water flowed, hot enough to cloud the air with steam.

Behind me, I could feel Aurelia watching as I poured a bottle of oil into the water. The scent of lavender filled the air.

When the bath was ready, I turned back to her.

"Come here," I said.

She came forward slowly as if she wasn't sure of this side of me. I didn't bother to admit that neither was I. I'd never taken care of anyone like this before. Never wanted to.

I stopped her with a hand on her hip.

"Look at me," I said.

She lifted her gaze. There it was—that flicker of trust she tried so hard to hide, softer than the rest of her, vulnerable and lethal all at once.

"We don't know what's coming next," I said quietly. "We don't know how long we have. So, if you want this, Furious... don't hold back. Don't brace for it to be taken away. Take it." I slid my knuckles along her cheek. "Take me. Just as I will take you—if you're still offering."

Something in her eyes broke open at that. She exhaled, a rough, shaky sound that might have been a laugh, might have been a sob, and nodded once.

"Let me undress you," I murmured.

Her breath caught, but she didn't argue.

She turned around, and I went to work on the laces of her tunic. When it was undone, I pulled the garment over her head, baring the golden line of her shoulders, the sweep of her back, the marks she bore. Scars. Freckles. Gods, she was beautiful.

"Turn around," I said, voice rougher than I intended.

She obeyed, and I reached for her trousers, unbuttoning them and shucking them down her legs until they were on the floor. Her undergarments went next, sliding away until she was standing in the soft candlelight in nothing at all.

For a long, delicious moment, I allowed myself to look. It was a gift I hadn't allowed myself the first time I'd come to her. Back then, everything had felt urgent and final. Like a goodbye. I couldn't bear the idea of looking at what I was losing. This felt like a beginning. And I was damn sure going to take my time saying hello.

Her shoulders were elegant, sloped like the promise of sunrise. Her breasts—full, soft, lifted slightly as she drew in a nervous breath—made heat coil low and hard inside me. Her waist dipped gently, drawing my gaze down the smooth line of her stomach to the flare of her hips... the place where tendrils of my shadows whispered greedily along her thighs as if they, too, wanted permission to touch her. To make her moan.

Gods. I had never wanted anything like this.

Her shoulders tightened under the weight of my gaze. "Say something," she muttered.

"I am," I said, unable to fight off the smile. "I'm just using my eyes."

Color flared high on her cheeks. "You're impossible."

"Yes." I brushed a thumb lightly over a faint scar at her ribs. "And you are perfect."

Her breath hitched.

I took her hand and led her toward the tub. Steam curled around us, wrapping her in warmth and scent. I steadied her as she stepped in, the water rising around her calves, her thighs, her hips. She sank down with a sigh that punched straight through my chest.

"That good?" I murmured.

She closed her eyes, letting her head tip back against the rim. "You have no idea."

I knelt beside the tub, ignoring the way the floor dug into my knees, and rolled up my sleeves.

"Sit up," I said gently. "Let me see you."

Her lids fluttered open. She shifted, turning slightly toward me, arms resting on the edge. Loose strands of hair clung damply to her neck.

I dipped a cloth into the water, wrung it out, and touched it to her shoulder. She flinched—not from pain, but from sensation, every line of her body tensing, then easing as the heat soaked into sore muscles.

"You don't have to—" she began.

"I want to." I dragged the cloth slowly along the curve of her shoulder, down her arm, over the small raised ridges of scars. "Let me."

She went quiet, her cheeks flushing deliciously.

I worked in silence for a while. Water lapped gently at the sides of the tub as I bathed her, every touch an exploration. The back of her neck, where tension always lived. The line of her collarbone, where I'd wanted to put my mouth too many times to count. The elegant shape of her wrist, fragile and deceptively strong.

Her breathing changed, growing deeper, more uneven. Every time my fingers brushed skin instead of cloth, a little spark jumped between us.

"Rydian," she said eventually, voice low. "This is... cruel."

At my next touch, a sound broke from her, half exasperated, half wild. "You—"

"Lean forward," I instructed.

She did, arms folding on the rim so she could rest her head on them. The movement bared her back to me—tension-strung muscles, fine lines of strength, soft curves that invited me closer. I let my palm follow the path the cloth had taken, the touch a bare whisper over damp skin.

She shivered.

It turned into a soft, involuntary sound when I found another knot and worked it loose.

"Better?" I asked.

She didn't answer with words, just melted into my hands.

I took my time with her back, cataloging every inch with my touch, my mind. When I finally let my hands skim down along her sides, just above the waterline, her breath stuttered.

"Still with me?"

She nodded against her arms.

"Good." I leaned in a little closer, letting my mouth hover near her ear. "Because I'm nowhere near done."

I set the cloth aside, dipped my fingers into the warm water, and let my hands explore more boldly. Over the curve of her shoulder. Down the slope of her spine. Along the edge of her ribs, where the rise and fall of each breath felt like a prayer under my palms.

She shifted restlessly in the water, thighs pressing together. Magic shivered under her skin, a low, restless hum that synced with the thrum of my own.

"You're shaking," I murmured.

"You're torturing me," she shot back, voice frayed.

"Not torture," I said. My fingers traced idle patterns on her hip, stroking slow, lazy circles. "This is worship."

"You're—" Her breath broke as I let my hands slide a fraction lower, still not quite where she wanted them. "You're impossible."

"You keep saying that," I said. "And yet, here you are."

She twisted, turning to face me. Water sloshed quietly. Her eyes were darker now, pupils blown, lashes clumped with steam. "Because I trust you," she said, the words spilling out like she hadn't meant to say them. "Even when I shouldn't."

My chest tightened. Gently, I reached up and cradled her jaw in my palm, thumb brushing the damp skin beneath her lower lip.

"You should," I said. "You can."

"You're going to die for me," she whispered, throat thick. "Someday. Because of that stupid vow. Because of my father. Because of everything I am. How am I supposed to live with that and still—"

"Love me?" I finished when she couldn't.

Her eyes flickered.

I huffed out a short, humorless laugh. "I've got news for you, Furious. You already do."

She glared weakly. "You're very sure of yourself."

"I'm sure of us," I said. "The rest can go to Hel."

She looked at me like she wanted to throw something. Or cry. Or kiss me until she couldn't stand upright. "What changed?" she asked quietly. "You were the one who kept saying we couldn't, because of your vow. Because you didn't want to tie me to a male who's already promised his death away."

"I went to Hel," I said. "Or as close as I could manage. I called your father and tried to rip that vow out of his hands."

Her eyes widened. "You what?"

"I failed," I admitted. "He wouldn't let me take it back. Wouldn't free me from it." My thumb dragged slowly across her cheekbone. "But I realized something. The gods aren't in control of me any more than they're in control of Heliconia. They can demand my death all they like. They don't get to dictate my life."

Emotion thickened her voice. "So you decided to live."

"I decided to live for you," I said. "For as long as I have." I leaned in, my forehead touching hers. "I am going to fight beside you. Bleed beside you. Sleep beside you. And no god, no queen, no throne gets to tell me I can't claim what I want before they try to take it away."

Her breath hitched. "You want me," she whispered.

"I want all of you," I said. "Every sharp edge. Every scar. Every reckless, infuriating, impossible part."

Her fingers rose from the water, trembling, and fisted in the front of my shirt. "Then take me," she said, voice barely more than air.

I smiled, slow and lethal. "With pleasure."

I bent and kissed her.

She met me with a desperate, ferocious hunger that knocked the air from my lungs. Her mouth opened for me, hot and sweet and familiar all at once, like something I'd been starving for and finally, finally gotten my hands on. Her wet fingers slid up into my hair, pulling me closer, dragging me in until there was no space left between us.

The world narrowed to her lips, her breath, the little sounds she made when I deepened the kiss, when I angled my head just right. My hands found her shoulders, then her back, then the slick, heated curve of her waist under the water. I hauled her closer, until she was pressed to the side of the tub and I was braced over her, half-kneeling, half-caged by my own need.

She gasped against my mouth, then kissed me harder, like she could crawl inside my skin and stay there.

"Rydian," she breathed when we broke for air, her lips swollen, eyes dazed. "Bed. Now."

I chuckled, low and dark. "Impatient, Princess."

"You've been torturing me for days," she said. "Weeks. Years."

"Fair point," I conceded.

I peeled my shirt over my head and tossed it aside, her gaze following the motion hungrily. Her eyes dragged over the runes on my skin, the scars, the shadows pooling at my feet like they were waiting for what would come next.

Her tongue brushed her bottom lip.

That nearly undid me.

I unbuckled my belt, watching the way her chest rose and fell faster with each sound of metal on leather. Boots. Pants. Every layer hitting the floor felt like scraping away the last restraints I'd ever had between us.

When I stepped out of the final piece of clothing, her breath caught —audibly.

"Furious," I murmured, stepping close enough that heat spilled between us. "If you keep looking at me like that, I'm never letting you out of this room."

"Good," she whispered.

I sank into the tub behind her, pulling her gently into my lap, her back against my chest. She gave a soft gasp as my arms wrapped around her waist. Her body melted against mine, head tipping back onto my shoulder in silent permission.

"I want to touch you," I said against her neck. "Every inch. Slowly."

I pressed my lips to the slick curve of her shoulder. And then her throat.

And then the place just beneath her ear. She made a small noise of pleasure, and my cock twitched. Gods, I'd never been owned by anything like I was owned by that sound.

My mouth brushed her ear. "You're mine, Aurelia."

Her fingers tangled with mine under the water, guiding them between her thighs.

"And you're mine," she breathed.

The vow settled between us—heavy, binding, consuming—and I lowered my lips to her neck as I slid a finger inside her wet heat, ready to worship her properly.

THE
LOVERS

Chapter Forty-Nine
Aurelia

Rydian's finger slid inside me, and I shattered into a thousand sparks of light. My back arched against his chest, head falling onto his shoulder as my body clenched around that single point of contact. The water lapped gently at my skin, warm and languid, but everything inside me was fire.

"Gods, you feel so good," Rydian murmured against my ear, voice like velvet and smoke.

I couldn't quite form words to respond before his thumb found the sensitive bundle of nerves at my center and all that came out was a broken moan.

His laugh was low, dark, insufferably satisfied. "That's it, Furious. Let me hear you."

The shadows he'd wrapped around the room pulsed in response—thick ribbons of darkness coating the walls, the window, every crack in the floorboards. No light crept in. No sound crept out. We existed in our own pocket of the world, sealed away from everything and everyone.

His free hand splayed across my stomach, holding me steady as he worked me with devastating patience. One finger became two, stretching me, filling me, curling just so until stars burst behind my eyelids.

"Rydian." His name came out half prayer, half warning.

"I've got you." His lips brushed the shell of my pointed ear, breath hot. "I've got you. Just feel."

So I did.

I let myself sink into the sensation of his body behind me—all hard planes and coiled strength, his erection pressing insistently against my lower back. The water was cooling now, but I barely noticed, not when his fingers moved in that relentless rhythm, not when his shadows crept along the surface of the water like curious things, trailing over my collarbones, my breasts, everywhere his hands couldn't reach.

"So responsive," he said, wonder threading through the roughness of his voice. "Every touch and you light up for me. Do you know how long I've wanted this? To see you come undone by my hands?"

I couldn't answer. Couldn't think. There was only the building pressure, the impossible tension coiling tighter at my core. My fingers gripped his forearm beneath the water, nails biting into muscle and ink as I chased something I couldn't name.

"That's it," he coaxed. "Don't hold back. You don't have to be composed. Not with me."

The words undid something in my chest—some wall I hadn't realized I was keeping up.

"Where do I please you, Princess?" he whispered, and gods, I remembered. I remembered him asking that question before, remembered the smirk on his lips, the challenge in his storm-gray eyes. Back when we were still pretending we didn't want this. Back when the idea of touching him felt like treason against everything I'd been raised to accomplish.

Now his fingers curled inside me, and I answered with a sound I didn't recognize as my own.

"Here," he breathed. "Right here. Isn't it?"

I panted, on the brink of coming apart in his arms.

His thumb pressed harder, circling with devastating precision while his fingers maintained that perfect rhythm. The shadows around us seemed to pulse with his heartbeat—or maybe mine. I couldn't tell anymore where I ended and he began.

"Come for me, Furious," he said, and it wasn't a request. It was a command. A royal decree from the heir to a throne who had chosen to kneel at mine.

I broke.

The release crashed through me like a wave, like wildfire, like the first rays of dawn splitting open a dark horizon. My body bowed off his chest, muscles seizing, every nerve ending igniting at once. I heard myself cry out—his name, maybe, or something wordless—and his shadows swallowed the sound whole, kept it just for us in this sanctuary he'd built from darkness and want.

His arms wrapped around me as I trembled through the aftershocks, one hand still pressed between my thighs, gentling me down. His lips found the curve of my neck, pressing soft kisses there while I remembered how to breathe.

"Beautiful," he murmured against my skin. "Absolutely beautiful."

I laughed weakly, still trembling. "I don't think I can move."

"Then don't." He turned me in his arms until I was facing him, straddling his lap in the cooling water. His gray eyes were molten in the candlelight, his dark hair curling damply at his temples. "I'll move you where I want you."

The promise in those words sent a fresh shiver down my spine. I reached up to brush back his damp hair, my heart already racing again as his erection pressed into my core. His eyes lit with that same awareness, but he didn't hurry to do anything about it.

Instead, he caught my wrist, bringing my palm to his lips. The tattoos that wound up his forearms seemed to shift in the flickering light—ancient runes of power and protection, a history written in ink. I traced one with my finger, following it up to his bicep, across the hard swell of muscle.

He was beautiful too.

All sharp angles and lethal grace, built like a weapon meant for war and somehow still gentle enough to wash my hair and knead the knots from my shoulders. The contradiction made something ache in my chest.

"Bed," I said, finding my voice again. "You promised me a bed."

His smile turned wicked. "Impatient."

"You made me impatient." I leaned in, brushing my lips against his jaw. "You made me a lot of things."

"Good things, I hope."

"Terrible things," I corrected. "Distracted during meetings with Spring emissaries. Pretending your touch was merely to help steady me as we cut through a thicket. Prone to staring at your shoulders when you were changing out of your leathers. These last few days have been torture."

"That was on purpose," he admitted.

"I know." I kissed the corner of his mouth. "I hated you for it."

"No, you didn't."

No. I didn't.

He stood in one fluid motion, lifting me like I weighed nothing. Water cascaded off us both, steam curling in the air, and I wrapped my legs around his waist on instinct. The hard length of him pressed against my center, and we both went still, breath catching.

"Bed," he agreed, voice strained.

He stepped out of the tub, shadows parting for him like loyal subjects, and carried me through the doorway into the adjoining bedroom. He laid me down like I was something fragile. Like I might break. Then he knelt at the edge of the bed, dark hair falling across his forehead in wild disarray. His hands found my ankles, thumbs tracing slow circles.

"What are you doing?" I asked, impatient and aching.

His grin was knowing. "I'm taking my time." His grip slid higher. Calves. Knees. The soft skin of my inner thighs. His shadows followed, trailing over my skin like phantom caresses, raising goosebumps everywhere they touched.

I let out a sigh.

Then his mouth moved higher, trailing along my thigh, and all thought evaporated like morning mist.

"Rydian—"

"Shh." His breath ghosted over my center, and my hips jerked off the bed. "Let me worship you properly."

He was merciless. Thorough. His tongue traced patterns against my most sensitive flesh while his hands pinned my hips to the bed, keeping me exactly where he wanted me. The shadows around us grew thicker, darker, as if responding to his focus, his intensity.

I fisted my hands in the furs beneath me and held on for dear life.

"You taste like sunshine," he murmured against me, and the vibration of his voice made me gasp. "I thought you would. I dreamed about this. Dreamed about you spread out beneath me, making those sounds, coming apart on my tongue."

His words should have been obscene. Instead, they felt like poetry.

He sealed his lips around that bundle of nerves and sucked, and I came apart for the second time with a cry that echoed off the shadowed walls. My fingers found his hair, gripping tight, holding him to me as wave after wave of pleasure crashed through my body. He worked me through it, gentling gradually, pressing soft kisses to my oversensitive flesh until I stopped shaking.

When he finally lifted his head, his eyes were dark with want, and his lips were wet. He looked like a man who had found exactly what he was searching for.

"Come here," I breathed, reaching for him.

He crawled up my body, shadows trailing in his wake, until his weight settled over me—solid and warm and real. His forearms braced on either side of my head, caging me in, and I wrapped my arms around his neck to pull him down.

The kiss was deep and desperate and tasted like me.

I felt him position himself at my entrance, the blunt pressure making my breath catch. His forehead dropped to mine.

"Look at me," he said softly.

I opened my eyes. Found his—gray as storm clouds, bright as lightning, full of something that made my heart clench.

"I love you," he said. "I should have told you before. Should have told you a hundred times instead of pretending I could let you go."

Tears pricked at my lashes. "I love you too. Even when you're impossible."

His laugh was rough.

He slid inside me in one long, slow stroke.

My back arched, a gasp tearing free as my body stretched to accommodate him. He was everywhere—above me, inside me, all around me. His shadows curled along my arms, my waist, threading between my fingers like they wanted to hold me too.

"Okay?" he asked, jaw tight with the effort of staying still.

"More than okay." I rolled my hips, testing, and we both groaned. "Move. Please."

He did.

Slowly at first—long, deep strokes that hit something profound inside me. His eyes never left mine, watching every flicker of sensation that crossed my face.

"So tight," he breathed. "So perfect. Made for me, aren't you?"

"Yes." The word spilled out before I could stop them. "Always."

His rhythm faltered, something raw and reverent flashing in his gaze. Then he kissed me, hard, and began to move faster.

I met him thrust for thrust, my nails raking down his back, over the tattoos that marked his ribs. He made a sound against my mouth—half growl, half prayer—and drove into me deeper.

The pleasure built again, impossible and consuming. Every nerve in my body sang where we were connected. His shadows writhed around us, responding to every catch of breath, every whispered word.

I came with his name on my lips, inner walls clenching around him, and felt him follow me over seconds later—his whole body shuddering, a groan tearing from his chest as he spilled himself inside me.

We stayed tangled together for a long moment afterward, breathing hard, hearts pounding in tandem. His shadows slowly receded from the walls, letting thin threads of moonlight creep back in through the shuttered window.

He rolled to his side, pulling me with him, tucking me against his chest like I belonged there.

"What happens tomorrow?" I asked quietly.

His fingers traced lazy patterns on my hip. "Tomorrow we face whatever comes. Together."

"And tonight?"

His smile was slow, wicked, full of promise. "Tonight, I'm going to make you scream my name so many times that even my shadows won't be able to muffle the sound." He pressed a kiss to my forehead. "Rest up, Princess. We're just getting started."

THE
LOVERS

Chapter Fifty

Aurelia

I woke slowly, rested and warm, for the first time in weeks. Rydian's arm lay heavy across my waist, shadows curled lazily along his skin like contented cats. His breathing was steady against the back of my neck.

For a long moment, I didn't move.

I didn't want to.

My body was sore in a way that felt satisfying.

Gods. Last night had been even better than our first, and that was saying something.

His voice came from the warm space behind my ear, low and rough with sleep. "Thinking of running off?"

I smiled into the pillow. "Not at all."

"Good." His nose brushed my shoulder. "Because if you leave this bed, I might burn the cabin down."

"Out of the two of us, I'm the one who could do such a thing."

"My shadows would restrain you before that could happen."

Heat pulsed through me at the way he said it—lazy, possessive, still half-asleep. A promise in the making. Or maybe a threat. With Rydian, it was hard to tell the difference.

I rolled onto my back. He propped himself on his elbow, hair tousled, eyes dark, with last-night's hunger muted only slightly by sleep.

He studied me for a long, quiet moment, brushing a loose strand of hair from my face.

"How do you feel?" he asked softly.

"Tired," I whispered. "Sore."

He smirked, satisfied.

"And..." I hesitated.

His eyes softened, and he waited.

"Different," I admitted. "I can't explain it. My magic feels... heavier? Or deeper. Like there's something else to it, something closer to the surface than ever."

His thumb brushed my cheekbone. "I can feel it." His gaze darkened as his hand slid beneath the blankets, trailing over my hips to my thighs. "And I can feel you."

My pulse jumped. "Rydian—"

A knock sounded, muffled through the shadows wrapping the door.

We both froze.

Then—

"Breakfast!" Vanya's voice squeaked through the doorframe. "Um—I mean—whenever you're, uh, done." A beat. "With... whatever you're doing."

Rydian grinned at me. "She's never going to look at me again."

"She barely looks at you now," I said, laughing despite myself.

He lifted his head, glared halfheartedly, and stole one more kiss that had my entire body arching toward him.

Then he climbed out of bed.

I watched him get dressed—slowly, deliberately, his eyes flicking to me every few seconds like he could feel my gaze trailing over the runes carved across his torso and arms.

"Stop staring, Furious," he murmured, pulling his shirt over his head.

"I wasn't."

"You were."

I sighed. "Fine. I was."

He smirked, completely insufferable. "Good."

I threw a pillow at him.

He caught it, laughing. And gods—his laugh. It was rare, rough, and it pulled something inside me tight. Maybe this cabin wasn't the safest place in the realm, but for the first time in years, I felt safe. Climbing out of bed at last, I dressed and set off in search of breakfast.

The smell of spiced porridge hit me first. Then the sound of clattering bowls. Then Callan's voice complaining loudly enough to wake the dead.

"Who the Hel decided rabbits are a food group? Has the realm forgotten proper cuisine? I am a king—"

"Fugitive king," Daegel corrected without looking up.

Callan glared. "I am a temporarily displaced monarch."

Keres snorted. "You're a refugee with an ego bigger than your—"

"Keres," Daegel warned.

I stepped into the kitchen.

Everyone froze.

Then all eyes snapped to Rydian following behind me. My cheeks flushed hot, but I kept my head high.

Keres smirked.

Daegel winked.

Vanya flushed crimson and stared down at her bowl.

Callan's eyes narrowed, flicking between Rydian and me like he was solving a riddle and hating every answer.

Rydian simply crossed his arms and leaned against the doorway, looking entirely too smug.

"Sit," Keres ordered, pushing a bowl toward me. "Eat."

I obeyed.

Callan stabbed his spoon into his porridge. "It's gritty. Why is it gritty?"

"Because we heard you hated gritty porridge and obviously went out of our way to prepare it so," Keres snapped. "Eat."

Callan scrunched his face like a toddler forced to choke down vegetables, then took a dramatic bite—and made a face.

Rydian sat down beside me and whispered, "I can kill him now. No one will blame me."

I kicked him under the table.

His hand brushed my knee in retaliation.

My breath caught.

Gods. This was impossible. Breakfast shouldn't feel like foreplay.

Daegel noticed and winked. Keres shot him a look sharp enough to cut stone. Lesha—propped up on cushions and sipping weak tea—offered me a small smile. Color had returned to her cheeks. Her wings... well. They weren't wings anymore. But she was alive. She was fighting.

And that was enough.

I relaxed into the morning for the first time in forever.

But peace in Menryth rarely lasted longer than five minutes.

A knock sounded at the front door—three sharp strikes that made the whole room go still.

Everyone reached for weapons.

Rydian's shadows surged forward like a living storm.

I stood.

Keres held up a hand. "Wait. None of our wards alerted us to a guest. We need to be sure it's not—"

The knock came again, and Rydian stiffened. He rose and went to the door, hand hovering over the latch. Shadows pooled at his feet, ready to spring.

He opened it a crack.

A scroll slipped through the gap, wrapped in black ribbon and sealed with—

Oh.

My breath hitched at the sight of the raven's wings. Midnight's crest.

Rydian inhaled sharply. He snatched the scroll, shut the door, locked it, reinforced it with a burst of shadow that climbed the wood like vines.

Callan stared. "What is that?"

Rydian didn't answer.

He broke the seal.

Unrolled the parchment.

Read.

And though Rydian didn't pale—not exactly—something shifted in his expression.

"Keres," he said quietly. "Everyone—arms down."

Callan looked offended. "I assure you, I do not take orders from—"

Rydian lifted a hand.

Callan shut up.

Everyone waited.

Rydian swallowed.

Then he read aloud:

To Aurelia Valeen of Summer and Callan Ashfall of Autumn. Queen Cadira of the Midnight Court requests your presence.

Rydian closed the scroll, voice steady but strained. "It's from my mother."

Callan frowned, looking from Rydian to me. "The Midnight queen wants to meet us. What's so bad about that?"

"Requests?" I echoed. "Or commands?"

Rydian's jaw tightened.

Daegel crossed his arms. "What does she want with Aurelia?"

"She doesn't say," Rydian replied, but there was something in his voice—something guarded—that made every nerve in my body spark.

Callan frowned. "Is she... safe?"

Rydian stared at him. "For you? No."

Callan blinked.

Rydian shoved the scroll into his pocket and dragged a hand through his hair. "She wants an audience. That's all I know."

"You think we shouldn't go," I said quietly.

Rydian's shadows wrapped around my wrist—not pulling, not restraining, but grounding. A touch. A promise.

"She will not harm you," he assured me.

I nodded.

But inside?

My heart pounded.

Because the Midnight queen saw me as a threat to her son. And if she knew Rydian and I had bound ourselves to each other last night, there might be Hel to pay. Then again, the prince of Midnight wasn't the only one who could keep a secret.

Thank you for reading! Aurelia's story continues in Crown of Thorns and Thistles! Find out what the Queen of the Midnight Court has in store for Aurelia, Rydian, and Callan.

If you are enjoying this series, don't miss the prequel story, A Glamour of Smoke & Shadow, and find out how Heliconia's magic and evil were both made in the same moment her friendship with Sonoma (Aurelia's mother) ended forever.

About the Author

Heather Hildenbrand lives in coastal Virginia where she writes paranormal and fantasy romance full of enemies to lovers and morally gray heroes. Her most frequent hobbies are cuddling with her 2 golden-doodles and avoiding killer slugs.

You can find out more about Heather and her books at www.heatherhildenbrandbooks.com.

Or find her here:

Also by Heather Hildenbrand

One Dark Spark

Two Blazing Hearts

Three Scorched Kingdoms

Dark Wolf Soul

Deadly Wolf Bite

Broken Wolf Heart

Savage Wolf Vow

A Glamour of Smoke and Shadow (Cursed Fae)

Kingdom of Briars and Roses (Cursed Fae)

Prince of Secrets and Shadows (Cursed Fae)

A Crown of Thorns and Thistles (Cursed Fae)

Protect Me (Immortal Vices & Virtues)

Hunt Me (Immortal Vices & Virtues)

Consume Me (Immortal Vices & Virtues)

To Hunt A Wolf

To Kiss A Wolf

To Keep A Wolf

Midnight Cursed

Midnight Hunted

Midnight Bound

Wolf Cursed

Wolf Captive

Wolf Chosen

Wolf Revealed

A Witch's Call

A Witch's Destiny

A Witch's Fate

A Witch's Soul

A Witch's Prophecy

A Witch's Hope

Twisted Tides

The Girl Who Cried Werewolf

The Girl Who Cried Captive

The Girl Who Cried War

The Girl Who Never Cried

The Winter Witch

The Spring Witch

The Witch's Heart

Midnight Mate

Goddess Ascending

Goddess Claiming

Goddess Forging

Kiss of Death

Knock Em Dead

Death's Door

Dead to Rights

Dead End

The Girl Who Called The Stars

The Girl Who Ruled The Stars

Alpha Games

Alpha Trials

Alpha Chosen

Dirty Blood

Cold Blood

Blood Bond

Blood Rule

Broken Blood

Imitation

Deviation

Generation

Heather also writes small town contemporary romance as Violet Stafford.

Stay For Summer

The Breakup Bet

www.ingramcontent.com/pod-product-compliance
Lightning Source LLC
Chambersburg PA
CBHW020451310726
48979CB00016B/2603/J

* 9 7 8 1 9 6 1 4 5 5 4 0 5 *